Fl

"Come here, Antonie," he commanded quietly, tired of the waiting game they had played. "I want to hold you."

"You might find me a very large armful, *gringo,*" she answered, her pulse jumping erratically at his words.

"I'm willing to risk that. I want you, I crave your touch. It's nearly an obsession with me. Come here to me, Antonie."

She moved closer to him, shivering beneath the warmth of his gaze. "It is a very big step, *querido.*"

Royal reached out and pulled her into his arms. "And I'll help you make it."

Her arms slid around his neck as he took her mouth in a deep kiss that revealed his hunger for her. As his kisses grew more demanding, a soft moan escaped her. It felt so good to hold him, her body pressed against his, his hands stroking her, stirring her to the point of mindless need. His caresses swept her away and she knew there was no use in fighting such fire. That this was her destiny to love this man, and destiny could not be denied. . . .

A TASTE OF FIRE

SARAH DUSTIN

ZEBRA BOOKS
KENSINGTON PUBLISHING CORP.

ZEBRA BOOKS

are published by

Kensington Publishing Corp.
475 Park Avenue South
New York, NY 10016

First printing: April, 1988.

Printed in the United States of America

Prologue

Shots. Even a child of nine recognized that sound. Suddenly it was no longer a fine spring day, the wildflowers no longer held her interest. The overgrown puppy at the child's feet even ceased its romping. For a moment an ominous silence reigned as if even the birds waited for a repetition of the sound that too often signaled death in the new Territory of New Mexico.

Standing like a small statue, the little girl tried to think. Was it Indians? Was it *banditti?* There seemed to be so many things to fear. Should she stay? Should she run? Should she hide? The only thing she had been told was where to hide if she was at home and there was an attack. No one had told her what to do if she was picking wildflowers out of sight of her home.

Another shot cut through the still air and her legs began to move. At first it was a slow advance, but then her small legs began to move faster. She had to know. The puppy clumsily tried to keep up with her as she raced toward home.

Juan Ramirez was sickened by what he saw. He was

5

a man of violence, but he prided himself on confining it to those he considered deserving or who could fight back. The men who rode with him knew he held firm to his rules. These poor settlers had nothing worth stealing, had been struggling as hard as any of his own people. This violence had gained them nothing and that infuriated him. It had also wasted time, another serious crime in his eyes. He stared down at the instigator he had just shot and was wondering idly if that would be enough of a lesson for his three men or if he should shoot them too. He stiffened and turned, his gun ready as were those of his men, at the sound of someone running.

The little girl who raced toward them seemed blind to their presence. He tried to stop her from getting inside the cabin but she neatly eluded his grasp. Cursing, he followed the child and stood in the doorway to watch her.

She stood and looked around at the destruction but not really understanding it. Setting down her flowers, she moved toward her mother's body wondering why she was nearly naked. With an odd dignity that struck to the core the man watching her, she straightened her mother's clothing and shut the woman's wide, staring eyes. All she could think of was that death meant burying. She had to dig two big holes and put her parents in them. That was what they had done with her brother and sister when they had died.

"Why are you still here?" she asked the man who blocked the door. "They're dead. You can't kill them any more. Move."

Not sure why, Juan moved. He stood scratching his beard as he watched her go to the barn. His men grew restless as they wondered aloud why they were not leaving. Juan continued to watch as she returned dragging a shovel that was too big and too heavy for

6

her to use.

He compared her to a china doll he had stolen once. Her long untidy curls were the color of cornsilk, her skin like cream and her stature delicate even for a child of nine. It was her eyes that really fascinated him, however. They were like amethysts, huge pools of purple in her small face, topped by delicate brows and encircled by lush lashes that were several shades darker than her hair. He had no idea what he would do with her but he knew he could not leave her behind.

"*Niña,* my men will do the burying." He took the shovel from her and handed it to one of the three who had helped in the killing. "You are too little, eh?"

It was a hasty burial. There was a very good chance that men were already on their trail. The border was not far, but Juan did not wish to be caught in a race for it. He left the child putting her wildflowers on her mother's grave and returned to the cabin to throw her few things into a saddlebag. When he went back outside he found her returning to the cabin.

"Juan," ventured Manuel, his right hand man, "what can you do with a little girl? This is madness."

Looking at the child who watched them, plainly not understanding Spanish, he replied, "Yes, it is, but she is my prize." He grinned at Manuel. "I will be a father but without the trouble of a wife. Is that madness?" He asked her in English, "Your name?"

"Antonie Doberman." She studied the tall, slim dark man. "Why did you kill my mama and papa?"

"I did not do this thing, *niña.*" He gestured to the body of the man he had shot. "This man did, so I killed him. I am a *bandito, si,* but I do not trouble those with nothing worth stealing." He watched her nod at the sense of that. "You come with us now, *chica.*"

7

"Sage. My dog." She clung to Juan's saddlehorn and looked down at the puppy who whined at the horse's hooves.

"Manuel will bring the dog." He chuckled over Manuel's curses as he mounted behind the little girl. "You will belong to Juan now."

Chapter One

She had not looked back that day as they rode for the border. And for a little while after Juan had taken her, she had missed her parents, but they had not been very affectionate, being too caught up in the struggle of living. For all his faults, Juan Ramirez gave her more love than her honest and peace-loving parents ever had.

Antione and Juan were rarely separated. The only time she did not ride at his side was when there was fighting. Then he would leave her with one of his trusted men at a safe distance. Even when he was with one of his whores in town, she was near. She slept outside the door with Sage and the guard whom Juan always posted.

It was not until she was thirteen that any change came into her life. Juan and his men had laughed heartily at her panic when her first menstrual period had begun. They had dragged a woman into camp to explain and to instruct her. However, it was a tall, young Texan who showed Juan that a little extra privacy was not all that should be done for her.

Profits from a raid weighing down their pockets, the men had sought out a safe town where drink and

9

women could be bought. As always, Antonie and Sage sat in a corner eating and drinking. There they would stay until Juan retired to a room for the night. Then Antonie would curl up on the floor with Sage outside the door and under the watchful eye of whoever Juan selected as a guard. She sat quietly watching the drinking, gambling and lewdness with eyes well accustomed to the darker side of life. No one bothered her as she sat there, for Juan was well known in this border town as was the swift and deadly justice he dealt out.

In an opposite corner sat Royal Bancroft, unaware of the dangerous company he had wandered into. Just twenty-one, he was drawn to the border towns by cheap liquor, cheaper women and that air of recklessness that prevailed. His jade green eyes had left the abundant charms of the woman by his side to rest upon a sight he had never expected to find in a border town cantina.

The girl made Royal think of a little china doll, despite the roughness of her attire and appearance. Her pale hair hung far past her hips, held in place only by a bandana, her low crowned, wide brimmed hat hiding little of it. The black of her shirt and pants only accentuated the creaminess of her skin. In profile her small straight nose and full mouth as well as the delicate bones of her face already held promise of a womanly beauty, sensuality and passion. Glancing over her black clad figure, Royal decided that so did her budding figure.

Royal did not like seeing a young girl in such a place. If she had any innocence left it would not last long. He could only think of his sister, Patricia, who was probably this girl's age. It was wrong for that child to be in the cantina and, even as he cursed the idealism and sense of right that drove him, Royal moved to do something about it. He stopped before the girl, a little stunned by her incredibly lovely eyes, and was about to speak when all the noise in the cantina abruptly ceased, accentuating the sound of the hammers on several pistols being drawn back. Slowly Royal raised his arms and just as slowly, turned around.

"You are young, *gringo,* so I let you explain yourself. Then I might shoot," Juan shrugged, "or I might not."

Wondering how to ease the deadly tension he had inadvertently caused, Royal said, "I meant the child no harm."

The word child eased the tension just slightly. "Then why do you approach my *niña?*"

Despite his best efforts to hide it, Royal knew his surprise was showing. The tall Mexican eyeing him so closely and coldly over the barrel of his gun could not possibly be the girl's father. It was an effort not to look at her again to reassure himself of her fair coloring.

"I was simply concerned about a child being in a place like this."

With a barely perceptible signal from the man, Royal was relieved of his weapons. Cautiously, as the other men put away their weapons, Royal obeyed the man's signal to come and sit at his table. He could not help but smile a little at the way the man roughly pushed the whore from his lap and, with another subtle gesture, summoned the little girl to come and sit there. The way the hard man's eyes softened when the girl drew near, as well as the way she snuggled against him so naturally, made the man seem less dangerous but Royal knew that was a very costly assumption to make.

"My *niña* always comes with me. She has seen many of these cantinas, eh?"

11

"Well, all I could think of was my sister, who's about your girl's age. I wouldn't want her in a place like this," he paused, "learning."

"She is a child. It is too early for her to learn."

"Her childhood is fading *señor*." Royal nodded toward the girl's chest.

The way she had put her arm around Juan's neck had stretched Antonie's shirt taut against her budding breasts. She scowled as Juan then Manuel looked down and both men's eyes widened. Ignoring her protest, Juan pulled out the front of her shirt to peer inside and gape at the small breasts forming there in total disbelief.

"*Por Dios*," he said softly, hastily letting go so that the shirt fell back into place. "Why did you say nothing, *chica?*"

"I hoped they would go away, then you could not laugh like you did at the blood. I do not like to be laughed at."

"Ah, *querida*, we did not laugh at you, only at you thinking you were dying. Calling for a priest and all, eh?"

The man looked around at his men pawing the whores and his face darkened. Royal could guess at his thoughts. The child was growing and soon her thoughts would catch up with her body. She could all too easily join the ranks of the women that now offered to pleasure his men for a few pesos.

"Look, just send her back to her room," Royal suggested gently.

"She sleeps near me, here, when I choose a room."

"My God," Royal breathed, shocked to his young soul. "You let her watch?"

"No," the man growled. "She sleeps outside the door."

"So she only hears," Royal said sarcastically.

12

"Oh, Juan does not make much noise. Only grunts a bit. Now Manuel . . ." Antonie's revelations were halted by Juan's hand over her mouth.

"We know how Manuel is. You should not," Juan said sternly as he removed his hand. "What do I do now, eh?"

Royal was about to offer a suggestion when his gaze was suddenly captivated by a fleeting image in the mirror behind the bar. There was a furtive movement outside, but he was not sure what it meant until he caught the gleam of a rifle barrel. It was taking aim at the man seated across from him, a man too deep in thought to sense the danger or defend himself. So, too, would the child with the lovely eyes get caught in the fire.

Yelling a warning, Royal hurled himself at the man and the child, bringing them all to the floor as the first shot was fired. Unarmed, Royal could do nothing but cover the girl and keep his head down as the battle raged. With a speed that Royal had to admire, Juan had the table and chairs placed as barricades. It looked and sounded like pandemonium but Royal noticed only two men in the bar were taken down and they had fallen in the first few seconds. The attackers, however, were bitterly defeated, and the others who were able to fled for their lives. He continued to sit on the floor with the girl and her mangy dog as some semblance of order was restored.

"Who was it?" Antonie asked calmly as she finally returned to her seat with Juan as Royal collapsed in his.

"Raoul and his scum." Juan looked at Royal. "I owe you, *gringo*, and Juan Ramirez does not forget a debt. Your name?"

"Royal Bancroft," he answered automatically, in shock at meeting a near legend and saving the life of

13

the man all of Texas was aching to hang. "Texas. Outside San Antonio." He absently accepted the return of his weapons. "Christ, they would hang me if they knew."

Juan laughed heartily. "*Sí, sí.* You would have not been so quick if you had known, eh?"

Sighing, Royal grinned and shook his head. "There is still the child. They aren't looking to hang her."

"No?" Juan rubbed his cheek against the top of Antonie's now hatless head.

"No." Royal took a long pull on his beer and decided to be honest. "They think you stole her and would like to take her back."

"It is as I thought. They have already tried but no one will take my *niña*. She is an orphan. Antonie Doberman."

"Hello, Antonie." Royal saw her smile shyly at him and could easily foresee her beauty.

"She came with me when she was nine. I am her father now. My men, her family. We see that she goes to church." Dancing black eyes returned Royal's grin. "We teach her all we know. She can ride, shoot, all of that, as good as any man." He frowned and looked around the cantina again. "I do not want her to learn of this life but this *bandito* knows of only *putas*."

It was not easy, but Royal hid his surprise. The man was the scourge of Texas and the Territory of New Mexico, swooping across the border to rob and kill and disappear back across the Rio Grande into Mexico. El Diablo was only one of the names given this hard man who eluded capture so easily. Yet, here he sat, as concerned as any father for the chastity of the girl he had picked up on some raid. Royal now thought it a lost cause, but he was willing to help if he could.

"You can start by keeping her out of places like

14

this. This isn't what she should learn of men and women."

Nodding, Juan stood up. "You come with me, *gringo*, and tell me more while I find a room for Antonie. Julio, I give you two hours to have your fun, then you come to the inn and take my place watching Antonie."

Two men, well armed, followed Juan, Antonie and Royal. It was evident that Juan had no intention of being caught out alone and unaware. Royal noted that the girl was calmly accepting of these precautions. As they walked, Royal obediently related all he could think of pertaining to the proper raising of a young girl. Having a sister gave him some insight but not much.

When they reached the room obtained for Antonie, a door away from his own, Royal kept his eyes averted as she got ready for bed. Once she was neatly tucked in bed, he sat at a small table with Juan to share a bottle of tequila. Royal could not fully shake the strangeness of talking about the proper raising of a girl with a man like Juan Ramirez.

"I did not do the killing of her parents."

That softly spoken statement made Royal flush guiltily. "I had wondered."

"You are an honest man. There are few left. They were *gringos*, but poor. I do not go after ones who have nothing or men whose hands are fitted to a plow, not a gun. They are a waste of my time, eh? Men come and go in my band. Not all follow orders. Four took a little, how you say, detour. They do the killing. I had just shot the leader as a lesson when the girl comes. She was nine and very tiny." He shrugged. "I decided to be a father."

"They think you stole her and they want her almost as much as they want you."

15

"*Sí*. They have tried. I left her with Manuel's woman once. She proved she was not to be trusted."

"What happened?"

"She sold my *niña* to the *gringos*. We did not kill her for that but Manuel took his sons. So, we follow and bring my *niña* back."

"Was that best?" Royal ventured to ask. "You are a *bandito*, living each day by your gun. God knows how many men ache to kill you. Maybe she'd be better off if she went back. There would be families ready to take in such a pretty child."

"Antonie is mine. The *gringos* could not hold her. She slipped away from them and we found her walking back to me. The child made her choice. She wants to stay with Juan Ramirez."

There was no more to say. Amazing though it was, Juan Ramirez plainly adored the little girl with all the ferocity of a true father, perhaps more. He was a hard man born of a hard life, but evidently the child filled some need, touched some long unused softness in the man. The child looked neither abused nor unhappy. She was clearly just where she wanted to be.

Deciding that he had had enough excitement and drink for the evening, Royal did not go back to the cantina. He crawled into his bed and quickly fell asleep. Although he knew it was morning when he opened his eyes, it was not sunlight he first saw but a pair of wide purple eyes staring into his. He was suddenly very conscious of his nudity.

"I brought you your breakfast, *señor*." Antonie sat down on the edge of his bed.

Gingerly he sat up, taking care to keep himself covered, the smell of rich hot coffee and food further waking him. "That was very kind of you, Antonie, but you really shouldn't be in here."

"I left the door open as I heard you say a lady

16

should."

Royal nearly choked on his coffee for the door was indeed open, wide open, letting anyone who walked past look in on him. "Yes, well, when I was speaking of rooms, I wasn't meaning bedrooms." The way she looked at him told him that she did not understand. "Ladies do not enter a man's bedroom." He decided to eat while he thought of a way to explain it to her.

She watched him while he ate. His thick chestnut hair was tousled from sleep but did as little as his youth to soften the slightly harsh lines of his face. He was not as dark as Juan but not as pale as some *gringos*. The deep green of his eyes, set beneath neatly drawn, vaguely winged brows, fascinated her.

"Kiss me," she abruptly ordered when he ate the last of his food.

After choking on that last bite for a minute, Royal gasped, "Don't be ridiculous." He suddenly found a knife at his throat.

"I said kiss me, *gringo*."

"Antonie," drawled an all too familiar voice from the door, "this is not the way to seduce a man."

Putting away her knife, Antonie groused, "I thought you were still with Maria."

Strolling up the the bed, Juan looked at her sternly. "Ah. So you thought to rush in here and learn to be a *puta*."

"I just wanted a kiss. None of that other business. Oro and Tomás are only two years older than me and they have done it all."

"They are learning to be men. Doing it all is part of becoming a man."

"I do not want it all. Just one kiss. I asked Oro and Tomás but they said no and threw me in the water. Last time I was at church the girls were talking about kissing. I just wanted to know. Everybody has done it

17

but me."

Juan stared at her. It was clear that her thoughts were already growing with her body. He knew how stubborn she could be once she got an idea into her head. Leaning against the wall by the bed, he took out a cigarillo.

"Kiss her."

"What?" Royal gasped. "She's just a kid, for Christ's sake."

"*Sí* and no." He lit his cigarillo and slowly drew on it. "She is thinking she is missing something, eh?"

"And you expect me to show her she isn't?" Royal did not feel very flattered.

"No. I expect you to answer what this question is in her stubborn mind. She will keep asking until she gets her answer and I do not want someone to tell her too much, *sí*? You kiss her."

"Oh for God's sake," Royal muttered and yanked her to him to deliver a brief kiss.

"That is all?" Antonie asked in disappointment.

"For you, *sí*. Now, vamoose."

"It does not seem worth all the excitement," she grumbled as she left, Sage at her heels.

"That should end that," Juan said with satisfaction.

"Are you sure?" Royal was trying not to be too insulted by her reaction.

"*Sí*. She does not like it when the girls at the church talk of things she does not know. Now she knows." Juan moved to the door. "Some day I will repay my debt. *Vaya con Dios, amigo.*"

Before Royal could reply the man was gone, the door shut after him. It was time to go home for a while. Things might be dull there but at least he did not find himself cheek to jowl with notorious *banditti* and precocious little girls.

An hour later he was mounting his horse in preparation of leaving, only to see that Juan Ramirez was doing the same. The girl sat on a huge black stallion flanked by two mounted youths who obviously had some Indian blood in their veins. They made an impressive trio, the two tall, dark youths beside the tiny fair Antonie. He returned their farewells as he rode past them on his way out of town.

When Royal reached his home several days later, he found that the girl still troubled him. She came to mind as he greeted his sister. Patricia was growing up wrapped in the protection of her family, enjoying all the innocent games and interests of a young girl facing womanhood. It was hard not to compare that to Antonie's life, steeped in violence and danger. It still did not seem right but he knew there was nothing he could do about it. Since he did not want anyone to know that he had saved the life of Juan Ramirez, he never mentioned Antonie to anyone, only listened more closely to any tales of Juan Ramirez that came his way.

A short time after his meeting with Juan and Antonie, war exploded within the country. Royal lost all interest in Juan Ramirez and his young charge, as he and two of his brothers rode off with many another young Texan to become mired in hate and blood. The second oldest of the three fell at Gettysburg while Royal and his brother Cole managed to survive until Lee surrendered. Bitter, scarred inside and out, they returned home after a year only to find their parents dead and Patricia and the youngest son, Justin, struggling to keep the ranch together. Cole joined the Rangers while Royal tried to forget the war by immersing himself in the fight to hang onto the ranch.

In the meantime, Ramirez still plagued the area,

dashing in to strike and then flitting away. Antonie grew into the lovely woman Royal had seen in the still budding girl and men died because of it. For lesser offenders, one warning was allowed. Not all of what Royal had told Juan was heeded, but Antonie's virtue was tightly guarded. Antonie often mused that Royal Bancroft was probably the only man who had kissed Juan Ramirez's *niña* and lived.

Antonie grew up lovely but hard. She rode and shot as well as a man, had an admirable skill with a whip and was almost unchallenged with a knife. What softness existed in her woman's body was kept well hidden and was rarely seen. Now and again she did wonder if one swift kiss from a Texan was worth so many nights of haunting by a pair of jade green eyes.

Chapter Two

"What the hell happened to you?"

Cole Bancroft eased himself into a chair and tried to grin at his elder brother. "Can I have a drink before I go into any details?"

Royal's anger hid his concern. He had lost one brother and had no intention of losing another. By the looks of it, the wound in Cole's shoulder had come far too close in succeeding in its clear intention of killing the lawman. Scowling, he handed Cole a drink.

"Don't you think four years of getting shot at is enough?" Royal snapped.

"Plenty, but I've got two months left before I get out. Damn, Royal, we almost had the bastard."

"Ramirez?" He forced away a sudden vision of wide purple eyes.

"Yeah. Still, we did him some real damage so that might be an end to it."

"How'd he get away?"

"That's the strange thing. It was the girl." He frowned briefly when Royal gave a sudden start. "She never gets involved. Never. We were closing in for the kill when she and those two Indians, or so they looked, came charging in. No one expected it. Threw us all off. They dragged off Ramirez and one other, though he looked dead. Gave the others left alive a chance to run."

"That when you got shot?"

"Oh yeah." Cole shook his head and took a drink. "I should be dead. I couldn't shoot her, Royal. I was the only one who had the chance but I couldn't. Funny thing is, she was ready to shoot me. Hank yelled for me to shoot but I froze."

"Jesus. Well, she missed. You're damn lucky."

"I'm not so sure it was luck. She was aiming right and steady at my heart, Royal, then suddenly upped her aim."

"Did someone say your name?"

"Come to think of it, yeah. Hank said, 'Shoot, Bancroft, or get your dumb ass out of there.' "

A small grin flickered over Royal's face. "Hell, and it's been at least seven years. Wonder if he'll consider that old debt paid now?"

"Think you might stop muttering to yourself and tell me what the hell you mean?"

"It's a long story."

"I ain't going too far too fast." Cole did, however, find a need to refill his drink as Royal told his story.

"I never told anyone as it's not a story I wanted to get around."

"Hell no. They'd hang you. Slowly. It hasn't stopped him from hitting our ranch though."

"Never really thought it was him." He held up his hand to stop Cole's hovering outburst. "I don't know who, though. Just felt it wasn't him." After staring into his drink for a moment, he asked quietly, "What's she look like?"

"Told the men I didn't know." Cole grimaced. "Just didn't want any of them setting out after her. She's something, Royal. Lord, is she something. Not very big but what there is of her," he shook his head. "Well, it's why I couldn't shoot her. Just stood there gawking at her thinking stupid things like how can a girl with hair like cornsilk shoot a man. She dresses all in black and her horse is a big black stallion. Startling. If Ramirez is like a father to her, I think she'll be an orphan again real soon."

Antonie had to face the truth. It was over and she knew it. She had even fetched a priest to give Juan the last rites. For eleven years she had held the love of and loved a man living on borrowed time. Now she would be alone again. Even Sage was gone. As she attended Manuel's and Julio's brief funeral then left Oro and Tomás to their grief, she wondered how much time was left before Juan left them too.

"*Niña,* come to me," Juan rasped from the bed. "We must talk."

"No. You must save your strength." She knelt by his bed and pressed his hand to her cheek.

"There is nothing to save it for, *querida.* Listen. You must pay my debt now. The *gringo.* Bancroft. I had plans made. You must carry them out. Vultures circle him, child. His land is good and a man is after it."

"I think his brother was with the Rangers. I could have killed him but I did not."

"Not enough. Two lives I owe him. To this man his ranch is his life. Juan Ramirez will give it to him."

"Who is trying to steal it and how can I help?" She was finding it hard not to cry as she watched the life slowly ebb from his body.

"A man close to him, but I have no name. Raoul is in his pay. Killed Bancroft's parents. Many raids. Much trouble."

She nodded and tried to keep the tears she could no

23

longer hold back from dampening his hand. "Weaken him until he is broken."

"That is the plan. Much trouble planned for cattle drive. Sister in danger. You will go to him. Take Oro and Tomás. Be his guns. Pay our debt, my angel." He felt her tears and smiled a little. "My child never cries."

"Please, Juan." She kissed his palm. "Please do not leave me alone. I love you."

His hand went to her hair. "As I love you, Antonie, and this I have said to no one before. You were the sunlight in my dark life and I thank you. Do not ask me to live, my pet, for if I do I would never rise from this bed and that is no life. Julio and Manuel wait for me. We will cause the devil a trouble, eh?"

"I am sure." She kissed his too-cold cheek. "I will name my first son for you, father of my heart."

"I will be remembered. That will be enough."

He slipped away, quietly, with a soft sigh. Antonie wiped her tears and saw to his burial. The journey he had told her to take was postponed for a while as she saw to the selection of headstones for Juan, Manuel and Julio. They had been hard men who had lived by their guns but to her, Oro and Tomás they had been beloved family.

As they finally prepared to leave for Texas, Antonie studied her companions. Oro and Tomás were identical save that Oro had a small scar on his finely hewn chin and was less jovial and talkative than Tomás. The Indian blood bequeathed them by their mother, who had been part Yaqui, had given a light copper tone to their skin and high wide cheekbones. Their straight black hair was always too long, making that heritage seem more prominent than the greater Mexican one. From the moment they had been taken from their mother they had been brothers and guards to

Antonie. She hoped that their constant presence at her side, out of the raiding and fighting, would mean that they were not wanted by the law.

They were a half day's ride from San Antonio and not quite a half day's ride from the Bancroft ranch when they began to look for a place to camp for the night. It was Oro who first sensed others nearby. He came riding up to Antonie and Tomás, who were collecting brush for a fire, and, although few others would have read anything in his face, she knew he had news.

"Five minutes' ride from here. Six men. Two captives. One girl, one youth. Raoul's men. I am sure."

"Juan said Raoul was working for the one who wants to break Bancroft. We'd better see to this."

Sneaking up on the campsite was not hard. The men were swilling tequila and loudly celebrating their success. Oro saw to it that one man who had wandered off to answer the call of nature would never be bothered by such trivialities again. His compatriots were too interested in the young girl to notice any absence or to care, and Antonie knew that would prove their downfall. The young man they had captured was badly beaten and Antonie wondered if that had happened during or after the capture as she slipped even closer to her chosen target.

Antonie watched the girl weep quietly as she was approached by her captors. Antonie did not need to see the frustrated fury and fear in the youth's face to know what was coming. Hearing the girl gag as one leering *bandito* tore the front of her dress and mauled her bared breasts, much to the amusement of his compatriots, Antonie threw her knife.

When her attacker suddenly went limp, grunting softly and falling on her, the girl whimpered as she saw the knife protruding from his back. Antonie could

25

see that the girl was nearly hysterical, fighting to get out from beneath the dead man, but the battle that ensued required all her attention. The others fell quickly as they shot into the dark in a blind panic. When Antonie and the twins emerged silently from the shadows, she could tell that the girl's terrified mind wondered what new horror had just arrived. Antonie knew that the three of them looked as much like *banditti* as the ones they had just killed.

Oro stared at the young girl, trembling and wide eyed in her panic. Her huge light green eyes never left his face as he calmly approached her and silently laced her torn bodice together with a piece of rawhide. Antonie wondered what was going through the girl's mind.

"Would it not be best to untie her first?" she drawled.

"No. She would just run away. See her eyes? She is like a trapped rabbit. See to the boy, little one."

"Yes, my general." She grinned when she saw the glare the young man sent Oro. "They understand what we say or some of it. At least, he does." She switched to English as she took out her knife, newly retrieved from the dead man's body. "I will only cut your bonds, *amigo*. Who are you?"

"Justin and Patricia Bancroft."

"You have a brother named Royal?"

"Yes. How do you know him?"

"We have come to repay a debt. We will take you back to him. Tomás," she called, "can you find some water in this sty?"

A moment later Tomás appeared with water and a fresh bottle of tequila. "One still lives."

"Can he make it back to Raoul?" She grinned at Justin's weak protest when she stripped off his shirt.

"*Sí*. I will give him a message to take to Raoul, eh?"

26

He chuckled as he strode back to the man who still lived.

Wincing as she ran testing fingers over his ribs, Justin asked, "You know whose men these are?"

"*Sí*. They are the men of Raoul Mendez, but a *gringo* hired them. What *gringo* I do not know. Oro, does the rabbit wear a petticoat? These ribs need to be wrapped." She took the petticoat from Patricia's trembling hand. "So the rabbit is loose."

"*Querida*, you are a hard woman," Oro said quietly. "I will help Tomás with the bodies. We can camp here."

"Who are you?" Patricia asked tremulously after Oro left.

"I am Antonie Doberman Ramirez. They are Oro and Tomás Degas. We will return you to Royal. Drink, Justin." She grinned when he choked on the tequila and then handed Patricia a dampened cloth. "Clean his face, little rabbit. Grit your teeth, *chico*."

He did and turned alarmingly pale but held onto consciousness with grim determination. Antonie knew he was staring at her but said nothing, feeling that he needed to concentrate on something as she tended his wounds. She thought that he looked very young and knew that he was deeply curious about how she knew his brother. Although she sympathized with that curiosity, she decided it was not really her place to satisfy it.

"How old are you?" he gasped as she hastily dabbed his cuts with tequila.

"Twenty. And you? *Dios*, but they pounded you, *amigo*."

"Twenty also. At least I am alive. They killed the two men with us. Lord, I feel like I've been in a stampede."

"You look it. Where were you headed?" She sat

27

back on her heels to study her handiwork.

"San Antonio. 'Bout this time every year Pattie goes shopping. What is this debt you keep talking about?"

"I think I will let your brother tell you. Did they steal your gear along with you?"

"Not sure. Can't see that they'd leave it behind."

"This is true. I will look." She strolled off to see about food and bedding.

"She said hardly a word to me," Patricia hissed.

"Well, she was probably just leaving you to calm down. How are you? Okay?"

"Yes." She shuddered. "I can't wait to have a bath. I feel dirty. So many bodies, Justin."

He took her hand in a comforting grasp. "It couldn't be helped, Pattie. It was us or them. They weren't the type of men you discussed things with."

"I know." She glanced toward the three setting up camp. "Are you sure we'll be safe with them? Two Indians and that odd girl?"

"Don't worry. We'll be fine. I think the men are only partly Indian, you know. A lot of Mexicans got some in them. As far as Antonie goes, she's probably led a hard life, that's all. Just raised different. I might be wrong but I think she was more comfortable talking with me. Might not have had much to do with ladies. Sorry about your shopping trip."

"I couldn't look at dresses now anyway. Let's just get home."

Antonie smiled faintly as she prepared a fire for their meal. She wondered if she should tell the pair how clearly their soft talk carried in the night, but decided not to. It never hurt to have an advantage. Covertly watching the young girl as the meal was prepared and the bedding laid out, Antonie thought that Patricia was probably what Royal had said a lady should be. Trying not to be critical, Antonie did concede that, despite the girl's lack of fight and her continuing nervousness, Patricia was holding up well. The girl was simply not hardened to the rough side of life as she was.

Antonie had the first watch and, noticing Justin's restlessness, went over to sit next to him. "In pain, *gringo?*"

"Somewhat." He accepted the tequila she offered him. "I really can't stand this stuff, but it does help."

"I like wine better. The rabbit has decided to trust us?" She met Justin's admonishing look with a grin.

"She's not really timid, you know." He stared at her in some surprise when she took a swig from the bottle and then handed it back to him.

"Mmmm. She is a lady. Juan tried to make me one. Some of it worked, some of it did not." She could see just when he started to put a few facts together.

"You're the girl with Juan Ramirez." He looked toward Oro and Tomás. "His men?"

"Mine. Oro and Tomás were my bodyguards, eh? They did nothing but watch out for me."

"It was Ramirez who killed my folks. He raided our ranch."

"No, not Juan," she replied, unmoved by his hissing fury. "He owes Royal and has never touched your ranch. It was Raoul."

Watching him as he digested her words, Antonie was relieved when he nodded, indicating that he believed her. It would be almost impossible to repay Juan's debt if the brothers, even just one of them, could not accept her or the twins. The battle they faced demanded close cooperation and trust.

"He shot my brother last week."

"No. I shot your brother last week. Go to sleep, *gringo.*"

She calmly walked away but had to grin at the look

29

of stunned surprise on his face. It was clear that Justin's brother had not told exactly how he had been wounded. When she saw him grin, she laughed softly. The brothers at home were clearly going to be pressed to do a lot of explaining.

In the morning, Patricia and Antonie went to wash up and change their clothes. Patricia was so clearly nervous that Antonie was sorely tempted to do something that would send the girl screaming back to camp but resisted the urge. She had no doubt that only Tomás would think it was funny. Instead she went quietly about her business and wondered crossly why the girl would not relax.

It was easy for Antonie to see that Patricia was shocked by the fact that she wore nothing under her clothes save for socks and men's underbriefs. Antonie covertly watched Patricia and decided that, shocking to a real lady or not, her underclothes were a lot more practical. She also decided that they were probably far more comfortable too. Seeing Patricia's beauty clearly, Antonie found herself praying that there would be no trouble with Tomás or Oro.

Royal sat down to share a hearty breakfast with a still healing Cole. "Stiff?" he asked.

"Yup, but it's going. Another week and I'll be nearly as good as new. Damn embarrassing. The men'll never let me forget it."

"Well, you've only got a short time left with them anyway." He frowned at the way Cole looked away and did not answer. "Don't you?"

"Hell, I don't know. Just might join up again. Don't scowl. It's a job that needs doing and you don't really need me here."

"You don't need a job either. You know the ranch was to be for all of us."

"I know, Royal. Pa bought plenty of land for each of us to have a piece even after you take your large chunk. I'm only twenty-three, not ready at all to settle and breed horses as I thought it'd be nice to do. Maybe in a few more years. Right now?" He shrugged.

"Right now you crave the excitement," Royal said with a touch of anger, then sighed. "I can understand that but, damn, I don't like you taking chances. I also hoped to have you help me for a while. I'm going on the drive this year."

That caught Cole's interest. "Nothing says I have to rejoin right away." He grinned. "Been wanting us to try a drive."

"Well, I'll be more than glad to have you." He pushed back his chair. "Best get to work. What the hell does she want?" he snapped as a familiar voice called a greeting from the hall and footsteps approached the door.

"You," Cole replied and grinned when Royal scowled even more. "Why don't you just surrender?"

Royal wondered the same thing as Marilynn Collins strolled in, kissed him briefly and sat down. She was lovely, with her rich auburn hair and hazel-green eyes. Although he had never made love to her, he would certainly have few objections to doing so. She knew ranch life, yet was as much a lady as any New Orleans belle. He even liked her most of the time. Somehow, though, that did not seem enough.

"What can we do for you, Marilynn?" Royal served her coffee, trying to hide his eagerness to get to work.

"Since Patricia isn't here, I thought you would need help for the dinner tonight. I've come to see that

31

everything goes well."

"There was no need. Maria has things well in hand."

"You know how those people are, Royal. They need someone to keep them moving. I'll just provide the needed push."

There was evidently no way Royal was going to talk her out of it so he just gave up. After several moments of idle conversation, he made his escape, Cole close behind him. The last thing he wanted was to be put to work on the dinner party and Cole clearly felt the same.

"Why didn't you defend Maria? You know she doesn't need help or prodding."

"Cole, Marilynn is her father's daughter. She thinks all Mexicans are lazy. You can't argue with their kind of prejudice. Believe me, I've tried. Next time I'll know enough not to let Pattie run off. I hope she gets home in time."

The ride to the Bancroft ranch was taken very leisurely, due to Justin's injuries. At midday they took a long rest. It was good for the horses as well as themselves to rest in the noon heat.

Antonie laughed when she, Oro and Tomás took a swim in the creek for it had Patricia covering her eyes or averting them for quite a while. In deference to the girl's sensibilities, Antonie wore a bandana around her breasts just to keep from shocking Patricia too much. She and the twins then sprawled on blankets spread on the grass to dry off in the heat. She was glad to be on the road again, however, for she wanted to reach the Bancroft ranch before nightfall. If Raoul's men had reached him, the man could well come looking for them.

32

"Don't scowl, Pattie. We'll get there before dark. About an hour yet," Justin soothed as the hour grew late.

"Just in time for dessert."

"Oh, hell, the dinner party. Clean forgot it."

"There a problem?" Antonie asked as she rode closer to the siblings, pulled a bottle of wine from her saddlebags and opened it.

"Dinner party at the house tonight. We were planning on being back for it but not in this state. Is that our wine?"

"*Sí*, Justin. Want some?" She grinned as she held out the bottle and he accepted it, taking a healthy swallow. "What about your sister?" she asked when he handed the bottle back.

"I don't drink. Well, an occasional glass of sherry, that's all." She watched a little enviously as Antonie had another long drink.

"Ah, *sí*." Antonie tossed Oro a bottle of wine. "That is a 'being a lady' lesson."

"One of the ones that didn't work?" Justin teased.

"Juan never taught it. He said it was stupid. That lady can then be made very drunk very fast by a man and be a lady no more, eh? He said women should know drink and drinking so that then they cannot fall into that trap."

"God, that actually makes sense." Justin took another drink. "Maybe we should creep in the back way."

"I don't think so, Justin. Cole and Royal must be wondering where we are even now. Dinner will be nearly over anyway."

"You're right, Pattie. We'll just walk in. Best way."

"No. I will announce you." A slow smile crossed Antonie's face as she thought of the perfect way to do that. "I too owe Royal." She edged over to Tomás who was beginning to look as if he knew what she was

33

thinking. "I just need a little instruction."

"*Sí, querida*, and you have come to a master," Tomás drawled and then gave her a lengthy kiss.

Emerging from the embrace a little breathless, Antonie mused, "That was not how he did it."

"He gave you a kiss for a child. Tomás gives you a kiss for a woman." He turned with her to look at Oro, who had made a mocking sound.

"You can do better, *amigo*?" Antonie asked with a grin, partly prompted by the shock on Patricia's face.

"Of course. Who do you think instructed Tomás?" He put his arm around Antonie proceeded to demonstrate his skill.

"Amateurs," Justin drawled when Oro lifted his head and grinned at the increasingly warm Antonie.

"Oho, the *gringo* challenges." Tomás laughed and was clearly as amused as Antonie was over Patricia's gaping face.

Moving next to Justin, Antonie leaned toward him and drawled, "Well, *amigo*?"

Gently and clearly savoring every minute of it, Justin kissed her, then asked a little huskily, "Well?"

"I think I'd best stop this lesson or I will fall off my horse." Antonie grinned when the young men laughed and then she took a hearty drink, for she was feeling decidedly warm. "This kissing is thirsty business."

"You're going to walk in and kiss Royal?" Patricia squeaked as she finally guessed Antonie's plan.

"*Sí*. I owe him one and I always pay my debts," she purred. "Come. If we move we will get there before the wine is gone."

They increased their speed just a little and Justin made no complaint. Antonie guessed that he was eager to get home. At the ranch there would be a soft bed to ease his pain.

Antonie kept an eye on Patricia, watching as the

34

girl tried not to look shocked by the increasingly free behavior around her. Even Oro grew less quiet and gentlemanly as the wine flowed. He joined Tomás in entertaining the less worldly Justin with some decidedly ribald stories. That Patricia had somehow managed to remain unaware of this side of men was very evident. Antonie was rather glad that she had not been raised as a proper little lady. It looked to have a lot of drawbacks.

She turned her thoughts to Royal Bancroft as they crested a rise and the ranch came into view. Except for jade green eyes and chestnut hair she remembered little of him. She was curious to see if he recalled her at all.

Chapter Three

"Don't worry so, Royal. I'm sure there's a simple reason for their tardiness. We just couldn't keep holding dinner, however," Marilynn said haughtily.

Royal thought twenty minutes a paltry delay but did not say so. "You're right, of course. Still, it'll soon be dark." He tensed at the sound of a commotion in the front hall. "Ah, maybe they're here at last."

He gaped as widely as his guests at the person who finally entered the dining room. That it was neither Patricia nor Justin was all that really registered in Royal's mind. Those two appeared in the doorway an instant later but he did not really notice them. He only faintly noticed that the ladies at the table were looking terrified and the men were gawking.

The girl wore snug black pants that nicely displayed her gently rounded hips and slim legs. Her black shirt fit equally well over her high, full breasts. Her corn-silk hair was gathered in one thick swatch, tied with a red bandana and brought forward over her right shoulder to hang in one thick wave past her hips. A single holster was at her tiny waist, sloping to her hip, and a knife hilt was visible over the top of her boot yet, strangely enough, none of it distracted from her

36

femininity. When she reached him, she pushed back her hat which gave him a brief glimpse of purple eyes, grinned as she sat on his lap and began to heartily kiss him.

Startled was not all that Royal felt. He forgot all about the guests seated at his table as her full breasts pressed against his chest, her long fingers stroked his neck and her honeyed tongue stroked the inside of his mouth. When she pulled away, he finally put purple eyes, black clothes and cornsilk hair together to make a name.

"Antonie," he croaked, hoping his guests would think he was dazed with surprise instead of white hot lust.

"*Sí, gringo.*" She wondered where her breath had gone. "Now we are even, eh?"

"No. I think you're a notch above me. I didn't kiss you like that," he said softly. "What are you doing here?"

"Royal," hissed Marilynn.

"Oh." He realized he was still holding Antonie on his lap and set her on her feet before him.

"I brought your sister and brother back, *gringo.*" Leaning against the table, Antonie nodded toward the door.

His eyes flew to the doorway where Patricia and Justin stood with a matched set of well armed men. Patricia was looking wide-eyed and shocked, but Justin was snickering along with the twins. It was that slight sign of camaraderie that lessened the threatening appearance of the well-armed twins. Justin's battered appearance told Royal that there had been some trouble, however, and, with Cole following suit, he started toward them. Antonie slid into Royal's seat and surveyed the table.

Patricia gave a small cry and ran to the ready

shelter of Royal's arms. "We were attacked. The hands were killed."

"Ramirez, the bastard," roared Henry Collins.

"No," Antonie said quietly as she helped herself to a piece of pie. "It was Raoul Mendez."

"Are you sure?" Cole asked as he helped Justin sit down.

"*Sí*," Oro replied as he sat on the arm of Antonie's chair and helped himself to some wine. "There were six of them."

"Nonsense," growled Collins. "Mendez doesn't come to this area. It was that damned Ramirez, I tell you."

"And I tell you, canyon mouth," snapped Antonie, "that it was Mendez. Ah, *por Dios*, strawberries." She stabbed one with her knife and rolled it in the sugar then popped it into her mouth, giving an ecstatic sigh.

"Ah, folks," Royal began apologetically after he had found a seat for Patricia, "I think we will have to call it a night."

He hastily cleared his home of guests. It was hard not to tell Henry just why he trusted Antonie's word on who the attackers had been. He replied to Marilynn's somewhat shrill demands about who Antonie was with the same vagueness. It was not only a need to hear what had happened that hurried him but an eagerness to feast his eyes on the woman Antonie had become.

"Never seen a house emptied so fast," drawled Cole as Royal strode back into the dining room.

"They'll find excuses to come by tomorrow, I've no doubt." He collapsed into a chair next to Antonie and sent her a mock glare. "Was it necessary to insult one of my guests?" Royal mused that the way she ate strawberries was positively lewd.

"Bah, that pig talks through his," she paused and

38

grinned, "hat. I know my *banditti*, eh, *gringo?*"

"Without doubt, but I am not about to tell Henry why that is." He glanced pointedly at the twins.

"Ah, Oro and Tomas Degas. Manuel's sons." She giggled when Royal groaned. "Oro has the scar."

"You said you were attacked?" he asked Patricia, taking her hand in a gentle grasp.

"On the way to San Antonio," she replied, her voice unsteady as she recalled everything, telling the tale with Justin's occasional help.

"You weren't hurt, were you, Pattie?" he asked tensely when she had finished, for the extent of the personal attack upon her was not made really clear.

"No, the rabbit is whole," Antonie replied when Patricia seemed struck speechless. "The bastard died—quickly."

"Thank you, Antonie. You and your friends must stay the night. Rest before you go back."

"We are not going back. Not yet. We are here to give you your ranch."

Royal's brows shot up. "How can you give me something I already have?"

"I put that wrong. I mean we are here to see that you keep what you have. That will clear Juan's debt. He told me to come here and to see to this matter. I promised him on his deathbed, so here I am, *gringo*, and here I stay until all is done."

"Ramirez is dead?" Cole asked.

"*Sí.*" She fought down a grief she had not really dealt with yet. "It is over."

"I am sorry for your loss, Antonie," Royal said quietly.

"Ah, well, he, Julio and Manuel will give the devil a good run, eh? Now I must clear his debt."

"There's no debt, Antonie. You could've killed Cole but you didn't and now you've helped these two.

39

That's more than enough."

"No, I told Juan I would come and help save your ranch. This I will do."

"Save it from what?" He tried to still the erotic images forming in his head as he watched her lick the sugar off her fingers.

"From whom. I do not know. Someone close, Juan said. Raoul is in his pay. He killed your parents and is the one who keeps raiding you. There is to be much trouble for you on this drive you plan. We will be your guns."

"Where did Juan get his information?" Royal had recently begun to think that his trouble was not all bad luck.

"This I cannot tell you. It was not for me to know. But, if Juan said you are to have trouble, you will have it."

"Much more trouble and there won't be any need to worry about the ranch," grumbled Justin. "We'll lose it for sure."

"Exactly," said Antonie. "That is how the game is played. Enough little cuts and you bleed to death, eh?"

"Colorfully put," Royal drawled, hastily pouring himself a glass of the wine that Antonie, Tomaś and Oro were drinking so much of. "Just the other day I was thinking that it couldn't all be rotten luck. We were being hit harder and more often than any of the others. It was as if our every move was known. This drive now. I've only talked to a few people about it, but Juan heard of it in Mexico."

"We've known the people around here since we were were born. Who the hell could it Be?" Cole wondered aloud.

"You must think who would gain most." Tomaś began to finish off the pie.

"Unfortunately, Tomaś, that could be any one of our neighbors." Royal suddenly became aware of the fact that even Patricia and Justin were eating anything left of the desserts. "I gather you haven't had your supper," he said dryly.

"No," Patricia replied and stood up. "I'll go talk to Maria, shall I? There must be something quick she can get us."

"Yes, do that, Pattie. Careful, she's not in the best of tempers."

"Oh." Patricia stopped at the door to frown at Royal. "Has Marilynn been here helping?"

"Excessively. We'll need some rooms readied too." Pattie nodded and left, so Royal turned his attention back to Antonie.

"This Marilynn, she was the one sitting next to you?" Royal nodded and Antonie grinned. "She is hot for you, *gringo*, eh?"

Sending a quelling look at his snickering brothers before replying, Royal said firmly, "She was being neighborly and helping with this affair."

Antonie made a mocking noise. "If you do not want to marry her, you'd best start running faster, *amigo*. She has set a claim on you. I see the way she stares when I greet you."

"The manner of your greeting would make anyone stare."

"Pretty good, eh? I think of that as we were riding here. Even practiced, eh, Oro?"

"*Sí*, but you never said which one of us was best, *querida*. You may admit it was Oro. The other two will take it like men."

Knowing she was being set up for an awkward situation, Antonie smiled slowly and leaned toward Royal, slipping her arm around his neck. "I think maybe it was this *gringo*. More practice than you or

41

the other two."

This time Royal was not restrained by surprise. He drank greedily from her strawberry-sweetened mouth. His hands ached to move over her gentle curves but the sound of the laughing jests of their audience restrained him.

"Por Dios!"

"Oh no, she's at it again."

Reluctantly releasing her, Royal turned to see Maria and Patricia in the doorway. He went to help them with the food they had brought. It was a diversion he needed to get his thoughts out of a decidedly carnal vein. Seeing that Oro had slipped into his chair as soon as he had left it, he sat between Oro and Patricia after a wide-eyed Maria had left.

As the others ate, Royal studied Antonie and the Degas twins. It was hard to evaluate what relationship existed there. That they were close was easy to see, but whether it was as friends or lovers was not. He acknowledged a somewhat furious loathing of the possibility that she was the lover of any man, but did not delve into the why of that.

Cole was right. The girl was certainly something. She was still small, still delicately beautiful, but now she exuded a subtle sensuality and possessed the woman's body to match it. There was a wildness in her, barely leashed, that called to a man, beckoned to him to test how it would affect her passion. He had sensed some of it in her kiss and was more than eager to savor it fully.

"Have you thought of who is after your land?" Antonie asked Royal, proud of how clearly her wine-tangled tongue had performed.

"No. It's going to need a great deal of looking into. I don't want to believe it of any of the ones I know." He sighed.

"Ah, well, there is time yet before your drive. It is too bad that Raoul's man knew nothing, but Raoul knows we watch now," Oro said coldly, his face briefly setting into harsh lines that made him look far older than his twenty-two years.

While Oro had spoken, Antonie had realized that she had passed her limit of wine. Juan had taught her well and she recognized the signs of impending collapse. With a graceful dignity that belied her inebriated state, she rose and walked to the door.

"I will go to bed now. *Buenos noches.*"

She made her way carefully up the stairs, meeting Maria and a young maid just coming out of a room. With extreme politeness, she inquired about which room had been allotted to her. Maria timidly directed her and watched wide-eyed as Antonie walked to her bed, lay down and promptly closed her eyes. Antonie made no reply to the woman's soft worried inquiries and heard Maria return to her work muttering about what sort of people the *patrón* was getting mixed up with.

"Is she all right?" Cole asked a little worriedly, after Antonie's abrupt departure.

"*Sí,*" Tomás replied with a grin. "Too much wine."

"Oh, yes, well, there were those four bottles we drank on the way here," mused Justin, oblivious to the startled looks of his elder brothers.

"But she doesn't know what room is hers," protested Patricia.

"I think Maria's still up there. She'll tell her," Royal said.

"That's all right, *amigo*, we'll see to it," Oro said as he and Tomás moved to the door. "The *chica* should at least have the right bed."

"And to be tucked in, eh?" Tomás added suggestively with a laughing glance toward a shocked Patricia as Oro urged him out of the room. "Must take her guns off, *sí*, and her boots. Ah, her hat," he continued irrepressibly as Oro quickly closed the door to cut off his words.

Patricia broke the silence a moment later. "No more. I won't have it. Not in my house."

She was out the door before Royal could stop her. He hastily followed, as did Justin, although he needed Cole's strong arm for some support. Patricia was just storming into the room as they reached the top of the stairs and they crowded in the doorway. Oro had just taken off one of Antonie's boots and Tomás was struggling to remove the holster from her inert body. Royal saw Maria edge her way into the room as quietly as possible.

"Get out! Out!" Patricia yelled, snatching the boot from Oro and pushing him toward the door. "You might not think there's anything wrong in taking clothes off willy-nilly but I do and I won't have it. Not here. You can't carry on like that here."

"Where is our room, eh? We go to bed now too," protested Tomás as he followed Oro in a hasty retreat out the door.

"Well it's not here," snapped Patricia, getting ready to slam the door.

"Two doors down on the left," yelled Maria even as the door slammed shut.

"*Caramba*," breathed Tomás. "The rabbit turned into the lion, eh?" He started to laugh.

Steering his giggling brother down the hall, Oro drawled, "Time for bed. *Buenos noches, señors*. Check the *chico*'s bandages before he sleeps."

"What bandages?" asked Cole as he and Royal took Justin to his room.

"My ribs got pretty badly bruised," Justin explained as he sat on his bed. "Antonie wrapped them."

Royal winced in sympathy as he and Cole undressed Justin and saw the bandaging. The wounds were not truly bad ones but they were the sort that could be very uncomfortable. By the time they had him settled, his bruised ribs rewrapped, Royal could see that Justin was in a lot of pain. He hastily got his brother a drink and was pleased to see Justin recover enough to talk for a while.

"Patricia wasn't badly hurt, was she?" Cole asked quietly.

"No. They ripped her bodice and one of them mauled her a bit but he got a knife in the back. I think the killing bothered her more. The two hands with us, then five more men downed right before her eyes. She's never seen the rough side before. Then those three stepped out of the dark and weren't looking much safer than the ones they just killed." He grinned slightly. "I think Antonie's calling her 'the rabbit' all the time snapped Patricia out of her shock quicker than anything else could have."

"Strange trio. Can't figure out what they are to each other," Royal mused, thinking Justin might have a clue.

"That's hard to figure. They act like brothers and sister but they sure didn't kiss her like brothers would. Yet, they thought it funny that she planned to kiss you and when she kissed me. That isn't a lover's way. Don't think so anyway."

"I'm beginning to feel sorely deprived," Cole drawled and the three brothers laughed softly. "What's all this about taking clothes off?"

"Ah, they went swimming. Stripped down right in front of us save for the underdrawers. Pattie kept her eyes covered which set Antonie and Tomás laughing although Antonie kept her chest covered which I think she does not usually do. They were just like kids, like

45

we used to be at the swimming hole, not like two men, who probably know three times what I do, swimming with a lovely, half naked girl. Except for seeing more skin than she's ever seen, they did nothing Pattie could not have looked at." He looked sharply at Royal. "Antonie said I was to ask you about this debt she keeps talking about."

Sighing, Royal reluctantly repeated the tale. "I've kept silent about it for seven years, then suddenly have to tell it twice." He savored a little of his brandy. "I never expected any payment. I reckon Juan was just waiting for an opportunity."

"Antonie said it wasn't Juan pulling the raids on us or who shot our folks."

"I never really thought it was, Justin. That's how I thought Juan was repaying me. It was Mendez, right?"

Justin nodded. "That's what they say, Royal. Still, how can they help us? They must be wanted."

"Not that I know of," remarked Cole. "Always stayed out of it 'cept that once when I got this."

"She flat out admitted shooting you. I couldn't picture it even though I think it was Antonie who threw that knife, 'cause she pulled it out of the guy, wiped it off and slipped it back inside her boot. She's just so dainty looking, though."

"She's spent eleven years with Ramirez," Royal pointed out. "He may have kept her out of things but she'd know how to fight if she had to."

"I reckon," agreed Justin. "She talked about how you'd told Juan what to do to make her a lady as we shared a bottle of tequila." He grinned when his brothers laughed. "Are they right about someone close to us being after our ranch?"

"It's a very reasonable explanation for our troubles," Royal answered as he collected the glasses.

"So they'll be staying around a while then." Justin could not fully hide a yawn.

"Yes. It ought to be interesting."

Antonie could hear voices as if through a thick fog but did not move as Patricia helped Maria slip a clean white shirt on her. As Maria tugged the sheet over her, Antonie vaguely sensed that she was being studied. She struggled to listen to what was said and hoped she would be able to remember.

"She's very pretty."

"*Sí*," agreed Maria, "but I do not think she is Mexican."

"No, but she grew up in Mexico, I think. She has the accent and all. Spanish is more her tongue than English."

"*Señorita*, why has the *patrón* let these three stay? They are *banditti*. I am sure of this."

"Perhaps, but they say they owe Royal and they've come to help us keep our ranch. I think they are a little wild," Patricia said with a weak laugh, "but I don't think that they're bad really. They were good to Justin and me."

"There can be good in anyone but maybe not enough. One dress," Maria muttered.

"She treats me just like I'm a child," Patricia said a little truculently.

"To her I think you are."

"But she's only two years older than me," Patricia argued.

"She has seen and done much more than you, *chica*. Maybe more than your brothers, eh? This makes her older than her age. *Buenos noches*."

"*Buenos noches*, Maria."

Hearing the door shut behind the two women,

47

Antonie stopped fighting to stay conscious. She had found out what she had wanted to know. Everyone was willing to at least give her and the twins the benefit of a doubt. Only one thing troubled her and that was the way that Patricia had constantly studied Oro. Antonie felt that that could lead to some real difficulties but, at the moment, she was too drunkenly exhausted to worry about it much.

In their bedroom, Tomás and Oro settled in for the night. As Tomás turned the covers down on the bed, he looked at Oro with a wide grin on his face.

"Like kings, eh, Oro?" Tomás asked with pleasure in his voice. "I did not expect to be treated as the guest."

"I think it is Antonie who gets us such good treatment. They cannot put her out with the hands so we do not go either."

"*Sí*, but I am not going to complain. I think there could be trouble with that Royal. He has eyes for the little one."

"The little one is now twenty, Tomás. It may be time to let her say *sí* or no."

"Maybe. That man is not one to take a woman who says no."

"This is what I think. Still, we will be sure that Antonie knows what her '*sí*' can mean before we relax our watch on her."

Royal stealthily moved away from the door. Cursing softly, he wished that they had said more, said enough to let him know if they were Antonie's lovers. He told himself to be content with what he had learned for they could have talked in Spanish and he would have come away with nothing.

He had felt relief when he had started past their door and heard the murmur of their voices. At least for now neither of them were sharing Antonie's bed.

48

Royal intended to fill the vacant space as quickly as possible. Her kiss had not been all fun, even though inspired by it. Passion had flickered in her lovely eyes and he wanted to turn that flicker into a raging fire, a fire as strong as the one that already burned within him. He hoped fervently that the twins would not convince Antonie to ignore that fire, that they would soon be relaxing their guard as they had said they would.

"Something tells me you're staking a claim," Cole drawled as he lounged in the doorway to Royal's room.

"Really? What makes you say that?" Royal took off his jacket and started to unbutton his shirt.

"Perhaps it's the way your mind's distracted but your body is at attention." He grinned when Royal laughed. "She could belong to one of the Degas twins. Maybe even both of them."

"Could but won't for long."

"Maybe a trip to the saloon would be safer."

"Safer but not half as enjoyable. Don't worry, I intend to be persuasive and I have reason to believe that she'll be persuadable. I also think that whatever does exist between her and the Degas twins is not ironclad. They watch and protect her but do not own her."

Cole shrugged. "You won't really know until you try, will you? Don't reckon I can talk you out of trying, can I?"

"Nope. Antonie's got the face of an angel and a body that could tempt a saint and I'm no saint," he said dryly.

"Just don't end up being a martyr," Cole retorted and left with a murmured good night.

As he got into bed, Royal wondered just how much he would be risking by pursuing Antonie. It was something he just had to test, for there was no way to know the true situation between her and the twins without trying. That they were in their own room did not necessarily mean all that much for Antonie was, after all, useless to a man at the moment. Neither did their apparent lack of possessiveness prove much, for they could be casual lovers, enjoying the passion and not suffering the jealousy.

To see a saloon girl to ease his ache would be safer but he had only resorted to that type of female when he had been desperate. It was not to his taste to use women any man with the right amount of money had access to. Even Louise's girls rarely got his business. Sighing, he gave in to sleep knowing that none of those outlets would do. At the moment his body craved Antonie and Antonie alone.

Chapter Four

Despite the disapproval Maria let show on her face, Royal brought Antonie her morning coffee. He slipped quietly into her room, set her coffee down on the table by her bed and then studied her as she slept. The urge to crawl into bed with her was almost too strong to resist. There was no doubting her womanliness, yet there was a childlike innocence on her sleeping face. He sat down on the edge of the bed, bent toward her and gave in to the urge to kiss her.

Antonie woke slowly as warm lips brushed over hers, their pressure growing more and more persistent. Even before she was fully awake, she knew it was Royal and her arms slipped around his neck as she murmured his name. Her lips parted to let in his tongue, her own tongue greeting his with unrestrained delight. A purr of enjoyment echoed in her throat.

"I brought you some coffee," he said huskily as his lips traced the features of her face and he tugged the covers down.

"You are very kind, *señor*." She savored the heat he stirred in her, wondering how he did it.

"You taste like honey," he whispered against her

throat as his lips edged down the open neck of her shirt. "Honeyed silk."

Her eyes heavy with mounting passion, she watched him unbutton her shirt, his mouth lingering over each newly exposed patch of skin. She realized that she should stop him but she did not want to. It felt so good. Her hands delved into his hair, finding it thick and soft even as she reprimanded herself for letting him continue. She suddenly recalled what had always happened in the past to men who had paid her too much attention and tensed, waiting for the gunshot and dreading it.

"What's wrong?" he rasped, looking at her even as his hand slid inside her shirt to cup one full breast.

"I was expecting you to get shot," she gasped, amazed at how her body was reacting to his light touch.

"Is that how Juan handled your lovers?" He exulted over the very evident passion he was stirring in her.

"*Sí*. He shot the men who would try to have me."

"Well, Juan is no longer here so I won't be shot, will I?" He readied himself to open her shirt so that his eyes could enjoy what his hands already relished.

"I would not bet on that, *señor*."

Royal wondered how the twins had gotten into the room without his hearing them even as he eased his body off Antonie's. Both young men stood there, guns steadily aimed at him, their handsome faces unreadable although their dark eyes were hard. He also wondered if they were really guarding her against him or against her straying away from them.

"Thank you for my morning coffee, *Señor* Bancroft," Antonie said calmly as he stood up and she pulled up the covers.

Keeping an eye on the twins, Royal made his way to the door. "Maria will have breakfast ready soon."

After he was gone, the twins holstered their pistols and sat on the bed. Propping herself up against her pillows, Antonie redid her shirt and reached for her coffee. She was glad they had interrupted what was going on, for she needed some time to think about her reactions to Royal Bancroft.

"He wants you, *chica*," Oro said quietly. "He thinks you are free for the taking."

"Maybe for him I am," she said carefully. "He makes me feel very good, eh? I did not want to say no."

"His wanting you does not mean he will love you or make an honest woman of you."

"That I know, Tomás. He thinks I am a *puta*. This he will see is not true if I let him have me."

"You cannot love this man," protested Oro. "You do not know him. It is your body that speaks."

"But so loudly, eh? Such a fire. I am thinking I might be foolish to pass it by. You tell me, a fire that burns the mind clear of all thought does not happen all the time, *sí*? With just one kiss I am burning and his for the taking. Is this usual?"

"No, little one, it is not," Tomás answered. "A fire like that can happen only once I think. It also means that, if you do not love him now, you may soon. That could bring you much pain. He is a man of money and you are Juan Ramirez's *ninã*."

She shrugged. "I must think on it. Maybe the pain will be a small price to pay to taste the fire."

"It is your decision," Oro declared and Tomás nodded, thus ending any interference they could cause and leaving Antonie fully on her own.

Wishing he could catch Antonie all alone again but lacking the time to wait for the opportunity at the moment, Royal got ready to head out and check his stock. He could not recall ever having been so instantly or so fully aroused by a woman, especially from just one kiss. He was determined to taste all of her.

Marilynn entered the front hall and Royal forced his features into a pleasant smile and greeted her. Seeing Marilynn while he had been envisioning making love to Antonie was slightly awkward. And suddenly the idea of taking Marilynn to bed was not so attractive. Royal told himself it was only a momentary aberration as he accepted her kiss.

Antonie paused on the stairs to study the couple's light embrace. It was little more than a polite greeting between them but she felt the sharp pinch of jealousy and grimaced. It seemed it was already more than passion that she felt for Royal Bancroft. She started down the stairs only to stop again as she fought to control her temper which soared over Marilynn's words, words that cut deeply.

"I'm glad to see that those *banditti* are no longer here."

"They're not *banditti*, Marilynn. They saved Patricia's and Justin's lives. More than that, they've warned me of a danger I did not really see."

"Are you saying that they are still here?" Marilynn gasped.

"Of course." Royal's irritation was not well hidden and he wondered why her remarks should bother him so much.

Marilynn was incensed, something she did little to hide. Her voice turned sharp. "You let that Mexican slut stay the night in this house?"

Still furious but in control, Antonie skipped down the stairs. Her temper was further eased by the clearly read anger she saw on Royal's face. She went up to Royal, pulled his face down to hers and gave him a lingering kiss which he did nothing to resist. Slipping

54

her arm around his waist, she ignored his questioning glance and looked at Marilynn.

"This slut at least knows her business, *señorita*. I never leave a customer unsatisfied." Stepping away from Royal just a little, Antonie let her hand run down his hip to linger briefly on his thigh. "Such a man as this needs a lot of satisfying, eh? A night is hardly long enough." Putting her hat on, she started out the door, Marilynn's shocked, red face providing her with great amusement. "*Buenos dias, señorita*. Oh, the Yellow Rose of Texas," she began to sing, holding her laughter until she was out of earshot.

Royal's chuckles were hard to stifle but he struggled to as he tried to soothe Marilynn's anger. "She was joking, Marilynn."

"Was she?" Marilynn asked coldly as he escorted her into the dining room. "I failed to see the humor."

As he poured them each some coffee, he restrained his annoyance over her attitude and replied, "She obviously overheard your remarks and was getting back at you for them. Now, what can I do for you this morning?"

By the time she met the twins, Antonie was again in a truly cheerful mood.

"*Chica*, you must see what Old Pete just showed us," Tomás said as he grasped her by the hand.

Allowing herself to be dragged along after a grizzled, bowlegged man, Antonie asked, "What is it?"

Before a grinning Tomás could answer they had reached a spot in the rear of the stables and Antonie was able to see for herself. There, nestled cozily in a bed of hay covered by a blanket, was a dog with puppies. With a gasp of delight she knelt in the midst of the tussling puppies who were evidently being weaned despite their reluctance. In a moment she had chosen one that reminded her strongly of Sage with its

55

golden coat, mournful brown eyes and large paws that, for now, made the puppy very clumsy.

"Is he not *magnifico*?" she cried, standing up with the wriggling puppy in her arms. "Could I have this one?"

"Can't see why the hell not," said Old Pete, "but I reckon you'd best be asking the boss as them's his pups."

Royal was trying to think of a polite way to send Marilynn on her way so that he could get some work done when Antonie burst into the room crying, "Royal, say *sí*. You cannot be so mean as to say no to me on this, eh? It is only a small thing I am asking."

"Wait," he protested laughingly as she flung a slim arm around his neck and she and the puppy dampened his face with kisses.

"No. You must say *sí* or we will drown you in slobber." She giggled. "*Por favor?* I will never ask for another thing."

"I gather you want that cur you're holding," he drawled, struggling not to laugh as he held her slightly away from him.

"Cur?" she squeaked. "This fine animal is no cur but a *magnifico* blend of breeding."

"Nicely put. Yes, you may keep the dog." He forgot all about Marilynn standing there and savored the long full kiss of gratitude Antonie bestowed upon him.

"You're easily pleased," he murmured as she pulled away.

"Am I?" she whispered huskily and slowly winked, a glint of impishness lighting up her eyes. "We shall see," she purred.

Even though he knew he was being baited, his passion soared so he hurriedly changed the subject.

"What will you name him?"

"*El Magnifico*," she announced grandly, then swiftly held the puppy away from her. "*El Magnifico* is *mucho* leaky."

"That is disgusting," Marilynn said coldly, interrupting their laugher and clearly not entirely referring to the dog. "Animals should not be allowed in the house for that very reason. If that is not cleaned properly, it will smell and ruin that carpet.

"Then I will buy Royal a new carpet," Antonie said calmly as she mopped up the wet spot.

"With what?" Marilynn snapped, ignoring Royal's hissed admonishment. "Where would you get that kind of money?"

"From what Royal pays me," Antonie paused and looked directly at Marilynn, smiling slowly, "for the use of my holster, *señorita*."

"That's enough, Antonie," Royal reprimanded softly when Marilynn gasped in shock, although he felt like laughing.

Sighing, Antonie moved toward a settee placed near the fireplace. "I will sit here and be very quiet and good, *patrón*."

He watched her doubtfully for a moment then turned back to talk to Marilynn. It was hard going for she was obviously in a snit. He breathed a silent sigh of relief when he was finally able to escort her to the door.

In a way, he recognized that Marilynn had, some right to act indignantly. He had done nothing to stop her growing belief that they were a match. Royal knew that his interest in Antonie was very evident. Nonetheless, Marilynn's attitude irritated him. It was becoming increasingly more difficult to stay calm and polite with her. Her leaving eased a tension he had only just begun to recognize.

Stepping back into the room where he had left Antonie, he studied her as he approached her. She was much akin to a child as she sprawled on the settee letting the puppy romp around her, giggling at his actions. He recognized that characteristic as just another part of her attraction for him. She was an ever-changing delight, a different side of her nature always flickering to the surface.

Sitting next to her, he said, "You really shouldn't bait Marilynn."

"I either bait her or I belt her, eh? Which do you rather?" She laughed as the puppy slid down her leg.

"Bait her, I guess." He sighed as he put an arm around her shoulders, his hand toying with a thick swatch of her hair. "There is no denying that she's insulting. It just puts me in a damn awkward position, that's all, having to always smooth ruffled feathers."

"And she is the one you are to marry?" Antonie found herself tensed for his reply.

"Damned if I know. It's one of those things everyone seems to expect or think I should do."

"But you have not said yes or no, *si?*" She sighed with quiet pleasure when his long fingers began to caress her neck.

"Exactly." He bent his head to kiss her throat, his tongue sliding over the increasing pulse there. "I don't love the woman."

"But there are advantages, eh? She would make a very fine mistress of the rancho. You have exchanged no vows?"

"Do you think I'd be doing this if I had?" His hand moved over her thigh.

"I do not think so but I do not know you well. Ah," she sighed with evident delight as his hand brushed over her breast.

"I have made no vows." His mouth hovered over hers as he undid her shirt. "What about your watch dogs?"

Her tongue traced his lips and his soft growl of pleasure delighted her. "They watch no more."

As his mouth possessed hers his hand slid inside her shirt. Her eyes were already heavy lidded, the purple deep and rich with passion. When his eyes fell to the full, creamy breasts he had exposed, he caught his breath. The rose colored tips were taut and beckoning, a lovely topping to her high breasts.

He traced each hard nub with his finger once before he bent his head to let his tongue flick over each one.

Antonie bucked slightly as pure fire shot through her veins. Her hands plunged into his thick hair as her body arched to his caress. When his mouth closed over one aching tip to draw on it with a slow greediness, she groaned, her hips squirming, restless with the fierce new feelings within her.

"You like that, do you, honey?" he whispered just before his hungry mouth latched onto her other breast.

Sí, sí," she gasped, holding his head close to her. "It burns down to my toes."

"Come with me now, Antonie," he urged between kisses that traced the fine lines of her face. "Let me love you."

"No, not now." She stood up in one lithe action, her unsteady fingers beginning to redo her shirt.

"Why not?" he rasped, trying to rein in his runaway passion.

Antonie found that question hard to answer. There was an ache in her that begged to be satisfied but she could not let it rule her. This was not something she could simply fall into. He was not a man promising love and marriage, only passion. She had to weigh the loss against the gain rationally and rationality was not something she possessed when he held her.

"Why not, Antonie?" he asked quietly, still burning for her but more in control of himself.

She put on her hat, picked up *El Magnifico* and looked at Royal. "It is a big decision, whether or not to take a lover. I cannot let the fire rule me. That would be unwise."

"You can't ignore that fire either, Antonie."

"No, I cannot," she agreed and started for the door, "but I must think on whether tasting the fire is worth the price."

He was not sure he understood what she meant. Shrugging, he stood and started to go outside, hoping to work off his frustrations. What mattered was that she had not said no. There was a chance for him yet. He intended to grab that chance for he had never wanted a woman so badly or tasted a passion so fierce before. This was something he could not let slip by.

After a short walk, Antonie found herself a well shaded grassy spot away from the ranch and sat down. She watched the puppy romp as she thought. When her quiet moment was interrupted by Marilynn's sudden appearance Antonie was not really surprised. The woman wanted Royal Bancroft. It was only to be expected that she try to warn off or scare off the competition whether it be for his body or for his heart. Antonie stayed seated, watching the woman dismount from her horse with cool, expressionless eyes, something that plainly annoyed Marilynn.

There was no denying that Marilynn was lovely, but Antonie felt that there was something not quite right about the woman. After a moment's consideration, she was confident that it was instinct and not jealousy that made her feel that way. Marilynn lacked warmth. There was a cold emptiness in the woman's lovely eyes, a stiffness to her soft, womanly figure. Even the anger Marilynn radiated was cold and controlled. Royal might find elegance and all the accomplishments of a lady in her but he would find little passion. Antonie wondered if he had already guessed that.

"You don't really know your place, do you, señorita?" The way Marilynn sneered the last word made it an insult.

"My place is where I am." Antonie was determined not to let the woman make her angry.

"How very clever. If you were wise, you would find your place elsewhere."

"Do you threaten me?"

"No. I'm merely warning you. Royal is mine. I will not allow you to take him away from me."

"Perhaps I only mean to borrow him for a while."

Marilynn smiled coldly. "And give up all this? You want me to believe you would not try to become mistress of this ranch?"

"It is but dirt, señorita. If I decide to try for anything it will be for the man, not the dirt he stands on."

"How very noble, but you do not fool me." She remounted, glaring down at Antonie. "I won't stand idly by and let you have your merry way. I intend to have Royal, to be mistress of this ranch and I won't let any little Mexican slut get in the way of that."

"Ah, *El Magnifico*," Antonie sighed after Marilynn had left, "that woman begs for to be shot. She has not tasted the fire."

A smile touched her face when Oro appeared at her side a few moments later. "I thought this a hidden place."

"The *gringo* bitch found you easily enough." He lay

down, crossing his arms beneath his head.

"She warned me to stay away from Royal."

"It is said that they will marry."

"Royal says he has made no vows, given no promises. I believe him. She hungers to rule over his kingdom."

"And what do you hunger for, little one?"

"The fire. I want to taste the fire. I think and I think and no reason dims that hunger." She settled into the same position as Oro. "I think that if I do not taste the fire I will always hunger for it, and always wonder about it: That could be a greater pain than what I might receive if my heart follows my body. Regret can be harder to bear than loss, eh?"

"Yes. Give it a few more days, Antonie. Be sure before you give away your innocence. It can never be retrieved."

"I know." She reached out to clasp his hand. "I will think on it a while longer. It is not a decision to make hastily, I know."

Royal saw them as he rode past. It was an innocent scene but it annoyed him. She claimed that her guard dogs were no longer watching over her but they were still too close for his liking.

Oro suddenly rolled on top of her. "Maybe you just need a man, little one."

She let him kiss her, even heartily participated. His skilled hand traced her curves as his mouth plied hers with slow sensuality. She was not unmoved, could even see that it could be very nice to make love with Oro, but it was not the same.

"There is not the fire. I could make love to you but I do not have to, if you see what I am saying." Seeing the warmth in his dark eyes, she suddenly worried if her words had hurt him. "Did you feel a fire, Oro?"

"Not as you mean. I am a man and you are lovely

62

and soft. It would be easy to feel passion for you, to make love to you." He sat up. "You are not just hungering for a man though, but one man. Royal Bancroft. Lying with me would not solve the problem." He smiled slightly. "I know what you speak of but I have never felt it. I am almost jealous. If you decide to lie with him, you will taste something I have never known for all my times of bedding a woman. I will not fault you if you do choose to go with the man."

"That is a comfort. It would pain me to disappoint you. Now," she smiled, "you must help me begin *El Magnifico*'s training."

He laughed heartily at her choice of name just as she had thought he would and the air of seriousness disappeared. They romped like two children as they played with the puppy, teaching him very little. For the moment, Royal Bancroft was completely forgotten.

Royal quietly rode away, still very confused and angry about the relationship that existed between Antonie and the Degas twins. For a brief moment, Antonie and Oro had certainly appeared to be lovers but the embrace had ended quickly, their air of innocence returning within an instant. He was still trying to answer his own questions when he met Cole, who had clearly seen where he had been.

"Did your little *señorita* need soothing after Marilynn spoke to her?" Cole asked.

"Marilynn spoke to Antonie?"

"Oh yes. Didn't hear much but it was plain as day that dear Marilynn was telling the girl to stay the hell away from you."

Royal swore softly. "Marilynn oversteps her bounds. I've made not one damn promise, not even hinted at one."

"We-ell, silence in the face of all the assumption could have been enough for her. You know what's been thought for a good long time about the two of you but you have never flatly denied it. You've given the woman free rein around this place. You can't fully blame her for thinking everything's all set."

"Perhaps not, but she's never shown this sort of possessiveness before and I've been far from faithful."

"No, but you've never brought any of your women to the ranch before. Neither have you ever been in such obvious heat."

"Is it that clear to see?" Royal was not all pleased to be so easily read.

Cole chuckled. "Air plain sizzles between you and the little *señorita*. She is a fine looking piece."

There was a not-so-subtle intonation in Cole's words that made Royal frown. The plan was to bed her not wed her and Cole's approval of the girl shouldn't have mattered to him. But it did.

"Don't you like Antonie?"

"Can't say. Don't know her. Still, she dresses like a man and shoots like one. That ain't the way of a lady."

"Don't forget, she was raised by a *bandito*," Royal said and was as surprised by the defensive note in his voice as Cole seemed to be.

There could be a chance that it was more than his loins being drawn to Antonie Doberman Ramirez. He was no snob, cared little what stock people sprang from, but the daughter, adopted or not, of a *bandito* who had been the scourge of Texas for twenty years or so was stretching tolerance a little too far. He could tell by Cole's face that his brother felt much the same way and Cole's next words confirmed that suspicion.

"I don't. Just don't you forget it," Cole said quietly. "I've seen her sensual side, her childlike side as well. Despite her clothes, she's damn feminine. You don't

64

forget she's a woman, that's for damn sure. I've also seen her pull a gun on a man with the clear-eyed intent of killing him. It don't matter one tiny bit that she wasn't born of Juan's blood. He raised her, taught her. She grew up with thieves and murderers. She doesn't live by our rules. Don't forget that for one minute, Royal. Enjoy her all you want, but don't trust her for one minute, not for an inch."

Watching Cole ride off, Royal thought about what his brother had said. It all made sense, was very sound advice, but he could not feel the same. He could seem to do little else but trust Antonie although he knew that that trust had barely been tested. Spurring his horse after Cole, he decided he would be wise not to disregard Cole's words. Whatever happened between him and Antonie, he would strive to remember who she was and where she had come from.

Chapter Five

Heavy with the unfulfilled promise of rain, the night felt as if it were pressing in on Antonie, choking her. Finding Oro, she told him she was going to the swimming hole they had been shown the other day. Not feeling inclined himself, he sent her on her way with a word of caution. Although things were peaceful, Antonie agreed that it would not be wise to ease her wariness. She was not even sure she could. It was too much a part of her.

It had been a week since Royal had last kissed her and Antonie began to think that he had changed his mind about wanting her. She also knew that he was the reason that she found the weather oppressive. He had left her with a deep restlessness.

Royal too found himself stifled by the night, something he had never suffered from before. A restlessness had taken possession of him in the last few days. He cursed softly and rose from the desk, where he had been trying to do some work, to go look for Antonie. A week was long enough for her to decide what she wanted. If she had not decided yet, he would do it for her.

Oro studied Royal as he asked of Antonie's whereabouts. "It might be wisest if I do not tell you."

"And why is that?" Royal immediately wondered if Antonie was with a man and frowned when the thought of that actually hurt.

"*Señor*, I am not stupid. You burn for the little one. Tonight the flame is very hot, eh?"

"Surely that is a matter strictly between Antonie and me."

Shrugging, Oro said, "*Sí* and no. It is her body so it is hers to do with as she wants. Then again, she is like a sister to me and you can understand how I feel. I do not want to sit back and watch her get hurt."

"I have no intention of hurting Antonie."

"That is easy to say, eh?" Oro sighed. "Ah well, it is out of my hands. Antonie herself asked that. She has gone swimming."

"Alone?"

Oro nodded.

"Where?"

"Justin said it was the place of your childhood."

Upon reaching the pool surrounded by a stand of cottonwoods, Antonie knew exactly what she might be getting into with Royal. A week of thinking about him and being his lover had not really decided her. It was when she thought that he might have decided not to bed her that her decision had been made. The thought that she might have already lost her chance was so painful that she knew she would give in if he asked her again.

Each time she had thought about his kisses that delicious warmth his touch created had curled inside her until now it seemed to be there all the time. Seeing him, even from a distance, was enough to fill her head with erotic images. The man was becoming a drug.

Shedding the last of her clothes, she dove into the water, relishing its coolness. While it eased the discomfort of the heat of the night, it did nothing for the heat within her. Swimming naked held its own sort of seductiveness. Yet again her mind filled with images of her and Royal making love. Antonie softly cursed the man for nudging awake feelings she could not seem to control.

Royal saw her as he reached the stand of cottonwoods. Her hair was like a beacon, in the way that it caught and held the moonlight. For a moment he simply watched her, enjoying the grace she displayed as she swam. Then, careful not to startle her with too stealthy a move, he approached the edge of the pool.

"Have you come for a swim?" she asked, careful to keep herself modestly covered by the water.

"Am I invited?"

"It is your pool."

He began to remove his clothes, pausing when he was stripped down to his underdrawers. Recalling that Justin had said the trio swam in their underdrawers, he decided it might be best to leave his on. To dive in totally naked would be presumptuous and the last thing he wanted was to make any wrong move or gesture.

As they swam, he noticed that she kept just out of his reach. The occasional glimpse of slim limbs tantalized him. He could not be quite sure of exactly what, if anything, she was wearing. Finally, he stopped, standing in water that reached to his waist.

"You swim like a fish," he remarked as she came to a stop far enough away so that the water covered all but her slim shoulders.

"It was a skill Juan thought good to know." Her hand itched to smooth over his taut skin as her eyes admired his lightly haired chest.

"Come here, Antonie," he commanded quietly, tired of the waiting game they had played. "I want to hold you."

Her pulse jumped erratically at his words even as she replied, "You might find me a very large armful, *gringo*."

"I'm willing to risk that. Antonie, I want to make love to you. No, I crave it. It's nearly an obsession with me. Come here, Antonie."

She moved closer, shivering beneath the warmth of his gaze as her breast slowly cleared the water. "It is a very big step, *querido*."

His eyes fixed hungrily upon her full breasts, the rose tips hard and inviting. He reached out and pulled her into his arms. "I'll help you make it."

The feel of her breasts pressed hard against his broad chest made her tremble. Her arms slid around his neck as he took her mouth in a deep kiss which, though slow and enticing, revealed his hunger for her, a hunger she shared.

As his kisses grew more demanding, his hands smoothed down her back. When he met no obstruction, he trembled, his hands gliding over the gentle curves of her backside and urging her hips against his. The soft moan that escaped her as she came into contact with the indisputable proof of his desire sent his passions soaring. When she moved against him in growing urgency, he found himself shaking.

"You can't turn away from this, Antonie. Let me love you," he groaned against her throat.

"*Sí.*"

As he scooped her up into his arms, Antonie knew that that one small word had irrevocably committed her. He set her down and spread out her towel and his shirt for her to lie on. She mused idly that a man had no right to look so good in wet, sagging under-drawers. When she sat down on their makeshift bed and watched him shed that last piece of clothing, she decided it had to be a sin for him to look so good without them. The man was strength, grace and virility perfectly blended.

His eyes never left her moonlit curves as he knelt before her. Softly kissing her, he urged her onto her back. When he released her mouth, he stayed crouched over her, surveying her as his hand lightly skimmed over her.

"You're lovelier than I had imagined." His hands cupped and weighed her full breasts. "I've thought of you like this since the day you arrived." After caressing her waist, his hands slid to her thighs, urging them apart so that he could kneel between them. "God, you're all cream and gold. It's going to be heaven, Antonie."

She did not argue, but simply held out her arms. A shudder tore through her when his flesh met hers. It felt so good to hold him. Her body pressed against his as he kissed her, his hands stroking her curves, stirring her to the point of mindless need.

Slowly his mouth made its way to her breasts. When his tongue flicked over each hard tip, her nails lightly scored his strong back. Her cry was a mixture of relief and desire when he finally took an aching nub into his mouth. Her hands buried themselves in his hair, holding him close as he hungrily suckled her breasts until she writhed beneath him.

When her hands began to smooth over him, she realized she was not alone in being swept away. His sounds of pleasure were as unrestrained as her own and his caresses grew more urgent. When his searching hand left her thighs to touch the very center of her heat, her hands clenched his taut buttocks. So strong was her passion that she only flinched slightly, then was fully caught up in her desires again. She opened to him freely, arching to his touch as she was swallowed up in the fire he created.

"Por favor, por favor," she rasped, clutching at him in a nearly frantic urgency. *"Te quiera.* I want you. *Te quiera, mi vida."*

When he gave her what she cried for, they both halted in surprise. Antonie felt her passion dim slightly as her innocence was somewhat painfully ended but she was surprised at how little it mattered, the feel of their bodies joined as one sending her passions soaring again. Royal was stunned into immobility, unable to believe that she was untouched yet unable to deny it.

"Antonie," he rasped, uncertain about what to do, yet knowing it would be impossible to leave her now.

"Ah, querido," she moaned, her hands on his hips urging him to move. *"Por favor, mi vida. Por favor."*

She cried out with pure delight when he began to move. Her arms and legs wrapped around him tightly as she caught his rhythm, her lithe body falling into perfect time with his.

Their cries mingled as they crested passion's heights. Royal drove deeply inside her to find his release even as her inner shudders had barely begun. He held her close to him as they trembled and shook with pleasure. It was quite a while before he could make his sated body move and his desire-fogged mind recall what he had just discovered.

"You were a virgin." He glanced at himself and winced slightly for even the dim light could not hide the signs of her innocence staining his body.

"Sí," she replied calmly as she sat up. "Do not all women start that way?"

He frowned as he watched her go to the stream to

71

wash herself, easing the slight discomfort he had caused her. After a moment, he too went to wash off. Then, taking her by the hand, led her back to their rough bed and sat down, drawing her down beside him. He felt uncertain and did not like it.

"Why didn't you tell me you'd never had a lover?"

"Would it have mattered?" She moved so that she faced him and reached out to let her fingers tangle in the light hair on his chest.

Looking at her, his eyes and body delighting in the way her thick hair draped over her body in a futile attempt at modesty, rasped, "No, I don't think so." When her hand trailed down the thin line of hair that led to his groin, he muttered "I would have been more gentle."

"I have no complaints, *querido*." She let her hand gently caress him low on his belly, then over his thighs.

"Are you sore?" He reached out to push her hair back over her shoulders, exposing her lovely breasts to his eager gaze.

"*De nada*," she purred and gently stroked his manhood, finding that not only his eyes were hungry for her.

"I saw you kissing Oro," he said thickly, his hands clenched her shoulders.

"We were seeing if it was only that I wanted a man, any man." She watched his eyelids droop and his breath grow uneven as her hand continued its intimate play. "There was no fire. It could be made but that was not what I hungered for."

"And this is what you hungered for?" he groaned as his hands moved over her breasts.

"*Sí*." This is what I craved. I decided it was worth the cost. And now that you have had me?"

72

"I will have you again," he answered as he pushed her onto her back and slowly eased into her.

"What a good idea. Ah, that feels so good. *Magnifico,*" she sighed, her hands smoothing over his lean body.

"Yes, it does feel good," he murmured as he brushed his lips over hers. "Better than I could have ever imagined."

When he kissed her, he began to move slowly. She was soon swept away again, lost deeply in her passion. There was no fighting such a fire and she knew there would be few regrets. Something told her that this was destined and destiny could not be avoided.

Afterwards they fell into a sated sleep, Antonie wrapped securely in his arms. She woke alert and tense and wondered why. Then she heard the mutter of voices and the soft sound of horses approaching at a slow walk. Nudging Royal awake, she grabbed for her clothes. Although not so quickly, Royal was soon as alert as she and they made for the cover of the trees even as they dressed.

"Raoul's men," she hissed as she crouched in their hiding place, her pistol drawn, and watched the group of five men water their horses at the pool.

"Are you sure of that?"

"*Sí.* I recognize the little fat one with the big scar on his neck. Juan gave him that."

"What are they saying? My Spanish is not good at all, just a few polite phrases."

"And they are not being very polite, eh? They plan to raid your stables. They ride there now."

"They'll never get enough horses to make it worth their while."

"They do not want horses, *querido*. They want to do you damage. Maybe kill a few men. Maybe set fire to the stables. Maybe set fire to something else." She

73

watched him frown then slowly cocked her pistol. "We will take them here. We will surprise them. We cannot warn the ones at the ranch," she pointed out when he hesitated. "They will run if they think they have been discovered. Raoul's men prefer surprise to be on their side."

He hated to admit it but she was right. Briefly he worried about her being in such a position, but then realized that she would think him foolish for worrying. She had spent most of her life in danger, finding herself in similar situations far too often. Nodding, he moved away a little so that there would be the semblance of a crossfire. At his signal they fired together.

Two men went down immediately and the others scrambled to mount, firing blindly into the shadows of the trees. Antonie cursed when a bullet seared her arm. A third man fell as the survivors fled in a direction away from the ranch. When they were sure it was clear, Antonie and Royal stepped from the shelter of the trees and approached the three bodies on the ground.

Royal watched as she searched the pockets of the dead men. She showed no signs of the hysteria he would have expected from a woman under such circumstances. Instead of tears, she was as cool-headed as he, perhaps more so. It was not until she stood up that he realized there was blood on her arm. Immediately he was at her side. To get a better look he tore her shirt sleeve.

"It is only a flesh wound," she protested only to be ignored. "They had no papers on them. I had hoped to find a name." She winced when he bathed her wound. "We still do not know who has paid Raoul to do these things."

"We stopped them. That's what matters. Perhaps if we stay lucky, Raoul will give up. Come on, we'd better get back to the house."

"Are you angry with me?" she asked as they walked, for there was an odd tone to his voice.

"No." Royal sighed. "I'm not angry at you. I'm angry that you heard them first and angry that someone is out to bring me down. I'll also have to get used to having a woman around who can fight like a man. You're not what I am accustomed to, Antonie."

"You would prefer that I weep or faint? I would not have lived long if I had done that. I learned how to fight so that I may live."

"I know, Antonie. I'm not faulting you, don't ever think that. It'll just take some getting used to," he repeated quietly.

When they reached the ranch, Antonie found herself shuttled off to her room, Maria hovering over her. She would have preferred to be with the men, discussing what had happened and what to do in the future in terms of defense. So, too, could she not help but wonder if what had happened between herself and Royal by the swimming hole was all there was to be. Deciding there was nothing to be gained in fretting over the matter, she let Maria baby her, tuck her into bed, and then found it easy to go to sleep.

After sending Oro and Tomás off to set up an extra guard, Royal poured himself a large brandy and sat down. Justin was already abed as was Patricia, so only Cole remained. Royal was not sure he even wanted Cole's company at the moment.

"And just how is it that you two happened to be caught unaware down by the swimming hole?" Cole asked. "Swimming, were you?"

"You know damn well what we were doing, not that it's any of your damn business."

"Good thing the *señorita* has sharp ears. Could have been embarrassing."

"Stop calling her that," Royal groused. "Her name's Antonie. Hell, you're wrong about her and you're right about her."

"Care to explain that a mite more clearly?"

"She was a virgin," he said quietly and nodded when Cole gaped at him in total astonishment. "I felt the same way."

"You didn't force her or, hell, I mean, take advantage of her, I reckon. She isn't going to be crying about being ruined, is she?"

"Not her. But, there I am thinking of her as a sweet untouched girl and, next, she's got a gun in her hand facing five armed men and calmly stating the advantages of attacking them there and then. Didn't blink an eye after it was over or even mention that she'd been hit. 'It's only a flesh wound,' she says. Calm and cool the whole time."

"Just like her adoptive father would have been," Cole remarked gently.

"Yes, exactly. Yet, what the hell's a girl like that doing being a virgin? The two images just don't mix."

"I'd feel damn flattered."

"Oh, I do, but, hell, those Degas boys have been with her for at least seven years, probably longer. I thought for sure they had had her."

"They started out together at a young age. That could make a difference. They feel more like siblings." Cole took a long sip of his drink, watching Royal's frowning face. "What do you do with her now?"

"What do you think?" Royal said dryly. "What I can't understand is her attitude. I had no hint that she was a virgin until it was too late. She decided she wanted me for a lover and that was that." He ran his hand through his hair. "I don't know her type. All the

76

women I've known act according to certain rules. She doesn't. I don't know which way to turn."

"Now that you have made me suitably envious, how about a little bit of advice. She thinks like a man."

Royal blinked in sudden comprehension. "You're right."

"She was raised by a man. Even I've seen that she's more comfortable around men. Oh, there's no doubt she's a woman and probably with a woman's quirks, but if you follow your own inclinations, I think she'll make sense to you more often that not. She's looking at this in the same way you are. Pattie's said several times that Antonie doesn't seem to know what to do around her, that they have little common ground. I'm sure Antonie has all the emotional twists and turns of any female but, in the main, she thinks like a man." Cole smiled slowly. "What would a man do now?"

"He'd be waiting in the bed for the damn woman to show up. Maybe sleep a little but still wait."

Royal heard Cole laugh softly as he quickly finished his drink and left. He saw the humor in the situation but also understood the concern Cole could not hide. Antonie was still Juan Ramirez's daughter, a *bandito*'s child. Royal knew that Cole felt he was headed for trouble. Even so, he mused with a little smile, he suspected that Cole would not mind a little of this sort of trouble.

Slipping quietly into Antonie's room, Royal fully expected her to wake up. Instead she slept on as if she knew there was no danger. It was evidently not any sound that alerted her to trouble but some sixth sense. In some ways she reminded him of a wild thing that would start at only a certain sound, movement or scent, quite often imperceptible to a man. Even while he could admire, actually envy, that skill, it was an unsettling one. If nothing else, it served as a strong reminder of the life she had led.

She also looked like a child with a sweet innocence on her face as she slept. Long, thick lashes, like a crescent of black silk, lay on soft cheeks and her full mouth was parted slightly. It was very hard to believe that her small, delicate hand, now curled gently under her cheek, had stroked him so boldly or held a pistol so calmly and expertly.

Quietly he undressed and slid into her bed, taking her into his arms. He was more than pleased to find her naked. Barely had he begun to enjoy that when her eyes opened and she stared at him with a sleepy sensuality that sent his pulse soaring.

"How's your wound?" he asked as his hand slid over the curve of her hip.

"It was only a graze. It is nothing to worry about." She snuggled up to him, delighting in his hard, sinewy warmth. "*De nada.* I have had worse." She drew his hand to a scar below her ribs and to her side. "This one nearly killed me."

Tugging down the sheet, he studied the scar that the dim light of the moon had hidden from him before. "How can you be so calm?"

"I did not die, eh? This too I owe to Raoul. Juan ached to kill him. Perhaps I will do that for Juan."

"Not if I beat you to it. That man's been a thorn in my side for too long. He also killed my parents."

"You will have him, *querido,*" she said confidently. "That dog's death is long overdue." Her hands slid down his leg and she smiled, deciding that enough had been said about Raoul. "Now that you know I am well, are you going to your own bed?"

"Not unless you join me there," he moaned as his head bent to her breasts.

"And what of your family?" she asked huskily, arching to his hungry mouth as it moved over her

78

breasts.

"It is my house," he stated with an ill-concealed arrogance. "You taste delicious. Honeyed silk." He gently nipped her taut stomach.

"It is my bed. I should kick you out. What would you do then, *mi amor?*"

"Come back here and convince you to change your mind."

"That sounds interesting," she purred. "Consider yourself kicked out of the bed, *gringo*. Now, convince me."

"My pleasure," he rasped as he prepared to kiss her.

"No, *señor*," she murmured against his lips. "I think *el gusto mio,* the pleasure is mine."

She made no secret of that, much to Royal's delight. If there had ever been a woman so open in her sensuality, he could not remember having her. The sound of her passion-thickened voice murmuring in Spanish and English sent his own passion to new heights. Fleetingly, he wondered if he was headed for trouble and entanglement, but the thought vanished as her limbs wrapped around him. such a journey was worth whatever fine a man had to pay.

When finally they lay sated and exhausted, Antonie sensed more strongly that with each time she made love to him she was in danger of losing far more than her much protected innocence. The sensation of being bound to him in many ways, not passion alone, grew with every kiss. She knew it would be foolish to think that such glory could come from her body alone. Antonie decided such pleasure would be worth the price.

She was sure that her heart was involved but not so sure of how deeply. She knew it would be risky, if not stupid, to lose her heart completely. Oro was right. Royal Bancroft was a man bred to land and money.

That sort of man did not give his heart nor his name to an orphan who had been raised by a *bandito*. He would search for a lady to be mistress of his big ranch and raise his children.

A wince crossed her face and she was glad Royal was asleep and unable to see it. It hurt to think of another woman sharing the important and the mundane with him. That was something she would have to watch out for.

The pleasure was all she would have. Antonie knew she had to face that. If any more came from their relationship, it would be an unexpected joy. To hope would be to bring herself more pain. Knowing that with such certainty told her she was already in far deeper than she wanted to be.

"Ah, Juan," she sighed, her eyes on the man whose dark head rested so nicely upon her breasts, "I think your *niña* has been a little unwise. I think she has stepped off a very high cliff. I pray that you are here in spirit, at my side at all times as you promised, so that you might cushion my fall."

Chapter Six

The cold water made Antonie shiver but she worked the pump handle once more, sending another burst of water cascading over her head. Standing up, she used her bandana to dry her face but let her hair stay dripping wet, the trickles of water from it cooling her a little more. Rounding up the cattle for the drive was hot, exhausting work but, as she leaned against the pump and saw Patricia sitting on the veranda, Antonie decided she preferred it to being idle. Patricia could do the work but was not allowed to unless the ranch was desperate for hands. Yet again Antonie mused that being a proper lady had a lot of drawbacks.

"Tony, I have some cool lemonade here if you wish some," Patricia called.

"Sí. That would be nice," Antonie called back as she moved to join Patricia on the veranda.

"I expect the others will be along soon," Patricia said as she handed Antonie a glass of lemonade and sat down again.

"Sí. They will be." Antonie savored the cool drink before adding, "Royal thought I looked too warm so he sent me back here."

Antonie knew that the girl studied her but pretended not to notice. It was no secret that she and Royal were lovers yet Patricia had thus far said nothing. However, Antonie had sensed a curiosity in the girl from the start. She had the feeling that that curiosity had grown to a strength that would soon overpower her extreme good manners.

"I've never met anyone like you before," Patricia suddenly burst out.

"Like me? How like me?"

Patricia blushed. "Well, I mean a woman who has a . . . a lover."

Laughing softly, Antonie shook her head. "*Sí*. You have. You just do not know it, either because it is kept quiet or they work to hide it from girls like you. It is a thing that is often hidden but it is there."

"Oh. I just don't understand. I mean, well, this is really none of my business, but don't you want a husband? Is that why you take lovers instead?"

"Lover not lovers. Only one. Only Royal."

"You mean, you were . . . you never . . . oh, dear, I'm stumbling. You were . . . ?"

"A virgin. *Sí*. I weighed it in my head for a week before I decided I would be foolish to turn away from him. I do not think I can explain it so that you can understand."

"I am not a child."

"No, but you are different. You are taught things I never learned. I think you see the world with different eyes. Ah, *chica*, sometimes there is a fire between a man and a woman, a fire so hot it burns away morals and sense."

"Is that what you have with Royal?"

"*Sí*. I know of men and women. These truths were not hidden from me as they are from you. I knew I had found something rare. Perhaps I am weak, for I succumbed to the strength of it. I did not want to return to Mexico without tasting it. The virginity you have been taught to cling to so tightly is maybe not so important to me, eh? I have no fear of living without a man. I do not like the thought of growing old alone without children but I do not fear it. If being Royal's lover now means no man will want me for his wife, then I am thinking there is no man worthy."

82

"It would seem that they should understand," Patricia said quietly. "Then again, it seems that they don't."

Antonie shrugged. "It requires a man who can understand that a woman has the same feelings as a man and that she is not a *puta* because she does. Maybe there are not many of them. It is also pride, I think. They do not like to know that another has touched what is theirs. Ah, here come the others. I hope you have a lot of this lemonade, *chica*."

The Bancrofts, Oro and Tomás soon joined them on the veranda. Antonie saw that Maria took care of the hands while Patricia served the ones on the veranda. She laughed when Royal leaned up against the railing and drew her toward him for his hair still dripped from his rinse under the pump. He shook it off like a dog, sprinkling her as he backed her up against him, then draped his arm around her shoulders.

As they discussed what remained to be done, Antonie noticed something she heartily wished she could have ignored or which did not exist. The interest Patricia had shown in Oro had not faded. It had clearly intensified. A fleeting look at the Bancrofts' faces told Antonie that the brothers had so far failed to notice how their sister studied Oro, the look in the girl's eyes when she did and the way Patricia constantly maneuvered herself close to Oro. She wondered how long their ignorance would continue.

A close study of Oro's face only added to Antonie's worry. He was not immune to the young girl. Antonie could almost feel the tension in him as Patricia constantly moved near him, sorely tempting him. Oro had always been able to turn casually away from the ladies if he felt it necessary or in his best interest to do so. More often, he simply did not notice that a lady was interested. The fact that he was not doing either now was, in Antonie's mind, very dangerous indeed. It could well mean that the fire Oro had said he had never felt was now licking at his heels.

An abrupt departure by Oro only confirmed her suspicions. Antonie tried to hide her concern. She did not want any awkward questions asked or cause any one of the Bancroft brothers to look more closely at the way Patricia acted around Oro. Somehow she was going to have to find time to talk to Oro, to try and find out just how bad things were.

"Come on," Royal said as he urged Antonie toward the door. "I need a bath."

"Need help, do you?"

"We-ell," he drawled softly, "I was hoping you'd offer to scrub my back and then I would scrub yours. It'd be easier to do that if we bathe together and think of the water we'd save."

Her thoughts, inspired by his invitation, had little to do with saving water. "And all the extra work we'll save Rosa and Maria."

"Royal."

The curse that hissed through Royal's teeth almost made Antonie smile. It did at least ease her annoyance with Marilynn's ill-timed arrival, for Royal was so clearly not delighted by the woman's visit, visits that were far too regular, Antonie mused crossly as she went into the house.

The woman thinks to keep Royal tied to her by constantly presenting herself, Antonie silently grumbled to herself as she went to her room and prepared for her solitary bath.

"That woman is here again," muttered Maria as she and the young Rosa brought in Antonie's bath water.

Antonie bit back a laugh for Maria never hid her dislike for Marilynn. "Perhaps she has some important news to tell."

"Humph. She is just trying to make sure she does not lose her place."

"Oh, I don't think she needs to worry about that,"

Antonie said quietly as Rosa and Maria started to leave. "She has only been set aside for a little while."

"Is that what you think, *señorita?* We will see. Come, Rosa, there is more water to heat."

Although it was tempting to think Maria's opinion was reason to hope, Antonie resolutely fought it. Maria hated Marilynn and would be pleased to see any other woman become Royal's wife. It was simply wishful thinking, Maria reading more into a temporary love affair than there was. Royal's attitude could have easily aided Maria in that self-deception.

Slipping into the steaming water with a sigh of pleasure, Antonie smiled crookedly as she thought of Royal. Although they did not officially share the same room Antonie never slept alone whether she slept in her own bed or his. He was openly friendly and affectionate and he liked her. Even Antonie had no doubts about that. Their relationship was not based solely upon lust, something everyone could see. But sometimes Antonie wished it was, then everything would be much simpler.

Grimacing, Antonie began to scrub herself clean, holding her breath and ducking beneath the water to rinse out her soapy hair. If Royal simply lusted for her, she would find it easier to quell her own errant hopes. Then she would know exactly where she stood, what he wanted from her and what he felt for her. Now she was too often confused, torn equally between hope and common sense, reading things into his every word or action and trying very hard not to.

Cursing herself for being an idiot did no good at all. Despite her best efforts, despite all her common sense, her heart was irrevocably involved. What should have remained an affair of the body had now become an affair of the heart, even if only on her part. That organ continually contracted and twisted every time Marilyn drew Royal's attention.

"Well, maybe he'll think twice next time," she muttered as she stepped out of the tub and started to dry off, "when he recalls how he missed some fun in the bath because he answered Marilynn's squawk."

Once dressed, she felt restless. Glimpsing Royal and Marilynn still on the veranda, Marilynn clinging to Royal's arm, Antonie decided to go out the back door. She had barely gone a few yards when she saw Oro and Patricia. Only briefly did she think about leaving them alone in what appeared to be an awkward moment. She wanted to know just how bad the situation was and if there was anything she could do to sort things out. Staying in the shadow of the house, she listened and felt her heart sink as all of her worst suspicions were confirmed.

"I just wanted to talk, Oro," Patricia said weakly.

"No, you did not." He yanked her into his arms. "This is what you want. This is why you haunt me, *chica*."

Antonie winced as Oro roughly kissed Patricia. He was not making any effort to be gentle, seductive or charming and that was not at all like Oro. He was clearly trying to drive the girl away and Antonie had the chilling feeling it was because he ached to pull the girl close and hold on tightly.

"Oro, you don't understand," Patricia said tearfully as he pushed her away.

"*Sí.* I understand. I am different, eh? Well, I am not that different, *chica*. If you keep inviting me, I will grab what you offer, use you and throw you aside as quickly as any Anglo. Stay with your flower-toting *muchachos, chica,* and leave me alone," he hissed even as he mounted the horse he had been leading. "You are not worth being shot for."

Quietly approaching the sniffling girl as Oro rode toward town, Antonie sympathized with Patricia's hurt. Oro's words had been cruel. Her sympathy, however, was severely constrained by annoyance. Patricia was dragging them all into a dangerous predicament.

"He is right, *chica*," she said quietly and smiled gently when Patricia faced her, blushing deeply.

"You were spying on us?"

"Not spying. Only watching. I saw how things were, guessed what was happening, and wished to see how bad it was."

"You mean how shamelessly I was chasing him, don't you?" Patricia snapped, self-disgust tinting her voice.

"Perhaps. Whether it is shameless or not, you must stop."

"Why? Because you want him?"

"I only want to hold one lover at a time," Antonie answered, recognizing the jealousy Patricia felt. "You will cease to tease him so, *chica*."

"And just who are you to tell me that?"

"His friend and, I am hoping, yours. Oh, you look at Oro a lot but you do not see very clearly. He is Mexican, *chica*, Mexican and Yaqui. Even many Mexicans would shun him."

"No one shuns him here."

"No, because we all fight for the same thing. He is a comrade-in-arms, eh? They do not treat him too badly in town for he works for Royal Bancroft. They do not forget what he is though, but I think you do. You close your eyes to it."

"It doesn't matter where he's from or what blood flows in his veins. Oro is a man first. People see that."

"If you think that, you are a fool. If someone said that to you, chances are that he is a liar. Fine sentiments but few follow them, especially if that man looks at someone's sister or daughter. Then they see Mexican or Indian or, worse in some eyes, a halfbreed. Then they don't care if they called him friend, drank with him or even if they owe him their life. They see only a Mexican, a halfbred, daring to look at a white woman. So, they shoot him or hang him or, if he is lucky, they only beat him badly. This is what you want to happen?"

"No! It won't," Patricia said but her denial lacked strength. "My brothers aren't like that."

"Have they ever been tested? Have you ever walked out with a Mexican or a halfbreed before?"

"Well, no, but — well, Royal is your lover. There, that shows it."

"It shows nothing. I am not Mexican or Indian nor even a little of each. My blood is Anglo. German to be exact. I am also only his lover. That is acceptable to people. In truth, I sometimes think they expect it because of what I am and where I come from. I make no secret of where and with whom I was raised. Even the sheriff knows."

She laughed and shook her head. "I think sometimes that they do not always see me as a woman. I am one they cannot understand. I act like a man but look like a woman. This confuses them. I speak like a Mexican but look like an Anglo. I do not fit any of their little niches so I think they do not hold me to their rules. Since the women do not have anything to do with me and Royal keeps the men away, I am not a worry either.

"However, you and Oro?" Antonie shook her head. "No. That will not do. Even if you are willing, that is no matter. One like Oro is not to touch an Anglo. That is a rule and one no one hereabouts will allow to be broken. If you keep after Oro and he weakens, he could well sign his own death warrant. You do not play at being his love but his executioner."

With a convulsive sob, Patricia dashed into the house. Antonie sighed, feeling the villian for a moment. She did not really want to hurt the girl but she also preferred Oro in one piece.

"Do you think she understood?" a deep voice asked in

Spanish.

Gasping in surprise, Antonie whirled to find Tomás behind her. "Just how much of it did you hear?"

Tomás shrugged. "Most of it. I saw how Oro ran off to town and thought to speak to her myself."

"You figured that it had to be Patricia who sent him scurrying away."

"Yes. It has been so for a while now. She presses and he runs. He goes to the saloon but he is not having a good time."

"No. He is hiding. I do not know if she understood what I was saying or if she believes it. It is hard to say because I am not sure of what she is feeling. Is it infatuation or is it more? Maybe she is just fascinated by Oro because he is different, perhaps even because she knows people will not approve. I wonder if she is more dangerous because she does not understand herself, what she is or is not feeling. Oro's words hurt her but it could be just a surface wound, eh? A little scratch that will quickly heal."

"What she could cause Oro would be no scratch, *chica*, and I am afraid it would never heal."

"It is that bad?" she asked softly, knowing he did not refer to the bodily wounds the bigots could inflict.

"It is that bad. I suppose we cannot just leave this place and the trouble she could bring?"

Antonie sighed and shook her head. "I must stay. I promised Juan. You and Oro did not. You may leave."

"Not without you, *chica*. Could you speak to Royal?"

"Perhaps, but I think I will wait. He does not see it. His brothers do not either. To mention this now could start trouble that could well be avoided. This may be the end of it. Oro was cruel, I was harsh and she has to know where he has gone."

"It may do it. I too would like to see trouble avoided. I also want to stay here for I wish to see an end to Raoul."

Nodding, Antonie smiled crookedly and asked, "Is *Señorita* Collins gone yet?"

Tomás laughed. "The talk of trouble makes you think of her, does it? She left a few minutes ago."

"I think I should shoot that woman. It seems it will be the only way to make her go away and be quiet," Antonie grumbled even as she started toward the house. "Take care of Oro, Tomás. I think he is in a mood to get into trouble."

"I am headed after him now," Tomás called as he strode toward the stables.

As she made her way up to her room, Antonie hoped that the uncomfortable confrontation with Patricia meant an end to the problem. If Patricia and Oro were meant to be together, she would like them to be, would like to help them instead of standing between them, but she could not ignore the ugly facts. While the Bancrofts did not seem to hold any prejudices, they had not been really tested. She did not want Oro to be the one to see just how far their tolerance would stretch.

Oro would be a good man for Patricia. He would work hard to give her a good and happy life. Although his father had been a *bandito,* Oro had not been dragged into that way of life. As Juan had, Manuel had recognized that the life of a *bandito* was not a good one and it was often very short. He had worked hard to convince his sons not to follow in his footsteps but to try for something better. Oro could probably find that something better with Patricia.

But no one will let him, Antonie thought sadly. The moment Oro and Patricia became any more than the boss's sister and a temporary hand, prejudices would boil to the surface. The fact that Patricia was the only daughter of a prominent family would only exacerbate the problem. Antonie did not know if Patricia could understand that, for she doubted that the girl had ever really seen prejudice in all its murderous ugliness. Considering the fact that Oro could be in the middle of it all, it was a thing Antonie hoped the girl would remain blissfully ignorant of.

Pausing by Royal's door, Antonie smiled as she heard the sound of splashing water. Quietly she entered the room and her smile grew when she saw the look of annoyance on his face. Marilynn's visit had plainly not put him in the best of moods.

"You are not pleased to get the dust off, *querido?*" she asked softly as she went to sit on his bed.

Royal started slightly, then looked at her, his eyes narrowing. Although he understood Marilynn's game, knew she felt her position in his life was threatened, it annoyed him. He had never said anything to make Marilynn think she had any position in his life greater than that of friend or neighbor. He supposed he ought to worry that he was hurting her feelings or even take some vain satisfaction in the hint of jealousy she revealed, but he only wished she would stop pestering him.

He suspected he ought to review those feelings far more closely. It certainly seemed that he would make a drastic mistake in marrying Marilynn, in succumbing to subtle outside pressures and expectations to do so. Royal admitted that he often found himself wishing that Marilynn would see that and discreetly fade away.

"I see you've already washed yours off," he grumbled as he searched for the soap.

"I was ready and the water was ready. I scrubbed my own back. What did Marilynn want?"

To interrupt things, Royal groused but only in his mind. Aloud, he answered, "She was curious about the drive. I reckon her father is contemplating one. It's a long hard trek and some people still wonder if it's worth it. It's still too new."

"It will be many months, eh?"

"Depending on luck and how hard we can push the herd without killing them—up to three months, maybe more."

"Do you think it is wise to leave the ranch for so long?"

Shrugging, Royal replied, "We won't be here and I think we're the ones this person's after, the ones he wants to get rid of."

"And he will have many months on the trail to do that."

" 'Fraid so. I'm hoping that Raoul's men are all he was able to hire and that they won't want to move so far away from the border."

"That is possible. Of course, the farther away from the border they get, the less they are known, eh?"

"You're supposed to ease my worries, not add to them."

"That is my job, is it, *querido?*" she asked with a little smile.

"Uh-huh. That and, "he looked at her, his brows lifting slightly as he held out the soap, "scrubbing my back."

She laughed and, rolling up her sleeves, moved to the side of the tub he was sprawled in. Even though his modesty was partly maintained by the soapy water there was enough of his lean muscular body in sight to warm her blood. Antonie was more than willing to touch him. She liked his body and felt no need to hide that fact.

When playfulness grew into passion, Antonie did nothing to stop it although she got very wet. He had touched off the wanting in her with his playful but sensual suggestion just before Marilynn had arrived and she was more than ready to satisfy it. She also craved the forgetfulness passion created. They were surrounded by troubles, a threat or danger around every corner, and she wanted to ignore all that for a little while, to revel in the temporary euphoria of passion. It was a goal that Royal proved very willing to help her reach.

Chapter Seven

"It is my turn, Royal."

Cursing softly, Royal ran his hand through his hair and then looked at Antonie in pure exasperation. "I didn't know there were turns."

"*Sí*, there are and this one is mine. For my two compadres I want Tomás and Jed Thayer. We will hold the fort, Captain."

"Take Oro too. I'd feel better if he's with you as well if you insist on staying here."

"*Sí*, I insist, but you take Oro. One reason we came here was because we know Raoul. He is an old enemy. Oro knows what to watch for."

Nothing Royal said could change Antonie's mind about taking a turn at guarding the ranch. He was not so sure he liked her choice of the young, good looking Jed Thayer either, but limited his jealous reaction to one long glare at his ranch hand. There was really no good reason he could give to stop her from taking her turn. He had hired her and the Degas twins together as extra guns. He had not expected her to take the job so seriously. Giving her a brief, slightly angry kiss, he decided to give up arguing and get to work.

"She's quite capable of doing the job and doing it well," Cole said as he rode up beside Royal.

"I know that."

"Hell, she's safer at the ranch than out here with us."

"How do you figure that?"

"Lots more places to take cover if there's trouble."

"True." Royal sighed and shook his head. "I just wish I could shake the feeling that there'll be trouble."

Antonie settled herself on the veranda rail, her back up against a post. So far, standing guard at the ranch had involved nothing more than being a chaperone for Patricia. This was the third beau to come calling on her and Antonie wondered a little crossly if Patricia had sent out some signal that drew all the aspirants to her hand like bees to clover.

Glancing at the young man seated at Patricia's side on the porch swing, Antonie inwardly grimaced. If that sweaty boy was the best the area had to offer, it was no surprise that Patricia was drawn to Oro. So far Antonie had not seen one of Patricia's beaus who was a quarter of the man that Oro was. Antonie feared that her hope that some young man from the area would deter Patricia from Oro was an empty one.

"Poor Hudson," Patricia said gently as she watched the young man ride away, "will never find a wife."

Moving to stand next to Patricia, Antonie asked, "Why do you say that?"

"He's terrified of girls. He sweats and stutters when he just passes a moment's idle conversation with a girl. I think he'd just keel over in a incoherent puddle if he even thought of making a proposal." She joined Antonie in laughing quietly.

It was after lunch that the fourth courting young man rode up to the ranch. As she watched the man's approach through the parlor window, Antonie sighed. She wondered if the young men in the area did any work. Antonie decided to return to her chaperoning when she had finished her coffee and not before. She moved away from the window.

"*Señorita?* Another young man has come."

Smiling at Maria, Antonie nodded. "I saw him. I'll go out in a moment."

"Do not leave it too long, eh?"

"Is this one not a gentleman then?"

"I have never seen him misbehave but," Maria shrugged, "I have this feeling about him, eh? I don't trust him."

"I'll get out there, Maria."

After the woman left, Antonie sighed and hurriedly finished her coffee. While Maria tended to worry too much about Patricia, Antonie did not want to ignore the woman's qualms. She did wish, however, that she had known how much of her time would be taken up with watching Patricia before she had insisted on taking her turn at standing guard at the ranch. The round-up was hot, exhausting and dirty work but it was not boring like this. Antonie was beginning to feel like a nursemaid.

She strode out onto the veranda and, after brief introductions were made, sat down on the top step. Sitting sideways, her back against the rail post, she was able to survey the horizon for danger as well as the young couple on the swing. Taking out a small pouch of tobacco and some papers, Antonie started to practice rolling a cigarette. She really had no inclination to smoke one but, after watching several hands roll one with apparent ease, she was curious as to how it was done.

"Antonie, you aren't taking up smoking, are you?"

Peeking at Patricia's shocked face, Antonie almost smiled. "No. I think not. I am just trying to roll one. It is not easy, eh?"

"Oh. Why?"

"Why not, *chica?*"

Even in that brief moment of looking directly at Patricia and her beau, Antonie decided that Maria was right to fret. The young man had looked at her with an expression in his eyes that Juan would have shot him for. Considering that he was sweet-talking Patricia at the time with a possible eye toward marriage, Antonie decided that was a good reason not to trust him. There was also the very good chance that he had only the seduction of a naive girl in mind.

Within a few moments, Antonie saw that her growing suspicions were justified. Young Clem Tillis clearly thought her too involved in her attempts to roll a cigarette to notice how his hands roamed over Patricia. It took Antonie another moment to see that Patricia was not calling for help or protesting because the girl was either too embarrassed or too frightened. The look on the girl's pale face was certainly not passion nor even reckless daring. Slowly, Antonie turned to face the couple.

"Move those hands, *Señor* Tillis."

"It's just a little cuddling, ma'am. Nothing to get all fired up over." His last words ended on a squeak when he suddenly found himself staring down the barrel of Antonie's gun.

"Move the hands, *gringo,* or I shoot you. Simple, eh?"

"Yeah, yeah, simple." He edged away from Patricia but then looked at the girl. "Now, Pattie, tell her it was nothing, hmm?"

Pattie opened her mouth to speak just as a shot rang out. Clem Tillis squealed and held his hands up. He lost all of his cockiness in an instant.

"Damnation! No need to shoot. I stopped touching her."

Moving with a swift grace, Antonie yanked Patricia

off the swing and pushed the girl down onto the floor of the veranda. "I did not shoot at you, *gringo*. They did." Peering over the veranda rail, Antonie indicated the large group of armed men riding straight for the ranch. "I think it is not safe in that seat now, *Señor* Tillis."

Throwing himself to the floor, Tillis made no move to draw his gun. "What the hell's going on around here?"

"Antonie? You all right?" Tomás shouted from his perch on the roof.

"*Sí*, Tomás." She neatly took down two men, curbing the attackers' advance.

The front door was flung open and for a brief instant, a frantic Maria was framed in the doorway. Antonie was surprised at how fast the plump woman prostrated herself when bullets shattered the door frame. From within the house came Rosa's screams of fright.

"Patricia?"

"She is all right, Maria," Antonie yelled in reply as she pinned down the attackers who were now seeking cover. "Get out of the way for we will be coming through in a minute."

"But it's open between here and the door," squeaked Tillis.

"That is all right, *Señor* Tillis. Patricia will be safe for I will keep this scum pinned down and you will be her cover."

"Now, wait just a damned minute . . ."

"*Señor* Tillis, you will do that and take a chance at being shot or you may stay here and be certain that I will shoot you."

"But, Antonie, what about you?" Patricia asked, in a trembling voice.

"I will be all right, Patricia. I will be right behind you. Tomás is on the roof and will cover me." Beginning a steady and deadly cover fire, Antonie hissed, "Go now."

Antonie almost smiled when Tillis scooped up Patricia and keeping her sheltered in front of him, bolted for the door. He had clearly believed her threat for he nearly hurled himself into the house. Considering the roughness of the rescue, Antonie was not sure Patricia would be too grateful. Very carefully, Antonie edged closer to her goal, readying herself to follow the couple into the house. She just hoped that going inside would really be safer.

"Tomás," she yelled. "I am ready."

After one last emptying of her pistol to aid Tomás in keeping the attackers pinned down, she raced for the door. It was not only the cries that told her a few had dared to break their cover. Several shots came too close, so close she felt them pass. One even tore through her shirt sleeve as she slammed the door shut.

Maria, a weeping Rosa, a pale Patricia and a clearly terrified Clem Tillis hovered in the parlor. It was certainly a pathetic little army, Antonie thought wryly as she moved to the window. When she smashed a window, all three squealed and she almost laughed. She forced herself to be stern, however, for she could not afford to let them be useless. They were all she had. With them she was going to have to form an adequate defense of the house that would cover all angles.

"Where is Jed and Old Pete?" she demanded even as she concentrated on keeping their attackers from getting too near the house.

"Pete is across the hall and Jed is upstairs," replied Maria.

"Good, good. Now, get me guns and ammunition. All there is in the house. And shut that Rosa up."

It took a few minutes but Maria finally got Rosa to calm down a little. Then, with the girl in tow, she left to get the weapons and ammunition Antonie had asked for. Antonie noticed that Clem Tillis was firmly settled behind a very solid chair and showing no inclination to lend a hand. She was going to enjoy changing his mind.

When Maria and Rosa had collected all the weapons in the house, Antonie was impressed. The Bancrofts had collected enough to supply a small army. Antonie just wished she had the small army to use them.

"Who can handle a gun?" she demanded as she helped herself to a goodly supply of ammunition.

"I am not very good but I can use a rifle," Maria answered. "Patricia can shoot but Rosa, she has never learned."

Nodding, Antonie silently indicated that they should choose their weapons then looked at Clem. "And you, *señor?*"

"Hell, this ain't my fight. I'm not risking my neck."

"*Sí,* you are." She calmly pointed her gun at him. "You shoot them or I shoot you."

"And how can you explain that to my folks?"

"You died in the battle. So tragic." Although he looked suitably unnerved, he made no move to pick out a weapon or use his own. So she coolly shot away the cigar he was just lighting up in a show of bravado that did not fool her at all. "You will choose a weapon."

"All right, all right. I can use a rifle better'n I can a pistol," he said, his voice a wavering falsetto.

"Patricia, you will go to one of the bedrooms and Maria will go to another. I want the sides watched. We do not want any of these dogs to encircle us. You, *Señor* Tillis, will watch the back of the house. Rosa, if there is a blind spot, you are to watch it, eh? You cannot shoot but you can watch and call for aid if any of the men appear. Carry enough ammunition to take to Jed and Old Pete. They must need some by now. And, Rosa, you are to help anyone who is hit."

Once the others were gone, she returned her concentration to the men outside. They were being cautious, exposing themselves to the deadly fire from the house as little as possible. That meant that they had accomplished little and Antonie wondered if, due to the stand-off, they would soon give up. If it did not come to that, then it would be a matter of who ran out of ammunition first, if the attackers managed to make a successful run on the house or if the men with the herd came back. It worked out to be about a fifty-fifty chance of winning. As Antonie continued to try and convince the men outside that it would be far too risky to rush the house, she decided to pray for the men to come in from the range. That seemed to her the best option she could hope for, the one that would bring about the quickest resolution to the trouble.

Royal frowned as he watched Justin race toward him pushing his horse at a reckless speed. He had heard no shots and seen nothing. In fact, everything had been progressing with a gratifying smoothness. By the look of things, they could head out on the drive by the end of the next week. He did not really want to hear that something had gone wrong but he had the sinking feeling that that was just what he was about to hear.

"Is there a reason for nearly killing that horse?" he asked with a false calm when Justin finally reached him.

"There's shots coming from the ranch, Royal."

"Shots? One? Two? How's it sound?" he demanded tersely even as he fired off three shots, the signal for trouble that would bring all his men to his side.

"It sounds like there's a damn war going on."

When his men were gathered, Royal led them at a steady ground-eating pace toward the ranch. It took nearly all of his willpower to rein in just out of sight of the house. The sound of heavy gunfire had him aching to charge right in, afraid for Antonie and the others, but he knew such a rash act could cost him men. He sent

Cole ahead to see exactly what the situation was so that they could plan an approach that would gain them the advantage.

"It looks pretty cut and dried, Royal," Cole reported when he returned. "There's about twenty men besieging the place but our people are in the house and have them pinned down. By the looks of it, our side's winning."

"The best way to handle it?"

"Straight in and shooting, Royal. The *banditti* are square between us and the house. We'll be coming in behind them."

Smiling grimly at this good news, Royal gave the signal to charge.

"Señorita! "Señorita!"

"Stay down, Rosa," Antonie hissed as the girl raced toward her. "Are they getting around us?"

"No, I see no one, but I did see one of *Señor* Royal's men. On the rise. The men are coming to save us."

"Tell everyone, Rosa. We do not want any of our own men shot by us. And keep your head down, *chica*."

When Royal and his men charged, Antonie simply watched. There was no hope for the ruffians outside. They scattered like frightened fowl before the onslaught. Not many got away, falling victim to the hail of bullets now raining on them from two sides. Even as the shooting sputtered to a halt, the other defenders of the house gathered in the parlor.

Briefly Antonie felt piqued when Royal and his brothers entered. Royal looked to the welfare of Patricia and Maria first. However, Antonie felt soothed when she saw how his eyes sought her out immediately and never left her as he gathered assurances that everyone was unharmed, only a few nicks and bruises. She was able to stay seated by the window and wait for him to come to her.

"Are you all right, Antonie?" he asked quietly as he crouched before her.

"*Sí*. Not a scratch."

He touched the place where the bullet had torn her shirt sleeve. "This was damned close."

"But not close enough, eh?" She picked up her hat and wriggled her finger in a fresh bullet hole in the crown. "Same here."

Clutching her tightly by the arms, his blood chilled by the evidence of such a close call, he rasped, "That's not funny."

"I know. I did not laugh, *querido*." She smiled faintly. "It was my favorite hat." When *El Magnifico* scrambled to her side, she laughed softly and scratched his ears. "Such a brave one. He hid beneath the settee."

"If there had been room, Clem would have joined him there," Patricia sneered.

"Here now, that ain't fair. I did my part."

"Only after Tony threatened to shoot you."

"There's gratitude for you. I don't have to stay here and take this." He strode out of the room, a chiding Patricia at his heels.

"Did you really threaten to shoot him?" Royal asked as he helped Antonie to her feet and led her to the settee.

"*Sí. Gracias*, Maria," she murmured as she accepted the glass of brandy the woman served her. "It made him obedient."

"I reckon it would. Raoul's men?" he asked, looking to both Tomás and Antonie for an answer.

Tomás shrugged. "Could have been. I recognized no one. Maybe just some hired dogs."

Rising slowly from his seat, Royal said wearily, "We'll deliver the bodies and the prisoners to the sheriff. Maybe we'll be lucky and he'll come up with an answer or two."

102

Shortly after Royal left, Antonie began to feel weary but she struggled to overcome it. She doubted that there would be any more trouble for a while but did not want to ease her guard. However, as soon as all the hands were back at the ranch for the night, she readily relinquished her position. After a light supper, she had a quick hot bath and speedily sought her bed, not rousing again until Royal eased into her bed and gently pulled her into his arms.

"I am not easing your troubles, *querido,*" she said softly, annoyed at what she saw as her failure to protect Royal and his ranch from being raided.

"Nonsense. We were losing before you came."

"We are not winning now."

"Maybe not but we're holding our own and it's costing them."

"*Sí,* it is costing them. The word will be put out that we are not easy prey. What happened here today will be told. Whoever sent these men will begin to find it hard to hire others. I say hard but not impossible."

"No, not impossible. I am not fool enough to think this will end it. The only way to stop all this is to get the one behind it and I haven't a clue to who that is."

"The sheriff knew nothing? Found nothing?"

"Nothing. Couldn't get anything from the prisoners either. Really don't think they know. Asking around town only told us that some of them had been seen in the saloon or the whorehouse. The usual places one goes to hire such scum."

"That is where they go. I would look for such men there. Men who do not know who or why, just how much, eh?"

"I can't quite figure out why they'd hit the ranch. Why not go for the men spread out on the range?"

"Because you are too spread out. That would take time. Maybe you would hear a shot. Then they must

103

face many armed men. True, you'd be out in the open but so would they. Here, they knew there were only few and mostly women. I am thinking they planned to kill us all, maybe burn you out. You come back to the dead and the ruin and maybe that is enough. You decide this land is worth no more dying, no more grief and you leave. It would work, *sí?*"

"*Sí*. Enough. More than enough. I was afraid that that was just what I was going to find. I was afraid for you."

"That is nice," she said slowly.

"Yes. Nice. But? I can hear the but, Antonie."

"I can take care of myself."

"I know. I came tearing in here, afraid for you, and you have handled it all unafraid."

"No. Not unafraid. I was afraid and I do not like the killing. I feel sick and I sweat."

"It doesn't show."

"No. Juan taught me to put it all inside until the danger is past, until the battle is over. He told me I can cry later, be sick later, grieve later, shake later. It will all be there, he said, and it is. He taught me to hold it back. It is the only way to survive. Some fear is okay, eh? It keeps you from being reckless. Too much fear and you panic, you make a mistake that gets you killed."

"That's what our officers always said. Only a fool is unafraid but a wise man controls his fear. Juan would have made a great general, I think."

"*Sí*. He was in a way."

"So, you're saying I shouldn't be afraid for you."

Struggling to keep her mind on the conversation as his hands began to move over her seductively, she clarified, "I was saying you do not need to be afraid, but I think I like it that you can be. *Sí*, it is very nice."

Unbuttoning the shirt she wore as a nightgown, Royal decided he was tired of thinking of and discussing his many troubles. "I think I can manage one or two other nice things."

Craving the escape from the world that his lovemaking offered, Antonie slid her arms around his neck and urged his lips toward hers. "Ah, *querido,* I think maybe you can too."

Chapter Eight

Even as he greeted the newest arrivals to his fiesta, Royal wondered where Antonie was. It was not like her to be late. Neither did she seem prone to all the primping that had nearly made Patricia too late to help him start greeting their guests. Nonetheless, with most everyone having already arrived Antonie was still no-where in sight.

As he went to get a drink, he wondered if she was purposely avoiding the festivities. It suddenly occurred to him that he had never seen her in a dress. It was quite possible that she did not own one. He was just cursing himself for not asking her if she needed a dress when he caught sight of her standing near where the hands were gathered.

She wore the dress of a Mexican peasant, although Royal could see that the material was of the best quality. The crisp white, lace-trimmed blouse, the black cinch belt and the red skirt was simplicity itself but she looked beautiful in it. Her lovely thick hair was loose, hanging in lush waves just past her slim hips, the front sections gently pulled back and braided. Royal felt desire tauten his body as he watched her lithe figure move in a subtle rhythmic response to the music.

Just as he started to move toward her, Marilynn arrived at his side. Royal struggled to banish the thought that her hand on his arm felt like a manacle.

Before all their mutual friends and neighbors he had to be pleasant to her. He simply hoped he could detach himself before too long and seek out Antonie, for he discovered that he heartily disliked leaving her with his hands and those from other ranches. Too many of those hands were young and single.

Antonie watched Marilynn tow Royal away and sighed. She had hoped that the woman would miss the fiesta for some reason, preferably a serious disease. Antonie knew she felt pure, fierce jealousy but she could not seem to subdue it. She also knew that Marilynn was of Royal's world, a far too constant visual reminder of just how different that world was from the one Antonie had known. The sensible part of her saw that as a blessing, for it could be used to still her fruitless dreams. But Antonie found that she was getting less sensible with each night she spent in Royal's arms. Fruitless dreams and foolish hopes were getting more and more plentiful.

It made her angry with herself. She had thought she possessed the strength and good sense to find pleasure and avoid pain. Instead, she seemed to be doing everything that would insure that she ended up being hurt badly. She would not be able to walk away from Royal without scars. Since she doubted he would suffer any, it seemed most unfair.

"Such a long face for a fiesta, *chica.*"

Looking closely at Oro, Antonie said carefully, "Your mouth is smiling, *amigo,* but in your eyes I see a face as long as mine."

Draping an arm around her shoulders, Oro briefly kissed her. "It shows, eh?"

"I am thinking it is not an easy thing to hide." She spoke in Spanish to ensure privacy.

"No. It cuts too deep. It is too much a part of you, I think, touching you from head to toe as if it flows in the

107

blood."

"*Sí, sí,* that is it. She has not stopped coming after you? I had thought she had."

Oro laughed softly, a sadness in his mirth. "She speaks to me only when she must and yet it seems there are more 'musts' than there is a need to be. She watches me, little one. I see it and I feel it and I ache to answer it. I want to shoot the sweaty Anglos who sit on that porch swing with her."

He looked at Antonie, his eyes narrowing. "Her anger with me is easing. She softens again. This night she has approached me twice and there was no must about it. The nearer she comes the harder it is to stay away."

"You are looking at me as if you have an idea."

"Yes, I have one but it could cause you some trouble."

"More trouble than we would face if you do as you so ache to do?"

"No."

"I am not afraid of a little trouble, Oro."

"Maybe she will pull away, very far away, if she thinks that there is one between her and me."

It only took Antonie a moment to understand what he meant. In less than that time she was able to clearly see what sort of trouble his plan could bring her. Nonetheless, she recognized the merit of his suggestion and the trouble it could bring her was certainly far less than what could descend upon them if Oro answered the invitation Patricia could not seem to stop sending him.

"Yes, she will. She has the Bancroft pride. She is also young and innocent, would not know how to fight the other woman."

"Darling, it will cause you trouble. You must see that."

"Oh, I see it, Oro, but it is not the sort of trouble that

108

will get me hanged or shot or beaten."

"But it could bring you pain and I do not wish to see you hurt."

"It is not a pain that will kill me. I believe it is not a pain I can avoid anyway." She looked at Royal, who was dancing with Marilynn. "There is the proof that I am but a passing moment. There is his world and I am no part of that."

"You think he will still marry that woman?"

"Perhaps not her but one much like her. An Anglo raised in the Anglo world. I am a Doberman by blood but Juan raised me and I am his child in all other ways. He cannot forget that. I think, not even when he holds me in the night."

"He is good to you."

"Oh, yes. He is. He is kind, gentle, a good lover and, I think, a friend. He does not hide what we share, or try to tuck it into the background as if he is ashamed of me or of wanting one like me. Perhaps he even trusts me enough so that, even though I cannot tell him the whole truth, he will believe me when I tell him you and I are not lovers, that all is not as it looks."

She wished she could feel as confident of that possibility as she tried to sound. Antonie strongly suspected that Royal was the possessive sort. It was not a character trait she was fond of but she had even recognized it in herself. His eyes would be telling him that he was sharing her with someone else. She would be asking him to ignore what he saw and, without any explanation, accept her simple statement that she had no lover but him. She was not sure she would be able to believe it if the situations were reversed.

For a brief moment, Antonie allowed herself the luxury of being furious with Patricia. If the girl had just left well enough alone, there would be no need for the subterfuge or the risk of pain. It was inconceivable that

109

the girl could not know the sort of trouble she was courting, what risks she was trying to tempt Oro into taking, especially after Antonie had explained it all to her.

With a sigh, Antonie shook her anger away. Patricia was no practiced seducer, no experienced woman who just sought a unique lover with no regard to his feelings or the danger her lust might inspire. As far as Antonie could tell, the girl really did care for Oro but was too innocent, too ignorant of the world to understand what Antonie had warned her of, that such a pairing could not be, that no one would let it happen. Even if, by some miracle, Oro and Patricia were allowed to follow their hearts, Antonie doubted that Patricia had any idea of what her life would be like, how hard it would be. Prejudice had to be suffered, tasted by its victim, before it could really be understood, and Patricia had clearly never experienced its poison.

When Jed Thayer asked her to dance, Antonie eagerly accepted. She was tired of her dark thoughts. With a festiveness that was tinted by desperation, Antonie set out to fully enjoy all the entertainment the fiesta had to offer. There was no escaping her worries or troubles, but she was determined to firmly push them aside, if only for a little while.

"Where is Antonie?" Cole asked Royal as he strolled up to stand by his brother and Marilynn, who still clung firmly to Royal's arm.

"With the hands."

"What's she doing there?"

"Why shouldn't she be?" Marilynn demanded. "She and the two halfbreeds are hired hands, aren't they?"

"I am paying them, yes," Royal said tightly, "but they never asked to be. They came here, unasked, to warn me and to help me."

"That was very good of them, I'm sure. However,

110

they didn't turn down your offer of pay, did they."

Royal decided there was no point in telling Marilynn about how hard he had had to work to get Antonie and the Degas twins to accept pay. Neither did he think he could get her to understand his feeling that he was getting them very cheaply. They worked as hard as the hands, acted as extra guns and guards and freely offered their experience with and knowledge of the type of men who kept harassing him, all on a hand's pay. Filled with intractable prejudices learned at her father's knee, Marilynn would undoubtedly belittle that and Royal did not want to risk losing his temper.

"Antonie looks pretty good in a dress," Cole observed. "Want me to go get her and bring her over here?"

"Oh, I don't think you should, Cole," Marilynn answered.

"Why not, Marilynn?" he demanded.

"Well, I'm sure she would be most uncomfortable. She's with her own kind, where she wants to be."

"Fine, then I'll go join her."

It was hard for Royal not to join Cole as he strode away. Unfortunately, he had a lot of guests and it was his duty to circulate, to play the charming host. That also meant that he would continue to be stuck with Marilynn's company.

He realized that he had lost all liking for Marilynn. The prejudices that he had more or less ignored now infuriated him. Her attitudes were no longer something to be tolerated as something she could not really help but something he actively loathed. What made it a lot worse was that he could do nothing about it.

Marriage to Marilynn was certainly out of the question. Somehow he was going to have to get that message across to her as gently as possible. Apparently, taking a lover beneath her very nose was not enough to deter the woman. She probably saw it as some final bachelor frolic that had little or nothing to do with their relationship. He knew that a number of women felt that they should stoically tolerate a man's indiscretions. Marilynn was evidently one of those, but Royal suddenly found that attitude distasteful, even insulting, for it hinted that he lacked the strength of character to be faithful. It also meant that he might have to get very blunt, even nasty, to shake the woman.

As the night dragged on, Royal found his mood growing darker and darker. He found it hard to stand idly by while Antonie laughed and danced with the hands. As far as he could see, the men were enjoying her company far too much. What really troubled him, however, was what appeared to be going on between Oro and Antonie.

Since Antonie had come to his bed, Royal had disregarded Oro. He had accepted that the twins were her family. But now he recalled all too well the kiss he had seen Antonie and Oro share, as their actions at the moment appeared far from familial. There was the air of romance, of intimacy. Royal found himself wondering what game was being played, but had no opportunity to investigate it. The demands of being the host tied his hands and he began to curse the fiesta.

Still laughing and trying to catch her breath after a lively dance, Antonie gladly accepted the cool drink Cole handed her. It took a moment to realize that Cole was looking rather stern. She suddenly had the sinking feeling that the performance she and Oro were putting on for Patricia had already been taken in by someone else. Patricia had already noticed, so Antonie decided it had been a little foolish to think or hope that no one else would.

"Why are you not with the guests?"

"Why aren't you, Tony?"

112

"Ah, they are not for me. A fiesta is to enjoy. With them I would only end up being angry."

"Probably." Cole looked away for a moment, sighed, then fixed her with a stern gaze. "What game are you playing?"

"Game *señor?*"

"Don't do that, Tony. Don't play dumb. I may not be decided firmly on a lot of things about you but one thing I do know for sure and that's that you ain't stupid, honey."

"Thank you."

"Antonie," he said with anger.

"Maybe I am just not sure what you mean, eh?"

"I'll clarify it for you. You belong to Royal."

"I belong to no man." Despite her annoyance, Antonie almost smiled at Cole's look of male exasperation. "I belong to Antonie Doberman Ramirez and only to her. Maybe I give myself for a while but I am never owned."

"Get off your high horse. So, okay, I put that wrong."

"*Sí.* You did."

"You are Royal's lover. Better?" he asked sarcastically.

"*Sí*, better."

"Thank you. So, you are Royal's lover yet tonight you've been hanging all over Oro."

"Hanging all over him?" Antonie felt somewhat insulted by his description.

"And he's been hanging all over you," Cole continued doggedly, "or near enough. I just want to know what you're stirring up."

"I am just enjoying the fiesta."

"I'm not blind, Tony."

"No, but maybe you do not see too clearly, eh? I have only one lover. I need no more. I want no more."

She met his long, studying look calmly. Her words had been the truth. It was easy to face him squarely.

Cole finally nodded. "Okay."

"Okay what?"

"Okay, I believe you."

"*Gracias*. Not that it is your business anyhow."

"No? We have a long cattle drive starting the day after tomorrow. Besides all the usual trouble we can face, we might also be harassed by Raoul or some other hired guns. A romantic triangle is a fine knot of trouble in itself and we don't need it. Royal goes and gets too involved in a mess like that and I might end up leading the drive and I sure as hell don't want that. Leadership's something I try real hard to avoid, even if it means sticking my nose into other people's business."

"There is no triangle."

"Well, maybe you ought to stop playing it so close to Oro."

"I will play it close to Oro if I want to. I will tell Royal what I told you."

"Yes? That might not be good enough, darling. I can be charitable. You ain't my lover. Royal might have a few doubts."

"That is his problem."

She moved away from Cole, not wanting any more discussions on the matter. It was far too tempting to give him a fuller explanation. Antonie knew how easily she could be seen as the villainess and she dreaded that. The last thing she wanted to be seen as was a fickle lover. She was glad when Cole returned to the guests near Royal for it meant an end to the matter. Antonie doubted that Cole would raise the subject again once some time had passed.

After a few Irish jigs with the O'Malley brothers and a tiring but sensuous Spanish dance with Oro, Antonie decided she needed to rest her feet. It had been a long time since she had danced. She had forgotten how exhausting it could be.

Sitting beneath a large tree, Antonie removed her shoes. She smiled a little when she saw that the path to the privy reserved for the women ran right by her. It was proving to be a well traveled path. Antonie gaily returned the greetings some women gave her and coolly ignored those who ignored her. It was as she was tugging her shoes back on that she caught a glimpse of a lavender skirt out of the corner of her eye. Inwardly she grimaced for she recognized the fine silk dress. Antonie looked up and met Marilynn's glare with a cool smile.

"I see you did not heed my words."

"Ah, those words were to be heeded, eh?" Antonie slowly stood up.

"Of course they were, but you didn't listen to a word."

"*Sí*, I did and I have seen that you spoke the truth. You are certainly not standing idly by." Antonie found some satisfaction, if small, in the fact that she was so clearly annoying Marilynn.

"Don't try to be funny. Now, for a while, I thought it would be to my advantage to let Royal get this frolic out of his system. A last bachelor fling is to be expected."

"Is it now?"

"Men will be men."

"I have never seen it otherwise, *señorita*."

"However," Marilynn hissed through tightly clenched teeth, "this nonsense has gone on long enough."

"I am thinking that it is not for you to say what has gone on long enough."

"Oh but it is. I am, after all, Royal's fiancée."

"Ah, he has proposed, has he?"

Antonie found it nearly impossible to keep her voice light. She felt cold and had a strong urge to scratch out Marilynn's hazel green eyes. Perhaps even to indulge in pulling out every strand of the auburn hair the woman was so proud of.

115

"My dear, we have been engaged for months. If he hasn't told you, well, that rather shows what a fool you've been. The man is obviously using you."

"Is he? Perhaps, *señorita*, I am using him."

"Whatever it is, it will stop."

"Do you threaten me, *Señorita* Collins?"

"You know full well I do and you'd be very wise to heed it and heed it well."

Watching the woman stride away, Antonie murmured, "*Sí.* At least that much we can agree on."

Briefly she thought about Marilynn's claim that she and Royal were engaged. Now that the first, strong heat of anger and jealousy had passed, Antonie could view it with more calm, greater clarity. Either Royal or Marilynn was lying about that relationship and Antonie felt pretty sure it was Marilynn.

Feeling a little better, Antonie returned to where the hands carried on a celebration almost completely separate from that of Royal and his guests. Only the foremen passed between the two groups with any ease. Even though she would have liked to respond to Marilynn's threat by neatly cutting the woman away from Royal, Antonie decided to stay with the hands. Just as she reached the group, Justin suddenly appeared at her side.

"Why are you staying over here, Tony?"

"I think for the same reason these men stay over here. It is more comfortable."

"It's not because of bigots like Marilynn and her pa?"

"A little, *sí*." Antonie grinned. "I think Royal would not like it if I shot one of his guests."

Justin laughed. "No, reckon not, though I know it can be mighty tempting."

"Very tempting. Is that why you are over here."

"Nope. I wanted a dance with you and I finally figured out that I'd best stroll over here if I'm going to

116

get one."

Glancing at a pretty little brunette she had noticed Justin paying marked attention to, Antonie teased, "Are you sure? I would not like to, how you say, queer your game."

"Hush your mouth, woman, and dance," he grumbled laughingly, his cheeks touched with a blush, as he swung her into a waltz.

Antonie laughed at the look on Justin's face when he discovered that he had to practically fight to keep her as a partner. They both laughed heartily at the antics of the men who danced with each other, the one in the role of the woman tying a bandana around his arm, overplaying their roles until they became pure farce. By the time the dance was over both she and Justin were breathless from laughing.

"Get out of here, Jed," Justin ordered with a laugh. "I want to talk to Tony for a while and I think she needs to catch her breath. Find another partner."

"Tomás," Jed called as he moved away, "you be the lady this time."

"Oh, *señor*," Tomás caroled in a high voice, "I cannot. We have not been properly introduced. Where is my duenna?"

"Tomás is mighty cheerful," Justin observed with a grin.

"Tomás is mighty drunk."

"He's still standing."

"*Sí*, but I have seen him pass out while he is still standing."

"I didn't think that punch was all that strong."

"It gets stronger when you add tequila as Tomás does."

"Ah, yes, that would stiffen it up a bit."

"Did you have something you wanted to talk to me about?"

Antonie hoped that she was not in for another uncomfortable discussion or a lecture. The night was only half over and she had already had two confrontations. Since the one with Marilynn was only a few moments old, she felt she deserved a rest before suffering through another.

"Oh, nothing really. I saw Marilynn corner you. Don't pay her any mind. She's a bitch."

"That bitch could become your sister," she said gently but smiled, finding his concern a pleasant change.

"No. I don't think so." He colored slightly and added softly, "Whatever might or might not happen between you and Royal, I think you've made him see her clearly, made him really look at the woman she is."

"Does he know you do not like her?"

"No, not really. I'm not really sure why I don't like her. She's never done anything to me or even said much to me. She's really prejudiced but so are a lot of others. I didn't ignore it the way Royal did, but I'm afraid I sort of accepted it. Royal doesn't do that any longer. He's really looked at it and he hates it."

"Are you sure?"

"Oh yes. Tomás wandered over there and was carrying on with Cole like they always do. Well, Marilynn made some remark about the halfbreed not knowing his place and Royal," Justin smiled, "told her not to be such an ass."

"I'm surprised she still stands by him."

"She's determined not to give you any room tonight. He's working himself into a foul mood because of it, I think."

Antonie thought so too. Several times she had caught Royal staring at her, a dark look on his face. She did not really believe it all had to do with Marilynn's tenacity, however. Some of Royal's darkest looks had come her way when she had been with Oro. She felt sure she was not going to be allowed any grace period.

"You know, there's another thing about Marilynn that's always bothered me some," Justin said, breaking into Antonie's thoughts.

"And what is that?" she prompted when he fell silent.

"She never laughs. Not really. Oh, she occasionally gives one of those pretty finishing-school titters but she never honestly laughs. Foolish reason to dislike someone, I reckon."

"No, *amigo*. What a person laughs at is as important as what she does not laugh at. It can tell you a lot about what is or isn't in her heart. A person who does not laugh?" Antonie shook her head. "It is a thing to notice and worry about."

"It is unsettling. Well, I'd best get back to Betty. I can see Clem sniffing around her."

"Ah, that one is all hands and no courage."

"Did he touch Patricia?"

"Not for long."

Justin grinned. "I'll bet." Growing serious, he said, "Antonie, I hope that, well, whatever happens between you and Royal, we'll still be friends."

She smiled and said gently, "Whatever happens between me and Royal is just that—between me and Royal. It will make no difference to us." She kissed his cheek. "*Sí*. We will still be friends."

As she watched him walk away, she smiled. It gave her a good feeling to know that at least one of the Bancrofts could look past her relationship with Royal, consider it a thing apart. She had a feeling that that attitude would be put to the test very soon.

Chapter Nine

"How could you do this to me?"

Antonie inwardly groaned as she faced Patricia. With so little time left to the evening, she had hoped that this was one confrontation she would be able to avoid. If nothing else, she was not really sober enough to handle it all that well.

"Do what to you, *chica?* I have not seen you all night, eh?"

"You know what I mean, Antonie. I'm talking about you and Oro."

"Me and Oro?"

"Oh, Antonie, you have Royal. What do you need Oro for?"

"I will always need Oro."

"But you knew I wanted him. You knew it."

"We cannot always have what we want."

"It was bad enough watching him run to the saloon all the time. Now you're going to make me watch him with you every day?"

"Don't look."

When Patricia gave a convulsive sob and raced off, Antonie sighed. She was really getting tired of making the girl cry. Even listing all the reasons for doing what she had done did not make her feel any better about it. She heartily wished that there was another way to handle the matter.

"What did you do to Patricia?"

"*Ay dios mio,*" Antonie groaned as she found herself face to face with an angry and protective Maria. "Nothing."

"Nothing does not make the *niña* run to her room to cry her eyes out."

After studying the outraged Maria for a moment, Antonie inwardly nodded as she came to a decision. Maria was a Mexican. The woman had a comfortable place in the Bancroft home, but Antonie knew that Maria had tasted prejudice, if only at Marilynn's hands. The woman would understand what was going on and why. Maria could prove a useful ally.

"Patricia wants Oro," Antonie said flatly and nodded at the horrified look on Maria's face.

"*Madre de Dios.* If that boy even touches her, he is a dead boy."

"I've tried to tell her that, Maria, but she does not hear me. She says her brothers are not like that."

"Well, I've not seen it in them. They are good men and they are fair. But, Patricia is the only daughter, the only girl in the family."

"And their goodness and fairness might not reach so far, eh?"

"*Sí.* Oro is a fine boy. I have seen this. I think that they have too. Still, he has Yaqui blood and his papa was a *bandito.* Too many things the Anglos hate all in one boy. Sí, it could be asking too much."

"And, even if it was not, there are all the neighbors, the people in town. Many who would no longer speak to her. Her brothers would face the trouble too for they would have let her do it. She does not see it, Maria. I have talked and talked and Oro has tried to drive her

121

away but —" Antonie shrugged.

"But now you must try to make her think there is another. I see it now. Ah, *chica,* they have put you in a very bad place."

"Better that than Oro hanging from some tree."

"*Sí.* He would take her, eh?"

"In an instant, Maria. She does not see it, I think, but he is hurting. He knows all the trouble it could bring and not just for him. He fights to stay away but she will not leave him be."

"I will talk to her."

"Please. Try to make her understand. She is very young and has seen little of the ugliness of the world."

"Which is why she cannot understand what you tell her but, still, I will try. A shame," Maria sighed as she started toward the house, "for they would have such pretty babies."

"And, Maria?"

"*Sí?*"

"Do not tell her how Oro feels."

"Ah, no, no. I will not. That could be much trouble. I see that."

Antonie decided she needed another drink. Just pretending to be the other woman was exhausting. She did not know how any woman could manage being in such an awkward, tension-ridden position for any length of time. Grimacing slightly, Antonie recognized that a lot of people probably saw her in that role with Royal. She hoped she was right in believing she was not.

When Tomás made his way to her side, she had to smile. He was walking with great care, a sure sign that he was far from sober. His actions and words always became very precise when he drank too much. She supposed he deserved to let loose for a while as he had worked very hard. Antonie just hoped he would not

122

suffer too much on the morrow.

"I am drunk," he announced as he leaned up against the tree she stood next to.

She laughed. "*Sí*. Very drunk. Ah, well, many are."

"*Sí*. They start to stagger home."

"Perhaps you should start to stagger to your bed."

"I think you and Oro are going to have to help me, eh?"

"*Sí*, I think so too. You will pay for this tomorrow."

"Ah, *sí, sí*. It is good tomorrow is a day of rest before this cattle drive."

"There look to be many who will be needing it." She nodded toward where Jed Thayer was being carried off to the bunkhouse by two less than sober companions.

"I drank him under the table."

"He just had the good sense to fall down sooner."

"That is all that matters, *querida*."

"If you say so, *amigo*."

"The Bancroft *niña* gives you trouble?"

"Some, *sí*. I have talked to Maria. She will try to make the girl see how it is."

"Try, *sí*, but I wonder if she can. I was thinking of how your lover, he sees all this. He watches you."

"I know, but there is nothing I can do about it. I will tell Royal that Oro and I are not lovers. If that is not enough," she shrugged, "then it is over. I will face that when it happens."

"I am thinking it will happen tonight."

Sighing, Antonie nodded in sad agreement. "I am thinking it will too. Everyone else has chased me down to talk to me, lecture me, warn me and accuse me. He is the only one left."

Draping his arm around her shoulders, Tomás said sympathetically, "Poor *chica*. So unfair."

"Well, some of it, maybe. Tomás, you are getting very heavy."

"I am forgetting how to stand up."

Laughing softly, she put an arm around him to support him better and signaled to Oro. When Oro arrived she was not sure that he was in any better shape. However, he did look well enough to get Tomás to bed at least. Calling goodnight to the men who still lingered, she helped Oro tow Tomás into the house.

When they dropped Tomás onto his bed, Oro then flopped down on his. Antonie began to tug off the now unconscious Tomás's clothes. She suspected she would have to do the same for Oro. He had not really passed out but he looked pretty helpless.

"What a sorry pair you are," she said, laughing.

"And you are sober, *querida?*"

"No, Oro, but I am not as sorry as you two."

"I felt like getting sorry."

She tucked Tomás beneath his covers and moved to start undressing Oro. "It will not help you in the morning."

"*Sí*, it will. I will be too sick to care about anything or anyone, eh?"

"I am sorry, Oro."

"No, I am sorry. I am sorry I am so weak that I must lean on you. It is my trouble but I make it yours and that is not fair but I can think of nothing else."

"Certainly not now. Your brain is dead, eh?"

He laughed sleepily but then sighed. "I wish my heart was dead too. Maybe soon it will be."

"No. You may wish it but you will see that it can heal, that you will want it to."

"Is that what you will do, how you will feel?"

"*Sí*. I know it will hurt. Already it has hurt. I cannot stop it. I think I do not want to. There is a lot of good too, even if it will be over. I thought about all this before I said *sí* to Royal. Foolishly, I thought I could keep my heart protected but I suspected it would not

124

be. I prefer my position to yours. I need only accept that it will end. You must accept that it can never begin."

His hand moved over her backside. "Maybe we can console each other, eh?"

Removing his hand, she tucked it under his covers as she pulled them over him. "I think that would solve nothing and help neither of us, at least not now. Besides, *amigo,* I think you are too drunk to be much good tonight."

"*Sí.*" He laughed and closed his eyes. "Much too drunk. Sleep well, *querida.*"

She watched him for a little while. It was not fair that his parentage should be held against him. Perhaps it was even cowardly to run from the prejudice, to succumb to the unfairness of it. Perhaps they should try to fight it.

Cursing softly, she shook her head and started out of the room. The odds were too great and to buck them was recklessness. All that would be accomplished was Oro's death. It was better to try to avoid such a confrontation at this time.

Quietly shutting the door behind her as she stepped into the hall, Antonie saw Royal coming toward her. Inwardly, she sighed, for he looked angry. It occurred to her that what was supposed to have been a celebration was rapidly becoming a total disaster.

Royal saw Antonie step out of the twins' room and cursed softly. He had watched Oro and her all night as they had carried on while he had been unable to do a thing about it. Noting her tousled appearance, he could not stop himself from wondering if the pair had carried on far more intimately in private. There had been enough time for it since he had watched her and Oro lead Tomás away.

Grasping her none too gently by the wrist, he

dragged her into his room. She had looked especially pretty at the fiesta, softly feminine and seductive, yet he had not even gotten a chance to dance with her. Every other male had seemed to, even his brothers, he thought angrily as he shut the door and turned to her.

There was a great deal he wanted to say but, as he looked at her, her hair loose and her breasts softly outlined by her lacy blouse, he decided talking could wait. Every time he had watched her during the fiesta his desire had grown a little more. All the other things he was feeling simply did not seem important for the moment.

As he pulled her into his arms, he studied her flushed cheeks and bright eyes. "I think you're drunk, Antonie."

"*Sí.* I think I am a bit too."

"You looked very pretty tonight." He undid the tie on the neckline of her blouse.

"But you are tired of the dress?"

"Yes, real tired of it. I've spent half the night thinking about how damn fine you look under it." He tugged her blouse off.

She made a soft sound of pleasure as he cupped her breast in his hand and teased the tip with his tongue. "And the other half of the night, *mi vida?*"

"Thinking about all I wanted to do to you when I got you all alone."

"And now you are going to do all of these things?"

"Oh, yes, all of them."

Her hands burrowed into his thick hair when he drew the hard tip of her breast into his mouth. As his mouth and hands played over her breasts with a tantalizing greed, she felt her knees weaken. Passion cleared all thought from her mind and she was glad of it. If everything was soon to fall apart, she would at least have this last moment with him.

Gently he maneuvered her so that she sat on the edge

of the bed. As he knelt to remove her shoes and stockings and then his own, Antonie struggled to get him out of his shirt. When she was finally successful, she gave a soft murmur of delight as her hands moved over his smooth torso with obvious pleasure.

Kneeling before her, he put his arm around her neck and tugged her mouth down to his. Antonie fully returned his hungry, fierce kiss, her tongue eagerly fencing with his.

Her hands gripped his shoulders tightly when he cupped her breasts in his hands and his tongue and mouth pleasured them. His hands left her breasts when he began to gently, steadily suckle but she was not really aware of how he was removing the rest of her clothes until his kisses moved to her abdomen.

With passion in full control of her, she cared little about how completely she was exposed to his eyes. As his kisses moved down her slim legs she clung to him for support. Feeling as if all her bones had melted away, she fell back onto the bed. There was no resistance from her as he gently parted her thighs so that his mouth could play more freely over her inner thighs.

Then his lips touched the soft curls adorning her womanhood. Antonie gave a convulsive jerk but his hands gripped her a little harder around her hips, holding her still. She protested but even as the words left her lips, she was no longer fighting the intimacy, was welcoming it, crying out her pleasure and arching into his caress. When she felt herself cresting, she called to him, tried to reach for him, but he ignored her, crying out with her as her release shook her and he savored it.

Still reeling, Antonie opened her eyes to find him standing. Her gaze moved lovingly over his naked body as he loomed over her. He pulled her up into his arms then tumbled them both onto the bed to begin another assault upon her senses. This time he heeded her pleas when her passion began to mount, driving into her fiercely when she called out her need for him. He joined her in finding the culmination of their desire and Antonie clung to him weakly as they both shook with the force of it for long delicious moments after it had passed.

Royal flopped over onto his back and tugged her into his arms. He did not want to think about anything but sleep and the pleasant satiation of his body, but disturbing thoughts began to intrude upon his euphoria. Although he felt sure she had not lain with Oro tonight, there was no ignoring how the pair had acted. Every one of their actions had been that of lovers or of ones seriously contemplating such a relationship. The mere thought of it brought back the anger he had nursed all night.

"You're mine, Antonie."

Very slowly, she sat up to look at him. There was anger in his voice, nearly a threat. She knew the time of peace had passed. For a little while, she had hoped that he would simply ignore what seemed to be going on between herself and Oro, but knew that had been a foolish hope. A perverse part of her was rather glad that he was unable to ignore it.

"I am my own person but I think you say more than that."

"Yes, I do. I watched you and Oro tonight."

"Ah, was poor Marilynn unable to keep you entertained?"

"Leave Marilynn out of this. She has nothing to do with it. I want to know what's going on between you and Oro."

"Going on? We were at the fiesta. We were celebrating."

"There was a hell of a lot more than celebrating

128

going on, Antonie. You are mine. Oh, don't start that about only belonging to yourself. You know what I'm talking about. You're my lover and I damn well don't like sharing."

"You are not sharing."

"Damnit, Antonie, I'm not a fool. I saw you tonight, the two of you. If you aren't lovers now you're damn well thinking about it."

He was not going to believe her. She could see that clearly. Even though she felt sure she was going to be hurting herself far more than she would hurt him by such a move, Antonie knew that she had to leave his bed. She rose and tugged on her blouse and skirt then started to collect the rest of her clothes.

"What the hell are you doing?"

"Going to my room."

"Your room?" He grabbed her by the wrist. "You sure?"

"*Sí*, I am sure." She neatly twisted free of his hold. "I go to my room and my bed. Alone."

"Now wait a minute, Antonie. Let's discuss this."

"We do not discuss it. You say what you think and when I answer, you say no, that is not right. You are unreasonable."

"For Christ's sake, Antonie, it's not unreasonable for a man not to want to share his lover."

"I told you, you are not sharing me."

"I'm not blind, Antonie."

"*Sí*. You are some." She stared at him and said precisely, "Oro is not my lover."

"Maybe not now but . . ."

"Bah. Keep your buts."

"Antonie, get back here."

"No. I will not lie beneath a man who thinks I am a liar." Clutching her clothes she left the room.

Royal winced when she slammed the door after her,

129

then he cursed fluently. He had handled that all wrong. Jealous anger was not the way to keep her at his side. Briefly, he contemplated going after her, but then decided that would not be for the best either. They were both too angry to solve anything tonight. Some time was needed to cool off, to regain some sense of calm reason so that they could talk without the discussion becoming an argument.

He frowned as he worried about the wisdom of leaving her free for the taking, then shook away that fear. In a day's time they would head out on a long drive. There would be little chance for privacy between Antonie and Oro and what little there would be, he felt certain he could easily prevent. While he did that he could also work to remove this sudden stumbling block. He hoped it would not take long for his bed suddenly felt achingly empty.

Antonie threw herself face down on her bed and indulged in a hearty cry. Her body still tingled from his lovemaking yet, even as they had lain in each other's arms, he had started to accuse her. Just as she had feared, he did not really have enough trust in her to take her at her word. He preferred to judge her only by what he had seen.

She was still sniffling and thinking of looking for a handkerchief when she realized she was not alone. With a soft cry, she sat up to face the intruder. When she saw Maria, she was both relieved and disappointed. While she had feared some dangerous intruder, she had also hoped that Royal had come after her. The woman set a cup of steaming, aromatic brew on the table by the bed and then sat down on the edge of the bed.

"Drink it, *chica*. It is good for you."

Sitting up more comfortably, Antonie picked up the

130

cup and gingerly tasted its contents. "Not bad. Tea?"

"*Sí*. With herbs."

"It is medicine?"

"A little. It will soothe and help you sleep. I gave some to Patricia."

"She needed a lot of soothing?"

"*Sí*, the poor *chica*. You are right. She does not understand. She does not think we lie but she thinks us wrong. Maybe a part of her believes but it does not want to. She is so young and she loves. She thinks all should be happy."

"Do you think she really loves?"

"*Sí*. And you? Do you love?"

"It does not matter."

"He will not believe you."

"No. I looked him in the eye and I said, 'Oro is not my lover' but he doesn't hear me."

"And so you leave him."

"I could not be with a man who thinks I am a liar."

"*Sí*. There must be a, how they say it?, a line drawn. With some women it is that he must not stray."

Antonie smiled weakly. "I would not stand for that either. That is why I can understand his not wanting to share. I could not share. He will not believe me, though, when I say I am not with Oro. He believes only what he sees and that is not really proof for he has not seen me in bed with Oro. If I say I have not been there, he should believe me. I do not lie."

"Ah, well, he is angry. Maybe when the anger cools he will see clearer and he will listen."

"Maybe. We will see. I will not return to him while he is thinking I lie. I ask for little from him but there should be trust." She handed Maria the now empty cup. "Thank you. It was good and I think I do feel a little better, that I can get some sleep."

Maria paused at the door, sighed, and looked back at

Antonie. "I thought to wait but maybe I'd better tell you now. It will be said in the morning and you can be prepared. Patricia wants to go on the drive."

"*Dios.* They will not let her. Will they?"

Shrugging, Maria replied, "After the ranch was attacked they might agree with her that she is as safe with them as she is here. She is also going to feed the *patrón*'s words back at him. He has told her many times that she should learn more about the running of a rancho, of the raising and the selling of the cattle. I could not talk her out of this. *Buenos noches,* Antonie."

"*Buenos noches,* Maria," Antonie replied distractedly. When she had gone, Antonie rose from bed to wash up and undress.

If Patricia went along on the drive, it would mean that the game would have to be played for every long mile on the trail. Antonie felt a strong urge to scream. She was not sure she could keep up the pretense for so long.

But there was the chance that her brothers would stand firm against Patricia's plea. Antonie decided she could put her mind to better use thinking up arguments to counteract Patricia's than in fretting over the consequences of the girl joining the drive. Even if she had no chance to intercede in the family argument that was sure to result when Patricia made her suggestion, Antonie felt sure she could get her ideas across to at least one of the brothers. She could only hope that she could come up with a few good ones.

She was honest enough to admit that it was neither Oro nor Patricia nor what was between them that really troubled her. With Patricia left behind at the ranch, Antonie had hoped to be done with the game she and Oro played. Without that going on she felt sure Royal would soon come to see reason, to believe her assertion that she and Oro were not lovers. If Patricia did join the

132

drive, forcing her to stay close to Oro every step of the way, there would be no chance of such a reconciliation.

Crawling into bed, Antonie fought the urge to indulge in another bout of tears. She was hurt and instead of having more time to be with Royal, it was over. She wished she could just leave, but her promise to Juan and her strong sense of duty held her firm. Somehow she was going to have to endure the long months ahead being close to Royal yet apart from him.

Her eyes closing slowly, Antonie realized that Maria's potion really did soothe her and despite her pain and worries, she was going to sleep. As she gave in to its strong pull, she wondered wryly if Maria had a potion to cure lovesickness.

Chapter Ten

"Well? What do you think of cattle drives?" Cole asked as he rode up beside Antonie.

"Hot. Boring. Dusty. Itchy. Uncomfortable. Dirty. Smelly. Boring."

"You already said boring, Tony," he pointed out with a grin.

"It is twice boring. Maybe even three times boring. It is five times dirty and dusty."

He laughed and shook his head. "Don't I know it! Still, I'm glad I came along even if there weren't the trouble we've been having. Hasn't been much so far. 'Bout twenty head gone, one man wounded and one dead. We're making damn good time too."

"*Sí*, but," she looked at the horizon, "he is out there. I can feel him, smell him."

"Mendez?"

"*Sí*. Mendez. He nips at our heels like a bothersome dog. It is true that not much has happened but we push hard because we know he is out there. We watch more because we know he is watching. We grow tired. Soon. Soon, I think. He will strike."

"Aha. He tries to wear us down so that we'll be easy prey."

Antonie nodded. "He prefers his prey weaker than he is so he can be sure to win. He likes to pick the ground and the time. He will come and we must try to be ready."

"Maybe you should go home. You've done enough. It's not your ranch or your herd."

"I promised Juan that I would see that Royal keeps his land, that the debt is paid. Juan knew it was Mendez and so I think I was also promising that I would see an end to that pig."

"An old hate?"

"Very old. They come from the same village. Mendez raped and killed Juan's sister. That was just before Juan found me."

"You think he was thinking of her when he took you?"

"I did once but he said no." She grinned. "He said his sister was fat, dark and very obedient."

Cole laughed. "No, you wouldn't remind anyone of a girl like that." He frowned, growing serious. "Do you really think he meant for you to end Mendez's career?"

"His life. *Sí*, I think he did. I will have no choice anyway. Raoul wants me dead, I think."

"You sure are carrying around a pack of troubles. And, speaking of troubles, what's between you and Royal?"

"Nothing."

"Nothing don't have him growling like a bear with a sore paw or sending black looks at folks. Thought you were going to tell him there was nothing between you and Oro."

"I did. He did not believe me."

"So you left him. Well, left his bed anyway."

"*Sí*. I left his bed and I will stay gone until he sees that I am no liar."

"Now, Antoine . . ."

135

"No. Do not talk about it. I will not stay with a man who thinks I lie."

"Well, I'm not sure I'm willing to leave it at that but I reckon I'll have to for now 'cause here he comes."

Antoine moved away from Cole's side and rode toward Patricia. The girl was sullen company more often than not but it was less painful to quarrel with her than it was to quarrel with Royal. It was cowardly to simply try to avoid Royal but, after being subjected to Royal's cutting remarks several times in the past weeks, Antonie decided she preferred cowardice.

"You chased her off again," Cole remarked when Royal reached his side.

Royal briefly glared at Cole then at the departing Antonie. "She doesn't run from anything."

"Runs from you, brother. Maybe it's from all those compliments you fling at her head lately."

"Oh, shut up."

"Look, Royal, your private life's your business . . ."

"Exactly. My own business."

"Except when it's making things tough for everyone else."

"And just how the hell am I doing that?"

"In a lot of ways and I think you see them clear enough. The thing is that Antonie and the twins came here of their own free will to give us a hand. We owe them Justin's and Patricia's lives. Owe them Patricia's life twice over because Antonie and Tomás were guarding the ranch that day. We owe them for saving the ranch that day, too. Our men are good but they're just cowhands, not soldiers, not gunmen. Antonie can outdraw and outshoot most every one of them. We need them and they've done good by us. For thanks, you hand her sarcasm.

"Now, any fool can see things aren't just right 'tween you and Tony. Oro's mixed up in it somewhere too.

Either get it sorted out or leave it be. We're fighting for our lives here and these personal problems seem mighty small next to that," Cole finished tartly, then rode away.

Cursing viciously and continually, Royal decided to ride ahead of the herd. Only Tomás was wandering that far ahead and Royal doubted he would even catch a glimpse of him. He needed to be alone for just a while.

Cole was right. He had to push his personal problems into the background. Everything their father had built was at stake. It was a poor time to let some female tie him up in knots and distract him.

That, however, was easier decided than done. He ached for her. Every time Oro touched Antonie, even in the most casual way, it made him see red. The only good he could find in the whole mess was that the pair could not be lovers now. There was no privacy and no real chance for them to find any.

He gave a short, harsh laugh as he stared at the water they would soon camp by. It was probably for the best that he and Antonie were estranged. Royal doubted that he would be in any better a mood if he had to spend night after night for weeks with Antonie yet not make love to her. He would undoubtedly grow reckless, try to find a private place and get them both into trouble. It was not safe to get separated from the others. Raoul Mendez was out there somewhere waiting for any stray—human or bovine.

For a moment, he was distracted from his own troubles. He studied the land around him but saw nothing. But Royal could feel Mendez's presence. Mendez's boss had to be paying him very well to get him to leave the proximity of the Mexican border. With each mile that Mendez trailed them he made his escape even more improbable.

"But who the hell is paying the bastard?"

137

"If we knew that, this trouble would be over, eh?"

Whirling to look at Tomás who was just reining in at his side, Royal shouted, "Creeping up on a man like that's a good way to get shot!"

"You always look first."

"I do?"

"*Sí*. Sometimes you look even before you draw your gun. Like now."

"I'm not so sure that's a good thing."

"Maybe not out here, but in most places it is good. I look too, but only when I am ready to shoot. Then the time lost in being sure the threat is real is very small. For me, it has usually been a threat, a big one, eh? It is a hard line to stay to though. I almost shot a priest once."

Tomás said it so sweetly, almost cheerfully, that Royal was surprised into laughing. "I'd think you'd be real careful not to hurt one of those."

"*Sí*, that is what the priest said, especially since I was sneaking out of the convent school at the time."

Still laughing, Royal said, "I think you are just a little bit crazy, *amigo*."

"*Sí*, just a little. I think it is a good thing to be."

"You may just be right."

"Maybe. I came here to tell you that I have found a place where the ladies may wash in privacy tonight."

"That's fine but is it also safe?"

"Come, see for yourself."

When Antonie saw Royal approach her after they had camped for the night, she inwardly groaned. There was no place for her to slip away to, no way she could avoid him without looking embarrassingly obvious. As he neared her, she decided that this time she would not let his nasty little remarks either anger or hurt her.

"Antonie, Tomás found a secluded niche where you and Patricia could have a bath if you're of a mind to."

138

She almost gaped at him. His voice was pleasant and there was no sign of the simmering anger that had seemed to have become a permanent part of him. It took her a full minute to realize what he had said.

"A bath?" she squeaked as she leapt to her feet.

"Yes, a bath."

"A full bath? Clothes off, soap and all?"

"Well, a cold one."

"*Por Dios,* who is caring?" she dashed off to get Patricia.

Royal almost smiled as he watched her run off. When she was acting so totally female, he felt confident with her. She was like all the other women he had ever known. It was usually a short-lived feeling, however. There was no question in his mind that Antonie was fully and undoubtedly a woman, but she had some twists and turns he had never encountered before, quirks that could leave him floundering, wondering just how to move or what to say.

He shook that thought away when Antonie and Patricia hurried up to him, their arms full of clean clothes and bathing necessities. The look on their faces made him smile. It was especially nice to see Patricia in good spirits. Since she had insisted on coming on the drive he had had little sympathy with her moodiness, but it was good to see her happy for a change.

"You wouldn't dare tease us about such a thing, would you, Royal?"

"No, Patricia. I wouldn't tease you about it. Come on, I'll show you the place."

"Tomás found it?" Antonie asked as she fell into step at Royal's side.

"While he was scouting the area he came across it. It'll give you two some privacy but still be guarded."

"You're standing guard?"

"Yes, Pattie. Go on, right through those bushes."

When they were gone, Royal leaned up against a tree and kept watch. He had contemplated handing the chore over to someone else for it was going to be hard to stand there knowing that Antonie was only a few feet away, shedding her clothes and washing her lithe body. However, Justin and Cole were already bedded down resting up for the midnight watch and he knew that Patricia would not feel comfortable with anyone else. He grimaced and admitted to himself that he would not have felt very comfortable letting somebody else stand so close to an unclothed Antonie. It was not going to be easy, but he was just going to have to grit his teeth and try not to think too much about what Antonie was doing just behind those bushes. If he did, he would be useless as a guard.

The water was cold but Antonie did not care. She considered it a luxury to totally immerse herself and scrub herself clean. Since it might be her last chance for a good bath for a long time, she intended to fully enjoy it.

"I can see why Oro wants you."

Startled by the girl's quiet statement, Antonie just stared at Patricia. "What?"

"I said I can see why Oro wants you. And Royal. And probably most of all the rest of the men around here."

Hearing the somewhat petulant note in Patricia's voice, Antonie returned most of her attention to getting clean. "You are silly."

"No I'm not. They do. Now you've cast aside Royal and picked up Oro. You used Royal."

Glaring at the girl's stiff, slim back as Patricia marched out of the water, Antonie said coldly, "I did not use your brother."

"Ha! You were with him all the time then you set your eyes on Oro and cast poor Royal aside."

140

Antonie thought the girl's words a little dramatic but they did succeed in making her angry. "The reason why I am not with your brother is none of your business, *chica,* but I did not use him. If you must throw that accusation at anybody, throw it at Royal. He takes me and does not hide the fact that I am his lover. That marks me. What does he give me in return for my innocence and so much else that I give him? Passion. That is all. Passion. No words of love. No promise of a future. Only passion. Now, who is using whom, eh?"

Patricia did not bother to answer, just grabbed up the bucket she had put her clothes in to soak and marched away. Antonie cursed and rinsed the soap out of her hair. She was still annoyed when, a few minutes later, she emerged from the water and began to dry off. The girl had almost succeeded in ruining the pleasure of a bath.

Just as she tugged on her drawers, Antonie felt the hairs on the back of her neck stand on end. Inwardly, she cursed fluently as she realized that she had not been on her guard. She saw her knife and reached for it, only to have a booted foot reach it before she could, her wrists neatly lassoed. Even as she opened her mouth to call for Royal, a grubby hand was closed over it and another painfully gripped her hair, twisting until she was forced to her knees.

She stared up into the face of the man who crouched over her, grinning in a way that chilled her blood. It was Jesu Miller, a half-Anglo, half-Mexican who went to vicious extremes to win Raoul's favor. Antonie searched her mind frantically for some way to get loose or to at least make enough noise to draw Royal's attention.

Royal straightened up from his relaxed slouch when Patricia marched out of the bushes. "Where's Antonie?"

"Just finishing up." Patricia paused when it was clear

141

that Royal was staying near the pool. "Well?"

"Well what?"

"Aren't you going to walk me back to the camp?"

"I'm waiting for Antonie."

"Oh, of course. Wait for Antonie. Everybody else does," Patricia said darkly as she stomped away.

Trying to puzzle out his sister's mood, Royal watched her until she reached the camp. While in plain sight of the men in the camp, Patricia did not really need a guard. By the time she was back in camp, he gave up trying to figure out what was wrong with her and turned his attention back to guarding and waiting for Antonie.

Several long moments passed with no sight or sound of her. His stomach began to knot with tension as he waited. Finally, he decided that preserving her modesty was not worth ignoring the sense of danger that had come over him.

Cautiously, he crept forward. To avoid making much noise, he went through the covering brush on his stomach. He briefly mused that he was going to feel like a fool if she was all right. Wryly he admitted to himself that there was truth in the old adage that it was better to be safe than sorry.

When the clearing first came into view, he found himself struggling against acting rashly. The sight of Antonie half-dressed and caught firmly by a leering man had him aching to use his gun. It took him a moment to clear the fury from his brain enough to see that he had a real chance of hitting Antonie as well, for she was between him and her captor. He was going to have to be patient and wait for a clear shot.

"There, Juan's child," Jesu sneered as he removed his hand then quickly gagged her, "now I can take you to Raoul. Ah, how he will praise Jesu for giving him this prize."

Antonie bit back a moan as he used her hair to pull her to her feet. She suddenly realized that she had a chance now, however small. Before he could step out of reach or move behind her, she brought her knee up hard into his groin. He gave a soft cry of agony and doubled over. Using her bound hands as a fist, she swung at his head. As her fist came down, she caught the fleeting glint of a knife blade as he pulled the weapon from his boot. With a grunt, he fell forward, face down on the ground. She hesitated to flee when she saw his body give a convulsive spasm then lie ominously still.

Hearing a sound, she whirled around expecting a compatriot of Jesu's. She closed her eyes briefly in relief when she saw Royal. When he cautiously turned Jesu over, Antonie gasped behind her gag. The man had fallen on the knife he had drawn. The weapon he had meant to use on her had neatly ended his own life.

"I should've known you could take care of yourself," Royal said as he undid her bonds. "Who is it? Do you know?"

"*Sí*. Jesu Miller. He was *loco*."

She moved back to the water and rinsed her mouth to remove the taste of the filthy gag. It had been too close. Hearing Royal drag the body nearer to the undergrowth, she shivered. Jesu had been right. Raoul would have praised him highly. Antonie thanked God that Raoul would be disappointed this time.

"It was close," Royal said quietly as he moved back to her side.

"*Sí*. Very close."

"If Raoul got hold of you, he would kill you."

"Ah, *sí*, he would kill me." She decided it was not necessary to tell him about Raoul's unique ways of killing his enemies.

Grasping her by the shoulders, Royal asked, "Are

143

you sure you're all right?"

"I am not hurt."

The mere touch of his hands made her tremble, desire careening through her body. It had been over a month since they had made love but she was a little puzzled at how desperate she was to hold him and be held by him. She was also a little afraid and tried to pull away from him. His grip tightened and when she met his gaze, she knew he had seen her need. When his mouth approached hers the only protest she could manage was a somewhat frantic shaking of her head which he neatly stopped by cupping her face in his hands and even that meek protest died the moment his mouth covered hers. She lost all urge to resist him as he hungrily kissed her and became an equal partner in the fierce coupling that ensued.

Her body still trembling faintly from the force of her release, Antonie stared dazedly at the man sprawled in her arms. They had not even bothered to get fully naked. His shirt was undone and her drawers were off but nothing else. It had been so fast and furious that she could remember little of it. However, as he eased the intimacy of their embrace, she had the chilling feeling that it had been a mistake.

"Can Oro give you that, Antonie?"

Cursing fluently, Antonie abruptly rose and started to dress. Whatever had driven her to go so mad in his arms, she should have fought. Instead, she had gone down as easily as any round-heeled piece of calico.

"Antonie, damnit," Royal struggled to straighten out his clothing, "will you calm down?"

"I am supposed to take this insult with a smile? Let you call me a *puta* to my face?"

"I didn't call you a whore. You aren't being reasonable." He reached for her but she slapped his hand away.

144

"Oro is not my lover."

"Well, I know you two haven't been together on the drive," he began.

"*Por Dios,* you do not listen. This was a mistake. It will not happen again. To lie with a man who thinks me a liar is to be no better than a *puta.*"

He cursed when she hurried away. The chance for a reconciliation had been in his hands and he had let it slip away. He should never have mentioned Oro's name but the man was foremost in his thoughts at the moment.

As he made a quick check of the clearing to be sure nothing was left but the body, he thought about how adamant she was in her denial of a love affair with Oro. That she did not lie was clearly a strong point of pride with her. Slowly he began to wonder if he was wrong. She had never lied to him before. It was very probable that she was not lying now. As he started back to camp, he promised himself that he would strive to quell his possessive anger and look at things more closely.

"Such a dark face," Tomás murmured as he sat down next to Antonie, "and so all by yourself. You sit this far away from the others because you are afraid the gun you clean will go off, eh?"

Antonie smiled crookedly and shook her head. "I had to do some thinking."

"What troubles you, *chica?* Talk to me. Sometimes other eyes can see the problem clearer."

Taking a deep breath and silently cursing the blush that flooded her face, she said softly, "I made love with Royal by a corpse."

"Ah. Jesu will be sorry he missed it. I made love beside a live husband once."

She was briefly diverted and surprised into a laugh. "How could you do that?"

"As I walked by this woman's house, she called to me,

145

invited me to pleasure her as I had done before. I went to her window but I saw her husband in the bed and suggested that perhaps this was not a good time."

"Very wise."

"*Sí*, but she said he was dead drunk, that nothing could wake him. She persuaded me to come in. Well, there I was going about my business when I see that her husband is awake. But, instead of killing me, he was inspired by my skill. He pushed me out of bed and took my place with his wife. I decided I would let them have some privacy and left."

"You are going to get shot one of these days," she managed to say as she laughed.

"Only the earth lives forever." He shook his head when the troubled look returned to her face. "I did not divert you enough."

"No. How could I do that? It is disgusting. Such disrespect for the dead."

"No, *querida*, and the dead like Jesu deserve no respect. You cared nothing for him so you were not mocking your grief."

"I don't know, Tomás. To do that with the dead only a few feet away," she whispered, shock evident in her voice.

"Maybe that is why you did it."

"That makes no sense, *amigo*."

"*Sí*, it does. You faced death. You knew it and Royal knew it. What better way to prove to yourselves that you are alive?"

"You think that is why we acted so?"

"Some of the why. Maybe you would have only thought on it except you have been apart for a long time. Sailors come home having fought the sea and won and they find a woman quick. Soldiers can love their woman before they go to a battle yet come home even a few hours later and have to have her again. They

146

have survived and they want to prove it.

"I think too that the violence can be part of it. If there is a woman near the battle, she will probably be raped. How can a man take a woman at such a time, you wonder? When you fight, you face death, the blood races, eh?"

"Like it does when you're loving someone," Antonie said quietly.

"Sí. I am no rapist but the times I have fought and faced death, if there was a willing woman near, I would have taken her even if I had needed to push the dead aside to make room. So? You and Royal are together again?"

"No. Only for that moment. He still thinks I lie when I say Oro is not my lover."

"Poor little one. And you cannot ignore that?"

"I will not lie with a man who thinks me a liar."

"That I can understand but think on it well, *chica.* You are losing time with your man. You are tossing away chances to pull more than a fever from him. Be very sure that the price you are paying is not too high. I think that somewhere there has to be a compromise."

Chapter Eleven

Grimacing, Antonie shifted in her saddle. She had never spent so many consecutive hours in the saddle before. Tomorrow she would return to driving the wagon for a while. Glancing at Patricia, she felt the girl would agree. Perhaps they could use a blanket or two to soften that seat. Antonie decided she was tired of hard saddles and the hard ground.

Royal and Cole rode by and Royal tipped his hat in greeting. He had not been so vicious with her lately but he still watched her constantly, especially when she was with Oro. The dark anger was disappearing from his face, however. She wished she could know why that was. It would be nice if it was because he was starting to believe her but there was another possible reason, one which twisted her heart. Royal could simply have decided that he was no longer interested in her and was willing to let Oro take her off his hands.

"God, this dust is terrible."

Almost desperately, Antonie latched onto the diversion of Patricia's complaint. "It would be better up ahead a way."

"Yes, you're probably right. Oh, you don't need to come with me. You can go ride with someone else.

Like Oro? Or is it my brother today?"

Antonie had to give the girl credit for persistence. No matter how often Patricia failed to get Oro's attention and failed to get a rise out of Antonie, the girl kept at it. It was very possible that Maria was right, that Patricia did love Oro. Mere infatuation would surely have withered beneath all Patricia had had to endure.

"It is you today. Do you forget? When you, how you say?, wheedled your way into coming along on the drive, it was decided that I would be your guard, that I would stay with you." Antonie started to move forward.

Keeping pace at Antonie's side, Patricia said, "Yes? Well, do you know what I think?"

"I am sure you will tell me."

"Royal only made that rule because he was worried about you."

"That is ridiculous."

"Oh yes? It keeps you in the background, doesn't it? You can't get in the middle of any trouble we might face because you'll be trying to get me safe and out of the way. He was just making sure you wouldn't get shot."

"But, of course, he does not worry that his only sister will be shot. You are silly, *niña*."

"Why do you always talk to me like I'm a child?"

"Because often, like now, you act like a child. Now, if you are so tired of eating dust, you'd better ride. The herd catches us."

Frowning as he watched Antonie and Patricia, Royal muttered, "What are they up to?"

"Getting ahead of the herd a mite, I'd say. Tired of the dust," Cole answered.

"Fine, as long as they don't get too far ahead."

"Antonie knows her business."

"Yes, she does, but today I'd like everyone to stay close."

149

"Think there'll be some trouble?"

"Maybe. I've just got this feeling that something's in the wind."

"The stink of Raoul Mendez. I would've thought we'd had enough trouble."

"Little stuff. As Antonie calls it — a wolf nipping at our heels."

"Well, maybe we'll be lucky and he'll stay at our heels."

"Luck hasn't been with us much lately, I'd say, so keep a close watch."

It was mid-afternoon when Antonie stopped for a moment and dismounted, Patricia doing the same. Antonie felt bone-weary, dusty and dry. Taking only a small mouthful of water from her canteen, she rinsed her mouth then had a small drink.

"This really is a boring business, isn't it?" Patricia remarked as she sipped from her canteen.

"Some, *sí*."

"Why are we stopping?"

"We have gotten too far ahead. The orders were to stay close, in sight. We will wait a moment until we are closer."

"Funny how the land goes along so flat, then you get a rocky outcrop like that over there."

"It might mean that soon the land will not be so flat any more. I cannot say. I do not know this land."

"Neither do I and there's a lot of times I wish I'd stayed ignorant."

"If this was just a trip and not a cattle drive, it would look better, I think. I do not mind the flatness. One can see far away. There are fewer places to hide. That dog Mendez must hate it. He likes to sneak up on his prey."

"Well, he's a *bandito*."

"He is the lowest of curs. He likes to kill, to hurt. He is not worth spitting on."

"How can you talk like that about a *bandito?* The man who raised you was one."

"*Sí,* but he, too, hated Mendez. *Chica,* Mexico is a poor place. If a man is not a *patrón,* he is a peasant. A peasant is nothing in Mexico. The soldiers trample him and the *patróns* work him like a slave. If he complains about his lot, he is usually shot or beaten. If he is lucky, he can scratch the dirt for just enough to survive from the day he is born to the day he dies, old before his time. If he is not, the soldiers get him, rape his women and ruin his fields. Maybe filth like Mendez comes to do the same. Then there are Indians and no one helps the peasant against them. Of course, he could be taken to the mines to die in the darkness and worked harder than a burro.

"Juan was a peasant. He chose to be a *bandito.* He was a thief and he knew this was not right but he never stole from the poor on either side of the border. No, Juan struck at the strong and the rich. Sometimes he would win and gain some pesos. Sometimes he would lose the fight. He never killed the unarmed, the innocent or the ones who surrendered. He did not want blood, only money. If there is such a thing as an honorable thief, Juan Ramirez was one."

"But Mendez is not?"

"No, he is a pig. He murders, he tortures, he rapes. Mendez is eaten with hate. You do not surrender to him."

"It is hard to understand people like that."

"You do not try to understand them. You kill them."

"Antonie!"

Antonie shrugged. "It is what you must do."

"I don't think I could."

"Maybe not, but if you face him, you'd better do it or face a long, slow death. Just think about all the people he has killed and will kill if he continues to live. He stinks of death. Not just men either. Women and children. He shot a baby once, right in the mother's arms, for he had the hangover and the baby was crying. You think about that if you ever face him."

Before Patricia could express her shock over that tale, the faint sound of gunfire reached them. "Antonie?"

"Get back on your horse."

Just as they started to mount, another sound came to them, freezing them where they stood. Antonie felt sure that she had gone as pale as Patricia as they both stared in horror in the direction of the herd. There was only one explanation for the sound they heard and it made Antonie's blood run cold.

"Oh my God, a stampede."

"Mount, *chica*. Now."

Even as they swung up into their saddles, the herd came into view, barreling straight for them. Antonie slapped Patricia on the back to shake the girl out of her immobilizing fear. She then pointed toward the rocks that were a little ahead of them. If neither of their horses stumbled, Antonie was sure they could reach the safety of the rocks before the herd got to them.

Once at the rocks, Antonie dismounted, ordering Patricia to do the same. She grabbed their canteens and weapons then slapped each horse on the rump to set the animal running. There was no room to shelter them in the rocks and Antonie knew the animals would have a good chance of surviving if they were let go.

Pushing Patricia before her, Antonie climbed to the top of the rocks. The outcrop was wide enough and tall enough that the herd would have to go around it. Tying a bandana around her face, an action Patricia quickly imitated, Antonie watched in horrified fascination as her theory about what the herd would do was proven right. She just hoped that the others would see that she and Patricia were safe.

The dust kicked up by the herd was stifling. There was almost too much noise to endure, the frightening combination of thousands of hooves pounding over the ground, the screams of the animals who faltered and were run down, men yelling frantically, sometimes fearfully and guns being fired either at an enemy or in an attempt to turn the herd. When Patricia started to cling to her, Antonie unabashedly clung onto Patricia. She had a need to know she was not alone in the midst of such madness. The stinging dust finally forced Antonie to close her eyes.

"Is it over?"

Hearing Patricia's dry, raspy whisper, Antonie eased her hold on the girl. "I don't know. I think I can still hear it."

"So can I, but I think it's only in my head."

Using her bandana, Antonie wiped her eyes then carefully opened them. It was a little hard to believe what her watering eyes told her. The herd was gone. The thunder of hooves she still heard was the echo of the stampede in her head.

"They are gone."

"What do we do now?"

Dampening her bandana with water from her canteen so that she could better wash the dust from her face, Antonie replied, "We head after them."

"But our horses are gone."

"You have feet, *chica*."

"Antonie, they could be miles ahead of us."

"Very true, but someone will come back for us."

"Then why not just wait here?"

"Someone started that stampede. I do not want to meet them."

"Oh. I hadn't thought of that," Patricia said quietly as she followed Antonie and climbed down the rocks.

"They'd follow, would they?"

"There is a good chance that they would."

Even as she spoke, a shot rang out, the bullet hitting the rocks to Antonie's right. She scrambled back behind the protection of the rocks and pushed Patricia down behind cover. Cursing softly and continuously, she looked out at what she estimated to be at least half of Raoul's private army. She wondered if Raoul himself hid amongst the pack.

"Oh, Antonie, what do we do now?"

"Stay behind these rocks. Take up your rifle, *chica*."

Patricia did so but said shakily, "We can't fight them all."

"No, but we can hold them off for a while."

"What good will that do?"

"It will buy us time, Patricia. Time for the others to come."

Royal felt as sweat-soaked and exhausted as his horse when they finally stopped the herd. As his men gathered, however, his weariness faded, replaced by fear. His eyes frantically searched the ones around him then the horizon.

"Where's Antonie and Patricia?"

"I saw them, boss. They were fine. Sitting up on some rocks as safe as can be. I was near the back of the herd too."

Relaxing slightly, Royal asked, "You're sure, Tom?"

"Sure as I'm sitting here. Rocks were high enough and wide enough to make the herd go 'round them."

"I've got their horses, boss. Sent 'em off to fend for themselves, I reckon."

"Well, hang onto them, Johnnie. We're going back for them. Half of you get fresh horses and come with me. The rest of you make camp."

154

"Why so many men?" Cole asked as they started out.

"Someone started that stampede. That someone might just follow along to see how much damage was done."

Just as Royal began to wonder if they had somehow missed the spot where Tom had seen the girls, he heard the sound of gunfire. As he had feared, the girls had been left far enough behind to be caught by the ones responsible for the stampede. He ordered Johnnie to hold back with the girls' horses, then led the others in a charge that reminded him strongly of the war.

"Antonie, here they come!"

Grabbing hold of Patricia before the excited girl could leap up, Antonie advised, "We are, how you say it?, not out of the forest yet."

"Out of the woods."

"Same thing. Keep shooting, *chica*. Keep shooting 'til these curs are out of sight or our men get in the way."

Antonie saw that Patricia knew this was a time to be silently obedient. The girl doggedly began to shoot at their attackers again. What amusement Antonie felt over the rebel yells and whoops of the cowhands faded when she saw Patricia turn ashen. A *bandito* fell to Patricia's bullet only a few feet from where they crouched in the rocks. Although Antonie suspected the girl's shots had hit others, they had been faceless and far enough away so that the girl could give little thought to where her bullets were landing. This one had been so close that his blood had splattered the rocks they hid behind. To save the girl any further shock, Antonie ordered her to put up her gun sooner than she might have otherwise.

As she waited for their men to come for them, Antonie kept a close eye on Patricia. The girl could not seem to stop herself from looking at the dead man. Neither did her color improve much, but, she showed no sign of hysterics.

"Are you all right?" Royal demanded when he finally reached them.

"Sí, we are not hurt. Just dusty, eh?" Antonie smiled faintly as she fruitlessly tried to brush the dust from her clothes. "It is good that you came. I was running out of bullets." She indicated her half empty bandoleras.

"Royal, I killed a man," Patricia said flatly.

Even as Royal put his arm around Patricia and opened his mouth to speak, Antonie said, "Him? Bah. You did not kill him."

"But, Antonie, he was coming right at me. I shot and he fell."

"You shot and you missed. I shot him. See? Clean through the chest. You are not that good." She patted Patricia on the back and said gently, "You are a very bad shot."

"A bad shot?" Patricia looked stunned then glared at Antonie. "Well, if I'm so bad a shot, why did you have me shoot at all?"

"Well, they did not know how bad a shot you are."

"I'm going back to camp," Patricia grumbled and strode away, her slim back stiff with indignation.

Following Antonie as she moved to search the dead man's pockets, Royal said quietly, "You lied."

Studying the fine gold watch she had just found, Antonie nodded. "Sí. I lied. She killed him."

"I thought you never lied."

"I told you that I do not lie about Oro and me. I never said I never lied. You did not see her face when she shot this man."

"She must have known her shots were hitting men. She was fighting for her life."

"Sí, and she will see that eventually. The others were far away. She could not know who she hit or if she did. She saw this man's face as he saw his death, saw his

156

blood flow, heard his cry of fear. Patricia does not know this way of life. This violence and death is new to her. Her mind and heart have not hardened.

"Me? I have seen many die. Some by my gun. Some by my knife. I know the fight to live. Patricia knows flattering beaux on porch swings and tea with the preacher's wife. I am used to seeing this but a part of me still curls up, sickened by it. Everything in Patricia was horrified. So, I lied to ease that horror, a horror maybe too big for her to accept. I lied to take that look out of her eyes. I think these men are making raids as they follow us."

Shaking free of his fascination with that brief look into how she thought, Royal became aware of the fact that Antonie was cleaning out the dead man's pockets. "Antonie! You're robbing the dead! Put those things back."

Standing up, Antonie pocketed the money, tossed the bandoleras over her shoulder and calmly continued to study the gold watch. "No. He has no need of them."

"That may be true but . . ."

"Besides, except for the bullets, none of these things are his. He is one of the Martinez brothers. This watch says, 'To William Deeds, thanks for the chance. Joe.' " She patted her pants pocket. "The money he stole too."

"That doesn't make it right to steal from a corpse."

"Better I take it than Raoul and his men. They will stop to pick over the dead. Besides, this pig is headed to hell and it would be a shame to have such a fine watch melt, eh?" She went to find her horse.

Royal frowned, his eyes following her even as he moved toward his own horse. He could not figure her out. She lied to protect a young girl's feelings then calmly robbed the dead.

When Cole rode up beside him, Royal was eager to be distracted from his thoughts.

"Where'd you get that knife?"

"A fine one, isn't it? Off one of the dead Mexicans back there."

"You robbed the dead?" Royal asked, surprised.

"Such sensitivity. He's got no use for it now. Raoul and the rest of his men will be along soon and they'll pick the bodies clean. Clothes and all. At least I won't use this to slit throats in the night."

"You're just making excuses," Royal said, disgust in his voice.

Cole shrugged. "Maybe. I doubt I'll lose any sleep over relieving some dead *bandito* of his knife, however. Why are you all fired up?"

"I just don't like the idea of taking things off the dead. First Antonie, then you. Probably some of the others too."

"No probably about it. Hey, it's not nice. I know it. Don't usually do it. Not even in the war. Sometimes you just can't let what the dead have be wasted and sometimes, with scum like this, you just don't give a damn. Especially when you can be pretty certain that what they've got is stolen goods anyway. Come on, we've got to get an exact tally of what damage was done."

Consigning the recent pilfering to obscurity, Royal set about the task of tabulating his losses. Considering all that had happened, he soon saw that they had come through it all miraculously unscathed. By the time he was able to sit down for a cup of strong coffee, he was exhausted. If Raoul kept harassing them as badly as today, Royal felt confident that they would all drop dead of exhaustion before the drive was over.

He watched Patricia wearily enter the wagon where she and Antonie slept. Royal suspected that Patricia had already begun to see through the lie Antonie had told, but she was holding up well. Part of him wished

158

she had stayed home wrapped in blissful ignorance but another part of him felt it might do her some good to see some of the harsher side of life. Texas was still young, wild and rough. If Patricia was going to make her life in the growing state, she should get a little harder, a little more worldly.

When Antonie came over to the fire, sat down and helped herself to some coffee, he gave her a tired smile. He almost laughed when he realized that the tug of desire he always felt in her presence was a weak, half-hearted thing at the moment. Even that part of his body was just too tired to get too enthused. Nevertheless, he found himself wishing that, when he finally crawled into his bedroll, she would be there for him to curl up with.

Antonie felt him looking at her and finally gave in to the urge to return that look. He looked very tired and a little sad, which puzzled her for she could think of no reason for it. When she found herself longing to hold him close and smooth away the lines of exhaustion on his face, she decided that she had better leave or at least start up a conversation so as to distract herself. She opted for the latter as she was momentarily too lazy to rise and she wanted to finish her coffee.

"Well, at least we did not lose any miles today, eh? The herd ran in the right direction."

Laughing softly, Royal nodded. "Fact is, I think we gained some miles. However, if the herd is too tired, we could lose that advantage tomorrow. Same with the horses and men. Well, we can only wait and see."

"Did you lose much?"

"About twenty head. Not as bad as I had figured it would be."

"But no men were lost?"

"No. The only dead man was one of the ones who started the stampede."

"Justice."

"Maybe so but it's an ugly way to die."

"They were hoping many of us would die so."

"True."

"Any injuries amongst your men? I have been too busy to look and see."

"None during the stampede which I figure is as close to a miracle as I'll ever get. Martin got shot, winged really, in the fight and Johnson fell off his horse during the charge."

"Oh, poor Johnson," Antonie gasped as she stood up.

"Poor Johnson? He's only bruised up a mite. Martin's got a hole in his arm."

"Sí, and I feel bad for him but Johnson," she shook her head. "To fall off your horse in the middle of a charge into battle? There is embarrassment. I will go see him."

Staring after her as she strode off, Royal had a feeling he was gaping. He shook his head and looked at Cole who was bent double with laughter.

"I don't think I will ever understand that woman," he declared then joined Cole in his hearty enjoyment.

Chapter Twelve

Watching Oro from where she sat by Tomás, Antonie could see his tension. She sighed, knowing it was not just the waiting for something to happen. He could not even ease the lustful part of his feelings for Patricia, his love and respect for her stopping him. Antonie understood what he was feeling, at least in part, and she ached for him.

Most of the time she could not really be angry at Patricia although she felt the girl could have refrained wheedling her way into joining the drive. She felt for the girl as well, even when she longed to slap her for torturing poor Oro by offering a love he could not take. It was amazing that Patricia's brothers had not noticed her longing looks toward Oro, but they might yet and Antonie waited for that event with dread. Love was proving to be an extremely tiresome business.

"I will go on a watch," Oro said abruptly and started for his horse.

"There's no need," protested Cole. "Plenty of men out there."

"I will go."

Oro had just reached the remuda when shots rang

out. Antonie saw him fall and felt her blood run cold. For a moment he lay ominously still but then she saw what she had been waiting so tensely for. In a long ago agreed signal, he put up his thumb to show her that he lived. Unable to go to him, she hoped that whatever wound he had suffered was not too serious.

Antonie threw Patricia to the ground just as the girl started to move toward Oro. "Stay down," she hissed.

"But Oro," Patricia choked out even as Antonie pinned her down so neatly that she could not move at all.

"See his thumb? It is up. That means that he lives. Stay down or you will not. Now, crawl. Under the supply wagon. Keep your backside down." Antonie roughly pushed Patricia's gently rounded rump down as they started to crawl. "Want it shot off, *muchacha?*"

This was the attack they had waited for and Royal looked to see Antonie herding Patricia to safety. Only once did she shoot, neatly taking down the man who had spotted them. Her gun stayed at the ready but silent so as not to draw any more attention to herself and her basically helpless charge, for this time Patricia was unarmed. He was glad he had assigned Antonie that chore for it meant that she too had to stay under cover.

Raoul had clearly hoped that the element of surprise would be on his side but it was failing him. Royal knew that seeing how his men were being slaughtered while few of the Bancroft crew fell, Raoul would realize that a full assault was plainly not the answer. It did not surprise Royal at all when, after a relatively brief if furious battle, Raoul rode off into the night, but the man left eight of his men behind, dead or nearly so.

As soon as the shooting had ended, Antonie leapt to her feet. "Stay here," she ordered Patricia.

162

Patricia clearly had no intention of obeying for Antonie heard the girl follow her. Antonie quickly ascertained that Royal and Tomás were in fine shape as she ran to Oro and knelt by his side. Easing his head onto her lap, she gently dabbed the blood away from what was only a graze on his forehead. She spared little more than a glance for Patricia as the girl knelt and touched Oro's arm. Oro groaned and turned his face into Antonie's abdomen to hide.

"*Por Dios,* will you go away? I do not need you."

Even as a white-faced Patricia retreated, Oro staggered to his feet and stumbled away. Antonie signaled a hurriedly approaching Tomás that Oro was all right and then set out after him. She was worried about Oro stumbling around with a head wound, upset as he was.

Royal had sensed the tension between Oro and Patricia but had thought that perhaps his sister was pestering the man with an infatuation. Hearing Oro's words and seeing the way they had devastated Patricia, he knew it ran deeper. Not sure what he intended to do, he followed Oro and Antonie.

Still dizzy, Oro collapsed to his knees just out of sight of the camp. Antonie feared that it was not really the pain in his head that troubled him most but a deeper, perhaps incurable one. She sensed that he was turning away something he ached to grasp with both hands and hold onto tightly and that he hated himself for hurting Patricia by turning her away. When Antonie knelt in front of him, thinking that she had not fully realized the depth of what she was involved in, he reached for her blindly.

"It hurts. God, it hurts."

She knew he was not referring to his head wound as she wrapped him in her arms, her cheek pressed against his hair. When his strong arms held her too tightly, she made no complaint but rocked him gently and wept for his pain. It all seemed so very unfair.

Turning away from the private and uncomfortably emotional scene, Royal slowly made his way back to camp. Suddenly the responsibility he carried seemed too much. Oro Degas was not a man he would have chosen for Patricia but did he have a right to decide that? Seeing that everything was under control, he sought out Cole and Justin. If nothing else he needed a sounding board for his troubled thoughts.

Seeing Tomás grab a bottle of tequila and go to Patricia, Royal briefly postponed locating his brothers. He hated eavesdropping but he needed to know what was going on. There was no way he could make any rational decision without knowing. Staying out of sight, he strained to hear what Tomás and Patricia were saying.

"Here. Have a drink." Tomás offered Patricia the bottle of tequila and smiled a little when she took a sip from it and grimaced.

"That stuff is disgusting," she gasped. "I think it has done real damage to my throat."

"It is Mexican. An acquired taste. Not every *gringo* likes it." He took a drink and offered her the bottle again.

"I'm supposed to read something in that, am I? By the way, it does get better or maybe I just destroyed my throat and can't feel anything any more."

"*Sí*, it does get better and, *sí*, I am trying to tell you something. *Chica*, a *gringo* will laugh with a Mexican, drink with him, whore with him and fight beside him. He will slap him on the back and call him friend. This does fine, but he does not want us to touch his sister or his daughter, eh? You are taking bigger sips now, *muchacha*. Now, did you listen to my words."

164

"Royal isn't like that."

"No? You have asked him?"

"No," she replied softly. "You three have made me doubt him and I'm scared to open my mouth."

"What will he do? Maybe send Oro away or send you away until Oro goes back to Mexico. What is that?"

"That is terrible, that's what that is. It'd mean I wouldn't see him any more."

"This, now, makes you happy?" he asked incredulously. "*Por Dios,* you both walk around bleeding. This is no good."

"Haven't you ever been in love, Tomás? Haven't you ever loved anybody?"

"*Sí* and no. I love but I have never been in love. I love Oro. I love Antonie. I loved my father, Juan and Julio. If I was making them hurt so, I would stop it. That is love. I would leave or I would let them go. I would not drag out the agony."

"I had hoped I could change his mind," she said in a small voice.

"This would not make him happy, *pobrecita.* It would not make you happy either, not in the end."

"It's just his pride."

"A man must have his pride or he is no man," Tomás stated firmly. "Pride is not 'just' a thing. *Chica,* he thinks of you too. To be Oro's you could lose the brothers you love, eh? To have them against them your man would hurt. You would give up too much. When men are set against each other and tempers run hot, somebody gets hurt. You would be in the middle. There would be no happiness there."

"I will talk to Royal and if he acts like you've said, I'll go visit my cousin for a while. At least I won't have to see him going to the saloon all the time or hanging around Antonie," she grumbled and did not see Tomás wince. "My tongue feels funny." She stuck it out.

"Looks fine," Tomás said gravely and smiled a little when she giggled. "Can you touch your nose with it?"

There ensued a great deal of nonsense and Royal realized that Patricia was suffering the false euphoria of the inebriated. As he quietly moved away, he suspected that it would not be long before Patricia had to be helped to her bed.

He now felt that he understood the problem everyone had worked so hard to conceal. He just hoped he would be able to solve it to everyone's satisfaction.

Royal sat down with Cole and Justin and poured himself a strong cup of coffee. He was not sure of what to say. It was still hard to accept that his baby sister was a woman capable of loving. He had to keep reminding himself that she was eighteen now.

"How is Oro?" Justin asked.

"A graze. A little dizzy is all." He thought of what he had just witnessed and sighed. "Cole? What do you think of Oro Degas?"

Noticeably confused about what Royal was after but willing to cooperate, Cole replied, "Well, he's quiet, keeps to himself a lot. Seen a lot in his years which has made him a little hard, but he's honest and he ain't vicious. He's a man of his word. Hell, I don't know what you want me to say."

"It's what you didn't say that I'm interested in. You didn't mention that he was Mexican or who his father was."

"Don't care about that. Got nothing against Mexicans and he isn't following in his father's footsteps. Always sat back with the girl. He said once that his father didn't want them to follow his ways but didn't want them to go away either. Understandable. No, the only fault I can find with Oro and it ain't really a fault, is that he's a little hard, a little too cynical maybe."

Running a hand through his hair, Royal said quietly, "That hard, cynical man is quite capable of being torn apart."

"Well, it's clear that he's real close to Tomás and Antonie," Justin said.

"No doubt of that, Justin. I even began to believe that he was damn close to Antonie, which was absurd." He refrained from explaining why. "He's been using her as a shield, being a hell of a lot more gallant or whatever than I think I could be."

"I think I've an idea of what you're talking about, but would you like to clarify it?" asked Justin.

"Well, how would you feel about Oro Degas becoming your brother-in-law?" He smiled crookedly when his brothers said nothing, just blinked. "At least it's not a resounding no."

"Are you sure that's what he's interested in? Pattie's nice looking. Could be just lusting."

"No, Cole. Lust or, rather, the inability to satisfy it does not have a man like Degas weeping like a babe. I shouldn't have been a witness to it but I heard him tell a frantic Pattie to go away, that he didn't need her, watched her walk away looking like someone had died and thought I ought to talk to him, though damned if I knew what I was going to say."

"How'd I miss all this?" Cole asked no one in particular.

"I wasn't any better. I thought it was just an infatuation. I keep forgetting that Pattie's eighteen, full grown really. Hell, I don't know what to do. I hate to see Pattie hurting and I like Degas enough not to want to see him hurting either. Still, he isn't what I'd envisioned for Pattie."

"I'd rather him than some of the ones sniffing 'round

her lately," Justin said firmly. "Least you know where Oro stands."

"That's true enough. Are you sure the law isn't after the twins, Cole?"

"Can't be bothered. They haven't got a warrant out on them. Never got close enough to be seen save that once and nobody got killed. Told them Juan and his top men were dead so they've turned their attention elsewhere. Can't arrest a man for his father's crimes or the company he keeps and that's all they could get on Oro or Tomás."

"I would think that the real question here is what'd make Pattie happy," Justin said quietly.

"Yes, I think you're right," Royal agreed with equal quiet. "It's Pattie's future, not ours."

"Going to talk to her tonight?" Cole asked in a serious tone.

"I don't think she's in any state to be sensible," Royal nodded toward where Tomás was helping their obviously drunk sister into her wagon.

"Damn, where does he keep getting that stuff?" Oblivious to his brothers' amusement, Cole strode off to intercept Tomás. "Tomás!"

"*Ay de mi*," Tomás sighed dramatically as he faced a scowling Cole backed up by his two chuckling brothers.

"Where the hell do you keep getting this stuff?"

"This stuff?" Tomás looked at his well drained tequila bottle innocently.

"Yes, that stuff." Cole failed to hide his amusement.

"An angel. "*Sí*," Tomás stressed when Cole groaned in disgust and the others started to laugh. "She looked down and saw that I was feeling very dry and 'foof,' she sent this to clear away the dust in my throat. I think I should tell the church of this miracle."

The nonsense and argument that followed kept

Royal from seeing Oro until he was already settled in his bedroll. He decided that the matter of his sister's tangled lovelife could wait until morning. Leaving Cole and Tomás to their never-ending dispute over the younger man's drinking on a drive, Royal settled down on his own sleeping roll and found that he had no trouble at all in falling asleep.

When Patricia woke up the next morning and found Antonie watching her closely, she gasped, "I'm dying. Tomás poisoned me."

Helping the white-faced girl from the wagon, Antonie scolded, "You should have known tequila was not a drink for you, a girl who has a little glass of sherry now and again. Now you pay for your foolishness, eh?"

Reaching the water barrel, Antonie deemed it clean enough and casually shoved Patricia's face into the cool water. The screeches of protest Patricia made were cut off by the water and Antonie easily controlled the girl's struggles with a firm grip on Patricia's wrists and hair. By the third ducking, Patricia's brothers had arrived. Antonie decided that Patricia had had enough by then and released the girl.

"Might one ask what you're doing?" Royal asked with a false casualness.

"She's trying to drown me," Patricia gasped as she sank down to sit on the ground.

"I was clearing her head of the tequila." Antoine frowned at her dripping patient. "I do not think it helped."

"No, it didn't help," Patricia muttered, her head in her hands. "I'm still dying but now I'm doing it wide awake and soaking wet." She spared a bloodshot glare for her laughing audience. "It isn't funny. God, I'm sure

Tomás poisoned me."

"Where is Tomás?"

Hearing the unspoken retribution in Antonie's voice, Royal answered not quite truthfully, "I don't know. Want some coffee, Pattie?"

"I'll get it," Justin offered when his sister groaned in the affirmative.

"You should have something to eat as well, *muchacha,*" suggested Antoine. "It will help."

"How can eating help when the mere mention of food is killing me?" Patricia wailed, rubbing her throbbing temples.

"It will pass. Then you eat. Now you can lie back down in the back of the wagon while I drive, eh? That may help." She shook her head as Patricia made her unsteady way back inside the wagon.

"I think Oro will drive the wagon today." Royal saw but ignored the way that young man, lurking off to the side, suddenly stiffened. "I don't think he ought to be on a horse, not with that head wound. You can ride up with me, Antonie."

"But it is my job to be with your sister," Antonie protested, trying to save Oro from such a trying situation.

"Not today." He took her by the arm and paused before Oro, looking at the younger man in a way he hoped would convey what he meant without getting too exact. "The wagon is the best place for Oro."

Oro's eyes widened slightly. "Are you sure this is what you want?"

"What I want has nothing to do with it but I do trust you like a brother."

"Yours or hers, *gringo?*" Oro rasped quietly.

"Why, mine, of course," Royal answered in a low voice. "Pattie neither needs nor wants another brother.

170

Come on, Tony."

"What was that all about?" she hissed as they walked away from the wagon and Oro. "It would be better for me to drive the wagon."

"Can't Oro handle a team?" Royal winked at a grinning Cole when Antonie swore in exasperation.

"You know what I speak of, *gringo*. Do not play stupid with me." She tried to dig in her heels but he dragged her along.

"I wouldn't even try. I thought I was giving everyone what they wanted. Saddle up, sweets."

"I am not your sweets." She began to saddle her horse. "He is Mexican."

"I noticed. I've nothing against Mexicans."

"He has Yaqui blood in his veins." She sent him a narrow-eyed look but saw no flicker of doubt or distaste.

"Well, as long as he's not dripping it on my carpets or my boots, I don't care what kind of blood he has. That is, of course, assuming his intentions are honorable," Royal said quietly but his eyes pinned Antonie to the spot.

"If they were not, *gringo,*" she swung up into her saddle, "he would have had her by now."

"I think she's probably right," Cole said as she rode off. "The girls at the saloon were reduced to hair pulling over him."

"The saloon? That explains Pattie's mood of late. That and Antonie." He mounted and stared in the direction Antonie had gone. "Where'd that little blond witch go?"

"Maybe you ought to hold back for a bit."

"Why? The truth is out now."

"Yes, but you didn't accept it from her lips." Cole reminded him.

"I guessed that something was up, that she hadn't been lying, just hiding something."

"I'd give myself some time to put that thought into a pretty speech," Cole offered.

"To soothe ruffled feathers?" Royal asked.

"She deserves to have a few."

"A few, but she was not being completely truthful, was she."

"No, but I can understand why. Oro's like a brother to her, remember."

"Yes, and the thing she was hiding could have caused a real messy stir-up."

"No doubt about it, Royal." Cole frowned, then shook his head. "The real sorry thing is that they had a right to think it could be downright dangerous if what was going on between Oro and Patricia was not only stopped but hidden."

Royal nodded. "If I hadn't seen how badly they were hurting, I can't say I would've been too happy to find out about it."

"There will be trouble. Maybe a lot of it."

"I know. I wonder if Patricia is really aware of what she will be facing?"

"Think what they feel is strong enough to survive it all?"

"With Oro, yes. Patricia? I'm not so sure." Royal finally spotted Antonie riding with Tomás and cursed softly. "Of course, I could've done without the matched set." He ignored Cole's hearty laughter.

Antonie glanced over her shoulder and saw Royal watching her. She wished she could guess what he was thinking. He did not really seem to be angry, but she was sure that he would not be pleased about the deception she had been involved in, no matter how well he understood or sympathized with her reasons. He

172

was not a man who tolerated games well. She decided to stay close to Tomás in the cowardly hope of putting off any immediate confrontation.

"Ah, Oro finally got up the courage to speak," Tomás said as they prepared to stop for a noon rest.

"Considering the shape your brand of sympathy left her in," Antonie drawled as she dismounted and reached for her canteen, "she has probably only just become able to be talked to."

Doing the same as she, Tomás said sweetly, *Querida*, I was only trying to take the sadness from her eyes for a little while."

"It worked. Those eyes were no longer sad, only bloodshot."

Tomás laughed softly. "She has no stomach for the drink. You know what would be sad?"

"What?"

"If Oro discovers that he succeeded in driving the little *chica* away."

"You can take that worried frown from your face, *amigo*. The girl is very stubborn. She has stuck like a burr."

"Good. It would be bad if, when he is so close, he finds he has lost her."

"Very bad. She will need some pretty words though. He has hurt her. We have hurt her," Antonie said.

"*Sí*. Words and loving. Oro does not know it, I think, but he is good with both."

"Now what do you frown about?" she asked in teasing exasperation when he scowled.

"Oro will now settle down. He will have a wife, a bit of land and babies to raise, eh?"

"You do not really think he could put you aside, do you, Tomás?" she asked gently. "You are more than brothers."

"*Sí*, I know this. It is jealousy, I am thinking. I am surprised. I was not expecting this to happen."

"I think we were unfair to these Bancrofts."

"A little, sí. But, *querida*, they will understand. Maybe they surprise themselves by being so fair."

"True. It is nice. Very nice. To them it is more important that people be happy, that the hurting has stopped."

"I hope the hurting has stopped, *chica*. I hope the little girl Oro has set his heart on has the strength to keep loving him when the poison starts. And it will. There will be trouble. The Anglos won't like this."

"The Bancrofts are a power in that area. That will help. They have said *sí* to the match and will support it," Antonie added.

"It will need support. Maybe a lot of it."

Antonie was very afraid that he was right. With marriage to Patricia, Oro would get a nice little piece of land right in the middle of all those Anglos. They were not going to like that. The few Mexicans who had managed to cling to some land from when Mexico had ruled, found it hard. A lot of people felt that Texas should only be for the Anglos.

She saw Royal making his way toward her, and knew she would not be able to mount her horse and get away without looking like a scared rabbit. She cursed and glancing at Tomás, scowled. He was deserting her. If there was any sort of confrontation coming, Tomás clearly wanted no part of it. Antonie vowed that she would think of some suitable revenge for Tomás's desertion. Just at Royal reached her, she mounted her horse in a somewhat frantic attempt to put at least a little distance between them and give her some option for escape if things became too tense.

Royal eyed her warily. She was looking very defensive, as if she expected a fight and had already made her plans on how to handle it. Things would not be settled just yet. He could see that clearly. Nevertheless, he felt a need to speak to her about the matter, perhaps even put the first real chink in the wall that had sprung up between them.

Seeing that Oro and Patricia were back on the wagon seat after their protracted absence, and noting their smiles and subtle loving gestures, he said, "It looks like they have sorted themselves out."

Looking at the couple for a moment, Antonie turned back to meet Royal's gaze. "You cannot go back now, *gringo.*"

"I don't intend to." He grasped her reins. "I don't like games, Antonie."

She knew he now referred to the way she had stayed so close to Oro, letting everyone think they were lovers. "It was no game. You were my lover. Oro is the brother of my heart. If your brother was in trouble who would you reach out to and who would you turn your back on and hope maybe that they would understand, trust and be patient?"

"You could have told me what was going on."

"To do so I would have had to tell too much. You asked if Oro was my lover and I said no. That should have been enough."

"It might have been if you hadn't shut me out."

"I told you I would not lie beneath a man who calls me a liar." She yanked her reins free of his hold and rode away.

"Oh, hell." Royal muttered, wondering how he could fix things, for he wanted her back in his bed.

175

Chapter Thirteen

"I was beginning to wonder if we'd ever get the damned beasts here."

Antonie smiled at Cole as they stood waiting for Royal to finish settling the deal for the cattle. It had been a long drive, especially with the need to always look over their shoulders. Although the last stretch had been remarkably free of trouble, she did not feel that Raoul had given up. He would merely change his tactics.

Her eyes went to Royal. Since the time that Oro and Patricia had been allowed to openly follow their hearts, Royal had played the beau. If it had not been for the lack of privacy, she felt sure he would have played the lover. Now that privacy could be found, Antonie had to decide what to do.

Inwardly, she grimaced as she admitted that, if he took her into his arms, the decision would be made for her. Her body was starved for him. She had grown used to feeling him at her side in the night.

Cole watched her face as she watched Royal. "Going to forgive him?"

She looked at Cole. "I am thinking on it. To be called

a liar?" She shrugged and wondered fleetingly when and how Cole's opinion of her had changed, for she no longer sensed a wary reticence in him.

"Pride goeth before a fall," he intoned piously, grinning when she laughed softly. "Maybe you should've told him the truth."

"I told him all the truth I could. I said Oro was not my lover. That should have been enough."

"Maybe. Then again, Oro's a damn fine looking young man whom you've known far longer than you've known Royal and you were sticking real close."

"Sí. This is the truth. I have begun to think about that and maybe understand it."

Before Cole could make any more gentle attempts to get Royal back into her good graces, Royal arrived. "That's done. Now to the hotel."

"You can leave me at the bath house," Antonie said as she suddenly found herself tugged along.

"You can have a bath at the hotel. In your room."

"I will stay with the men outside of town."

"No, you won't. You're staying at the hotel like Oro and Tomás are." Seeing that she was about to protest, he added ingenuously, "Aren't you supposed to protect us? You can't do that with us in a hotel and you way outside of town."

Even though she had a good idea of why he wanted her in the hotel near at hand, she could not think of an argument for his logic. By the time she had thought of one, they were signing in. The clerk's initial reluctance had been quickly assuaged. Money, cold green eyes and a low threatening voice had a way of curing prejudice, Antonie noted cynically.

Just as they started toward their rooms, they met an elegant young man escorting three lovely ladies. Antonie silently sighed for these woman were like Marilynn and, like her, they were interested in Royal. Baird

Dumfrey introduced his sisters Charlotte, Margaret, and Barbara in order of age, and acted very familiar with Royal. The way Charlotte glanced at Antonie and quickly dismissed her as insignificant, stung. When a dinner was arranged, Antonie almost groaned. Baird Dumfrey's blatant interest in her did little to better her mood, for she was only partly aware of it and not at all interested.

Later, after a much enjoyed bath, Antonie let Patricia into the room. She idly mused that the girl was positively glowing. Even though she was honestly pleased for Oro and Patricia, she admitted to a twinge of jealousy.

"We're going to see about getting Oro and Tomás each a fine suit. Want to come along?"

Antonie's eyes flew to the dress she had spread out on the bed. "New clothes!"

"Yes. Would you like a new dress?"

"Can I get a dress like what these Dumfrey sisters were wearing?"

"I can't see why not."

"I do not know," Antonie mumbled even as she got dressed. "A dress is not all it takes to be a lady."

"Antonie, you are a lady."

Patricia was still arguing that as they stepped out to meet Oro, Tomás and Justin. The ease with which they guessed why she wanted a new dress made her fear she was all too obvious in her feelings for Royal. She did not, however, waste any time in denying what they thought.

Justin took Oro and Tomás off while Patricia dragged Antonie into a shop. Antonie was amused, both at Patricia's eagerness and the initial dismay of the shopwoman. It was clear that they both thought her quite a challenge. Then the woman's professionalism took over. She even decided it was a delight to dress

178

someone with Antonie's coloring and lithe figure. Antonie began to find herself with far more than a dress.

"What are all those things you pile up?" she asked Patricia as she stood while the dressmaker pinned her into a dress.

"Underthings. How do you like this?"

"What is it?"

"A nightgown, Antonie. It's very frilly and enticing."

"Then you buy it for your wedding night." Antonie slowly grinned. "Although Oro does not need enticing, I am thinking."

Blushing furiously, Patricia set the frilly nightgown aside. "I thought you might want one."

"Why?"

"Well, it is just not right to sleep naked."

"Oro will change your mind."

"Antonie!"

"If I am sleeping alone, I do not care for them. If I am not sleeping alone, I have no need for one, eh?" She exchanged a laughing glance with the seamstress. "I do not see buying something that will, I hope, get ripped off."

The groan that escaped Patricia suddenly stopped and she frowned at the pale green nightgown she held. "Ripped off?"

"In eagerness, but," Antonie said quickly as Patricia looked ready to put the nightgown back, "a girl should have a nightgown on her wedding night, especially a girl who has never known a man and never slept naked. What is my way is not yours, eh, *chica?*"

As Antonie breathed a sigh of relief when they finally finished in the shop, she realized that Patricia was watching her closely. She inwardly winced for Patricia wore an expression that she now easily recognized. Considering that Patricia was to be married soon, Antonie had a good idea of what Patricia would be

179

asking. After a moment's thought, Antonie decided she would not try to avoid the questions for Patricia did not really have anyone else to ask.

"We began to think we should send out a search party for you," Justin drawled as Antonie and Patricia stepped out of the shop.

"I did not know that buying a dress involved so much," Antonie groaned as she let Tomás take a few of her packages.

"There is more than a dress here," Tomás said dryly as he eyed the number of packages Antonie held.

"I needed to buy all the things to wear under the dress." Antonie shook her head. "So many things. *Gringo* ladies do not dress for comfort, I am thinking. I am surprised there are any babies. A man would be too tired to make one after getting his woman out of all this." She joined the young men in laughter and even a blushing Patricia giggled.

Royal and Cole, heading for the bank, met them at the door of the hotel. "Shopping?" Royal asked.

"*Sí*," Antonie replied calmly. "Is that not what money is for?"

"What have you bought?"

"None of your business." She held her packages out of his reach.

"Furbelows," Royal said firmly.

"Are they those frilly things with the drawstring at the waist?"

"Antonie," Patricia groaned and hurried to drag Antonie into the hotel away from the laughing men.

Starting out for the bank again, Royal frowned. "It sounds like Patricia has been supplying Antonie with all the usual lady's attire."

"Afraid you'll have to do more unwrapping than usual?" Cole asked with a total lack of sympathy.

"Hell, yes. Didn't realize how troublesome all that

180

folderol was until I met a lady who didn't wear it."

"But is still a lady?"

Looking at his brother curiously, Royal quietly said, "Yes. You've changed your tune."

Cole shrugged. "Couldn't help but do so. Yes, she's learned from Juan but he'd plainly intended that she not lead the life he had. Hell, even Hank went quiet a moment when I told him Ramirez was dead. The man was the last of his kind. Oh, he was a *bandito,* no question, but he had a sense of honor. Never hurt the innocent, none of this torturing Mendez delights in or shooting someone just to hear them fall. He hit the rich and the ones who could fight. Never, never took people to sell them."

"In other words, she and the twins took the good and left the bad."

"Right, and I think Juan and Manuel made sure they did."

"Is all this because you think I'm not looking at her as if she's a lady?"

"Are you?"

Royal shrugged. "I don't fault her for what she is."

"So what do you intend to do about her?"

"For now, get her back where she belongs. In my bed. I haven't gotten any further than that," Royal answered and was glad that Cole recognized his tone indicating that the subject was now closed, and quickly changed it.

Antonie noticed that Patricia was not in any great hurry to go to her own room as she put away her things. She also noticed that the younger girl seemed just a little nervous. Pouring them each a small glass of the wine she had had sent up, she handed it to Patricia and then sprawled comfortably in a chair. It was clear that

Patricia wanted to talk now. After a few more minutes of silence, Antonie gave her a nudge.

"What is it, *chica?*"

Sighing, Patricia sat on the bed. "I want you to tell me what happens between a man and a woman."

Smiling gently at the girl's blushes, Antonie asked, "You know nothing?"

"A little. Not much though. Mothers usually tell their daughters about such things when they are to be married."

"You have brothers, though."

"They aren't about to tell me anything. It's not like with you and the twins. I'd also be too embarrassed to ask them."

"Have you ever seen a man naked?"

It was hard but Antonie refrained from laughing at Patricia's shocked face. Then, very gently and with as careful a wording as possible, she told Patricia just what to expect on her wedding night. The younger girl's expressions told Antonie that, whatever Patricia had known, it had not been quite enough to prepare the girl for the whole revelation.

"Does it hurt?" she asked timidly.

"A little the first time. I think Oro can make the fire hot enough so that you do not care."

"He is probably very experienced."

"He is a man."

"But if he is used to a lot of women, how can he be happy with just one? An inexperienced one?"

"You will learn. He will teach you."

"Oh, I don't know, Antonie. I have been so sheltered and then suddenly I'm expected to roll about naked and do things I was always told I shouldn't know about."

"You will like being naked with Oro. He has a fine, strong body. Very handsome."

"Antonie, you don't understand . . ."

182

"*Sí*. I do. You are afraid. It will be new. But, you love Oro, Oro loves you and you share a fire. It will be fine."

"What if I'm one of those who doesn't like it?"

"Do you like kissing him, him kissing you, the touching and the holding? Do you want to hold on when he pulls away?" Patricia, her cheeks bright red, nodded. "Then you will like it. It is beautiful, *chica*. The excitement of anticipation, the time when the fire engulfs both of you until it is all you know and the lull after when you stay close, remembering and recovering. All of it. It is beautiful."

"Is that what you have with Royal?"

"I would not be his lover if I did not."

"Then, you will get married."

"No, I think not, *chica*."

"How can you share his bed if you know he won't, er, make an honest woman of you?"

"Because I would rather be a dishonest woman now than a regretful, unhappy one later, eh?" She smiled when Patricia frowned in slight confusion. "I know more than you, *chica*. I knew the fire when I tasted it, what it was and what it meant. It is something that is rare, comes but once in a life if at all. So, I said to myself, 'Is saving your innocence worth not tasting this?' and I had to say no."

"But, well, men expect their wives to be virgins."

"As I think I told you, *chica*, if I find a man I want to wed, a man who wants to wed me, I think he will understand what I did for he will know me."

"Do you love Royal then, Antonie?"

"Of what matter is that? When this business is done, I will be gone."

Antonie could sense that Patricia wanted her to clarify that ambiguous statement, so she hurriedly changed the subject. It was not too difficult to do, for Patricia was in love and looking forward to being married. All Antonie had to do was mention Oro and Patricia forgot whatever else she had been talking about.

She was relieved when Patricia left to get dressed for dinner, however. The girl was far from stupid and would soon see that she had been cleverly diverted. Antonie was glad their time alone was ended before she had revealed her intentions.

Smiling as her bath water arrived, Antonie tried to pretend that she was well accustomed to such service and to taking two baths in one day. She knew the women of Royal Bancroft's world would be. Unfortunately, such moments made her all too sharply aware of the difference between herself and those women. That took away a great deal of the pleasure of being waited on.

As she relaxed in her bath, easing the stiffness of standing in place so long for the dressmaker, she tried not to think about such things. It was a time to enjoy, not mope or worry. They had come through the drive nearly unscathed. Royal now had the money he needed to further thwart the plots of the one who tried to ruin him. That was cause for celebration and she was going to act accordingly. She certainly did not want anyone to think she was anything less than delighted over Royal's success, if for no other reason than they might start asking awkward questions like Patricia had.

Most everyone seemed to accept that she was Royal's lover, no more, no less. No one seemed to fault her for that and, if they thought she would become anything more or that she ought to do so, they kept that opinion to themselves. That was just how she liked it and how she wanted it to stay. She knew that the moment she ceased to be content and accepting of that position, some well-meaning people would start to meddle, eager to set things right. That was the very last thing she

184

wanted, for it was the sort of thing that caused more trouble than it cured.

When she had made the decision to become Royal Bancroft's lover, she had known of the risk involved. She had known that she would be taking a chance at being hurt, that she was not the sort of woman a man like Royal looked at as wife material. People accepted her as Royal's lover because they also saw that that was all a woman of her background could be to such a man. She only had herself to blame for the fact that more than her passion was now at risk. It simply made the gamble she was taking a greater one. She and Royal could love each other or they could hurt each other. No one and nothing could alter that, she told herself firmly as she dried herself.

However, Antonie found that she could not fully stop herself from nourishing some elaborate plans to change the course of things. She hated to think of leaving Royal. She hated even more the thought that when she came to visit Oro, as she fully intended to do from time to time, she would have to see Royal with his new woman, perhaps even a wife and children.

She sighed as she set out the clothes she would wear to dinner. Once she had started on the road of loving Royal she had known that she would have to walk it to the end. Antonie just wished that there was happiness at the end, not pain. She had already had a taste of what it was like to be without Royal and did not like it at all. It was hard to accept that soon she might feel that pain for months and for years to come instead of for just a few weeks.

For a brief while, she had contemplated staying aloof from him. His attitude and accusations concerning Oro had hurt. Somehow it seemed weak to simply fall back into his arms as if the past weeks had never occurred.

But weak was what she fully intended to be. She had already lost weeks of her precious, fleeting time with Royal. It seemed stupid to lose more just to make a point. He knew he had been wrong. That was enough.

Looking at the finery laid out on her bed, she grimaced. If he took Charlotte as his lover, Antonie knew that that would put an end to it. It would no longer be a matter of getting him to voice an apology. She would be his lover willingly but to take him back into her arms after he had been with another woman would, in her mind, make her no better than a whore. She would lose all respect for herself and, she suspected, what little he had for her.

Squaring her shoulders, she decided she would not be set aside without a fight. Charlotte Dumfrey would not find it so easy to walk away with the prize. Antonie intended that Royal would be aware that he made a final choice when he crawled into bed tonight. If he reached for Charlotte Dumfrey he would do it knowing that he would not reach for Antonie Doberman Ramirez on the morrow.

Royal greeted the Dumfreys in the lobby and wished fervently that he had made some excuse to forego the evening. Charlotte was lovely, charming and elegant but, at that moment, he was not the slightest bit interested. His mind was fully on a little blond who could probably outdraw him. He had no intention of doing anything with Charlotte for he knew it would mean a complete end to what he had with Antonie.

"They're a little late," he grumbled when there was still so sign of Antonie, Oro, Patricia, Tomás and Justin.

"Want me to go and see what's keeping them?" Cole offered.

"No never mind. Let's go in and have a drink. They'll be along and they know where to find us. Strange

186

though. Antonie's usually very punctual."

"She is dining with us?" Charlotte asked in barely hidden dismay.

"She and the twins," Royal answered curtly as they took their seats at the table.

Royal began to wonder if it was a mistake to let Antonie join them. This was not a style of life she was accustomed to. It could well turn out to be a painfully embarrassing interlude for her and that was the last thing he wanted.

Looking at how the Dumfrey sisters were dressed, he nearly winced. As far as he knew, the only dress Antonie possessed was the one she had worn at the fiesta. She had looked lovely in it, but it was not much more than a Mexican peasant's Sunday best. Even he could see how out of place it would be in the elegant dining room with the ladies in their satins, silks and lace. He hoped that when she had gone shopping with Patricia and that she had bought a suitable dress.

His mind went to what would happen when the Dumfreys left. He knew what he intended and that was to get Antonie into bed and begin to make up for lost time. The question was whether she would let him.

Although he detested the thought, he could not ignore the fact that they had been estranged for a while. For all he knew, that fire she had so enjoyed could have cooled. In a way, he had insulted her by insinuating that she had lied. Royal knew that to Antonie's way of thinking, that was probably one of the very worse insults he could have ever given her.

There was the problem of how much of an apology he would have to deliver. He did not think he should make a very large one for she had been playing games. If he had erred by what he had thought, she had been wrong in not giving him a fuller explanation for her actions. In a way, she had insulted him by thinking him too prejudiced and narrow-minded to understand.

Sighing mentally, he acknowledged that he might well have taken the news of a budding romance between Oro and Patricia adversely. He liked the younger man but had foreseen a far different mate for his little sister. Until he had had his eyes opened to how much each of them was hurting, he would have viewed a match between them as unsuitable. It was a little disconcerting that Antonie could read him better than he could read himself. He was plainly not as free of prejudice as he had thought.

Suddenly he wondered if those prejudices were prompting his current concern for Antonie. What did it matter if she was not dressed in satin and lace? She looked lovely in her peasant dress. She also had beauty, grace, intelligence and wit. He felt just a little ashamed over worrying if she could hold her own against the Dumfrey sisters or would embarrass herself and him.

Turning to look at Charlotte in answer to her less than subtle bids for his attention, Royal felt a little surprised. Charlotte Dumfrey had been one of the women he had considered as a possible wife. He should have felt slightly embarrassed about being so caught up with another woman, perhaps even offending Charlotte so that she would refuse any courtship overtures he might decide to make, yet he was not. Smiling politely, he exchanged polite inconsequential chit-chat and continued to wonder what was keeping Antonie.

Chapter Fourteen

When the knock came at her door, Antonie swore with relief. She let Oro, Tomás, Patricia and Justin in. Patricia looked at Antonie who was dressed only in a miniscule camisole and lacy pantaloons and sighed. Antonie almost smiled for she knew the girl would probably never understand her feeling that she was adequately covered in such attire. It was Antonie's opinion that if you were not naked you were decent. The three young men sat on her bed, grinned at her and helped themselves to the wine. She just hoped they would save a little for her.

"You three look very fine," Antonie said as she viewed the young men's finery.

"It won't do them any good if you don't hurry and get dressed. What's taking you so long?" Patricia asked.

"You look very fine too, Pattie. I did not know there was so much to put on. What is this?" She held up a corset.

"A corset," Patricia snapped trying unsuccessfully not to blush. "I don't think you need it anyway. Put on your petticoats."

The three gentlemen watched in unhidden amusement as Patricia helped Antonie to get dressed but Antonie was too annoyed to be bothered by it. She kept up a running complaint about the fussiness and multitude of clothing. When she was finally seated by an exasperated but amused Patricia, who was clearly not sure of how to style Antonie's thick mass of hair, Antonie was more than ready for the glass of wine Tomás served her.

"Simple, I think. A very simple style," Patricia mumbled to herself as she brushed out Antonie's hair. "Do you have any jewelry?"

"Sí but it is not very rich." She looked at Patricia's pearls. "Not like yours."

"Oh. I thought maybe Juan," she blushed and faltered to a stop before she could finish.

"Stole some for me?" Antonie asked with a grin. "No. He and Manuel bought us everything. The money was stolen, this is true, but what we have was bought. Tomás, can you get me my things from my bag? They might not suit."

When Tomás set the earrings, necklace, ring and bracelet on the table, Patricia gasped and murmured her appreciation. They were intricate works of turquoise and silver. Antonie was pleased that Patricia thought they were pretty.

"They will do beautifully. There," she stepped back from Antonie and surveyed her handiwork, "what do you think?"

"It is neat," Antonie ventured as she studied the thick chignon while Patricia put her necklace on her. "Will it fall down?"

"I hope not. It suits you, Antonie. Truly," Patricia soothed as Antonie put on the rest of her jewelry.

After putting on her shoes, Antonie went to view herself in the mirror. "I do not look very much like me."

190

"You look lovely," Justin said with indisputable conviction.

"Maybe, but I do not look like Antonie. Maybe this was not such a good idea. This is not what I am."

Handing Antonie her shawl, Patricia said, "What nonsense. How can it not be what you are? That is you."

"This can be me if I want it to be, *sí*. I can play at being the fine lady but not always. If this is what Royal is seeking then I am not for him. I could not play this game all the time."

"You can be anything you want, Antonie," Patricia said. "A little practice and this would stop being a game."

Antonie looked at her friend. "No. I would play it easier but it would still be a game. I have watched the ladies and I know I could not always be like them. A lady does not talk of the stock or the men's business. She does not shoot or wear pants to ride as one should, astride. She does not admit to liking her man's kisses. There is a lot she does not do. I would feel choked. I could not be happy like this. To make Royal think so is to lie and lies are always revealed."

Oro stood up to put his arm around Antonie and to drop a kiss on her cheek. "To try to be what you are not is bad. You are right, *querida*. So, you will be Antonie dressed in her finest and showing her best manners, but still Antonie, eh?"

That sounded eminently reasonable to Antonie. She would also show Royal that she could look as fine as any lady and that she would not shame him in public. However, if he desired fluttering fans and giggles then he could have that but not from her. She would not be false to herself, not even for Royal.

She was glad of the cheerful company as the five of

191

them made their way to the hotel dining room. Although she held firm to her decision, she could not help but worry that the real Antonie was not what Royal wanted. She feared the pain his rejection would bring her. When she saw Cole and Royal with the other women, her courage faltered as did her steps, but Tomás firmly pulled her along.

"Jesus," Cole breathed as he caught sight of Antonie but then his eyes went to Royal, not wanting to miss his brother's reactions.

Lifting his glass to his lips, Royal's eyes idly went to the doorway and stayed there. His whole body froze at the sight of Antonie. Occasionally he had wondered how she would look if she was all dressed up but his imaginings had not come anywhere near the truth.

The deep mauve color of her dress accentuated her fair coloring. Her lovely slim neck was fully exposed by her hairstyle and the low cut of her gown. Many a male eye was drawn to her slim figure, lingering on the full breasts that swelled gently above the neckline and cushioned the unusual necklace she wore. Her dark escort, Tomás, was simply a foil for her beauty.

Noticing the stunned look on Royal's face before he struggled to hide it, Antonie felt nervous, for she was not sure how to interpret it. She smiled when she noticed the narrowing eyes of the ladies, however. Possibly it meant that they had seen the competition and were displeased. She thought the Dumfrey sisters were insurpassable in their beauty and elegance but hoped that now she could at least give them a good run for their money.

Royal was not pleased when Antonie was seated between Baird and Tomás. Baird's dark eyes were fixed on her as if she were the meal. Royal had not noticed the man's interest earlier in the day.

"That what you bought today?" he asked, thinking that she was showing far too much bosom even though he knew she was revealing no more than any other lady there.

Antonie wondered at the strange note in Royal's voice. "Sí. The dress I had was not suitable, eh?"

"It was a lovely dress," Cole said, "but tonight you look like a princess."

A faint color touched her cheeks but she grinned. "A princess, Tomás. You must kiss my hand in homage."

"Only your hand?" Tomás murmured as he pressed a lingering kiss to her palm. "What do I get to kiss if you become a queen?"

When Antonie gave her husky laugh, Royal scowled. If possible, Baird looked even more eager. The man would have to think again if he thought Antonie was his for the picking. Reluctantly, Royal turned to Charlotte when she demanded his attention.

Conversation was idle as they enjoyed the main meal. It was not until the dessert was served that the Dumfrey sisters homed in on their attack. Antonie had been waiting for it. She had garnered too much attention. Oro had eyes for none but Patricia but what little attention he had had to spare went to her. Tomás had no interest in the Dumfrey sisters, so he used his special brand of charm to quell the nerves he knew assailed her. Cole seemed interested in Royal's reactions, although Antonie was not sure why. Royal seemed to spend most of his time trying to interrupt her and Baird every time they started to converse. That left very little for the Dumfrey sisters to work with or bask in, for Justin was still too young to matter to them, and Antonie could see that they were angry.

There were undoubtedly other reasons for the coming fray that Antonie sensed was imminent, but she

193

could only guess at them. She assumed that Charlotte, in her bid for Royal, was planning to make her embarrass herself. Firmly resolving not to let her temper flare, Antonie braced for the assault.

"What do your people do in Mexico?" Charlotte asked.

"Nothing that I know of," Antonie drawled. "They are dead, *señorita*," she added quietly.

"Oh, dear. So you are an orphan," Margaret consoled with false sympathy. "Where is your family's land?"

"There is no land." Antonie saw no reason to dance about the truth.

"How do you live?" Barbara asked.

"Barbara," Baird hissed reprovingly but was halted by Antonie's light touch on his arm.

"I work, *muchacha*." Antonie sensed that Barbara, merely seventeen, was mostly curious, not vindictive.

"You work for Royal?" Charlotte asked, her hand resting on his arm.

Quelling an urge to break that woman's fingers, Antonie took a sip of wine. She knew what Charlotte insinuated. A woman was usually in a man's employ for one reason only. She sensed that Oro and Tomás had heard the insult behind the soft question. Their dark eyes had hardened and their handsome faces had tautened. Even Royal looked annoyed. Strangely, that soothed Antonie's temper.

"*Sí*. I keep an eye on Patricia. There was much trouble on the drive."

That change of subject was seized upon by the gentlemen. Antonie knew that the Dumfrey sisters had not finished however. She wondered if it would be best to make a strategic retreat but then decided against it. Antonie felt that that would be admitting defeat.

Watching Charlotte charm Royal, constantly touching him and monopolizing his attention, was putting a severe strain on Antonie's determination not to lose her temper. Baird's flirting was soothing and flattered her sorely bruised vanity. She responded to it naturally. Tomás helped too with his usual outrageousness and constant friendly arguing with Cole.

As confirmation of Royal's desertion and that he had seen her as not more than idle amusement, Antonie saw that he did nothing to protect her from the constant subtle insults of the women. She had no trouble protecting herself or hiding how their continuous references to all she lacked stung. However, her honor was being scorned and she was hurt. If Royal had any feeling for her at all, he would not be able to stay silent, let alone continue to charm her attacker.

Royal was working himself up into a glorious rage. He knew the Dumfrey sisters assumed Antonie was his mistress, and thought he was angry over her presumptuousness at sitting with them. However, he reluctantly recognized the jealousy and that spurred his anger and cursed the fact that the others did too. Even Baird was finding it amusing.

He could not stop himself from viewing Antonie's responses to Baird's indisputable charm as blatant flirting. Every time she laughed, he ground his teeth. Whenever she leaned forward he was torn between wanting to drag her to his room and belting Baird for letting his eyes linger so hungrily on her well exposed breasts. So intent was he on controlling the violence that surged inside him that he was mostly unaware of the Dumfrey sisters genteel persecution of Antonie. When he did notice, he said nothing for he feared that he would only join the attack in his present mood and with remarks that were far more direct and cutting.

It was a combination of elements that finally snapped

195

the control of the tension at the table. The free flowing wine made Charlotte utter a remark that was less than subtle, about Antonie's morals. Antonie tossed off the last of her wine and slowly rose to her feet, her eyes dark purple with fury.

"I have had enough. I put on my finery and display my best manners, for what? To dine with a *maldita perra. Cui bono?* For what use? *Madre de Dios!* I will go drink with those who do not play these games, ones who, when they insult you, do not expect a sweet smile and soft answer. Good manners are wasted here where there are so few."

"Good manners?" Charlotte demanded. "What does one like you know of good manners?"

"More than you, *señorita*. Where I come from one does not share food with a person then ply him with insults," her voice lowered slightly, "not if one wishes to stay alive." She smiled a little when Charlotte paled slightly.

"Where the hell are you going?" Royal snapped when Antonie began to walk away.

"First to change my clothes. After that?" She shrugged. "It is not really your business, is it, *Señor* Bancroft?"

Tomás hurried after her. Before Royal could blink, Cole and Justin hastily excused themselves and left as well. At a glance, he could tell that Baird was seriously contemplating deserting his sisters to follow the blond siren. It did nothing to improve Royal's deteriorating mood.

Antonie stormed into her room, her three escorts trailing behind her. She grabbed up her clothes and stepped behind a dressing screen. The three gentlemen sat on her bed and she heard them help themselves to the wine left from before dinner. Antonie kept up a tirade as she changed her clothes.

"Bah! So much for finery." She tossed her new dress over the screen. "I do not know why I kept my temper for so long. And I did well keeping my temper, did I not, Tomás?" She peered around the screen. "Was I not the model of patience?"

"*Sí*, Antonie. I did not recognize you, you were so patient." He saluted her with his glass of wine.

She nodded and went back to changing her clothes. "Well, I will not do that again. There is no satisfaction in swallowing insults."

"Charlotte was plain jealous, Tony," Justin said. "She wants Royal."

Stepping out, dressed in her pants and shirt, Antonie began to search for her boots. "She had him. When he looked at me it was only to scowl. Well, if he is to scowl at me even when I am behaving then I will not behave, eh? I do not like this lady business."

"You were ten times the lady any of those Dumfrey gals were," Cole said as Antonie tugged on her boots. "Your tongue can have a razor's edge, honey, but you didn't stoop to their game. That's the mark of a lady. Not her clothes or what fork she uses."

Putting on her gun belt, Antonie mulled that over for a moment. "They were like Marilynn and she is a lady, *sí?*"

Standing up, Cole handed her her hat and draped an arm around her shoulders as they headed out. "Darlin', I've known a fair number of ladies. Even so, I've never really listened to them talk, one lady to another. Tonight I was listening and, damn, it was nasty. Now, I'll admit I wasn't all that partial to you when I first met you. Because of the way you dressed and acted, I set you apart from other ladies. Even before tonight I knew that was a damned ignorant thing to do."

"*Gracias, señor.*" She grinned at him when he gently flicked her cheek with one long finger.

"Tonight I saw why I had no trouble thinking of you as a lady even as well armed as you are now."

"What did you see?" she asked when he did not continue.

"For a start, sweets, you're honest. I've met few so-called ladies who are. They play games, darlin'. You don't. Hell, I'd take that over a pretty dress, fluttering eyelashes and a flicking fan any day of the week. There is one thing though." They stepped outside of the hotel.

She eyed him a little suspiciously as they paused. "*Si?* What is this one thing?"

"We-ell, you ain't exactly fair, Tony." He turned to face her, still keeping an arm around her shoulders.

"What is this?" Although she could see the teasing glint in his eyes, she could not guess what the jest would be.

"I've been left out and I'm feeling sorely deprived. You've kissed Tomás, Oro, Justin and, of course, Royal, but not me."

Laughing along with Justin and Tomás, she slipped her arms around his neck. "I cannot let such an injustice continue."

"Damn right," he murmured and thoroughly indulged himself in a brief taste of what he knew he could never possess.

"A little public, isn't it?" gritted an all too familiar voice.

Once the others had left, Royal could tolerate very little of the Dumfrey sisters. He politely but firmly hastened their departure from the hotel. With Charlotte clinging to his arm in a way that made him grit his teeth, he stepped outside and came to an abrupt halt at the sight that confronted him. When Cole and Antonie ended their embrace at his curt statement, he saw their surprise as guilt.

It hurt and he was loathe to examine why. He told himself it was because Cole was taking unfair advantage of the misunderstandings that had thus far kept Antonie out of his bed. A man had a right to a sense of possession.

"*Sí*, you are right, *Señor* Bancroft," Antonie said as she stepped out of Cole's hold. She moved to where Royal stood, eased Charlotte's clutching grip and placed the woman's hand more demurely upon Royal's arm. "Much better. Save the groping for later, *señorita*."

Bidding a hasty good evening, Antonie and Tomás joined Royal's brothers in making a hasty and less than dignified retreat. Royal indulged himself with a fierce glare at their rapidly disappearing backs. Out of the corner of his eye, he saw Oro and Patricia hastily disappear and knew his anger was very obvious but found that he did not really care. He rather curtly ushered the Dumfrey sisters into their carriage and climbed in.

The fact that Baird and his own brothers found amusement in his anger only soured Royal's mood more. He was sure that the fact that he had never had any trouble with a female before only added to their enjoyment of his current difficulties. He intended to make sure that their amusement was very short-lived.

He decided that it was all Antonie's fault that he now found himself in the uncomfortable position of playing the jealous lover and having provided the night's entertainment. She might have a good reason for being distant from him, but that did not mean she had the right to turn to another man. Even though a small inner voice suggested that he was being somewhat unreasonable, Royal did not care enough to alter his opinion. He did not really wish to look too closely at the reasons for the way he was feeling either. It was much safer to think that she had purposely set out to annoy him and that he was only acting accordingly.

Yet again he cursed the luck that had brought the Dumfreys into his path. If he had not dined with them, he could have spent the evening wooing Antonie, soothing her ruffled feathers. Instead he had had to watch her in all her new-found elegance being wooed by Baird then sit and watch her walk away with Cole. What should have been a pleasant evening was turning into a total disaster. Instead of he and Antonie exhausting themselves in his bed or hers, she was out carousing with Tomás and his own brothers and he had to endure Charlotte.

Royal was seeing that he could easily lose his chance with Antonie if he did not quickly mend things with her. It had been too long since he had reaffirmed his possession. The predators were beginning to sniff around. He was going to have to rectify that and brand Antonie again as his as soon as possible.

"I thought that woman was supposed to be watching your sister?" Charlotte remarked, breaking into his thoughts.

Even as he wondered if the buggy could move a little faster, Royal answered, "Oro's watching her now."

"Perhaps," Charlotte said with a cloying gentleness, "she should be protected from him."

"Why?" He eyed the woman coldly. "He's Pattie's fiancé."

Charlotte and her sisters gasped. "He's a Mexican."

"Certainly is. He's also a damn fine young man."

"But, if this man Oro protects your sister, why did you hire Antonie?" Barbara asked.

"Antonie protected Patricia's life on the drive. We

200

were harassed the whole way. That little lady was the best damn guard money could buy. I never had a moment's concern about Patricia and things got nasty several times."

"I'm sure that she was, and that justifies your putting your sister in the company of such a woman," Charlotte said with a less than subtle sneer.

In a clear attempt to avoid an acrimonious confrontation, Baird said smoothly, "Pull in your claws, sister dear. Your attempts to belittle Miss Ramirez this evening only showed that she is very much the lady."

That admonition clearly exasperated Charlotte and she lapsed into a sullen silence. Even though the others chatted idly despite her withdrawal, Royal felt it was a long, somewhat tedious ride to the Dumfrey house. When they did arrive, Royal politely, if reluctantly, accepted an offer of coffee. Idly looking around, Royal decided that the Dumfreys had done well by getting in on the start of this new stage in the cattle business and might well never come back to Texas and the hard work of the other end of the business.

It was impossible for Royal to relax. His mind kept drifting to Antonie out carousing with his brothers who seemed to think she was free. Worse, Antonie seemed to think she was free as well. That sense of being unattached would communicate itself with predictable results.

The mere possibility of another man tasting her passion put him into a rage and twisted his insides. Seeing her in Cole's arms had made him realize that he had not really believed his own accusations concerning Oro. He had sensed that something was being hidden from him.

Suddenly he frowned into the dregs of his coffee. He had resented the loss of her full attention. It was plain

201

that he felt possessive about far more than her lovely body. Royal was not sure he wanted to understand the implications of that.

"Give me a minute to change and I'll go looking for them with you."

Royal frowned at Baird. "What makes you think I'm going to look for them?" He frowned even more when Baird just laughed softly.

While he struggled to entertain the sisters, Royal studied Charlotte. Lovely and much like Marilynn, she had been another real possibility as a wife. Both ladies were the sort he had envisioned as the mistress of his ranch. Suddenly the idea was so unattractive as to be almost distasteful. They would decorate his house but not be a true partner. Both women were from ranches but he suddenly saw that, while they had an idea of its workings, they were interested it little more than the profits and the frills ranch life provided.

When Baird returned, Royal was more than ready to leave. He would have preferred to look for Antonie alone but, even though he knew Baird was fully aware of that, he would not admit it aloud. The man had already been given enough amusement. Unfortunately Royal could not deter him and they left to go to the hotel.

"It Patricia really marrying Oro Degas?" Baird ventured as he sat on Royal's hotel bed while Royal changed his clothes.

"Yes. Soon as we get home."

"Sure that's wise? There might be some difficulties. My sister's reaction was not unusual."

"No. I realize that. To be blunt, Pattie was throwing herself at the man and he was doing his damnedest to stay out of the way, even though it was the last thing he wanted to do. It finally hit me that they were both hurting."

"And you asked yourself why."

"Exactly. There wasn't one damn good reason. I'm sure there will be disapproval but she has her family behind her." He put on his hat. "Shall we go?" He did not wait for a reply but headed out the door.

"Are you sure it was wise to let Antonie go off in the beginning?" Baird asked as they walked toward the end of town which the drovers frequented.

"As if I could've stopped her," Royal grumbled. "Antonie can take care of herself. Also, Oro and Tomás grew up keeping an eye on her. They've got a second sense about when trouble's brewing. She's had a rough life. She understands places like these."

"So why are you looking for her?"

"Damned if I know." Royal scowled at his chuckling friend and then he smiled crookedly. "Hell, I'll be honest. The girl belongs to me."

"Does she know that?"

"It appears not."

"Then maybe you're wrong. Maybe she doesn't belong to you."

"Oh, yes, she does." He peered into a saloon but did not spot his prey amongst the rowdy crowd. "If she doesn't know it now," he said angrily as he headed toward another saloon, "she'll know it by the time this night's over."

Chapter Fifteen

"There was little air to breathe in there," Antoine gasped as she and her three companions rapidly exited a noisy, crowded saloon.

"Like a damn cattle pen," Cole grumbled as he took her arm and led her down a side street.

It was a little quieter down the side street. At the bottom stood a small, two-story building that proved to be another saloon. One glance inside told them that it was what they wanted. It was only interestingly crowded and the noise was lively, not deafening. The hails that greeted them told them that other men from their crew had also preferred an atmosphere a little less insane.

Antonie recognized Royal's married hands as well as the older men. Looking around and paying close attention to Cole's and Justin's replies to the greetings, she realized there were more men from the neighboring ranches. The three saloon girls would undoubtedly have as much business as they could want but only their companionship was what was really wanted by most of the men here.

"Hey, Tony, I thought you were going to have yourself a real fancy night at the hotel."

Smiling at Luke Cousins, Royal's foreman, she replied, "Fancy nights end early, Luke."

"Well, darlin', sit yourself down and we'll do our best to keep you entertained until as late as you like."

She laughed softly when he grinned and pointedly shuffled the cards he held. "I intend to keep what little is left of my pay, or most of it."

"I'm not greedy, darlin'. Where's the boss?"

"He stayed with the Dumfrey family," Cole replied as he set a beer in front of Antonie and sat next to her.

No more mention was made of the boss and that suited Antonie just fine. She hoped to forget Royal for just a little while at least.

The level of betting was kept low and Antonie joined in the card game. She drank the beer which flowed freely but did not seem to mix badly with the wine she had indulged in earlier. It did, however, begin to make her a very gay companion.

When Royal finally located the saloon where Antonie was, it was not as peaceful as she had first found it to be. He was not overly surprised to see Antonie had challenged Luke about who could produce the fancier footwork in accompaniment to Charlie Foster's fiddle playing. With a shake of his head, he got himself and Baird a glass of beer and joined the others at the table, ignoring their knowing grins.

"I call it a draw, Tony," Luke gasped as they collapsed into their chairs. "I'll work on a new step and win next time."

"Ha!" Antonie looked at Royal, not daring to think that he might have come looking specifically for her. "Where are your ladies?"

"Tucked up safely in their beds," Royal drawled, "as all proper young ladies should be."

"*Carramba!* It is glad that I am not 'a proper young lady' " she said the last four words in a falsetto tone. "So boring to go to bed so early."

"Depends on where you go to bed." Seeing the light of mischief that brightened her lovely eyes, Royal purred, "Don't say it."

"Pity," she pouted and took a drink of beer. "It was good." She laughed with the others and indulged in several minutes of nonsense before turning back to Royal. "Well, what did you think of Antonie's lady, eh? My dress was pretty."

Royal found it hard to stay angry with her, especially when she was in so ebullient a mood. "Very pretty. The color suited you."

She flipped off her hat to display her still done up hair. "I could not take down the hair. Pattie worked so hard."

Tomás chuckled. "You cannot leave it up forever, *chica.*"

Putting her hat back on, she grinned at Tomás. "*Sí,* or it might walk away on its own, eh?" She frowned. "What is the time? Maybe these ladies do not go to bed as early as I think, eh?" She pulled out Juan's watch, one of his few possessions he had left to her.

"Look at that. There's a catch there," pointed out Baird. "That usually means there's a little compartment."

With a little work and Baird's assistance, Antonie got it open. There was a small piece of paper inside and enfolded in that was a lock of her hair. On the paper, in a scrawl that she immediately recognized as Juan's nearly illiterate attempt at writing, was written: "From my child's beloved head when she was ten."

A grief she had never given full vent to welled up inside of her, choking her. Very carefully, she replaced the items, shut the watch and put it away. Somehow, the sentimental gesture by a hard man touched off the pain of loss even his burial had failed to. She regretfully admitted that the drink which had cheered her was now making her more despondent than she might have been.

"I will leave now." She stood up. *"Buenos noches."* She strode out of the saloon without a backward glance.

"I better go to her," Tomás said, surging to his feet.

Grasping the young man's arm, Royal also stood. "I will."

"She needs comfort now, not angry words, *señor.*"

"I know." He tossed off the rest of his beer. "It was Juan's watch."

"Sí." Tomás sat back down. "She has never really grieved for him."

"Mmm. And she is not as tough as she'd like us to think."

Tomás looked directly into Royal's eyes and, clearly referring to more than Antonie's grief, said quietly, "No, *señor,* she is not."

Refusing to acknowledge that he understood, Royal muttered his goodnights and strode off after Antonie. He would mull over Tomás's words later, for he knew it would entail a fair amount of soul searching. Right now, however, his main concern was Antonie.

He found her halfway along the main street. With her head bent, she was striding toward the hotel. It was hard to tell if she was crying until he reached her side. Then, when he glanced beneath the brim of her hat, he saw the tears on her cheeks. He fell into step beside her all the way to her room.

"I never cry," she said in a voice thick with tears as she sat on her bed and buried her face in her hands.

"It is nothing to be ashamed of." He took off her hat

207

and then knelt to pull off her boots. "You loved the man."

"He was very good to me."

"Yes, he was and, despite what he was and how he lived, he loved you. I saw that years ago."

She watched his hands undo her holster. "He taught me all I know. He tried to make me a lady."

"Honey," he cupped her tearstained face in his hands, "you're very much a lady. You haven't failed Juan in that way."

"No? I became your *puta*," she said quietly, looking into the jade green eyes that could so easily melt her.

"My lover," he corrected sternly as he sat beside her and took off his boots.

"There is a difference?" She made no attempt to stop his preparations to spend the night in her bed.

"Oh, yes." He tossed his hat onto a chair and pulled her into his arms.

"You say that to make me happy so that I will not refuse you, eh?" She slipped her arms around his waist.

"Not at all. I would not insult your intelligence by mouthing nonsense. If nothing else, I am honest with you."

That he was, she mused, not stopping him as he undid her shirt. She even arched her neck to allow his warm lips better access to her throat. He wanted her. He never hid that fact. Neither did he fill her ears with empty promises and words of love that he did not mean. That hurt even though she preferred a lack of love to deception and false hope and all the pain that could bring her.

In all honesty, she had to admit that she wanted him — desperately. She could not blame him for the fact that her heart was involved as much as her body was. He had not asked for that. She had not really asked for that either. Passion had been what she had been looking for, not the pain of a love unwanted and not returned.

Glancing up at him as he removed her shirt, she saw the half-smile that touched his face. "What is funny?"

His appreciative but amused eyes ran over the frilly camisole she wore. "All this lace beneath the men's clothes."

"I thought it was very pretty. I have never worn such lacy things before." Her fingers slowly began to undo his shirt.

"Incongruous but lovely." He removed her pants, smiling again when he revealed her frilly drawers.

She tumbled back onto the bed and he leaned over her, resting on his forearms. The look in his eyes told her exactly what he wanted. A shiver of desire tore through her lithe frame. There was no fighting that warmth.

Brushing his lips over hers, he murmured, "It's been a long time. Too long. I've missed you."

"I did not send you away." She finished removing his shirt then let her hands roam lovingly over his muscular torso.

"No, I kept myself away," he murmured as he began to unpin her hair. "I resented the loss of your full attention."

"That was the cause of your anger?" she asked curiously as she undid his trousers so that her hands could slide down the back of them and smooth over his taut buttocks.

"Yes. He ran his hands through her thick silken hair. "You're mine. I didn't like sharing any part of you."

"I belong to no one," she said quietly, edging his trousers down over his slim hips.

Slowly, he stood up and removed the rest of his clothing, seeing her statement as a challenge. "I put my brand on you that first night, sweet thing."

"A brand on me?" she gasped, scrambling to her knees on the bed. "I am not one of your cattles."

"Cows or cattle, not cattles. No, you aren't but the principle's the same. You're mine, honey." He pushed her down onto the bed and gently but firmly pinned her there with his body. "I was noticing tonight that my brand was fading a bit. It needs remarking."

Glaring at him but not indulging in any useless struggling when he held her wrists over her head with one hand and began to untie her camisole with another, she snapped, "I am not a possession. I am a woman."

"Very much so," he said quietly as he removed her camisole and let his eyes feast on her full breasts.

It was a struggle to recall that she was annoyed over his attitude when his tongue began to flick over the peak of each breast. "You do not listen to me, *gringo*." She winced at the way the word emerged sounding suspiciously like an endearment.

"No. You don't listen to me." His tongue continued to circle her breasts as he removed the rest of her clothing. "You're mine, my little blond witch, and here and now I intend to prove it." His mouth covered hers before she could offer any further argument.

She knew she lost whatever battle she had been fighting. The intoxicating power of his kiss, his stroking plunging tongue, erased any anger she possessed. As if to be sure of that surrender, he kept on kissing her until she had no thought in her head save for the pleasure he could give her, was giving her, and how much she wanted him.

"Skin like silk and tasting of the sweetest honey," he murmured huskily as his eager mouth slid down to her breasts.

Her hands delved into his thick hair as his lips

210

feasted on her breasts. He left the tips of her breasts taut, wet and throbbing and moved his attentions to her stomach. His hands stroked her legs, making them burn and grow heavy. No coercion was needed to make them part, allowing his seeking hand full access to her. The way he fondled and probed her so intimately had her muttering words of passion and love but a remnant of caution had her speak in Spanish, a language he was not proficient in.

"*Ay de mi*," she gasped in shock when his mouth suddenly took the place of his hand, his tongue replacing his fingers. She was still unused to such intimacy and he held her firmly when she tried to pull away, Very soon though whatever shock she felt faded beneath waves of passion. She arched to him, crying out in the heat of her desire.

"Now, *querido*, now. I want you with me," she moaned, clutching him and dragging him into her feverish embrace.

His possession of her was swift, his hungry mouth devouring her cry. She barely heard his words but they drove her wild. Her hands clutched at his slim hips while her legs wrapped around him tightly. Their cries of release mingled as they crested passion's heights together. Clinging tightly to each other, they floated back down into sanity. It was a long while before their sated bodies parted even slightly, Royal staying wrapped securely in her arms, his face tucked into her neck and his hand cupping her breast.

"You can't expect a man to want to share something like that, Antonie. You are mine."

"And you are mine, Royal Bancroft?" she asked softly. "As you claim your brand marks me, does mine mark you?"

For a moment, he did not answer. The idea was not

211

as distasteful as he had expected. It was also fair. Although she was asking for a commitment of sorts, she was not seeking vows of love or promises of marriage. If she wanted that, he felt she would have asked outright. He frowned when he found that he was more than a little disappointed that she did not speak of love. Shaking that away as foolishness since he was not about to offer love or marriage, he brought his mind back to the matter at hand.

"Yes, I believe it does. I haven't had the slightest urge for another woman since you walked into my life."

"Do you know," she murmured, fighting to hide her delight over his words, "I always remembered you, your hair and your eyes."

He chuckled sleepily. "Same here. Purple eyes and cornsilk hair came to mind every time someone said Juan or Ramirez."

"Perhaps, *mi vida,* we were fated.

"I'm beginning to wonder."

Her arms held him close, her cheeks resting against his hair. It was wonderful to have him back with her. A sense of possession was not love but it did indicate that he was not without some feeling for her. She loved him so much that that was enough to stir hope and bring her delight. He was caught in passion's trap as strongly as she. For as long as it held him, he was truly hers.

Although half asleep, Royal sensed something in the way she held him. It was a possessive touch but it was not stifling. He did not feel trapped. Somehow he knew she would not cling if he wanted to leave, no matter how she felt about it.

He knew he had to give some serious thought to how he felt about her beyond his passion for her and his wanting to possess her. However, he was too tired at the moment. When she had left his bed, he had developed difficulty in sleeping. The restless nights spent aching for her caught up with him now that he was back in her arms, his needs momentarily satisfied. Royal knew that he should think about that too, that there was some message there, but he decided to sleep first.

Antonie suddenly woke up. Instincts developed during eleven years of living with a man on the run brought her out of her sated sleep wide-eyed and alert. Royal slept on still wrapped in her arms.

She moved one slim arm away from him, her small hand slipping beneath her pillow to clasp her gun and ease it out. Her eyes searched the darkness, found nothing and then went to the door. She was not surprised to see it stealthily open; she only tensed, ready to fight.

A darkly dressed man slipped into the room, and silently closed the door after him. In his hand was a pistol which, as he neared the bed, he raised and aimed at her and Royal.

From beneath her lashes, Antonie saw their erstwhile assassin smile. She knew he had seen their guns placed at a safe distance, out of their immediate reach, and thought them helpless. When he cocked his gun, she cocked hers and wondered how one of Raoul's men could believe her to be so foolish as to go to bed unarmed and helpless. She knew Raoul favored murders in the night.

When he readied his aim, she acted swiftly, her sudden movement startling the man. Antonie fired, taking his pistol neatly out of his hand, then fired again, wounding him high on the arm. The man screamed and tried to go for the door. Antonie stood up for a now wide awake Royal was in her way and shot the man in the leg. She finally accomplished what she had aimed to do. He was unable to escape but was not so badly wounded that he could not talk, perhaps give them some much needed information.

"Christ! Get something on," bellowed Royal, tossing her his shirt. "Those shots will have everybody racing for this room."

She barely managed to get his shirt on and Royal was doing up his pants when the door burst open. The twins and Royal's siblings were the first to appear, all in various states of undress. Behind them began to form a curious crowd attired in hastily donned robes.

Royal had just finished telling the twins and his family what had happened when the sheriff, called by the hotel manager, elbowed his way into the room, his deputy in his wake. It was not so easy for Royal to repeat his tale to the sheriff. The man did not know Antonie as her friends did. He saw a lovely woman only, one who hardly looked able to lift a pistol let alone shoot it so well.

"Had to hit him three times, did you?" the sheriff asked Antonie.

"Sí. I got rid of the gun he had. Then I shoot him in the arm to make sure he stays but his legs still work, eh? So, when he ran to the door, I shoot him in the leg. Then he stays. We need to ask him questions."

"Get rid of the people in the hall, George." When the deputy left, the sheriff said, "I ask the questions around here."

"Look, this man and others like him have been dogging me for months," Royal said. "I want to know why and for whom."

After a moment of thought, the sheriff nodded. "Fair enough. Ask away. This sort doesn't usually talk much though."

The sheriff proved right. Raoul's man stayed silent. Only Antonie and the twins knew it was not loyalty but fear that kept him silent. She watched for a while then stood up, picked up her knife and approached the man. The way to break Raoul's hold was to put, if not a greater, a more immediate fear into the man.

"May I try?" she asked Royal. "You will agree that I know these people better than you."

"What's the knife for?" the sheriff demanded.

"Persuasion," she purred. "Oro? Tomás? Stand him up." She saw Royal murmur to the sheriff and knew she had free rein to paly her game. "Now, you dog," she said to the would be assassin in Spanish, "you will tell me who pays Raoul to do these things to Bancroft."

"I will tell Juan's whore nothing," he spat and screamed when Oro and Tomás twisted his arm, aggravating his wound.

"Oh, you will tell me, swine. I know you fear Raoul's anger but I could do worse than kill you." She gently ran the point of her knife down the front of his trousers letting it come to rest at the base of his manhood and smiled when he broke out into a sweat. "He would only leave you dead. If you do not tell me what I want to know, I will leave you less than a man."

"*Señorita*," he squeaked when she applied enough pressure to the knife to cause him a slight but frightening twinge.

"Slowly. I will do it slowly. Inch by inch." She chuckled and grinned at Oro and Tomás who also chuckled when she said, "Three slices ought to do it."

The man was too frightened to be insulted. "I know nothing. I swear it. I only do as I am told."

She pressed hard enough to draw a little blood and hoped he would break for this was as far as she would take the game. "I think it is not all a secret. You see and

215

you hear, eh?"

"Yes, yes," he squawked, trying to scramble away from the knife she held but unable to break the twins' firm hold.

"Well?" She reached for his belt, neatly cutting it with her knife.

"A *gringo*. A Texan pays Raoul. I do not know the name. No name. I swear it, *señorita*."

"Why does this Texan hire Raoul and his dogs? What is the plan?"

"To ruin the Bancrofts. Tonight I was to kill you. He thinks you and the Degas twins spoil his plans. He wants you dead."

Antonie shrugged. "He has always wanted us dead. This is not new. You did not mean to kill Royal Bancroft?"

"To wound him if he was with you. Only to wound him. I was to make him think that he was to be killed but that the attempt failed. You were to die. The Texan wants you dead but I was not told why. You are much hated." He looked at Antonie as if he had a very good idea of why that was.

"Tomás, Oro, release him. Say nothing of the plans for me," she said in Spanish as the sheriff collected his shaken prisoner. "What Raoul has planned for us is part of an old hate and a private one." The twins nodded reluctantly and she reverted to English to tell what she had learned.

After lengthy explanations and some debate, Royal and Antonie were again left alone. Royal bolted the door then moved to lean against the bed post to look quizzically at Antonie. Idly, he mused that he had never seen a woman before who could look so good in a man's shirt.

"Not so sure I like the idea of sleeping with a woman

216

who keeps a loaded gun under her pillow," he drawled.

She smiled, slid her arms around his neck and kissed him. "It used to be a knife but that can only be used once, when thrown, eh?"

"Oh, yes, a pistol's much more useful," he mumbled as her lips moved down his throat, her hands caressing his chest.

Perhaps it was the brush with death or the threat of it which continued to hang over her head but Antonie was suddenly desperate to make love. Her kisses moved down his chest. She paused to tongue and suckle his nipples, his sounds of pleasure stirring her more.

His hands tightened in her hair as she kissed his taut belly, her tongue dipping into his navel. Her hands neatly undid his pants. As she slowly lowered them, her mouth moved down one strong leg, tasting and nibbling. When she had fully removed his pants, her mouth edged its way back up his other leg, her hands lovingly stroking every place she could reach. Without pause, she began to pay homage to his virility.

Royal could do little more than brace himself against the bed post and groan her name, his hands clenched in her thick hair. Her mouth, her tongue, her teeth and her hands all worked with a gentle thoroughness to bring him more pleasure than he had ever known. If he had not had indisputable proof of her innocence, he would have thought her well trained.

Suddenly he could stand no more. He grasped her beneath her arms, tossed her onto the bed and hastily stripped his shirt off her. She lay sprawled beneath his crouched body, open, unresisting and very evidently ready. He glanced up to her face, saw her tongue slowly lick her lips with a voluptuous relish and with a hoarse cry, kissed her fiercely.

There ensued an onslaught upon her senses that, at

times, Antonie feared she would not survive. He left no part of her untasted or untouched. At times he was so fierce she was sure she would be bruised but it brought her only pleasure. He kept her riding the crest until she thought she would weep with her need for release. Her hands clutching at him, she tried to pull him into the embrace she craved.

Then he was there, driving into her with a force that made her cry out. But a moment later, he rolled over, keeping them united so that she was on top of him. Her need was at such a height that she needed no prompting. She took control with a delighted vengeance. For the second time that night, they burst through desire's barriers, their cries of release blending into one voice.

Wrapped securely in each other's arms, it was a long while before they had the strength to speak. The tremors of residual delight took many moments to fade from their sated bodies. Antonie lay sprawled on top of Royal with neither the inclination nor the energy to move.

"That was incredible," Royal finally said, his husky whisper breaking their contented silence.

"*Sí*," she agreed sleepily. "I do not think we can better that, eh?"

"We could always try."

"I do not think it would be good for our health, *mi amor*," she teased.

"You're probably right." He kissed her briefly. "You are the lover every man dreams about."

As she nuzzled his neck, she smiled slightly. Pleasure and disappointment arose at his remark. It was a lovely accolade but she would rather he thought of her as his love, not just his lover. Feeling droopy-eyed, she scolded herself as she let sleep take over. You could not make love come no matter how much you gave it or wanted it. She had received more than she had planned on already. She would make herself be content with that.

d blouse. It was not an Antonie won but
se she liked her new dress or her pants. It
rr taking her for a walk about the

Chapter Sixteen

"Hey, lazy, move those bones."

Very slowly, Antonie opened her eyes. She gave an unfriendly look to the grinning man by her bed. This was her first time in a soft bed in three months and she did not really appreciate him cutting that time short.

"Go away. I want to sleep." She put the pillow over her head.

Royal took the pillow away. "Come on. Up and at 'em. Don't you want to see the town?"

"What's to see? Saloons, whorehouses, a jail and shops. I have seen these before."

"Well, you can see them again. Rise and shine. I'll go order breakfast. Better hurry or it'll get cold," he said as he left.

She glared at the door for a moment, then cursed. There was no sense in staying in bed when he had succeeded in waking her up. Grumbling about his inconsiderate behavior, she got up and began her regular morning ritual.

After a moment's indecision, she decided to wear her

skirt and blouse. It was not an outfit an Anglo wore but it was all she had besides her new dress or her pants. If Royal was serious about taking her for a walk about the town, she would give him the courtesy of wearing a dress. He seemed quite accustomed to her wearing pants but she knew he preferred her in skirts.

Just as she was about to leave her room, she hesitated. With a shake of her head, she buckled on her gun. One of Raoul's men had managed to get into their room last night. The man was near and she could not take the risk of being caught unarmed just to play the lady for Royal.

Royal looked up as she entered the dining room in the hotel. His smile widened when he saw that she had worn her dress and fixed her hair the way she had for the fiesta. When she reached the table, he finally noticed the gun.

"What's that for?"

"The gun?" she asked as she sat down, smiling a greeting to Cole and Justin.

"Yes, the gun. We're only going to stroll around town."

"*Sí*. and last night we were only going to sleep, but one of Raoul's dogs found us. I remembered that as I started to leave my room and decided to wear my gun. Raoul is near and it is good to be careful."

"Reckon you're right. Coffee?"

"*Sí*. *Gracias*. Where is Tomás?" She smiled faintly when her question made Cole and Justin look uncomfortable.

"We-ell, he went back to the saloon," Cole replied finally. "At least, that's what he said he was doing."

"Maybe he did, although, he would have to pay a saloon girl and Tomás says he will never pay for it." She grinned when Cole and Justin laughed and Royal

221

shook his head. "You sure he went back into the saloon?"

"You don't really want to know about Tomás's private life, do you?" Royal asked.

"Well, *sí* and no. Sometimes it is good not to know what Tomás is doing but then he does ask for trouble. Officers' wives, *patrón*'s daughters, even a marshal's wife." She shook her head. "He will get shot." Her eyes narrowed as, though the door to the dining room, she saw Tomás jauntily descending the stairs. "If he went back to the saloon, he did not stay long. Not long for Tomás anyway."

"Ah, coffee. *Bueno*," Tomás said ecstatically as he joined them at the table.

"What have you been doing?" Antonie demanded, recognizing the self-satisfied look on his face.

"Can a man have no privacy, little one?"

"*Sí*, as long as she has no jealous husband."

"She doesn't, so you may relax."

"That is a nice change."

Shaking her head, Antonie concentrated on her meal. The food on the drive had not been bad but it had not equaled what she had become used to at Royal's ranch. Sighing in satisfaction, she sat back to savor a second cup of coffee.

She frowned when she saw Oro approach, only to be accosted in the lobby by a burly, very angry gentleman. "Um, Tomás?"

"*Sí, querida?*"

"You said no jealous husband, right?"

"*Sí*. No jealous husband."

"Ah, I see. Then it must be a brother or a father who is preparing to beat Oro to a, how you say, pulp."

When Tomás cursed and rushed out into the lobby, she joined the others in laughing at the fracas that ensued. It was ended when a well-rounded brunette and a skinny blonde rushed into the lobby. The two women soon led the burly man away and Tomás hurried after a scowling Oro, who strode into the dining room.

"She had better been worth my nearly getting my face broken, Tomás," Oro grumbled as he sat down.

"*Sí*, she was."

"Could you not find a nice, unwed orphan?"

"But I did, Oro, and still you complained."

After frowning thoughtfully for a moment, Oro glared at his brother. "Convent girls. *Ay de mi*. I would rather be beaten or shot than prayed over by irate nuns and priests."

"Come on, Antonie, let's go," Royal said quietly.

Even as she let him help her out of her seat, she protested, "But, I was listening to that argument."

"I suspect it's one you've often heard."

"*Sí*, I am afraid that is so." She linked her arm through his as they left the dining room. "It is usually Tomás who plays and Oro who gets blamed for it too."

"Never the other way around?"

"No. Oro goes to saloons and whores. He thinks he cannot charm and seduce a woman like Tomás can."

"A man who reduces the girls at the saloon to hair-pulling over him?"

Looking around her as they started through town, Antonie nodded. "He thinks they only act like that because he is kind to them and they don't get much of that. It is one reason he found the situation with Patricia so hard. She was looking at him, wanting him. No charm used, no seduction. Others have looked at him like that but he did not see it. Not until Patricia."

"Strange that twins should be so different."

"Oh, they are a lot alike too. When Tomás finds his

woman he will be as Oro is with Patricia. He will give her everything."

"Or turn her away if he thinks it's for the best?"

"Sí. That too."

"You couldn't trust me to see him as just a man, to judge him as just a man?"

"I wanted to. You seemed fair, clean of the poison of prejudice, but," she shrugged, "even Maria was not sure if that went deep enough to let Oro and Patricia be together. I just wonder if you know how much trouble there could be."

"Oh, I know what's coming. I also feel confident that plenty of our friends and neighbors are fair minded enough to let it make no difference. The ones that matter will accept it."

"Sí, and Patricia has a big family to help ease the sting. What is this place?"

"The bank. Come on."

"No. I will wait here. When I go into a bank I get the urge to stick my gun in the teller's face and demand money."

His lips twitched as he looked into her impish face, her eyes alight with laughter. "Funny. All right. I'll only be a few minutes."

Leaning against the outside of the building, Antonie watched the people walking by. It was evident that the so-called respectable citizens of the town felt it was safe to walk the streets when the sun was out. Her amusement grew when she realized that they all stopped at some invisible line, never crossing it. On the other side of that line were the saloons, the whorehouses and the cowboys. Obviously, even in broad daylight, they did not dare to venture into that area.

"Ah, señorita. All alone?"

She grimaced with distaste when a less than sober

224

and less than clean cowboy draped an arm around her shoulders. When she tried to slip free of his grip, his hold tightened and he and his friends laughed. It was clear that getting free of this entanglement was not going to be easy. She could only hope that there would be no scene.

"I am not alone. My man is in the bank."

"She's blond and blue-eyed. You sure she's a *señorita*, Joe?"

"Sure she is. No white woman'd wear this beaneater outfit."

"Let me go," Antonie demanded, angered by his derogatory remarks. "My man will return soon."

"Well, now, darlin', old Joe can show you a better time. I wouldn't leave you standing alone outside no bank." He tried to nudge her in the direction of the saloons. "Come on, sweetheart, let me and the boys show you some fun."

Digging in her heels, she turned toward him and pulled her gun, smiling coldly when he blanched as she pressed the barrel into his groin. "If you do not leave me alone you will have nothing to show me some fun with, *gringo*."

"Hey, Joe, you all right?"

"Tell your friends to stay where they are," she ordered.

"Don't move, you two," Joe squeaked.

Royal stepped out of the bank and tensed. Anger flowed through him when he saw the cowboy holding Antonie but he fought to stay calm. He did not know exactly what was going on. Since Antonie was not struggling, he calmly stepped up behind her and wondered what made the cowboy look so ill.

"Having trouble, darling?" he murmured.

"Jesus, mister, don't startle her or nothing," croaked

the cowhand, his horrified gaze falling to Antonie's gun.

Following that look, Royal almost laughed. "Ah, I see you have everything under control."

"*Sí*. These men were just leaving." She holstered her gun even as the trio bolted down the street.

Draping his arm around her shoulders, Royal drawled. "You realize you denied me the pleasure of acting the protective male."

She grinned at him. "Had a hankering to punch a nose, eh?"

"Some. Was he much trouble?" He started walking again. "I can see I'd better not leave you alone."

"Ah, the cowboy thought I was a *señorita* and that of course meant that I was a *puta* to be dragged off."

Hearing the bitter anger in her voice, he briefly tightened his hold on her in a gesture of sympathetic understanding. Her Mexican peasant attire marked her in a lot of eyes. He was surprised that her blond hair and blue eyes had not given the cowboys a moment's pause, even though that alone did not guarantee her a minimum of respect. Not every Mexican peasant girl was a whore just as not every Anglo woman was a lady. He had even met some Mexican whores who were far more genteel than some Anglo ladies.

"I thought we'd stop in at the sheriff's office."

"Why do we want to do that?"

"Well, maybe he's got more information out of that fellow."

"Maybe. He might have remembered something."

"Er, Antonie?"

"*Sí?*"

"Do you think you could ease up on threatening a fellow's, well, manhood?"

"Make you nervous, *querido?*" she teased.

226

"Hell, maybe. It just seems so, well, vicious."

"I have never carried out such a threat."

"You sure as hell make a man think you will. You had me and the sheriff sweating some last night."

"That is the trick. Juan told me to always make them believe you. He also taught me that to threaten that which makes a man a man is almost always successful. It is a man's weakest point, he said. Not only in his body but in his head. But, if it troubles you, *querido*, I will try to think of something else."

"No. You do what works, what keeps you safe."

Royal almost grinned as they walked into the sheriff's office. The man looked very surprised. When that look changed and became grim, Royal was no longer amused. He suddenly wondered yet again if Antonie was being hunted by the law. They were pretty far out of *bandito* territory but wanted posters were spread wider and farther every year.

"Funny you two showing up now," the sheriff said.

"We came to see if the prisoner did any more talking," Royal said.

"He didn't and he won't," the sheriff added as he headed toward the cell, signaling Antonie and Royal to follow him. "Don't suppose you know anything about this?"

There was no need to look beneath the haphazardly spread blanket to know that the man was dead. The amount of blood visible could only come from a fatal wound. Antonie felt slightly ill. The man's death had been messy and she could not help but wonder if that had been intentional.

"Raoul," she whispered, turning away and striding back into the sheriff's office.

"You all right, Antonie?" Royal asked gently as he joined her.

227

"*Sí*. Just a little sick feeling. It passes."

"You said something, ma'am?" the sheriff asked as he sat at his desk.

"You sit down, Antonie. You look a little pale. I can answer any questions."

She nodded and sat down. It puzzled her that her stomach should be so sensitive. She was no stranger to death even at its most gruesome, although she was usually spared the worst. Idly, she wondered if being with Royal was softening her in some way.

"I heard a name."

"You did, Sheriff. Raoul. Raoul Mendez. Heard of him?"

"Hell, yes. He ain't in this area. 'Course the tales come up with the cowboys."

"Well, I'm afraid Mendez came this time."

"He's here?" the sheriff asked, frowning.

"I was surprised that he would get so far away from the border too but, yes, he's here."

"He's the one trailing you. You mentioned it last night."

"He's trailing us, but someone is paying him to," Royal added.

"Who?"

"That's what I've been trying to find out. No luck so far. How'd this happen?"

"Someone must've come to the cell window. Fool probably thought he was getting rescued. They shot him. Used a damn big gun too. I heard him cry out, then there was a shot. Went running in and found a Godawful mess. Shot him square in the face. No sign of who did it. I'm just waiting on the undertaker. Was he a Mexican *bandito?*" the sheriff asked quietly as he studied a fine watch.

"*Sí*. I have seen him with Raoul before but I have no

228

name for him," Antonie replied.

"And why should you be knowing any names, ma'am?"

"I told you. I know these people. I am from Mexico."

"Ah. Well, don't reckon his name is Douglas Saunders, hmm?"

"No, it is not. I am sure of that."

"Don't happen to know anyone named Saunders, do you?"

"No, Sheriff. Royal?"

"Nope. Found the watch on him, did you?"

"Yup. Reckoned he'd stolen it."

The sheriff calmly pocketed the watch and Antonie put a hand over her mouth to try and smother a giggle. Royal shot her a quelling, scolding glance and then looked at the sheriff.

"Shouldn't that stay with the body, sir?"

"Why? He ain't going to need it. Ain't his either. I've been needing me a new watch. Now, you meet up with a fellow named Saunders who has lost himself a watch, you send him to me. I'll give it to him. I ain't letting that damn undertaker get this one. Undertakers are the biggest damn thieves there is," the sheriff said emphatically.

"Now, you ain't done nothing wrong so I can't be running you out of town or arresting you. However, I've got me enough trouble and work to do and enough crooks to tussle with that I don't need any brought up from Texas. Since this Mendez feller followed you up here, I reckon he'll follow you home too."

"*Sí*," replied Antonie as she stood up and moved to Royal's side. "He will."

"Well, then, when are you leaving?" the sheriff demanded.

Antonie could tell that Royal was angry as they

229

walked away from the sheriff's office. She had trouble keeping up with his long strides and he did not say a word until they stopped abruptly before the mercantile store. It was difficult to know if she should just be quiet and let him wrestle with his anger by himself or if she should try to pull him from his mood with conversation. When he solved her dilemma, she was glad for she wanted a return to the cheerful, easy camaraderie they had been enjoying before their visit to the sheriff's office.

"This is the first time I've had a sheriff ask me to leave town."

"He just asked when you were leaving," Antonie pointed out.

"Antonie, you know damn well he would've asked us to leave if I hadn't said we were going tomorrow morning."

"*Sí*, but he really wasn't asking you to leave. He wants Mendez to go away."

"I know and Mendez goes with us. Here, what do you think of that hat in the window?"

"It is silly."

"Silly? The sign says it is the latest Paris fasion," Royal said, shocked at her flippant remark.

"What's it doing out here?"

His mood gradually improved and Antonie was glad of it. For a little while it was nice to put aside their troubles, forget about the dangers and act like a carefree couple. Sometimes he even made her feel as if she were being courted, which sent her into blushing confusion but she loved it. She even allowed him to buy the frivolous hat.

That night as she held him close, both of them struggling to recover from a somewhat wild lovemaking session, she found herself wondering if they had really settled what had kept them apart. They had tumbled into bed and there had been a lot of talk about possession. She suddenly realized that he had said nothing to show clearly that her simple denial of being Oro's lover had been enough. Their reunion had occurred when the truth about Oro and Patricia had been revealed. She hit him.

"Yow!" Royal sat up abruptly, rubbing the arm she had punched. "What was that for?"

"When did you start to believe me?"

"About what?" Royal asked, puzzled.

"About Oro. I said I would not be with a man who thought me a liar. You never said you stopped thinking it. You didn't say much of anything about it at all."

"Antonie," he warily lay down at her side and took her into his arms, "I was starting to believe you before that."

"I did not see that."

"No, I was thinking about it. Before the fight at the rocks. Actually, from that day you got jumped while bathing. I got to thinking that you'd never lied to me. I decided to try and push the anger away and take a closer look at things."

"And you saw that I did not lie." She slid her arms around him, her hands moving lovingly over his strong back.

"We-ell, I got to thinking that you weren't lying about Oro and you but that you were hiding something. I'd just started to look closer at Patricia and Oro when the truth came out."

"Ah, I see. Okay, then I compromise."

"Compromise?"

"Sí. You said you did not think I lied but you did not fully trust me. This I can understand. So, it is all right now. I compromise like Tomás said I should." She

231

twined her leg around his and pressed the full length of her body against him. "Do I get a reward?"

"Call it a reward if you want to. You were going to get it anyway."

"*Sí?*"

"*Sí.* The ride home will be hard and fast and none too private. There won't be a chance for this."

"Ah, how sad. I will miss this soft bed." She giggled when he moaned and pushed her onto her back. "You did not mean the bed, *querido?*"

"No, I did not mean the bed. Let me show you what I meant."

"What a good idea."

Antonie aimlessly swung at the hand shaking her by the shoulder and tried to snuggle further into the bed. "Go away."

"There's nothing I'd like better than staying tucked up in that bed with you, honey, but we have to get going."

"Oh." She rolled over onto her back and stared sleepily at Royal even as she wondered why she was finding it so hard to wake up in the mornings lately. "Time to go back."

" 'Fraid so. If you get moving we can have a good breakfast. It'll be trail fare after this."

"I will be along quickly. You know what I like."

"I know what I like too, but I'll go order breakfast instead."

She giggled and, as soon as he was gone, hopped out of bed. Gasping slightly, she quickly sat, then lay back down until the swimming in her head had passed. Grimacing, she rose cautiously. Her physical problem was not going away as she had hoped it would. Whether

232

or not she liked it, she would have to see a doctor when they returned to the ranch and the long ride back would give her enough time to quell her fears about what the doctor might say was wrong.

As they got ready to mount outside the hotel, Royal studied Antonie. She had looked very pale when she had come down to breakfast, and a full meal had not improved her color much. He almost blamed himself for keeping her awake and exhausted with his lovemaking but he suddenly remembered a number of other mornings when she had looked distinctly wobbly and he had not touched her for weeks. Moving to her side, he helped her into her saddle.

"Are you all right, Antonie? Perhaps we could wait just one more day."

"No. Everyone is ready now. Besides," she nodded toward where the sheriff watched them, "someone waits for us to go."

Royal cursed softly. "And Mendez with us."

"We cannot blame him for that."

"No, reckon not. Are you sure you're all right?"

Sí, querido. Some fresh air and I will be better." She smiled faintly. "All this honest work is harder than I thought it would be."

"Cute, Antonie. Well, let's go then, but if you feel the need, we can slow down or even stop. Remember that."

"Sí, patrón."

After giving her a repressive glance, he went to his own horse. As they rode by the sheriff's, he tipped his hat and the man returned the gesture. When the sheriff looked at the watch he had taken from the dead *bandito,* Royal heard Antonie laugh and he shook his head.

By the time they took a brief rest at noon, Royal decided that Antonie was fine. The long drive and all the trouble they had faced probably accounted for her

233

fatigue and her paleness. A few hours of fresh air had indeed brought improvement and Royal decided he had been worried about nothing.

Antonie breathed a sigh of relief when Royal finally stopped keeping such a close watch on her. She felt a lot better just as she always had before. The sick feeling and the dizziness never lingered for long but she knew she would have to hide it better than she had been if it continued. She was very concerned about what ailed her, and she really did not want someone else hovering worriedly over her. Sighing, Antonie decided it was going to be a long ride back to the ranch.

Chapter Seventeen

"Well, there is your ranch, *amigo*. Safe and sound," Antonie said quietly.

She had sensed Royal's and his family's growing tension as they had neared the ranch. Although all their neighbors had assured the Bancrofts that they would keep an eye on things, the ranch had been left mostly defenseless. The victory of getting the cattle sold would have been severely diminished if they had come back to find only ashes.

"Let's just hope that everyone in it is, too," Royal murmured as he spurred his horse down the small rise where they had stopped.

A grinning Old Pete greeted them as they reined in before the house and quickly made Maria's boys, Sancho and Carlos, see to the horses and the gear. Royal and the rest of the party had barely stepped inside the house when Maria and Rosa rushed to greet them.

"Darling! I am so glad to see you back safe and sound. How lucky it was that I chose to stop by today."

Lucky was not the word Antonie would have chosen as she leaned against the stairpost and watched Marilynn rush into a startled Royal's arms. The only thing that kept her jealousy in check was the look of helpless embarrassment Royal sent her even as Marilynn kissed him. His swiftness in ending the embrace also pleased her. She had no idea of what, if anything, Royal had decided to do about Marilynn but she was glad to see that he was at least trying not to play both sides of the fence.

"You've been coming here?" Royal asked as he disentangled himself from Marilynn's embrace.

"Of course, darling. I told you I would watch out for everything."

Antonie choked back a sneer when Maria rolled her eyes heavenward.

"Now," Marilynn continued blithely, "I can assure you that your homecoming will run smoothly. We can talk while Maria and that girl heat the water for your bath. There's so much that happened while you were gone."

"Couldn't it wait? Look, why don't you go home and . . ."

"Nonsense, dear. I can help."

Seeing that it was going to take him a while to extract himself from Marilynn, Royal looked at Antonie. "Why don't you go and have your bath, Antonie?"

"Are you saying that I stink, *amigo?*"

"You smell about as good as I do."

"*Ai yi yi.* You'd best heat enough water for three baths, Maria," Antonie said, and laughing at the mock glare Royal sent her, dashed up the stairs.

Even as she entered her room, she heard the others hurriedly deserting Royal. Antonie thought sadly that, if Royal did wed Marilynn, the house would lose a great deal of its friendliness. Royal would find that his family would begin to drift away and she knew that that would hurt him. She shook away that distressing thought and started to get ready for the bath she knew would soon arrive.

Watching Maria closely at the woman filled the tub, Antonie wondered just how often Marilynn had come around. Marilynn did seem to act as if she had free rein over Royal's home and Maria had to find it an ordeal to constantly swallow the woman's attitudes and the deriding of all the work Maria did.

"I don't think Royal would fire you if you just told that woman to shut her mouth," Antonie said quietly.

"I am not sure if he would or not, but there would be some trouble and it is not worth it."

Slipping into the water with a sigh of pleasure, Antonie looked at Maria who was gathering up her dirty clothes. "Is there a good doctor in the area?"

"You are ill?" Maria asked fretfully.

"I am not sure."

"How can you not be sure?"

"It comes and goes."

"Oh? You tell me. I have seen a lot of sickness and do a little doctoring. Maybe it is a thing I have seen."

"Well, I would prefer talking to you. The doctor is a man, eh?" Maria nodded. "This is a female trouble I think."

"Ah, *sí, sí.* You do not want to talk to a man about such things." Maria sat on the bed. "You tell me. It hurts bad? You bleed too much maybe?"

"Right now I do not bleed at all. I did not think on that until the ride home. I was worried about the other things but then I remembered that I did not bleed once on the drive. Then I think these things are all connected, *sí?*"

"What other things?"

"I am so tired. A lot am I tired. Always I wake up

237

quick and alert but no more. It is so hard to get out of bed." Antonie shook her head. "And if I get up too quick I feel sick and my head, how it swims. It takes time to go away." Worried by the odd look on Maria's face, Antonie asked nervously, "I have heard that a growth can stop a woman's flow. Do you think I have one of these?"

"Oh, a growth," Maria choked out and then started to laugh. *"Por Dios,* a growth, eh?"

"Maria? Maria, this is not funny. What is wrong with me?"

"Wait, wait," Maria gasped, struggling to stop laughing.

"I was not finished. I think it is bad," Antonie said weakly as Maria started to calm down. "My stomach moves. It wiggles." She was dismayed when that only caused Maria to start laughing again. "I could be dying and you laugh."

"Oh, *chica,* forgive me," Maria said as she moved to the side of the tub and briefly hugged Antonie but she still shook with an occasional chuckle. "Stand up, *chica. Sí, sí.* Not so slim here now, eh?" she murmured as she put her hands on Antonie's waist. "Ah," she sighed as she rested her hand on Antonie's stomach. "There is the wiggle. *Sí,* a strong one."

As she sank back down into the water, Antonie asked shakily, "You know what is wrong with me?"

"Sí. You are with child."

"A baby?"

"Sí. The *patrón's* baby."

"The baby wiggles?"

"A strong child."

Antonie was stunned. Placing her hand over her stomach she felt the movement from the outside as well as the inside. A baby had been the last thing she had thought of but, as the knowledge took hold, a deep sense of joy flooded her.

"A baby, eh?"

"*Sí, chica*. How is it you could not know?"

"No one told me about babies. Juan got a woman to tell me about bleeding but not until I had started and thought I was dying. She did not tell me much, although she did say it had to do with babies. She wanted to get away from us, I think. She was frightened. Otherwise, no one told me anything. I was raised by men."

"*Sí*. They would not think to tell you. Now, I am wondering when we will see this baby. When did your bleeding stop?"

"Why, when I got here," Antonie said in some surprise. "At least, I think so. The last time I can remember clearly was when I took care of Juan after the rangers shot him. I was bleeding then. Since then? No, I do not think so."

"Ah, so soon. It was after then that you got with child. Maybe even the first time you lie with the *patrón*. Six months, maybe less, maybe a little more." Maria shrugged.

"But I am not very fat. Ladies with child get fat."

"Some. Some do not. Soon it will show. Maybe only a little, maybe a lot. A first baby does not always round the belly too quick, eh? Slide up. Rosa has just set more hot water outside the door and I think your bath cools."

By the time Maria had added the extra hot water, Antonie had come to a decision. "Maria?"

"*Sí?*"

"You are to say *nada*, eh?"

"*Sí, nada*. It is for you to tell the *patrón*."

"Or not."

"Not tell the *patrón*?" Maria gasped. "You must tell

239

him about his own baby."

"It is my baby too."

"*Sí,* so you will marry."

"Will we?"

"He wants that woman no more."

"He does not want her for now." She smiled crookedly when Maria's expression became worried. "Even if he decides he does not want to wed her, that does not mean that he wants to wed me. I must think about this, study this problem. It is not simple. No, not simple. So, say *nada* to anyone, Maria."

Maria finally nodded in agreement but Antonie knew that it was a reluctant concession. When she left, Antonie relaxed in the hot water, her eyes slowly closing. Although she was happy about the baby, she ruefully admitted that she did not need yet another thing to worry about and, depending on how things went with her and Royal, a child could be a very large worry indeed. There were now new decisions to make and several new possible futures to contemplate.

A brief cool draft touched her shoulders and she gradually opened her eyes. The dark look on Royal's face changed quickly when his gaze came to rest on her. She briefly wondered what had annoyed him as her body immediately responded to the desire that brightened his eyes. Stretching languorously in the tub, she smiled an invitation and laughed gently when he began to hurriedly shed his clothes.

About an hour later, Antonie lifted her head from his chest to glance toward the tub. "There is a lot of water on the floor," she murmured.

He playfully nuzzled her neck, making her giggle, then lightly slapped her backside before gently pushing her aside and sitting up. "And all my clean clothes are in the other room."

Her modesty returning, now that her passion was momentarily sated. Antonie clutched the sheet to her breasts as she sat up. "There is a spare towel. Wrap that around you. I will mop up this mess."

After giving her a brief kiss, he rose and fetched the towel. "I'm torn between staying here and starving."

"I will help you decide. I am hungry."

Laughing quietly, he started out of the room. "Then you'd better get dressed quick. I reckon dinner's being served right now."

As Antonie entered the dining room she realized that neither of them had mentioned Marilynn. She was relieved to see that the woman was gone. When Justin made a comment about Marilynn, Royal's answer was vaguely curt. He then skillfully and rapidly changed the subject. Although Antonie was not particularly eager to discuss the woman, she was curious about what had put Royal into such an odd mood. She decided that, as soon as they returned to their room, she would ask.

Maria was thrilled to hear about Oro's and Patricia's marriage plans and the evening was spent planning the wedding. Antonie noticed that Royal was careful to go over the guest list person by person and that he pressed Maria for an explanation each time she seemed at all cautious and hesitant. It was clear to Antonie that Royal wanted to try and avoid any chance of unpleasantness at his sister's wedding. She was not sure he would be able to, however, for some of the worst bigots were his closest neighbors and had been the Bancrofts' friends for years. In trying to avoid the chance of a shadow touching Patricia's wedding day, Royal could easily offend some of the more important people in the area.

"Invite them," Oro said quietly. When Royal had

241

rejected the Collinses, another prominent family.

"Oro, you know what they're like." Royal sighed and shook his head.

"*Sí*. Mexicans are dirt and breeds are even worse. *De nada*."

"They could get pretty nasty."

"No, they probably *will* get pretty nasty. That does not trouble me. If you do not invite them, that could be trouble for you, eh? So, ask them. If they do not come, the insult is theirs, not yours. This is better."

After a moment of deep thought, Royal nodded. He silently hoped that the Collinses would not come, but at least everyone would know that he had delivered no insult to the family, that he had not excluded them from an important family occasion. If they did choose to come as did others with similar prejudices, Royal just hoped that they had the common decency and good manners to keep those prejudices silent. Patricia would eventually have to face those attitudes, but not on her wedding day.

Inwardly, he shook his head, afraid that Patricia did not understand. It was going to take a lot of strength and a lot of love to survive the darts of far too many bigots and there could be far worse than nasty words flung at the couple. With that in mind, he kept Patricia with him when everyone began to drift off to bed.

When they were alone, he began carefully, "Pattie, about this marriage . . ."

"You can't change your mind now. I'm marrying Oro."

"I'm not changing my mind. Calm down."

"You're thinking of changing mine though, aren't you?"

"Only if you want it changed. Just listen for a minute."

242

"Okay, I reckon I can listen."

"I like Oro. He's a good man. I also don't believe in holding a man's blood, religion or relatives against him. I'm one of few though, honey. In that one slim man there's Mexican, Indian and a *bandito* heritage. That's three separate things that can rouse up a hell of a lot of hatred."

"Well, not many know who his father was," Patricia said with defiance in her voice.

"True, and the few that do know won't yap about it. It's there though, and it could easily come out, become widely known. There's never been a chance to hide the Mexican and Yaqui mix."

"Everybody's talked about it, Royal. Tomás, Antonie, Maria, and Oro. They've all told me about the prejudices."

He gently grasped her by the shoulders. "They told you but do you really understand? Once you marry him this family might be the only ones who'll speak to you. There'll be a lot of people snubbing you, pretending they don't see you, that you're beneath their notice. There'll be nasty remarks. Some folks'll think you are a whore for marrying him. Three cowhands thought Antonie could be treated as one just because she wore a Mexican dress. Those pretty manners you're so used to won't be around any more.

"And Oro may be treated worse. Oh, some of it'll come from petty jealousy. The men who were after you won't like it at all because he's supposed to be beneath them, yet you chose to marry him, so what the hell does that make them? There might be fights, maybe even a shoot-out or two. People are going to hate him even more for crossing the line that they drew."

Even though he could see the tears swimming in her eyes, he hardened himself to them and pressed on.

243

"What about your children? They'll hear it too. There'll be folks who won't let them near their kids. They'll have to suffer the hate too.

"You'd better like that piece of land you've got because you might not leave it much. It'll probably be the only real safe and peaceful place you can find, save this house, and that just might be because it abuts this place. There won't be any invitations any more."

"I don't care. I love Oro and our children will love him and be loved."

"It had better be a strong love, darling. It's going to take a lot of beating."

"It's strong. It survived Oro being nasty to me, nearly vicious. It survived him going to the saloons and coming home stinking of those girls. It survived Antonie and my thinking they were lovers. I think it can survive the pettiness of people who aren't worth knowing anyhow. I'll have Maria, Rosa and the permanent hands like Old Pete. I'll have Oro's family — Antonie and Tomás. I'll have my brothers. I'll have Oro and the family we'll build. That's more than enough for anybody."

He hugged her and kissed her cheek. "All right, honey. The whole family will be behind you and that's no small thing. Even with the troubles we've been having, we're no small power around here."

Antonie watched Royal closely when he slipped into her room. He looked worried yet oddly satisfied. Even though it was a family matter, she could not restrain her curiosity. In a way, it was her business too, for Oro was her family.

"You had a talk with Patricia about Oro?" she asked as he slid into bed and pulled her into his arms.

"In a way. I tried to tell her about prejudice. It seems she's heard it before."

244

"Sí. We have all talked to her."

"So she said. Well, I talked some more. I tried to make her see how it will be. The snubbings, the isolation, the insults. I told her how it could all be directed toward her children. Told her how Oro might well be in fights. I even said she might find that we're the only ones who'll have anything to do with her and that that patch of land might be the only place she'll see, well, besides here."

"Did she listen?"

"Yes, but she didn't falter."

"Did you want her to?"

"Hell, I don't know. I like Oro. I want Patricia to be happy. Yet, it's going to be hard, real hard."

"Sí. Now she will taste the hate."

"I know and I'm afraid of what it'll do to her," Royal said with sadness.

"A lot of people taste the hate and it does not change the good that is inside them. Look at Maria."

"True but then Maria's never been the belle of the town. If she married a man like Oro, her whole life wouldn't change."

"So Patricia makes a new life. Her life becomes Oro, the land and their family. She will be loved. Oro knows what is to come. He will watch and protect her and he will soothe the hurts with love. It will not be easy but I do not think it will break her."

"She said she'd be all right, that she'd have Oro, his family, her family and the folks here. She said that'd be enough, that the ones who turned away or turned nasty were not worth knowing anyways."

"Ah, she has seen the truth. She will be fine. And," she smiled, "she will have pretty babies. Maria says so. It made Maria very sad to think Patricia and Oro could not be married."

245

"I can't help being a little insulted that you all thought it had to be hidden from me."

"She is your only sister, *querido,* the only daughter of a rich Anglo rancher. Even Maria did not feel sure about it."

"Yes, and maybe some of that's my own fault. I've turned a deaf ear to Marilynn's nastiness, let the woman treat Maria badly. I'm going to put a stop to that."

"I told Maria to tell Marilynn to shut her mouth."

"Good idea."

"But Maria was unsure. She was afraid you would fire her."

"Fire Maria? That's absurd. Her father and my father worked together to build this place. Her family's as much a part of the ranch as the Bancrofts are. Hell, she's family. You don't fire family," Royal said in anger.

"You tell her that. She will be glad to know. She wants to tell Marilynn to shut her mouth and get out of her kitchen. If she is sure you won't fire her, then she might not care if it causes a little bit of trouble. It must be hard to have that woman come into the kitchen to tell poor Maria she is not doing right what she does so well."

"And Marilynn does just that. I never noticed just how much she acts as if she owns this place. It hit me squarely when we arrived to find her here. It's also making things awkward."

"Awkward?"

"Yes. I started to wonder about her and everybody's expectations when we started keeping company."

"Wonder what?" she asked in a low voice as her hands began to move over his lean body.

"Whether I was getting pushed into a corner that I was going to wish I'd have the sense to get out of." He tightened his hold on her. "But I don't want to talk about that now."

"No? What do you want to talk about?"

"About how you're going to ravish me until I collapse from exhaustion."

As her fingers slid up his thigh to trail tantalizingly over his groin, she murmured, "I do not think I know how to ravish a man."

"Well, you just give it a try and I'll let you know how you're doing."

At first Antonie played the game warily, shy and unsure about her ability to be the one in full control of their lovemaking. The other times she had been aggressive were when their emotions had run high. His approval and evident delight erased that uncertainty. She grew daring, trying things she had imagined in the midst of her erotic daydreams. When he tried to equalize their positions, she deterred him. She found her passion stirred more than sufficiently by making love to him. For as long as she could, she held them both at the razor's edge of completion. As she collapsed in his arms, she wondered if he could possibly feel more sated and wrung out than she did.

It was a long time before Royal regained his power of speech. He had never known a passion like what he had found with her. Even his toes tingled, he thought, a slow grin forming on his lips. She was the best he had ever known and he became surer each time he held her that he would be the greatest of fools if he let her go.

"Not bad," he said, drawing out each word.

Antoine lifted her head from its comfortable resting place on his chest to frown at him. "Only not bad?"

"Well, let's put it this way, in a couple of weeks you can try again."

"A couple of weeks?"

"Yes, I oughta be recovered enough to live through it by then."

Laughing gently, she curled up in his arms, getting comfortable, ready to fall asleep. "You should be more careful about making such challenges, *mi vida*."

"Ah, I see. Well, it was a hard ride here and the next few days will be busy, eh?"

"Very busy. A wedding takes a lot of planning."

When a few minutes had passed and he said nothing else, Antonie lifted her head to look at him. She smiled softly when she saw that he had fallen asleep. Sympathy filled her as she saw how the worry lines did not fully leave his face even when it was relaxed in sleep. Instead of coming home from the hell of the war to find peace, he had come home to another fight. She knew it was no longer her promise to Juan that drove her to help Royal see an end to the troubles that plagued him.

That end would have to come soon, she thought wryly, as the baby in her womb moved. Soon the child would force her to step back from the battle, could even force her to leave. She was rather surprised that Royal had not suspected her condition but he could well be as ignorant as she had been. He was also weighted down with so many troubles that he had no time to notice that anything lurked on the horizon. He had been unaware of the truth about Patricia and Oro and he could easily be blinded to the signs that indicated he would soon be a father.

She sighed and settled herself comfortably again, closing her eyes. A decision was going to have to be made soon. Maria had said that the child would soon round her belly and even a distracted Royal would notice that. Antoine did not want her few choices to be decided by the confrontation that would result if Royal did guess.

Of course the perfect solution would be Royal's deciding he wanted her for a wife before he knew she carried his child but Antoine knew that little in life was perfect. In what little time remained, she had to get a clear idea of how Royal felt about her. If all he felt for her was a fever of the body and a sense of duty, she would return to Mexico.

Chapter Eighteen

Smiling at her own foolishness, Antonie wiped her tears away and handed Maria her handkerchief for Maria had already soaked her own. Antonie suspected that her pregnancy had a little to do with her easy tears. Maria had warned her about that aspect of her condition. Nevertheless, she knew that the wedding also prompted tears. As she had watched Oro and Patricia exchange their vows, she had been deeply touched, joy for the couple bringing tears to her eyes.

There was some envy too, she admitted reluctantly, not overly proud of the feeling. She wanted what Oro and Patricia had found but it remained out of her reach. Though Royal's words could be sweet and inflaming, he did not speak of love or of a future for them, only of passion. Nothing he had said spoke of his love and commitment to her.

Tomás disrupted her dismal thoughts by draping himself on a tearful Maria and wailing about having lost his brother. For a moment, she and Maria listened to his nonsense, then, exchanging glances, they simultaneously cuffed him.

"Such sympathy," he grumbled as he rubbed his abused ears but then he grinned. "Stopped your tears though, eh?"

"They are going to have such pretty babies," Maria said with a sigh.

"Perhaps we ought to let them have their wedding night before we start counting the brood," Tomás added, chuckling.

"You are a naughty boy," Maria scolded, giggling when he gracefully eluded her swat at him.

"Naughty? I am goodness itself, eh? I even took Oro aside for a man to man talk."

"Who did you ask to be the man?"

"Tony, how you wound me," Tomás said in an injured tone.

"Hah. I think I should worry about what ideas you gave Oro and warn Patricia."

"I but gave him the benefit of my great experience and my skill."

"He, of course, listened with rapt attention," Antonie said with sarcasm.

"As one should when a master speaks."

"Your vanity is beyond belief."

He laughed, then rubbed his hands together in a gesture of eager anticipation. "Ah, they stop talking to the preacher. Now the drinking will begin."

"Are you planning on getting drunk again?" Antonie asked.

"Sí. It is a custom to get drunk at a wedding," he announced airily even as he started toward the punch bowl.

"Just remember that I will not have Oro to help me

put you to bed."

"Just leave me where I fall, *chica*. I will forgive you."

"How gallant," she muttered then laughed along with Maria.

Antonie started toward Royal, hesitating only briefly when she saw Marilynn sidle up to him. She decided she no longer wanted to retreat every time that woman was around. All things considered, it was time to do a little fighting for Royal. If Marilynn was no longer around, Antonie knew she would find it a little easier to judge exactly where she stood with Royal."

"I think this was a mistake, Royal," Marilynn said quietly.

"Oh? I don't think so," he replied as he took Antonie's hand, almost smiling at the anger that glinted in her eyes at Marilynn's words.

"This marriage will be the ruin of Patricia. You must see that."

"Love cannot ruin a person," Antonie said quietly.

"I am sure it is only an infatuation. If you had held firm, Royal, it would have passed."

"You don't know what you're talking about, Marilynn," Royal said coolly.

"Really? Many a woman has felt a slight fascination with a man not of her class or her blood. Patricia is simply too young, too naive, to differentiate between fascination and love. You should have given her more guidance in this."

"Marilynn, I invited you to a wedding not to lecture me on what you feel is my failing in raising Patricia."

"I'm just saying what a lot of others are or will be. Really, Royal, he's a half-breed and not even half-white."

"His mother was the half-breed, *Señorita* Collins," Antonie said coldly. "Be correct in your insults."

"She's all done making insults, aren't you, Marilynn," Royal said, a cool threat hidden in his voice, and he smiled crookedly when she strode away. "I wonder if that'll shut her up."

"Do not count on it, *amigo*. She feels she is right and that you are foolishly blind."

"So do a lot of folks but not as many as I'd feared," he murmured as he glanced at the guests.

"Do they accept or do they come to call you fool like Marilynn?"

"No, they've accepted the marriage. I've talked to most of them. Some are uneasy about it but they figure we know what we're doing. He's Patricia's choice and we've clearly approved it and that's good enough for them."

"And it is not their daughter or their sister," she murmured, smiling faintly.

Royal laughed. "I wouldn't be at all surprised if that's in their minds. They probably wish I had a sister for Tomás."

"*Sí*. They keep a close eye on their *niñas*. Do not worry. Tomás promised to behave."

"Kind of him."

"It was a great sacrifice but he was willing to make it for Oro and," she grinned, "after I convinced him that it would be very good for his health, eh?"

"I don't think I'll ask how you did that."

"It might be best, *querido*."

Antonie smiled politely when Mr. Paul Greaves approached them. He was a short rotund man with a kind nature and his small family was much like him.

She did not know him well but instinct told her he was easy to like.

"A fine looking couple," Mr. Greaves said sincerely. "Pattie looks real happy. Yup, real happy indeed."

"She is, Paul. It won't be easy but," Royal shrugged, "what is?"

"Not much, son. Are they going to live on her land? That's the section at the north end of your place, right?"

"That's right. Yes, they're going to live there. Probably be settled there by this time next year if all goes well."

"That's good. It's too empty out that way. Be sure to let me know when it's time for the building, that'll be needed."

"I will. Thanks, Paul."

"No thanks needed. Now, where'd that wife of mine go?" he muttered as he wandered off.

"A nice man."

"Yes, they don't come much nicer. He lives the Golden Rule. Want a drink?" Royal asked.

She nodded and watched him disappear into the knot of people around the punch bowl. When she saw two young girls and a young man talking and laughing with Patricia and Oro it made her feel good. They would have friends and that would further strengthen them against the ones who could not look past their prejudices.

As if that thought had needed physical embodiment, Marilynn approached her. When Antonie saw that Royal was nowhere near returning to her side, she realized that Marilynn intended to have a private conversation with her. Antonie braced herself for what she knew would be a trying confrontation. She was

254

determined not to cause a scene at Oro's wedding.

"I suppose you think this will help you get your hooks into Royal."

"My hooks?"

"It does you no good to play the fool, *señorita*." Marilynn sneered the word, making it an insult. "You think this marriage will get you closer to being mistress here. It won't work. If this marriage has given you an advantage, it won't last long. I doubt that fool halfbreed will live out the year."

"You threaten him, *Señorita* Collins?"

"I state a fact. Oh, people might've looked the other way if it was just some girl lowering herself to marry a breed but she's toting a large piece of good land in her dowry. People don't want his sort holding such good land and breeding a family on it. They'll soon dispossess him, shall we say."

"You'd best hope it does not happen, *señorita*. Shall we say," Antonie sneered, "your life depends upon it."

"Mine? I told you I don't need to do a thing."

"*Sí*, but I think I will forget that. I think I will only remember that you told me what would happen. Then I will think about the Bible. It says an eye for an eye, eh?"

"Something happening to Oro would give you a good excuse for getting rid of me, wouldn't it. You could say it was justice but it would simply be getting rid of the competition."

"I hadn't noticed you giving me any."

"Well, I certainly would not lower myself to offer Royal my body as freely as you do."

"Ah, *sí*, that is probably for the best. How embarrassing for you when he turns you down."

"Would he? Maybe we should put that to the test."

255

"Go right ahead."

"I just might."

Antonie slowly expelled her breath when Marilynn walked away. She was confident that she had held her own during the verbal duel but it troubled her. Her dare to Marilynn had been pure bravado, perhaps even recklessness. Antonie prayed that the woman did not take her up on it. She did not want her situation with Royal resolved by his bedding Marilynn.

"What was that all about?" Royal asked as he reached Antonie and handed her a drink.

"What?"

"Marilynn was talking to you and it didn't look like friendly chit-chat."

"It was about hooks and land."

Before a puzzled Royal could press for a clearer explanation, he was distracted by one of the guests. Only half-listening to the man, Royal watched Antonie start to dance with Tomás. He had the feeling that Marilynn had given Antonie a hard time and had probably been doing so for quite a while but he doubted he would be able to get Antonie to admit it. It was the sort of thing Antonie would feel was her problem and her problem alone.

As he danced with Marilynn, Royal wondered if he should say something but decided that it was neither the time nor the place. He ruefully admitted that he dreaded a confrontation with Marilynn. When she expressed a need for some fresh air, claiming a faintness due to the heat, he reluctantly escorted her outside. He was startled into immobility when she suddenly flung herself into his arms and kissed him with none of the cool delicacy she had always maintained in the past. Finally, shaking free of his shock, he disengaged himself from her hold with more haste than tact.

"I thought you were dizzy."

"Oh, Royal, how can you treat me so? Flaunting that woman in front of me," Marilynn said tearfully as she put her arms around his waist and pressed her body against him.

Royal was nonplussed that he felt no desire for her, only a somewhat frantic need to get away. He was also a little shocked. Marilynn was moving against him with a subtle seductiveness that was totally at odds with the virginal pose she had always maintained. Suspicions began to seep through his mind as he again disentangled himself from her embrace.

"What's between Antonie and me is none of your concern."

"None of my concern? How can you say that? Oh, it's my fault, I suppose. A man has needs and I ignored yours, but I've been raised to believe that a lady suppresses such needs until she is married. I did not mean for it to drive you into the arms of another woman."

"I wasn't driven." He could not shake the feeling that he was watching a very good performance.

"Lured then. The fault is mine but I am willing to correct that error."

Even as she reached for him and he readied himself to elude her, Cole strode up to them. "The newlyweds are getting itchy."

"Delicately put," Royal said, stepping away from Marilynn and closer to Cole, ignoring his brother's amused glance.

"We better tell them what we planned for them," Cole said.

"Hell, yes. Let's get going." He was relieved when Cole neatly cut off Marilynn's attempt to put her arm through Royal's.

"What have you got planned?" Marilynn asked, irritation in her voice as Cole escorted her inside.

"You'll see," Royal answered a little distractedly as he spotted Antonie and headed straight for her, outdistancing Cole and Marilynn.

Antonie had seen Marilynn and Royal leave the room. Every moment they were gone felt like an hour to her. All she could think of was how she had challenged Marilynn and wondered if she had taken up the challenge. She waited, terrified that, once Marilynn offered Royal more than passionless kisses, he would find that he no longer needed her. Anger also ate at her, an anger caused by his desertion before so many witnesses.

Those feelings were only eased slightly when he returned, with Cole escorting Marilynn. But Antonie quickly reasoned that Cole might have simply interrupted things. Yet the harried look on Royal's face soothed her. It was hardly the look of a man impassioned or contemplating something enjoyable. She tensed when he reached her and linked her arm through his, holding her close to his side.

"You're staying right here all night," he hissed.

"What?" Antonie croaked and watched him glance at Marilynn as if she were some frightful thing ready to spring at him.

"I'll explain later. Just stay close."

"You mean like protection?"

"God, yes. Come on. Cole said he thinks it's time to spring our little surprise on the newlyweds."

Clearly showing their confusion, Oro and Patricia

allowed themselves to be urged outside where a beribboned buggy awaited them. A grinning Maria put a food basket and a small bag of clothes in the buggy. The guests piled into wagons or on their horses and Antonie found herself mounted in front of Royal as he led the gay entourage.

The group stopped before a small hut that served as a way station for cowboys on the range. It was freshly painted with flowers strewn on the doorstep. A laughing Oro carried a blushing Patricia over the threshold to the crowd's cheer. Antonie helped Maria carry in the bags and smiled as she glanced around. She had known what was planned but had had little to do with the surprise as she had kept Patricia too busy to find out about it.

Everything had been scrubbed clean. Pretty curtains decorated the windows and a lacy cloth covered the table where Antonie set the basket of food. A big, soft bed dominated the room and caused Patricia to blush. Laughing quietly, she kissed Oro, then Patricia and helped Maria clear the cabin of teasing guests, closing the door after them.

When Royal swung her up onto the saddle and mounted behind her, she looked around at the guests starting back to the house and said quietly, "There is no need of this. Marilynn's gone."

"Gone?" Royal looked around and saw that the Collinses' buggy was missing. "Odd."

"Perhaps they thought that celebrating the bedding was more tolerance than they could bear," Antonie said absently, smiling as she glanced back at the hut and saw that the light in the windows had already dimmed. "Why the dog?" she asked when she saw *El Magnifico's* father tied by the step.

"Protection."

Tensing as she suddenly realized how isolated Patricia and Oro would be, she asked, "You think this is a good idea?"

"Maybe not, but a couple's wedding night ought to be private."

"And safe."

"Yes, I know. There's a double guard set out."

"I do not see them," Antonie said with worry lacing her voice.

"Neither will Oro, but they are there. It was a hard thing to decide on. I just thought they ought to have something a little special, something more than a room at the house. This was a compromise. Privacy but a well guarded one. Chance is a good watchdog and I've put some of my best men on watch. If there is trouble, it will be quickly handled. Cole put enough guns and ammunition in the place to hold off an army."

He smiled ruefully as they reached the house. Helping Antonie dismount, he watched his guests pour back inside and he and Antonie followed them in. "I think it will be a while before the celebrating ends."

"You do not like celebrating?"

"I don't mind it, but there's something else I've got a hankering for."

Her face reddened as she read the look in his eyes then laughed. "Jealous of Oro and Patricia, eh?"

"Damn right."

When a man approached them and began to talk about the trail drive, eager for information, Antonie left Royal's side. She walked over to where Tomás and Jed Thayer leaned against a wall. One look told her

260

that they probably needed that wall to support them. She wondered how they had made it out of the honeymoon cabin and back without falling out of their saddles.

"I hope you two are not part of the night guard."

"Nope," Jed answered. "Out last night and Royal said Tomás ought to be free to celebrate well."

"He has done that all right," Antonie said, amused.

Draping an arm around her shoulders, Tomás said, "I will need to find someone else to help you put me to bed."

"Maybe you could just stop celebrating so well."

"No, no, *chica*. Do you ask me to be a teeter-totter?"

Laughing along with Jed, she said, "You mean a teetotaller, *amigo*."

"Strange language, this English."

"Even stranger when you speak it," she added.

Seeing the way she kept looking out the window, Tomás said, "They will be all right, little one."

"*Sí.* They probably will be. They are guarded and they have shelter. It is just," she sighed and shook her head, "well, every step we take is known and now we have set two of our own out there almost alone."

Tomás nodded. "There is a danger. We cannot ignore that. Ah, but, *chica*, it is their first night together. It is her first night, eh?" he said gently. "Something special was needed. This was a compromise. They are not safely here but they are not all alone. Come, stop worrying and enjoy." He grinned rakishly. "Oro is." He laughed when she gave him a punitive nudge.

It was past midnight when Royal finally ushered out the last of his guests. Antonie was a little surprised that none of them had accepted his offer of a

261

bed for the night. She wondered if, with all Royal's troubles, the people felt that they were as safe, perhaps even safer, traveling the dark roads as they would be at his ranch.

Glancing up the stairs, she grinned. Cole and Justin almost had Tomás to the top of the stairs. A crooked smile curved her mouth for she understood some of the feelings which drove him to such overindulgence. He was happy for Oro but he was also faced with a drastic change in what had been a unique brotherly relationship. Tomás was sensible enough to know that Oro and he would always be tied in a way few brothers could be, but now Patricia shared Oro's life.

"Alone at last," Royal said as he pulled her into his arms and kissed her. "You're looking very serious." With his arm around her shoulders, he urged her up the stairs.

"I was just thinking of how Tomás must feel."

"A little jealous maybe."

"*Sí*. A little."

"I've heard that twins can be close, closer than siblings usually are."

"Tomás and Oro are. They share feelings, thoughts too. Each has always been the most important person in the other's life."

"I think you're pretty important to them."

"Ah, *sí*, but not in the same way." She looked at him and smiled teasingly as he followed her into her room. "You still need guarding, *querido?*"

"Don't laugh. I wasn't joking."

"No?" Antonie asked, smiling.

"No. I'll have you know I was almost raped, woman."

262

Even though there was a humorous note in his voice, Antonie could read panic in his eyes. She bit her lip but it did no good. Bursting out laughing, she fell onto the bed. She knew some of her amusement stemmed from a release from the fear that he might be willing to accept Marilynn's overtures. It was, however, also simply funny to think that such a lean, virile man could be so upset by a beautiful woman's advances.

"Think it's funny, do you?"

Watching him advance toward her, she nodded. "*Sí*. Very funny. I thought you liked to be ravished."

"Only when I ask for it," he said as he sat down and tugged off his boots.

"I did not hear you cry out in alarm."

"It was a close thing," he said as he started to remove her shoes and stockings. "Is that what you'd do?"

"I do not know. I have never been ravished."

"Maybe we should try it and see."

Reaching up to unbutton his shirt, she purred, "What a good idea. How do you keep having such good ideas?"

"Inspiration," he murmured against her mouth and proceeded, with her full cooperation, to prove that she did indeed cry out while being ravished, but not in alarm.

After they had fallen into a deep sleep, the sound of someone crashing into her room made Antonie wake up instantly, her hand reaching for her gun. She recognized Tomás immediately but her eyes widened in surprise as a cursing Royal lit the lamp by the bed. Tomás was wild-eyed yet looked fairly sober. He was also stark naked.

"We must go to Oro. Now."

"What is it, Tomás?"

"There's trouble, *chica*. Bad trouble."

Even as Royal rose and pulled on his pants, Antonie slid out of bed to yank on her camisole and pantaloons. She could not be sure how much of Tomás's feeling was a true sixth sense and how much was some panicky delusion brought on by too much drink. Since she had been worried about Oro and Patricia when they had left the couple, she did not fully trust her own judgment.

"Tomás, you had a lot to drink tonight," Royal said carefully.

"*Sí*. Too much. But I am cold sober now."

"Are you sure?" Antonie asked quietly. "You forgot to put your clothes on."

"What matter is that?" He grasped Antonie by the shoulders. "Oro is in trouble. I feel it. He is in trouble and he is hurt." He gave her a little shake. "I can feel it and I saw it in my head. We must go."

"Maybe it was just a bad dream."

"I said that to myself but it is no good."

"Look, there's men out there. If there was trouble, they'd tell us."

Even as he spoke the words, a commotion from downstairs froze Royal in place. He saw that it had the same effect on the others. Antonie felt a tremor go through Tomás and put a comforting hand on his arm. She knew he had had such feelings before, was more prone to them than Oro, but she was finding it hard to believe him. Inwardly grimacing, she admitted that she did not want to believe him. For all her worrying she did not want to think that Oro's and Patricia's wedding night could end in tragedy. She tensed as footsteps came pounding toward their room and suddenly Cole appeared in the doorway. He spared only one brief startled look at Tomás.

"There's someone attacking the cabin."

Chapter Nineteen

"Wait here," Royal ordered Antonie when they came within earshot of the battle. "You stay here with Justin."

"But, Royal," Antonie began to protest only to have her words stopped by a brief hard kiss.

"Please, for my own peace of mind. Stay back here."

There was something in his voice that held her in place despite her concern for Oro. He meant it when he spoke of his need for peace of mind. She knew he had no doubts about her ability to handle herself in times of danger but he would still worry about her. Nodding, she watched him smile fleetingly then ride off with the others. She was glad her wait was brief for, only a few moments later, Cole signaled that all was safe.

The moonlight illuminated the casualties which appeared to have been all on the attackers' side. As Antonie dismounted at the cabin, she felt her blood chill. The men standing around looked grim. When she stepped inside and saw that Patricia and Oro were

266

not dead, that Oro was only wounded, she felt weak with relief. Then she felt concern for the wound in Oro's leg and for the terrified Patricia. She went to Patricia and enfolded the girl in a comforting hug.

"Justin, you go for the doctor," Royal ordered and the young man quickly obeyed.

"I told you, Tony," Tomás said quietly. "I felt it."

"Sí, you did, and I should not have doubted."

"However," Royal added, "your words'll carry more weight if you remember to put your pants on next time."

Royal's gentle humor helped ease the tension. Antonie smiled faintly and Patricia gave a watery giggle.

"Lucky you saw them when you did," Royal said as he and Tomás carried Oro out to the buggy.

"Luck had nothing to do with it. The dog was growling and I had to piss," Oro ground out.

"I want to ride with Oro," Patricia protested as Antonie started to lead her to Royal's horse.

"Royal and Tomás will take the buggy. You are too upset to drive it well and to watch that Oro does not slip out if he faints."

Realizing that mentioning Oro's welfare was the way to keep Patricia in hand, Antonie used that ploy again when they arrived at the house. Antonie persuaded Patricia to sit in the parlor and drink a brandy instead of rushing upstairs to hover over Oro. When the doctor arrived shortly after, Antonie was relieved. Patricia needed the reassurance that Oro was getting quick competent care. So did she and she waited as tensely as Patricia for the doctor's prognosis.

"Hell of a thing to happen to a man on his wedding night," Doctor Fowler said as he strode into the parlor, the Bancrofts at his heels, Royal moving quickly to get the doctor a drink.

"Will he be all right?" Patricia asked shakily.

"He will be. Just be sure he takes it easy on that leg. It's a bad wound, no mistake about it, but he'll live. I can't promise he won't have a limp but, if he's real careful, he might not."

"I'll go sit with him."

"If you could wait just a minute, Pattie. The doctor gave him something. He's sleeping and Tomás is with him. I want you to tell me what happened."

Antonie, with Maria's help, tried to keep Patricia's impatience curbed as the doctor gave his instructions for Oro's care while savoring his drink. Despite the lateness of the hour, the doctor had come quickly and Antonie was grateful. She was also as happy as Patricia seemed to be when he left.

"I'm sorry, Pattie. I know you want to go sit with Oro," Royal apologized as he returned from showing the doctor out.

"It's all right, Royal."

"Look, *chica*, maybe you should take a potion too. Get some rest," Antonie suggested.

Patricia shook her head. "No. I don't think even a potion would help me sleep tonight. I'd rather go sit with Oro."

"Can you tell me anything that happened? Did you see anyone?"

"Not really, Royal. I woke up when the shooting started. Oro shoved Chance into the house then dragged himself in. He was wounded outside the door. He tried to get me to go under the bed but I wouldn't. When we started to fight back they tried to burn us out. That's when you arrived. Did Tomás really feel something warn him?"

"*Sí*. He burst into our room and tried to convince Royal and me to go with him to check on you. We thought he was still drunk, eh? Especially since he was naked. Only a few minutes later we got word of the attack."

"They knew we were there. They had come to kill us."

"Are you sure of that, Pattie?"

"Yes, I am, Royal. One of them even called to Oro."

"What did he say?" Antonie asked.

Blushing deeply, Patricia replied, "He said, well, something about hoping Oro had enjoyed his Anglo bride for it would be for the last time. They knew about the wedding and that's strange."

"I reckon it's been talked about a lot around here," Cole said.

"Perhaps. Oh, there was one other thing. Someone watched. From the rise. There was a lone horseman there until just before you came."

"The one who hired them?" Antonie looked at Royal.

"Most likely. You didn't see anything recognizable about the horseman?"

"No, Royal. I'm sorry. He was too far away and in the shadows."

"It's all right. If nothing else, at least we know it was the same ones we've been fighting all along. Go on up to Oro, honey." He gave Patricia a quick kiss and frowned as he watched her leave. "It seems our surprise was no surprise and nearly killed them."

"No. It was a surprise. It should have been safe because one cannot plan around surprises."

Royal nodded slowly. "You're right, Antonie. This

269

was a hastily put together attack."

"Do you think it was people who did not like the marriage?"

"For a little while, I did, darlin'."

"But not now?" Antonie asked.

"Nope. For one thing, our people wouldn't call Pattie an Anglo."

"And they wouldn't call Oro by name. Not that name anyway," Cole added.

"No. It would have been 'beaneater' or 'halfbreed,' " Antonie agreed tiredly, fighting a yawn.

Smiling faintly, Royal helped her stand and urged her toward the door. "Get some sleep, honey." He kissed her briefly. "Oro's going to need a lot of care. I'll be along soon."

"Think our enemies are getting a little desperate?" Cole asked as soon as Antonie had gone.

"This did seem a little rash," Justin agreed. "If they knew about the wedding and the cabin they must've known about the extra guard. Hell, according to Henry, they just missed running into him and Tom."

"Whoever planned this was in a hurry and didn't wait to get all the information."

"Do you have any idea, Royal?"

"Some, but I want to think about it some more, Cole."

"Well, if you don't mind, I'll leave you to do that thinking alone," Cole said as he stood up. "I'm dog tired."

"Me too, I'm afraid. Don't need me for anything, do you?" Justin asked.

"No, Justin. Go on to bed, you two." He smiled at Maria. "You too, woman. Pattie'll need you in the next few days."

Pausing as she followed Cole and Justin out of the room, Maria said quietly, "It was one of the guests."

"Yes, I'm afraid it was. Well, that narrows it some."

"Someone who left early, eh?"

"Early enough to contact their hired guns and mount an attack and too early to know that the cabin was guarded. I should've kept a closer watch on my guests' comings and goings."

"I will think on it."

"Thanks, Maria. Go on. Off to bed. Oh, and by the way, you have my full permission to yell at Marilynn and boot her out of your kitchen." He smiled when she flushed, then giggled and hurried away.

Sighing wearily, he went to sit down. He still had to wait for Tom to report in. Royal doubted that the sheriff would find out anything except that the dead men were *banditti* but there was always that chance. He needed some hard proof.

Sipping his brandy, he tried to push away the suspicion that was rapidly gaining strength. He did not want to face the truth that was fighting to be accepted. It would make him look like a complete fool and he was certainly beginning to feel like one.

"Marilynn," he hissed, making the name sound like a curse.

Forcing his anger aside, he tried to examine the proof he did have. It was all circumstantial but it fell into place too neatly to be ignored. If he had only once thought of the Collinses it would have been clear a lot earlier.

The Collinses lived right next to him. If they got his ranch they would have the biggest stretch of land in the county. They would also have control over most of

271

the water in the area. Even they had to turn to his land when things got a little dry. They would also be the greatest power in the area, controlling almost everyone, if they had a mind to. It was an arrangement that could tempt many a man, and that was enough motive for mayhem and murder. It had provided one often enough.

Marilynn might be the informant, the insider who gathered all the needed information. She had been around and privy to all sorts of information for a long time. Juan had said it was someone close to him and Marilynn was the closest of all their friends. She had known when his parents would be traveling to San Antonio. She had known about Pattie's planned trip, even to the number of men riding with her and Justin and the route taken. Marilynn had known about the cattle drive when it was only an idea, then when it was definitely planned and even his route, for he had wanted someone at home to be able to reach him if there was trouble.

He shook his head. All these facts made a strong case but he had not seen it, not until tonight. Marilynn's attempt to seduce him was a small part. She had seen her place in his life, vital to the plan, slipping away. The incident in the garden had been a desperate attempt to reestablish her intimate role with him. He had sensed that she had been acting a part. The really incriminating thing was that she and her father had left immediately after the surprise for Oro and Patricia had been revealed. They had left in plenty of time to contact their hired guns and arrange the attack. In fact, they were really the only ones who could have.

It was frustrating for, while everything pointed

toward Marilynn and her father, he had not one piece of evidence. He was not sure there would be any to be had. At least one of the hired men had to know who hired them. Certainly Raoul had, but so far none caught alive had had that information. Without proof he had nothing but suspicions and they were worth nothing against the Collinses.

Yet he still felt an inkling of doubt. He knew that it stemmed from not wanting to see what a fool he had been but, for whatever the reason, the doubt was there. There had to be a way to erase even that doubt or prove his suspicions were wrong.

"Sir?"

Shaking free of his thoughts, Royal waved Tom into the room. "Want a drink?"

"Won't say no."

"Help yourself. I'm too damned tired to play host," Royal said waving toward the brandy bottle.

"Had enough of it, huh?" Tom asked with a laugh as he poured himself a small brandy.

"For a few years anyway."

"Didn't find a thing, I'm afraid, boss."

"I'm not surprised, although I had hoped to be."

"Well, the sheriff thinks he has seen one of the men in the saloon and he's going to ask around. Doesn't promise anything though," Tom said tiredly.

"No. He'll probably only find out that he was right, that he had seen the man there."

"Yes, the people in the saloons don't much care who you are or about much else so long as you pay and don't cause any trouble. Still, I got a feeling it can't go on much longer."

"What makes you say that?" Royal asked, surprised.

"Tonight. It was rash. Not thought out at all. A

stupid move really. The kind that'll give them away."

"Or make them sit back, look close and be even more careful."

Tom sighed and set down his empty glass. "Or that. Sorry, I wish I could've brought you something, boss."

"You did your best, Tom. Get some sleep. The morning's all yours to do what you want."

"Thanks, boss." Tom paused in the doorway. "Oro's still all right?"

"Doc said he'll live and, if he's real careful, he might not limp either."

"That's good. He's a good man. 'Night, boss."

" 'Night, Tom."

As soon as Tom had gone, Royal indulged in a long bout of swearing. It left him feeling only somewhat better. He was still left with only a pile of suspicions and no proof. There was also a vast unorganized collection of half formed ideas about how to finalize those wavering suspicions and some of those were almost laughably wild.

Finishing off another brandy, he decided he was too tired and probably too drunk to think straight. If there was a solution he would have to look for it another day. Checking the house for any smoldering fires and that everything was secured, he decided to go to bed.

Quietly, he entered the room where Oro had been put. Patricia barely glanced at him, her gaze fixed on the restlessly sleeping Oro. Moving next to the bed, Royal studied his new brother-in-law and was a little surprised at how young he was. Stripped of all his *bandito* paraphernalia, most of his hardness had disappeared but Royal suspected that it was still there. The life Oro had led made sure of that. Royal felt certain

274

that, in some ways, Oro was older than him.

His eyes moved to Patricia. Inwardly he laughed when he found himself trying to see some difference in her. All he could see was a young woman who was worried sick about her husband and hating to see his pain.

"Well, at least you'll never forget your anniversary."

Patricia looked at him in shock then laughed. "What a terrible thing to say."

"I know but, well, you looked so lost. I just wanted to take that look away."

"You did. I do feel a little lost. I was there with Oro feeling warm and happy, thinking it was the first night of the rest of our lives together and suddenly everything changed horribly. It was as if God had thought I had forgotten about such things as mortality and wanted to remind me. I had gone to sleep," she blushed, "well, you know, and woke up to Oro's cursing and yelling at me to get down, his leg bleeding so badly and bullets flying everywhere. I'm surprised I didn't faint."

"You're stronger than that, Pattie."

"Yes, I guess I am. Funny, it wasn't until it was all over that I fell apart."

"That's when it doesn't matter."

"Antonie lied to me," Patricia said with a slight edge in her voice.

"What?"

"That day at the rocks. I am not a bad shot. I did kill that man."

"She was trying to save your feelings," Royal said gently.

"I know. I took it hard that day but this time it wasn't so bad. Oh, it's not easy, even though they

275

were trying to kill us, but some of the horror was gone. Maybe it's because Oro was there bleeding, and that kept in my head clear. I knew that this was a fight for our lives." She smiled faintly. "But you know all that. You've been through it."

"Sadly, yes. Look, Pattie, don't wear yourself out sitting here. If you feel tired, get some sleep. There's plenty of us to take a turn and he'll need you strong."

"I know. Just tonight. Go to bed, Royal. I'll be fine. You need your sleep too."

After giving her a brief kiss, he left. Standing in the hall, he wondered for a moment which bed he should crawl into. He ached with weariness and knew he would not be making love to Antonie tonight. They still maintained separate rooms even though they never slept apart. He knew he should probably go to his own bed rather than disturb her for she was tired too and needed her rest. Even as he thought that, he moved toward Antonie's door, his need to hold her overcoming his good intentions.

Slipping quietly into Antonie's room, he glanced at the bed and smiled. The arrangement of the pillows and the way she had fallen asleep partially sitting up told him that she had tried to wait up for him. He felt something melt inside him as he stripped off his clothes. He slipped into bed beside her as she murmured his name, turning toward him.

Antonie struggled to awaken as she felt Royal gently pull her into his arms. However, she was simply too exhausted to do more than partially rouse herself. The difficulty she had waking up in the morning evidently affected her any time she slept. Yet, as she snuggled up against Royal's warmth, she continued to try to wake up.

276

"Sorry," she mumbled. "Fell asleep."

Caressing her thick hair, he said, "It's all right. Go back to sleep, Antonie."

"It's late."

"Almost dawn."

"Tom find out anything?"

"Nope." He laughed softly when she yawned widely. "Don't fight it, Antonie. I probably should've gone to my own bed."

She moved closer. "No. Like you here."

"And I like being here. Hell, I need to be here. I certainly did tonight."

Inwardly, Antonie cursed her inability to fully clear her head. She sensed that he was in a mood to be very open with his thoughts and feelings. Here was her chance to get answers to some of the questions that plagued her, the answers that could well decide her future, yet she was no better than half-witted with exhaustion. Well, at least she could listen, she thought crossly, and hope that he continued to ramble on.

Feeling her stir in his arms, he kissed the top of her head. "No. Don't try to wake up. Funny, I'm too tired to make love but I had to hold you. I've gotten too used to you in my bed, I reckon."

"That's bad?"

"No, not bad. I realized it when we were apart. I hated sleeping alone."

"Me too."

"Good," he said, laughter tinting his voice, and he kissed the small fist she sleepily swung at him. "I hate to suffer alone. Did you reach for me, Antonie, reach for me in the night?" he asked gently.

"*Sí*. I reached for you." She felt his chest move with a sigh.

277

"I told myself I was crazy when I did it."

"So did I."

"Funny how you can get used to something like that so quickly. I've slept alone all my life but, after a few weeks with you in my bed, I found that I hated it."

Sensing that he was talking mostly to himself, Antonie said nothing.

"I've never slept with any of the women I've known. Didn't want to. I got what I wanted and left, even if it was in the middle of the damn night. Here I only have to go one door away and I don't even think of doing it."

For a while he silently wondered about that. He had recognized that sudden change in his habits before, but only briefly. It had been made very clear to him when they had been apart and especially tonight, when he did not even want to make love to her yet sought her bed.

He needed her and for far more than to cool the fever she could stir in him. Royal had sensed it growing, had not really fought it but, suddenly, he could see it more clearly than he had before. He was troubled and he felt betrayed so he turned to Antonie, needed to hold her to soothe the sting of betrayal by others he had thought his closest friends. Only a fool would fail to recognize that it was far more than lust behind such a need, especially when lust wasn't even there.

Uncertainties nibbled at him and he hated it. Antonie never spoke of more than the fever they shared. She never hinted that she would stay after his troubles were solved. He sensed that there was more than passion behind her feelings for him but, after being fooled so completely by Marilynn, he no longer completely trusted his instincts. Suddenly, he needed words, not necessarily words of love, but some sort of verbal declaration that it was not only passion and a promise to Juan that kept Antonie by his side.

"Antonie?"

"Mmmm?"

"Is it really your promise to Juan that holds you here? I mean, I know that's why you came here and that you will see all this through to its end but is it only the promise that keeps you helping me?"

She hesitated a moment before replying. Her answer could tell him more than she really wanted him to know. However, she could hear an urgency, a need to know, in his voice and feel the tension in his body. If her answer could ease that, she was willing to risk a little exposure. The very fact that he had asked and wanted an answer gave her a hint that his feelings for her could well run deeper than she had thought.

"No. I fight for you, *querido*. Perhaps my promise to Juan would keep me here if you tried to stop me from helping you but it is you I fight for. It is just convenient that my promise is fullfilled at the same time." She felt his hold on her tighten as she spoke.

"Thank you for that. I really need you to be on my side. I don't like you taking risks but I want you fighting for me. Contrary bastard, aren't I."

"*Sí.* Very contrary." She kissed his chest and sleepily rubbed her cheek against his skin.

"And when the fight is over?"

"When we win?"

"Yes, when we win. Will you return to Mexico?" he asked hesitantly.

"If that is what you want," she said cautiously.

"And if it isn't? If I ask you to stay?"

279

"I will stay." Something in his voice penetrated her sleep-fogged mind and she asked, "The fight will end soon? You have found out something?"

"I have found out nothing but I have some clear suspicions now. Some damn strong ones."

"What are they?" she asked even as she yawned, losing the fight against the sleep that sought to reclaim her.

"No, I won't tell you now. I want to think about it some more."

"Okay."

"Sleep, Antonie."

"*Sí,* I think I must."

He stared down at the woman in his arms even as sleep started to close his eyes too. Every moment that the battle continued, she was at risk. That thought gave him all the incentive he needed work on a plan that would irrevocably prove his suspicions right or wrong.

Chapter Twenty

"If you keep swearing so, Oro, I think God might slap you down," Antonie said teasingly as she helped him walk around his room.

She bit back a laugh which only made him curse more. He did not really need any help in walking now, even though his leg was still stiff and pained him. She was there to see that he did not try to do too much too quickly, to remind him that the doctor had ordered him to go carefully in order to lessen the chance of a permanent limp.

"Sit down, *amigo*, and have a drink."

Easing himself into a chair, Oro sighed. "Now Patricia is not only laden with a poor halfbreed but a cripple."

"Idiot."

Antonie handed him a glass of brandy, then sat down on the bed facing him. He looked tired and she knew that the lingering pain in his leg disturbed his sleep but he refused the potions which could ease that. She also knew that he was pushing himself.

"The doctor said I will have a limp."

"He said you might have a limp. You might not if you stop pushing so hard," Antonie admonished him.

"I am sick of this room. I am sick of being useless."

"I think you are sick from not making love to your wife."

"Do you peep in our keyhole that you can know this?"

"So grouchy you are."

"She complained to you that I am not man enough," Oro demanded.

"And so stupid. No, she did not complain to me. I just guessed."

"One time. One time I have with my bride and now I cannot love her."

"Why not?"

"*Chica*, you are innocent no longer. How can I mount my woman with this leg so bad, eh?"

"So let her mount you," Antonie said quietly and ignored the blush that heated her cheeks.

Oro's eyes widened. "*Por Dios*. Certainly an innocent no longer. Ah, but Patricia is innocent."

"Thought you said you had her once."

"Once. Such things as you speak of must be gently introduced."

"Bah. That is maybe true if all was normal but it is not. I think you baby her but she is your wife," Antonie said.

"*Sí*, my wife."

"Did I hear my name called?" Patricia said cheerfully as she stepped into the room.

"This growling bear wonders if you mean to stay up all night," Antonie answered as she stood up.

"Ah. Well, here I am now. You'd best go to your

growling bear, Antonie."

"Growling, is he?" Antonie asked laughingly as she started out the door.

"Like a bear with a sore paw."

Laughing, Antonie shut the door and started toward her room. She found it easy to be happy. Since the night of the attack on Oro and Patricia, she had felt sure that Royal was growing fond of her. With each passing day, she saw more and more behind his actions and his words than passion. The only shadow on her happiness was Marilynn.

Frowning slightly, Antonie could not stop herself from wondering why Royal allowed that relationship to continue as it had. She knew that the Collinses had long been close friends of the Bancrofts. Marilynn was after far more than friendship however, and acted as if the expected union between the two families was still a strong possibility. What bothered Antonie, what kept her from feeling really confident about her place in Royal's life, was that he did not seem to be doing anything to disabuse Marilynn of that notion. He pulled Marilynn no closer but neither did he push her away.

"What's that dark frown for?" Royal asked as Antonie entered the room.

Her eyes widened when she saw him and she quickly shut the door. He was lying on top of her bed, his arms crossed beneath his head and his feet crossed. One foot idly moved to some inner beat. She decided to ignore the fact that he was stark naked. It was a little hard to ignore the fact that he was also aroused. Struggling to maintain a casual demeanor, she moved to the mirror and began to unbind her hair.

"How's Oro doing?"

"Fine but he does not think so. It troubles him that he might limp but he pushes himself so hard that he could end up with just what he fears. Do you know what he said?"

"Nope. I wasn't there."

She ignored that. "He said that now Patricia was not only laden with a poor half-breed but now a crippled one."

"And what did you say?"

"I called him an idiot."

"Very sympathetic. This isn't working out like I'd planned."

Smiling softly to herself, she began to undress very slowly. "What isn't, *querido?*"

"You were supposed to see me in all my glory and leap upon me in a fit of unbridled lust."

"Ah, unbridled lust, hmm? Exactly what is this unbridled lust?" She let her skirt slide gradually over her hips and then draped it over a chair.

"That's when you hurl yourself into my arms and ravish me."

Removing her petticoats with the same seductive leisure she had her skirt, she asked, "You are all recovered from the last time I ravished you, eh?"

"Completely."

Keeping her back to him, she eased off her pantaloons. Dressed only in her blouse which just skimmed the top of her thighs she put out the lights until only the lamp beside the bed still burned. Standing by the bed, she smiled at Royal who was no longer sprawled so casually on her bed. He lay on his side, propped up on one elbow and stared at her, his eyes dark with desire. Very slowly, she began to untie the drawstring at the neck of her blouse.

"Are you certain of that, *mi vida?*"

"Why don't you try me and see," he challenged her.

"What a good idea," she purred and, with a subtle wiggle, sent her blouse sliding down her body to the floor.

With a moan, Royal yanked her onto the bed. Her soft husky laugh played over his skin like a caress. His little game had become hers but he did not mind at all.

Antonie took him at his word and proceeded to do her best to ravish him. Her hands moved over his body in a tactile expression of appreciation. As her fingers played over his chest, teasing his nipples into hard points, her mouth covered his. She kissed him in every way he had taught her and improvised a few new tricks of her own. His chest was already rising and falling rapidly by the time her lips and tongue eased their way down to suckle his taut nubs.

Royal fought to maintain some control over his soaring passion. He wanted to enjoy her soft kisses and stroking tongue for as long as he could. When she responded to the subtle lifting of his hips and engulfed him slowly with the warm moistness of her mouth, he knew he would not be able to hold on for much longer.

Her own passions racing through her, Antonie was only vaguely aware of his hoarse words but she knew he neared his crest. She straddled him and, as her mouth covered his, she slowly joined their bodies. For a little while she kept the pace slow but when he tightened his grip on her hips and urged her to a fiercer rhythm, she was more than ready to comply. Even as she cried out from the strength of her release, her hips pressing down in reaction to her body's greed for him, she heard him cry out, his hips lifting from the bed as he fought to bury himself within her as deeply as possible.

"Next time I get to ravish you," Royal said, his voice still husky as he reached out to turn off the light.

Snuggling up against his side, she murmured, "Ah, I am not sure, *mi vida*. Ladies are not supposed to like to be ravished."

Wrapping his arms about her, he drawled, "Turnabout is fair play, love."

Her heart skipped a beat at the endearment. Reaching almost desperately for some common sense, she told her heart to behave itself. She would not let herself make judgments based upon endearments whispered by a man sated with passion. After all, she thought wryly, it did not seem right for him to call her Tony at such a time but he had to all her something.

"Well, you'd best let me recover from ravishing you first."

"Mmmmm, I think I could do with some recovering myself."

She felt the baby move with a strength that somewhat startled her. Since her stomach was pressed against Royal, she was terrified that he had felt it too. Although she was far closer to a decision than she had been when she had discovered she carried his child, she was not quite ready to tell him. Suddenly, she wanted just a few more hours before that decision was final. She did not want it forced upon her now when she was not really prepared.

"Antonie?"

"What?" she whispered.

"Don't take this wrong, but I think you're putting

286

on some weight."

"*Sí*, a little," she said weakly, wishing he would move his hand from her waist. "Being your mistress . . ."

"No. Don't call yourself that."

Slowly, she released the breath she had not even realized she had been holding. He had not felt the baby move. Now her comment had diverted him from the somewhat dangerous topic of how her waist was thickening. She had her reprieve but she knew it was a short one. He could not continue to be unaware of such things, especially not when her baby was changing her body with increasing rapidity. If he had noticed the thickening of her waist, she was surprised that he had not noticed that her belly was no longer concave, was in fact rounding out.

"What am I then, *querido?*"

"My lover."

"Lover, mistress, there is a difference?"

"Maybe only in my head but, yes, there is a difference. A mistress is just a fancy name for a whore. She just gets paid better than a saloon girl. She's just something on the side for a married man who's made a bad marriage or one that he just can't be bothered working at. A mistress is a rich man's toy, something to be used and discarded when he tires of her or finds something he thinks is better. That's not how it is with us, Antonie.

"You're not just here to assuage my lust although," he smiled against her hair and that smile was reflected in his voice, "you do give me a pretty powerful case of lust. There's more than that with us," he continued seriously. "I don't just hop into bed with you, ease a need and scurry off to my own bed. I don't even know why we keep separate rooms. It certainly isn't because we're trying to hide our relationship. I haven't tried to from the start."

"I thought you wanted to keep separate rooms."

"Me? What gave you that idea? I don't ever sleep there and I don't use it to slip into in the wee hours of the night in some hypocritical attempt to pretend we aren't lovers. I thought you wanted separate rooms so you could have someplace to go and sulk like you did before the drive."

She lifted her head and saw the teasing look on his face but still said sternly, "I did not sulk. You were being an idiot."

"An idiot, is it?" he demanded but the kiss he gave her was far from punitive. "Enough impudence from you, woman. Tomorrow we'll pick one of these two rooms. Yours or mine."

Settling herself comfortably against his chest again, she said, "Yours. The bed is bigger."

"You want a bigger bed?"

"*Sí*. When you go to sleep, you start to spread out. Soon I have little room."

"Why don't you just nudge me out of the way?"

"You do not nudge good. Just grunt."

"Grunt?"

"*Sí*. Grunt. Sometimes curse."

"I don't think I want to hear any more of this. We'll move to the bigger bed."

"If you are sure. Maybe it is not worth the trouble, eh? Soon I think this fight is ended." She felt his arms tighten around her.

"You said you'd stay."

"*Sí*, if you want me to."

"I do. You're staying."

"*Sí, patrón*," she drawled, then ruined the effect of

her dry sarcasm by yawning.

"Go to sleep, you impudent brat."

"Brat, eh?"

"Brat, but that's all right. I'm finding that I have a real fondness for brats."

"A fondness?"

"A fondness. Get some sleep, Antonie."

She did not want to go to sleep. She wanted to find out a little more about what he meant by a fondness. Unfortunately, she discovered that her body was not interested in anything but rest. Even as she felt Royal press a kiss to the top of her head, she reluctantly gave in to sleep.

Royal closed his eyes. He was aware of a need to clarify his relationship with Antonie but he was not sure of how or in what manner. There was not enough time at the moment to give the situation the careful consideration it deserved. With so much else to be thought about, he had to just let things continue as they had. He knew that was not good enough any longer but he was not certain of the next step to take or in which direction to go.

Antonie had been a virgin. In the normal course of things, he ought to consider marrying her, but things were not normal. She was not just any young woman but the foster-daughter of Juan Ramirez, a *bandito*, a man who had lived and died by the gun. Eleven years of her life had been spent riding with the man, her mind formed by him. It was true that the man had succeeded in keeping her from following in his footsteps but she could still fight as well as any man and better than many and she often revealed that she thought like Juan. She was certainly not the sort of woman he had ever contemplated as his wife.

He grimaced when he recalled the woman he had thought of in that role. The one he had thought a finely bred lady, a woman who would grace his home, was the one who was trying to kill him and his family. Marilynn was coolly using him to enrich herself and her father. She did not care who died in the building of her empire. Even Juan Ramirez would not have stooped to the treachery and callous murder that Marilynn employed.

Shaking his head and feeling sleepy, he decided he had to finish the fight, clear away these weighty problems, before he could think about Antonie and himself. Marilynn was coming by in the morning and then he would put his suspicions to the test. Within a week he could well have the whole messy business cleared up and brought firmly to an end.

The next morning, waking slowly, Antonie realized she was alone. She stared groggily at the clock and was surprised at how late it was. Royal had evidently slipped away quietly and let her sleep. Not liking to waste a day in bed, she quickly got out of bed, noting idly that the dizziness and queasiness she had suffered had apparently left her.

And she went through her morning ablutions, she found that she had come to a decision. She would no longer play the game of wait and see, risking an ill-timed exposure such as she had briefly faced last night. Neither could she wait for the fight for the ranch to be resolved. She simply did not have the time any longer. Today she would tell Royal about the child.

She felt nervous and a little afraid but not as much as she had expected to. The past few weeks had strengthened her confidence. All her concerns were still intact, but she was no longer so overwhelmed by them. They no longer had the power to hold her back.

Royal had been more open with her lately. He really wanted her to stay even when the fight was over. He wanted them to move into one room, erasing the separateness they had kept by having two rooms. It was no declaration of love but Antonie was sure that she meant more to him than a fever in the blood, that his feelings ran deeper than lust. He had said as much last night.

Love was what she wanted from him but she was willing to settle for less, at least for now. Her love for him was so strong it almost frightened her. It also made her willing to compromise. If he offered marriage, she would accept. She would have his name, his passion and his child. If luck was with her, she could make that more, much more. He was a man who believed in the sanctity of marriage and that would be to her advantage.

Squaring her shoulders, she started down the stairs. She wanted the confrontation over now that she had made a decision. However, she was also ravenously hungry. As she tried to decide whether she should have something to eat before she confronted Royal, she became aware of the fact that the downstairs hall was not empty.

Marilynn had arrived. That was not only inconvenient, it was annoying. She greeted Royal with a kiss as always which extremely irritated Antonie. What held her rooted to the spot and made her ready to gasp aloud from the sharp pain that struck her was that this time Royal did not coolly accept the greeting and quickly step away. He kissed Marilynn back with evident hunger and enjoyment.

"Royal?" Marilynn gasped in confusion when he finally released her.

Hoping that he looked appropriately bestotted and not as completely unmoved by the embrace as he was, Royal said, "I have been such a fool, Marilynn." He put his arm around her shoulders. "Come on. We'll go in my study and talk. We can have some privacy there. There's so much I have to say to you."

A little voice told Antonie not to follow them but she ignored it. Today was the day of decision and the brief scene she had just witnessed seemed to tell her that she had made the wrong decision. It was tempting to simply close her eyes to what she had seen, to go to the kitchen and have breakfast as if Marilynn's arrival was only a slight intrusion. Antonie knew that would be the coward's way out. She had to find out just what was going on even if it meant that she would be hurt.

With a stealth learned at Juan's knee, she moved past the study and slipped into the small library. There was a small connecting door between the two rooms and Antonie moved toward it. Silently she eased it open a crack. She had meant to simply listen but to her dismay, she could see the couple clearly. Royal sat on the edge of his desk and pulled Marilynn into a light embrace.

"I don't understand, Royal," Marilynn said. "At the wedding . . ."

"I acted like an idiot. I reckon I was shocked. A lady doesn't express ardor in such a way, doesn't suggest what you did and you are a lady, Marilynn." He caressed her cheek with his fingertips. "That was foolish of me. I suddenly saw how badly I had mistreated you. I'd driven you to act so rashly by carrying on with that girl without a thought for your feelings."

"Oh, Royal, I can forgive you. The little slut bewitched you."

Royal had to fight to keep up his pose of a repentant beau, to suppress the fury that flashed through him when she referred to Antonie so insultingly. "I can't believe I was so stupid as to risk losing the woman I want to spend my life with for the sake of, well I really don't know what."

"Spend your life with? Are you asking me to marry you, Royal?"

"If you'll have me after I've treated you so abysmally."

"Of course I will. I mean, if it is really over between you and that whore?"

"She'll be leaving, Marilynn."

"Yes, yes, I'll marry you. As soon as possible. I've waited for so long."

"I know, darling." He kissed her, struggling to produce some semblance of desire required of a man who had just proposed and been accepted.

Shutting the door and moving away, Antonie felt icy cold, torn between pain and fury. There was no time to give in to either emotion, however. The decision she had made this morning had been that of a fool beguiled by sweet words and passion. She now made one that she believed was valid, was in fact the only one she could make.

Still employing her skillful stealth, she started back up the stairs. She had very little time. Just as with the now discarded decision she had made earlier, this one had to be put into action immediately. It was simply good luck that this decision required far less prepara-

293

tion than the other.

Slowly breaking off the kiss, Royal studied Marilynn. There was a coolness in her eyes that told him she was as unmoved as he was. She was putting on a good act of a woman enflamed by love. If his performance was lacking in any way, he doubted she had noticed as she was too involved in her own role.

"This Saturday. We can be married this Saturday."

"Ah, Marilynn, how I want to, but it's impossible."

"Why?"

"Sunday I ride to San Antonio. I'll have to leave fairly early in the morning." He moved his hands over her hips with skillful seductiveness. "I don't want to cut short our wedding night."

"I could go with you."

He shook his head. "It's business, darling. On Monday I meet with a Pinkerton man."

"What for?"

Taking note of the sudden sharpness in her eyes, he continued blithely, "Well, guns haven't stopped this trouble I've been having so I've decided to try brains. This man is said to be the best at what he does. He'd better be. He's costing enough. He's already written me that his preliminary investigation has proven promising."

"You leave Sunday morning, meet him on Monday and then what?"

"If all goes well, I'll return on Tuesday, probably bringing him with me."

"Well, just be sure you aren't tied up with business too long. Let's make the wedding for the following Saturday."

"All right. You can start making the arrangements."

For as long as he could bear it, he kissed her and

caressed her. It was hard to suppress the urge to rage at her, push her away in disgust, for her duplicity and coldbloodedness.

Pushing her away with a great show of reluctance and, anger giving his voice the appropriate huskiness, he said, "That's enough of that. We're going to follow the rules in this, love. Come on, time for you to go home." Taking her by the hand he led her outside to the veranda.

"I'll come around tomorrow, darling, with the first draft of the guest list."

He murmured all the appropriate responses to her suggestions and farewells but inwardly cursed. If Marilynn was going to play the game to the hilt, it would be hard to keep it a secret. As he went back to his study, he realized that he would have to tell Antonie what was going on. He would rather face a possible argument now than the sort of misunderstandings that could arise later. He would go talk to her in a while but first he wanted a drink to wash the bad taste of Marilynn from his mouth.

Chapter Twenty-one

"Leaving?" Patricia gasped, stopping short in her stroll around the room with Oro.

"Sí. Now. Immediately."

"What about your promise to Juan?" Tomás asked as he got up off the bed.

"I think Juan will understand," Antonie said with conviction.

"What about Royal?" Patricia asked.

"Royal does not matter."

"Doesn't matter? Antonie, how can you say that?"

"Easily. He has just proposed to Marilynn. I must go."

Antonie hastily left Oro's room and went to her own. It did not surprise her when, as she tossed her bags on the bed and started to pack, Patricia and Oro arrived. They would not change her mind but she supposed she ought to give them more information and, perhaps, a clearer explanation. She would be leaving abruptly enough.

"Sit down, Oro. You must rest that leg," she said

calmly.

Even though he sat down, Oro said, "The day has just begun, *chica*. I have not had time to tire yet."

"You really are leaving," Patricia whispered as she watched Antonie continue to pack.

"*Sí*. I am."

"Tomás is packing. He will go with you."

"That is not necessary, Oro."

"He and I think it is. You are sure that Royal has asked Marilynn to marry him?"

"*Sí*, Oro." She sighed and shook her head, "I saw him kiss Marilynn hello as he never had before. So, I followed when he took her into his study. I listened and watched through the door in the library. He asked her."

"I don't believe it," Patricia said, aghast.

"Go down the stairs and look, Patricia. They probably are still making the plans."

"Is it not cowardly to run, *querida?*"

"Maybe, but I do not think so. I had two choices, to stay or to go. This morning I went down stairs thinking I would stay but that has all changed."

"Maybe if you talk to Royal," Patricia began.

"There is no time to play his games. I am with child." Since her audience was struck momentarily speechless, Antonie continued, "If it was just Marilynn, I might stay. My promise to Juan would hold me even when Royal set me aside. I would feel I had made a gamble and I lost. But this," she placed her hand over her stomach, "changes everything. I was foolish and I thought he had chosen me but he chose Marilynn. So, I leave. Even now the baby starts to change my shape. I have no time."

"No, you do not, *chica,*" Oro agreed.

297

"Oro," Patricia gasped, "she should tell Royal."

"Why? He has chosen. There is no place here for Antonie and her child. Do you go back to Mexico?"

"*Sí.* To our village. If the old house cannot be used, there will be other places." When Tomás appeared in the doorway, she kissed Oro then Patricia. "I will let you know where I am.

"*Sí,* you had better, *chica,*" Oro said quietly.

No one paid any attention as she and Tomás saddled their horses. She was glad of Tomás's silence as they rode away from the ranch. When just out of sight of the ranch they met Marilynn, Antonie inwardly cursed. It was as if the woman hads known she was leaving, but the way Marilynn sat on her horse, looking all around made Antonie realize that the woman was already savoring the possession of the land she was surveying.

"Well, I must say, I hadn't realized that Royal would send you off so quickly."

"Royal has not sent me off as you put it, *señorita.*"

"No?" Marilynn glanced at the saddlebags on Antonie's and Tomás's horses. "You always pack so well for a casual ride?"

"Ah, I did not say I was not leaving, only that I was not sent away."

"Back to Mexico, hmmm?"

"*Sí,* by the straightest possible route."

"Yes, you might as well, seeing as you can't have Royal."

"Ah, but, *señorita,* I have already had him. *Adios.*"

Antonie did not look back as she rode away from Marilynn. The flash of fury in the woman's eyes had given her little satisfaction. Her verbal bravado did not alter the fact that she had lost the game.

"Are you sure this is what you want?" Tomás asked quietly.

"It is not what I want. It is what I must do."

"You could fight this *puta* who tries to take your place."

"You have that wrong, Tomás. I took her place but only for a little while."

"I do not understand this. I had thought that the *gringo* had put that one aside, that he wanted you."

"So did I. I let myself be fooled by pretty words and passion. Last night he talked of how we would stop this game of keeping two rooms and have only one. He asked me again if I would stay even if the battle was won. Yet, today?" She shook her head. "Why speak of such things when he planned to ask Marilynn to marry him?"

"I cannot tell you. It makes no sense."

"Nor to me."

"Maybe you should have waited and asked him these things."

"No, although I would like to know the answers. You did not know it all, Tomás. I carry Royal's child."

For a long time Tomás said nothing. The way he kept looking at her almost made Antonie smile. It was clearly a complication he had never thought of. He also looked a little fearful, as if he expected her to give birth immediately.

"If you told Royal of his child I think he would marry you," Tomás said at last.

"I think he would too, but that would be no good."

"You would have a name for your child."

"*Sí*, but that is all I would have. When I got out of bed this morning, I had made a decision. Since we came back from the cattle drive I have known of this

299

child and so I watched Royal, listened carefully to his words. Then I decided to tell him of the baby because I felt that, even though he did not speak of love, there was a chance. The baby might be the reason he married me but we had enough to make a good marriage. Then I found out that we have nothing.

"If I tell him of the child, he would probably marry me but it would be no good. I would have forced him to put aside the woman he wanted. I would have a name for my baby but I would also have Royal's resentment. Soon, I think, it would even kill the fire we share. Then I would only have the name. I will give the baby my name."

"He would be a bastard."

"I know but what can I do, eh?"

"You could marry me."

She stared at him in speechless surprise. "What?" she croaked after a moment.

"Marry me."

"Tomás, I love Royal."

"I know this, but you love me in a way too, as I love you."

"But not as lovers."

"I think we could be lovers. This, I think, we have always known but we did nothing."

Antonie thought about that for a little while. She realized that it was true. It had been easy to see when they had been young, their bodies' needs beginning to awaken. Time had erased it. The feelings she shared with Oro and Tomás were good ones and could easily be extended to include desire. It was a desire that would have to be coaxed, however, if only at first.

"Sí, I can see it. It is not the same though."

"No, I know this. It would not come with a look or

one kiss, not at first. I would understand if you did not want to be my lover at first. You hurt, eh? Maybe too much to turn to another so soon."

"Sí. I hurt. I knew I would, but I made it worse by letting myself hope, by letting myself be fooled into thinking there was more there for me than a strong lust."

"That is not your fault. I, too, watched and listened. He let you think there was. If he played a game, he played it well. I was surprised when you said he had chosen Marilynn. I was fooled and it was not my heart involved."

"Your heart would not be involved in this marriage either," she said quietly.

"Not as you feel for Royal, no. But it could come. It could come for you too."

"And if it did not? It is not fair to you."

"Because this baby is not mine? We could make one of mine later." He smiled. "Or more. We are young."

"Sí. Young. You could find someone. Someone who makes you burn, one that puts the fever in you," Antonie said, looking at Tomás.

"And maybe we find that with each other. Who knows? If I find this fire you speak of, do you think I would leave you?"

"No, and that is what is not fair. I have tasted the fire and, even though it has hurt me badly, I have known it. If I marry you, I make it so that you never can, so that you can never take the gamble and win like Oro did with Patricia."

"Ah, sí, that is fine, is it not. Because of what Royal did for Oro, I think," Tomás shrugged and shook his head. "Men can be so fair with men but not always with women, eh, querida?"

301

"No, not always with women."

"You think about what I ask, *chica*. I think I would be a good father."

"*Sí*, you would be."

"If it worries you that you may take too much and I may lose, I will promise to tell you if the one you speak of comes to me," Tomás said decisively.

"You would?"

"*Sí* and we could speak on it. I would tell you before I did one thing about it. Does that make you feel better? You think about it, *querida*. The baby needs a name. To be a bastard is a hard thing and Degas is a good name."

"*Sí*. Degas is a good name."

As they rode along at the somewhat leisurely pace that Tomás insisted on, Antonie thought about it. One reason she had been willing to accept less than love from Royal was to give her child a name. Tomás was right. To be a bastard was a hard thing and she had been ready to compromise her own wants in order to save her child from carrying that mark.

Marrying Tomás would solve that problem but she feared it would create a lot of others, mostly for Tomás. There had been a chance of a good life for him in Texas but, if he married her, he would not be able to grasp it. They would not want to be near to Royal, to risk the chance that he would find out that the child Tomás had claimed was his. That same reason would make it difficult for Oro and Tomás to visit each other. They would not be so far apart but, when there were families to care for, land to tend and secrets to hide, travel became a luxury that could not be afforded very often.

Thinking on the secret that they kept from Royal,

Antonie wondered if she had just left Oro and Patricia with a problem that could do some very real damage to their marriage. It was the very last thing she wanted, but she could see how that trouble could grow. Oro would feel bound to protect her and to keep her secret. Patricia would feel that her loyalty was to Royal, that she had to tell her brother about the child. Oro might understand that but he might also feel that Patricia should follow his way and then there would be trouble.

"I must send word to Oro and Patricia," she said suddenly.

"*Sí*. When we get to Mexico. Oro will want to know where we are."

"There is something else I must tell them. I must beg them not to let my secret come between them."

Tomás frowned for a moment then his dark eyes widened in understanding. "Ah, *sí*, there could be trouble."

"A lot. I will tell them that they must follow their hearts and not fault each other for it. This is my trouble. Not theirs."

"Have you decided to make it mine too?"

"I am still thinking. It is hard."

"The hurt is still too fresh?"

"*Sí*. Too sharp."

"There is time." He looked up at the sky. "We will look for a place to camp soon. A place that will stay dry when the rain comes. I would not like to sleep on the wet ground."

It was nearly dark before Antonie roused from her thoughts enough to look around. She had a feeling that Tomás had a specific place in mind. Just as she looked at him and prepared to ask him where they were going, a shot rang out.

Antonie stared in horror as Tomás's body jerked convulsively. Even in the dim light, she could see the dark stain start to spread on his shirt. He righted himself and was drawing his pistol when another shot was fired. Tomás cried out as he fell from his saddle to lie still in the road.

Juan's voice sounded in Antonie's head as she sat frozen, staring at Tomás. He yelled at her that she must not let emotion rule now. Grieve later, cry later, rage later but act now. To hesitate is to die, to let others die.

"Like Tomás," she whispered as she started to pull free of her shock. She could hear horses approaching and found the strength to draw her gun. Even as she aimed her pistol, she realized that she had been encircled. She and Tomás had ridden into a trap. Antonie knew that she had lost her chance to avenge Tomás's death when a blinding pain exploded in her head before she could fire her gun.

Royal sighed, stood up and stretched. He had accomplished a great deal of paper work but he knew he had just been hiding. Considering the way Marilynn had been acting when she had left, Royal was surprised that people had not already begun to stop by to offer congratulations on the engagement. He would have to tell Antonie about his plan, that he had asked Marilynn to marry him as a ploy. There was no telling how Antonie would react if someone else told her of his marriage plans. It was better to face her annoyance now than to try and sort out matters later. Just thinking of what could happen finally gave him the impetus to start looking for her. If he was lucky, he could talk to her before dinner.

When Maria called them all to dinner, Royal had still not found Antonie. The last any hands had seen of her was when she and Tomás had ridden off around noon. That was all he had found out from Oro and Patricia too.

He started to get really worried, yet seemed to be the only one who was. It was dark now and, although it was not impossible to ride in the dark, it was not a particularly safe thing to do. There was also a storm brewing. Even as he strode into the dining room, he heard the wind grow stronger and the rain start to hit the windows.

As he moved to his seat, he wondered if Oro had told him everything. There was little to read in the young man's face. Patricia, however, was acting suspiciously. She would not look at him and answered his greeting with a very weak monosyllable. Even Cole and Justin had noticed her odd attitude for they were looking at her curiously.

"Antonie is out riding with Tomás?" he asked Oro again as he sat down.

"Sí."

"In the dark and the rain."

"Sí."

"And just where were they going that they've had to be gone for more than half a day?"

"Mexico."

The forkful of tender beef Royal had raised to his mouth clattered back onto his plate. Oro was coldly meeting his stunned gaze. Royal felt a chill creep up his spine.

"Why are they going to Mexico?" he demanded as

305

anger, born of a fear he did not really want to examine, overtook his shock.

"They go home."

"I asked why, Oro."

"Because she will be your lover but not your *puta, gringo.*"

There was such fury in Oro's voice that Royal was momentarily taken aback. He had the distinct feeling that it was only the man's love for Patricia that kept him from putting that rage into action. The feeling that something was very wrong grew so strong that Royal had to clench the arms of his chair to keep from grabbing Oro and shaking some answers out of him.

"What the hell are you talking about?"

"She will not be your piece on the side, eh?"

"On the side of what?" Royal bellowed.

"On the side of your marriage to Marilynn Collins."

Royal froze even as Cole demanded, "What the hell? Are you marrying Marilynn?"

"I thought that idea had died," Justin said, surprised.

"It did, Justin," Royal said almost absently, his gaze never leaving Oro. "What makes you think I'm marrying Marilynn?"

"I do not think. I know. Antonie knows."

"Did she speak to Marilynn?"

"She saw you, Royal," Patricia answered quietly.

"Saw me? I haven't seen Antonie all day. Last I saw of her she was sleeping peacefully."

"*Sí*, and so you leave her bed and run to the Anglo bitch."

"Oro, please," Patricia whispered.

"Why don't you just tell me what happened, Oro?"

"Good idea," Cole interrupted with some annoyance. "You two are going back and forth without saying much. It's gotten damn confusing."

"Antonie got up and she went to find you. She found you kissing Marilynn at the door."

"Marilynn always kisses me when she arrives," Royal said defensively, but he knew that the very thing he feared had happened.

"You kissed her back this time. Antonie said so. She said that is why she followed you. From the library she saw and she heard."

"And then ran. Well, I'm going after her," Royal said as he stood up.

"No. You will leave her alone. I stepped back when you took her for your lover although I do not like it but it was what she wanted. I will not let you play these games with her. Marry your Anglo and stay away from Antonie," Oro threatened him.

"I am not marrying Marilynn," Royal ground out.

"Royal, sit down for a minute," Cole suggested. "I think you haven't finished explaining and you can't blame Oro for thinking what he is. You ain't going after Antonie now anyway. No sense in breaking your neck. I'm sure Oro can tell you right where they are going to be."

Slowly, Royal sat down. Cole was right. Oro was due an explanation. He was simply protecting Antonie. An explanation would also stop everyone from looking at him like he was the lowest of snakes, he thought crossly, as he looked around the table. It struck him as unfair that even his family would jump to the worst possible conclusion.

"I am not marrying Marilynn."

"You mean Antonie misunderstood?" Patricia asked eagerly.

"In a way. Look, I suddenly started to think and put two and two together. Every move we make is known."

"That could be a lot of people, Royal."

"I know, Cole. However, because of what happened at the wedding, I started looking at one person. Marilynn cornered me. To put it bluntly, she offered herself, to replace Antonie, of course. She was acting. I know it, could see it in her eyes. I started to ask myself why. I came up with a lot of sensible explanations. You know the sort. Maybe she's afraid of being a spinster. That kind of thing."

"It's very possible."

"So I thought, Justin. Then we presented Oro and Patricia with their surprise. That was a family secret, a closely kept one."

"*Sí,*" Oro agreed slowly. "Patricia and I never knew it was coming. This is so, *querida?*"

Patricia nodded. "Never heard a whisper."

"Yet an attack came," Cole said.

"It did and it was kind of ill-planned, don't you think?"

"We figured that out that night," Cole agreed.

"I know, but with so many guests?" He shook his head. "I thought I'd never guess. Then I remembered Antonie pointing out that Marilynn and her father were gone even as we left Oro and Patricia. They might not have even come all the way to the cabin."

"You mean you've known who's behind all this since then?"

"I've thought so, Justin. No, I'm sure of it, but I've got no proof. No proof at all. All I've got is the fact that Marilynn's always around. She knew the route we'd take on that drive. Just think a minute of everything that's happened right from the murder of our folks and who's always there?"

"Marilynn," Cole hissed.

"So why ask her to marry you?" Patricia asked in confusion.

"To set her up, eh?"

"Yes, Oro, to set her up."

"But after being with Antonie for so long . . ." Patricia began.

"Why would she fall for it? She's vain, Pattie. Hell, even I hadn't realized how vain. She also sees Antonie as a Mexican. That made it easy for her to think I'd choose her. So, I took her into the study, groveled a little, acted besotted and she bought it. I then told her, as exactly as I could without looking suspicious, about a trip I'll be taking Sunday. I told her I'm going to meet a Pinkerton man in San Antonio who's already got some information for me."

"And if she's the one we want, she won't want you getting there."

"Exactly, Justin."

"We'll only get the men she hires, *amigo*."

"Maybe, Oro. Maybe, because it'll be done close to home, someone will want to watch."

"Like they did the attack on the cabin," Patricia breathed.

"Right. That'd be sweet good luck we couldn't count on though. Nevertheless, Marilynn will know I set a trap. She'll know that I know. However that makes her act, we'll have her. Her and her father, for I know he's in it too. If nothing else, that knowledge can might them powerless."

"That's not good enough," Cole said icily. "They have to pay for killing Ma and Pa."

"They will. It make take some time though. Unless one of the pair falls into this trap or we finally get a man who'll talk, give us some proof, we'll still have some work to do to bring them to justice."

"I think Antonie would like to be in on that."

"Yes, she would, Cole." Royal looked at Oro. "I'll go after her first thing in the morning."

Oro slowly stood up. "*Sí*, you do that, *gringo*. I think there is something else you must be doing too."

"Really? And what is that?"

"I think that, when you go to bring Antonie back, you think real hard about why you do it."

"That should be obvious."

"Some of it, *sí*. A man does not like to lose such loving, eh? But Antonie is not *puta*."

"I know that," Royal said tensely.

"Good. So, you think, *gringo*. The battle is nearly over, eh? Life here will be back to what it was. Before you drag Antonie back, you think real hard on what you bring her back to. You figure out what you want, *gringo*."

Chapter Twenty-two

Burned into her mind's eye was the sight of Tomás sprawled in the road, his blood darkening the dirt. Her eyes flew open despite the blinding pain in her head. It was a moment before Antonie was truly aware of her surroundings and began to remember.

She was no longer on the trail but secured by her wrists to a musty smelling bed. A quick glance relieved her mind a little for she was still dressed. Frowning as she struggled to guess where she was, her eyes went over the adobe wall, gray with dirt and pockmarked. Her gaze flew to the door of the room as it opened and widened in shock when she saw who entered.

"So, the little bitch has finally woken up," Marilynn drawled as she strode into the room behind Raoul Mendez.

"Such a hard woman," Raoul mourned dramatically as he sat down on the bed across from Antonie.

"Correct me if I am wrong, but are you not the woman who wanted to marry Royal?" Antonie asked blandly.

"Of course I want to marry him and I will, now that you are out of the way."

"Then your association with this rabble escapes me." Antonie winced when Raoul gave her an ungentle prod with his foot.

"Royal has no real need of a wife. He could yet change his mind about the wedding. He also has no need to sell his land, land my father wants."

"Ah, I begin to see. If he is hurt badly enough, you will be sure to gain both. He will marry you for your fortune to save his land and then the land will be nearer to your papa through you. You have forgotten his brothers and Patricia. They share in it."

"I will see to that little problem in time," Marilynn said coolly as she extracted Raoul's money from the saddlebags she had tossed onto a rickety chair. "Count it if you must," she said as she handed it to him. "It's all there."

"*Sí,* the money is good." Raoul's dark eyes settled on Marilynn. "Now the rest, eh?"

"Raoul, we are not alone," Marilynn hissed. "Why not use her?"

The panic that seized Antonie faded abruptly at the look that flashed through Raoul's eyes. She could only describe it as terror. His next words gave her a good idea of why he was frightened and she almost laughed.

"She is Juan's *niña.*" He glanced around as if he expected him to appear. "No. I want the usual, *gringa.*" He pulled a knife, holding it menacingly aimed toward a wide-eyed Marilynn. "Move along, *gringa,*" he purred as he urged her back toward the door.

Marilynn began to obey but protested, "I don't like this, Raoul. The money should be enough."

"We make a deal, *gringa*. I think it would be wise if you keep it, eh?"

"I made no such deal."

"I say you did. Move."

When Marilynn hesitated, he grabbed her by the hair and forced her through the door before him. The smile Raoul sent her way before he shut the door after them told Antonie what he intended to do with the struggling Marilynn. Despite her feelings about Marilynn, this form of humiliation touched Antonie and she engaged in a fruitless struggle to get her wrists free. She had to try to help her.

Just as she admitted that there was no chance of her aiding Marilynn, Antonie realized that she could hear everything through the battered thin door. She felt her stomach churn as she heard Marilynn give a heart-rending cry. Her eyes widened with horror when she heard other men's voices. The poor woman was being forced to serve more than Raoul's animal lust.

After several moments of agonizing over the abused woman, Antonie suddenly tensed, listening to what she had just tried to deafen her ears to. There was no doubt in her mind that some very rough sexual activity was occurring in the other room. Raoul was highly vocal in his pleasure. What really caught her attention, however, was that Marilynn's tone had changed.

Antonie gasped in shock when she could no longer deny what she heard. Marilynn was enjoying herself. Her cries of protest had become ones of undisguised passion. She no longer screamed for her assailants to leave her alone but urged them on.

It was clear that she was not the cool, poised lady she played for Royal. She liked her sex play rough and plentiful. They had played a game and Antonie realized that she had almost fallen for it. If she had not listened more closely, had not succeeded in blocking out what she had first thought was a vicious rape, she would never have guessed at Marilynn's aberration. It was still hard to believe, even though the evidence kept beating away at her ears. She simply could not understand how any woman could subject herself to such treatment, let alone enjoy it.

Again Antonie's stomach heaved, only it was not with horror or disgust. Knowing what could exist between a man and a woman, she felt sickened by the twisted example of the act that she could hear being performed. She felt sure that Royal would share her disgust for he was a civilized man and what was going on in the other room was nothing less than barbaric.

Royal needed to know about this, she thought, and then sighed. Even if she got out of the mess she was in, Royal had made his choice. Antonie knew she could not tell him about Marilynn. He would not believe it. It sounded too much like a tale from a woman scorned. She wondered why she felt sorry for him and the trouble he was headed for, instead of consigning him to the devil.

"Well? Now that you have had your fun why don't you do what I have paid you for? Kill her."

Antonie tensed and strained to listen more carefully. She would worry about Royal later.

"Not now, *gringa*. At dawn. *Sí*, at dawn. If it rains? Mañana." Raoul laughed. "She can go nowhere. You men go. I need you no more."

Marilynn stomped her foot. "Damn you. I've paid you well. I want her killed now, so that I know it has been done."

Antonie did not need to hear Raoul's reaction to know that Marilynn had gone too far. Raoul took orders from no one. Despite his use of her body and the taking of her money, he saw Marilynn as a *gringa,* one of the race he hated.

She winced as she heard him spit a vicious curse then the sound of a blow striking flesh. By the sounds of it Marilynn was putting up a valiant defense. It did not surprise Antonie at all when the rough fight she could overhear soon became something else. It seemed a natural extension of the sickness that Marilynn and Raoul had already displayed.

When Raoul bellowed for one of his men to bring tequila, Marilynn protested, "I don't have time for frivolity, Raoul."

"We must celebrate, *gringa.*"

"The job's not done yet. She's still alive. I want to see her dead."

"You will. I told you when I would do it. You can come and see your proof then. And bring the rest of the money, eh?"

"You expect a lot for killing one girl."

"She is Juan's *niña.*"

Antonie almost smiled but her humor was bitter. There was really nothing funny about the fact that two people whose sanity she seriously questioned were discussing her death. It was costing Marilynn a lot but Antonie knew that Marilynn would feel her money well spent when she found out exactly how Raoul killed his enemies.

She was almost glad when the tequila arrived along with a couple of Raoul's men. It became evident that Marilynn was to entertain them again but this time Antonie ignored the woman's protests. Within moments those protests turned to words of enjoyment and encouragement as a rowdy, lewd celebration ensued.

For a while Antonie listened to the proceedings in an almost horrified fascination, but then closed her eyes. By action and sound, Marilynn gave herself away. Sudden insight told Antonie that the touch of honest panic she had heard in the woman's voice at first had not been because of a fear of what would happen but the knowledge that she would thoroughly enjoy it. Marilynn was plainly one of those women who could not get enough of men, any man, and, Antonie suspected, the rougher the better. She cared little about the man's looks, cleanliness or character as long as he had the right equipment. Marilynn was a whore and her actions with Raoul and his men made it hard for even Marilynn to deny that. By taking this woman as his wife, Royal would be dooming himself to a lengthy hell on earth. Antonie wondered sleepily why Marilynn and Royal were not lovers and decided it was probably because Royal was not crude enough to really stir her passions.

"You did not like the entertainment provided?"

Antonie opened her eyes, blinked and looked at Raoul. She could not believe she had fallen asleep during the raucous and decidedly crude goings on in the other room. Wincing over the continued throbbing in her head, she decided that the wound probably had a lot to do with it.

"Such things grow tedious. I have no interest in whores."

"*Sí*, the *gringa* is a whore. She will marry Royal Bancroft and you will die knowing that your lover takes a whore as his wife," he said with evident satisfaction. "She will cause much trouble for him and his family." He stood up and untied the end of the rope that bound her hands to the bed. "It is time that you eat."

"My last meal?" She struggled to eat the beans set before her while her hands were still bound together.

Raoul nodded. "If the day is fine, we will kill you at dawn."

Thinking of the new life she carried within her, Antonie wanted to cry. She held back her tears for several reasons. The main one was simply not wanting to give Raoul the pleasure of seeing her weakness. She also knew that such a feminine weakness would work to make him see her less as an equal, perhaps even lessen his fear of Juan's specter. No good would come of crying, not even in easing her pain. There were not enough tears for that, not in the whole world.

"If the weather is not fine?"

"Then the next day. I have thought long on this. It will be dramatic and very painful. Juan's child will die slowly."

"Dead is dead." She refused to let him see her fear.

He shrugged. "We will see how you think when I begin. I hope Juan's child proves worthy of my talent."

"I'll do my best," she drawled. "Marilynn stays to watch?"

"The *gringa* has gone home. She will return, for she is eager to see you dead."

When he had left her again, she found that death was not an easy thing to face. She was only twenty and carrying the child of the man she loved. They were the strongest reasons to live.

There was so much pain to ignore but to let it free would weaken her and she needed her strength. Tomás lay dead and Oro would suffer the loss of his twin and the sister of his heart. That knowledge deeply hurt her as well as knowing that Royal would give his name to a woman who would destroy him and those he loved.

Hope would have helped, but she had none. By the time anyone suspected that anything was wrong, it would be too late. Even if Tomás's body was found, there would be no way for anyone to know where she was. When sleep again claimed her, she welcomed it as an escape from her despair.

Rain greeted her when she woke up and she was almost disappointed. It would mean another day of waiting. She could not see a way to work up the hope that it was buying her valuable time.

Royal stared out at the rain and cursed. He had wanted to get an early start in trailing Antonie. The rain made it impossible for he was sure that she and Tomás would have sought shelter and it would be too easy to pass them by. The road would soon be a quagmire, making travel nearly impossible.

Oro had just hobbled into the dining room with Patricia's solicitous help when there came a thunderous knocking at the front door. Wondering who would be fool enough to come out in such weather, Royal hastened to the door. He did not take much notice of how curiosity brought Oro and Patricia along behind him.

At the door was a huge man wearing a voluminous coat. He held a well wrapped bundle and without a word, Royal motioned the man inside. One look at Oro's face told Royal that this man was an acquaintance and one Oro was pleased to see.

"O'Neill," Oro breathed as he hurried closer.

"Sure and that's just who it is, although your brother here thought I was of a higher calling. After riding with me he ought to know better."

"Tomás?" Oro paled as he saw how still the bundle

318

O'Neill held was. "He is hurt, old *amigo?*"

"Sorely, lad, I'm sorry to say. Got two bullets in him though I'm thinking I stopped the bleeding right enough. Heard the sad news about my compadre Juan and I've been looking for you three for a time now, but I would've been pleased not to find you at all rather than find this."

"Bring him in here. Pattie, get Cole and Justin out of bed and call Maria," Royal ordered.

O'Neill laid Tomás down on a carpet before the fire. With Oro hovering close by, he unwrapped the young man, revealing a bandage at the shoulder and waist. Miraculously, Tomás had stayed dry.

His blue eyes dark with concern, Liam O'Neill said, "I would have stopped to take the bullets out but he was having none of it. Said he had to get here quickly as possible. Something has happened to Juan's wee lass."

Royal felt his blood chill and had to clench his hands to keep from shaking Tomás awake, demanding to know what had happened. She had been returning to Mexico. He had thought she would be safe at least, if only because she would no longer be working for him. Looking at how badly Tomás was injured, he knew a numbing fear for Antonie's safety.

"Oro?" Tomás croaked even as Patricia was returning with her still dressing brothers in tow.

Clasping his twin's hand, Oro rasped, "*Sí*, Tomás. I am here."

"Raoul's got Tony. Set on us on the road. Knew where we'd be."

"Is she hurt?" Royal asked, dreading the answer.

"No, I think not." Tomás closed his eyes for a moment as pain washed over him.

"Do you know where they took her?" Oro pressed,

319

paling when he saw the shadow of delirium in Tomás's eyes.

"Devil's Hollow. Raoul will hurt her. They hit her, Oro."

"They will pay, brother. I will make them pay."

"So little. Could lose the baby. She was worried about the baby." He gave a parody of a smile. "Decided she'd better have a husband. I would have been a good father to her baby. *Cristo,* Oro, it hurts. It burns."

For a moment Royal could not catch his breath. He felt as if he had been hit squarely in the stomach by a powerful blow. The way Oro looked at him, even though it was a brief glance, made Royal feel sure that he looked as completely stunned as he felt. Royal suspected that he had gone a little gray around the edges.

"Did I see that devil O'Neill?"

"You did, Tomás," Oro replied. "Our old compadre has come at a good time, eh?"

"*Sí.* I think we have much need of him."

It was a tremendous battle for Royal not to try and force Tomás to speak to him. Only the terrible pain he knew Tomás was in, a pain so clearly shared by Oro, kept Royal from demanding information. He wished there was some way to get Tomás to simply repeat what he had said but Royal could not bring himself to ask it.

"Get my guns, Patricia," Oro said in a voice that made her turn ghost white.

"Your leg, Oro," she protested shakily even as she stood up.

"My guns." He watched her run from the room and then looked at Royal. "I am going after Antonie."

Buckling on the gun belt Justin had just fetched,

320

Royal said, "Not alone."

"All of us?" Oro's lips moved in a slight smile when the three brothers nodded.

"Sure and don't be forgetting O'Neill." He set down the glass of whiskey he had been served after tending to Tomás's wounds and reached for his coat. "I came this way thinking to visit a bit with the lass and visit I will, even if I must fetch her first."

"It will be good to ride with you again, *amigo*." Oro took the guns a trembling Patricia held out and buckled them on. "Antonie will be glad to see you, too. We will owe you much."

"Not a thing, Oro. I've had my scarred hide saved by you three more times than I can count."

"Oro," Patricia ventured, "your leg has barely healed. "Must you?"

"*Sí.* It is what I must do."

"Well, take some more men. I'm sure there are many who would want to go."

"I am sure too." He kissed her. "They must stay behind. In this a few is best. Take care of Tomás, *querida*."

Patricia grabbed him, holding on tightly for a moment. "Good luck and take care."

Looking at the grim-faced men he would be riding with, Royal knew he could find none better. He did not know O'Neill but he trusted Oro's and Tomás's judgment. If nothing else, they were good judges of whether a man would be an asset in a fight. At the moment, that was the only aspect of the man's character that Royal cared about.

Seeing the way that Oro gritted his teeth and paled slightly as he mounted, Royal said carefully, "Pattie is right. Your leg is barely healed."

"Raoul tried to kill my brother, may have succeeded

for I am not foolish enough not to see how badly wounded Tomás is. The dog also holds Antonie. My leg is of no matter. You understand, eh?"

"Yes."

"Then let us ride," Oro said even as he spurred his mount on.

Royal was deeply afraid for Antonie. Try as he would to block his fears from his mind, thoughts of all that could happen to her preyed on him. She was strong but she was so small.

He wished he had acted on his suspicions, not worried so about having facts before moving against a neighbor. There was little doubt in his mind who told Raoul where to find Antonie. Marilynn would pay dearly for that.

Tomás's words kept reverberating in his head. Antonie carried their child. He now understood why she had not waited when she had thought that he had chosen Marilynn. Depending upon how far along she was, time was something she might not have much of. Thinking that he was set to be married, she would not want him to know of the baby.

The rain had eased by the time they had reached the spot where O'Neill had found Tomás. Royal suspected that thinking of how his twin could easily have bled to death in such a barren, muddy place made Oro eager to leave it. They moved further down the road before pausing to talk about what they should do next.

"Devil's Hollow is two hours' ride from here. To the east."

"That'll put us there close to dawn, Oro," Cole observed. "Is there cover to be had?"

"*Sí*, but it is also hard to reach the cabin without being seen. This is why Raoul chose it."

"Well, let's get to the point where there is no more cover to be had and then decide," Royal said curtly.

"Aye," Liam agreed. "See what they're up to and what men they got. We can't plan blind."

Devil's Hollow was little more than a depression in the ground. A rough cabin sat in the middle just far enough from the few shrubs and rocks that provided cover on the encircling rise. A man would have to expose himself to get a good shot at anyone in the cabin. Without artillery, the best that Royal thought could be accomplished without a lot of casualties was a stand-off.

Two men, unfortunately alert, stood guard. If the number of horses was any real indication, Royal figured that there were at least six more men inside, if not eight. The odds could be as much as two to one.

"What's that thing? Looks like a cross." Justin looked as if he wished he had not asked when he saw Oro's face.

"It is Raoul's gallows. He has it built for Antonie. Raoul honors her. He intends her to die slowly. Raoul takes too seriously the drop of Apache blood his mother's rape gave him. Since nothing hangs there, then we know that Antonie still lives."

"He would torture a woman?" Cole hissed, casting a worried look at a decidedly gray Royal.

"*Sí*, but he sees Juan in Antonie, I think. Antonie is not just a woman to him but an old enemy."

"What if we rush the place?" Royal asked.

"If we live?" Oro shrugged. "Raoul might kill her before we got to the cabin. He might not. He is a one-thought man. He has decided to test her strength so he might not want to see her harmed in any other way, would not think of any other way."

"Would he still do this if he knew she is with child?"

323

Royal tensed, waiting for Oro to deny what Tomás had said.

"I do not know. If Raoul guesses that she carries a baby he will know that it is yours. A *gringo* baby? It could go badly for her. Also, it would make him see her too clearly as a woman and less as Juan's *niña* and an old enemy. That could bring its own troubles."

"It would have been nice if someone had told me about the child," Royal snarled.

"Antonie only told me moments before she left. We thought you had chosen *Señorita* Collins."

"I never would have played that game if I'd known she was carrying my child. I'd at least have warned Antonie what was going on. Hell, by the time I reached her in Mexico, she and Tomás would've been married."

"That was plan I did not know about. It was Tomás's." Oro's face tautened with pain as he said his twin's name.

Cole grasped his shoulder. "Tomás'll be fine. Anyone who can drink that poison like water won't be laid low by a little lead."

"Here, lads, something's about," O'Neill warned.

"They bring her out. Ah, my poor little sister, it must be hard to be brave when she thinks of the child she carries."

"Justin, you're staying with the horses. Someone has to," Royal said when Justin got ready to argue. "A watch must be kept as well. You're the one with the least fighting experience. The choice is obvious." Justin nodded, unable to fight that logic.

"How do we play it, lads?" O'Neill clearly felt a need for action as he watched Antonie being brought out of the cabin.

Oro glanced at Royal then said quietly, "We wait."

"Wait?" Royal demanded even while common sense told him that it was the only effective tactic to use.

"*Sí*. Wait. When Raoul begins, his men will watch."

"All of them?" Cole asked as he checked his weapon.

"Raoul strips his victims," Oro said, sighing even as Antonie was roughly undressed.

"All of them." Cole winced at the black fury on Royal's face. "Poor kid."

"If we wait too long, she could lose the child. The shock or pain could cause her to miscarry."

"The babe has survived much, Royal. It is four months along. Maybe longer. She did not say." Oro clasped Royal's shoulder. "I too worry and hate to see this happen but, if we move too soon, both could be lost and we as well. We will do her no good dead."

It was all true but, as they moved into position so that they could come up behind Raoul and his men in a semicircle, Royal found the waiting the hardest thing he had ever done.

Chapter Twenty-three

Antonie felt a strong sense of acceptance of her fate as she was led out into the dawn. Feeling removed from it all, she was stripped of her clothes. Her emotional detachment however wavered a little when she was tied to the rough wood, her feet several inches off the ground and her legs parted by lashing her ankles to small stakes in the ground. She struggled to eradicate the sudden clear memories of the remains of others Raoul had executed in the same manner.

"Easter already?" she murmured.

"Your blasphemy is ill-timed."

"I think, Raoul, that you blaspheme when you use this style of scaffold."

He shrugged as he checked his branding iron, then placed it back in the fire. Antonie knew that where he put his brand would be the one part of her that would remain otherwise unblemished. Raoul liked to have any who found his victims know just who had left them. It was a successful way to breed fear and Raoul liked to be feared.

She tried to ignore that slowly heating branding iron but even though she averted her eyes the image of it was clear in her mind. So too was the image of what it would do to her skin. It made her stomach churn and reminding herself that it would be the least of the pains Raoul would inflict before death rescued her was no help at all. She stared at Raoul, hatred clearing the fear she suspected had shown briefly in her eyes.

Royal's body jerked violently when he saw the branding iron. The thought of how it would soon touch Antonie's creamy skin made him want to bellow with rage and challenge the beast who threatened her. Only a gray-faced Cole's grip on his arm stopped him from running to her. He watched Oro still inching down the rise but his face was white and a fine tremor ran through his slim frame. It was clearly as hard for Oro to continue cautiously as it was for him. The fear that they would not be in time to save her from all Raoul planned made caution a hard won thing.

"You will last a long time, I think," Raoul said as he tested the sharpness of his knife.

Praying that God would mercifully stop her heart before she suffered too much, she spat on him. A fierce rage blazed in his eyes but he fought it. That was not something she found encouraging. She wanted to drive him into such a fury that he killed her quickly but it was clear that he had guessed her plan and was prepared to fight it.

"If the knife is hot when it slides through the flesh there will be not so great a loss of blood," Raoul chatted amiably and tested the sharpness of his heated blade against her shoulder, breaking the smooth skin. "Do not think to escape by swooning. I will wake you and continue."

"When you die as you surely must," she said coldly, fighting to ignore the sting caused by the shallow cut, "Juan will be waiting for you in hell." She smiled grimly when he paled. "Julio and Manuel will be at his side. Manuel owes you for Tomás."

She saw him fight to hide his fear from his men as he pressed his knife point to the inside of her arm. It was a shallow cut but it stung, making Antonie grit her teeth. She pulled herself together enough to glare at Raoul as he did the same to her other arm.

"The soles of the feet can be used to bring a person much pain," Raoul murmured, his gaze on the blood that trickled from the cuts on her slim arms. "Marco, the coals."

She could not fully control the shudder that tore through her when Marco picked up a small shovelful of hot coals. The reasons for the hollows beneath her feet were now apparent. It would be a slow process, the heat of the coals gradually searing her tender feet, the agony slowly increasing and, because it was going to be a slow process, the pain would last a long time.

Just as Marco straightened up from filling the second hollow with coals and raking his eyes over her, a shot rang out. Antonie watched as Marco's look changed from a lustful grin to one of surprise. His body fell over the hollow, his blood flowing over the coals, cooling them before the heat had done any more than uncomfortably warm the soles of her feet.

Antonie realized that her fate had become of very little concern to Raoul. The surprise attack and four good shots had neatly lessened Raoul's strength by four. The four men left thought only of escape, although they fought fiercely in their futile attempt to flee. When a bullet tore through Raoul's chest, Antonie watched, the knowledge of his impending death

328

showing clearly on his face. She tensed when he turned toward her for he obviously thought of taking her with him. But even as he started to aim his pistol at her, another shot tore through him and he fell.

She stared at him, feeling almost weak with relief that he would never again threaten her. For one brief instant she bitterly resented the quickness of his death but violently pushed that thought aside. She would not sink to his level.

It was Cole who reached Antonie first, the two men between him and her quickly dispatched. He kicked sand over the coals to further insure that they were no danger even as he bent to cut her feet loose. Sheltering her with his body, he cut loose one arm and caught her as she slumped. Cutting free her other arm, he lowered her gently to the ground, her back against the wooden scaffold.

Despite her aches, Antonie was feeling exhilarated. She was rescued. By some miracle, they had found her before Raoul had gone too far in his nefarious plans. The cuts on her arms and shoulder stung and her body ached all over but she smiled brilliantly at Cole, thinking how beautiful he was.

"Honey, I don't know where the hell you get the strength to smile."

"It is easy. I am alive."

He smiled back at her. "You are that." He then sobered. "I'm no good at doctoring."

"It can wait. My hurts are small. May I have your shirt?"

"Sure thing, sweet."

The other three men arrived just as he was helping her into his shirt. Royal weakly returned her smile, aching to talk to her but needing privacy. He knew there was a lot of explaining to do, his feeling enhanced when she blinked at him as if recalling something and hastily looked away. She still thought no doubt that he had chosen Marilynn over her.

"Tomás," Antonie began, tears filling her eyes as she sought the words to tell Oro of his twin's death.

"Is alive. O'Neill brought him to the ranch. Our compadre was sent by fate, I think."

She briefly closed her eyes in relief then looked at the big Irishman crouched at her side. "It is good to see you again."

"And you, lass. While you're getting better, I'll bore you with tales of what I've been doing this past year. Now," he stood up, "I'll get our horses here. In my bags is something that might do for doctoring your wounds."

"Is there a bed in that shack?"

"Sí, Cole. Two. I . . . I cannot walk. I have been tied too long."

"No one expected you to walk," Royal said as he picked her up.

There was something in the way he held her that made Antonie's heart soar, letting her believe that he cared. So strong was the feeling that it was a struggle to remember the scene she had witnessed between him and Marilynn.

When the memory finally came, she felt her hopes die. She was caught between the proverbial rock and a hard place. If she said nothing, he would marry Marilynn and she would lose him, knowing what he would suffer. Yet, if she told him all she knew of Marilynn, even if he believed her, he would undoubtedly hold it against her. Few people can forgive the one who shattered their dreams. There would always be the question of how deeply her own rejection had motivated her.

330

"Do you want to sit or lie down?"

"I will sit, Royal. O'Neill will tell me how he wishes me to help in the doctoring."

"We had to wait to rescue you, little one," he said hoarsely.

"*Sí*, I know this. Surprise was your best weapon. There is nothing to be sorry for. Raoul did little to me."

Thinking of what had driven her from the safety of the ranch, Royal winced. "Antonie, we have to talk about . . ."

"Here we go, lass. I have all that's needed to fix you up as fine as ever." O'Neill looked at Royal. "Why don't you go and send that fool Oro in here. He's clearing away signs of the fight, pushing his leg further than it should go. If the fool doesn't get off the bloody thing and rest it, it'll never heal right. Sure 'n that is a pure fact."

Antonie watched as Royal left and then sighed. She had not gotten away and now knew that distance would never free her. Although she felt she had always known that, she had managed to ignore it for a while.

"Don't look so sad, lass. It'll turn out fine."

"No, it will not, O'Neill. He is a rich man or can be again, a man of property. Juan Ramirez's *niña* is not for him."

"Then he's a fool and not worth your grief. Ah, Oro, glad you saw reason."

"I had little choice, *amigo*." Oro limped toward the bed.

"Settle yourself with the lass. I'm going to be doctoring her soon and I might need her held still. Your arms are still useful."

"Your flattery humbles me," Oro drawled as he settled himself on the bed with Antonie.

331

"How's the baby feeling?" O'Neill asked as he tended to her shoulder wound first.

Gasping a little from the sting of the whiskey O'Neill used to clean her wound, she finally asked, "You know?"

"Could see it clear enough when you were hanging out there buck nekked but, also, Tomás kept babbling about it."

"Then Royal knows."

"*Sí*," Oro replied, holding her with a gentle firmness. "He was not pleased to hear of Tomás's plan, eh? Not when he was headed out after you."

"He was coming to find me? But why?"

"You did not say goodbye."

"Oro," she hissed then flinched as O'Neill touched her feet.

"Speak to him, little one. It is not for me to say. In the middle is not where I wish to be."

"He's right, lass. Settle it yourself. Your wounds aren't bad, love. Still, you've had a shock and a bad knock on the head. Best to stay off these pretty little feet for a few days."

"Feet are not pretty," she said weakly as she turned to lie on her side, her head on Oro's strong thigh.

"Depends on whether they are running to or from a body. They're real pretty when they're a woman's, bare and toe upwards, set either side of a man's, bare and toes down. Aye and when they start curling with delight."

"You're a rogue, Liam O'Neill."

"Sure 'n don't we all know that."

"Are they all dead?" she asked.

"Not all," Oro replied.

"Think some will talk?"

"*Sí*, maybe, but I think the Bancrofts will find out

very little."

"Ah, that will not please Royal."

When Royal arrived to help Cole drag one of the dead men around to the back of the building, Cole asked, "How's Antonie?"

"Damn hard to tell. She's so damn stoic. Have you talked yet to any of the ones who are alive?"

"Only one of those left. Best do that before he goes too." Cole moved to crouch before a man whose wound was slowly but definitely mortal. "Who hired you?"

"A *gringa*." The man's expression was a ghastly parody of a smile. "A fine looking *puta* and hungry, eh?"

"That doesn't tell us a hell of a lot."

"Red hair, tall. Pretty." His voice grew weaker as he lost his battle against encroaching death. "Collins. *Señorita* Collins."

"Well, there's your suspicions confirmed. Dear Marilynn and her darling Papa have been behind all this."

"The word of a dead *bandito* won't hang anyone for our parents' murder, not when we're the only ones who heard it."

"Could do to scare them far enough away so that they can't bother us any more."

"True, but they'll find other victims. Maybe there's something in the cabin."

"Let's finish this first. If anyone sees this mess, they'll know something ain't right."

"Think someone might be coming, Cole? More men?"

"Can't say. The only one who could've is dead now. It can't hurt to be too careful though."

As he continued with the grisly work, Royal's mind

was on Antonie. He had made a lot of mistakes with her. The biggest had been not taking an honest look at how he felt. Blindly he had stumbled along, thinking only of possession and need. Passion and jealousy had directed his every step.

Worse, in the back of his mind, he had never forgotten her background. He had not let her erase whatever taint there might have been and there was no ignoring the fact that she had sensed that. It was undoubtedly the reason why she had been so quick to believe that he would make love to her one night and propose marriage to Marilynn the next morning.

Picking up a shovel, he joined Cole in digging a shallow grave, after searching the bodies for papers. There had been nothing. With Cole having worked for the law, their word might be enough to put the Collinses in jail, if not hang them. Royal still wanted hard proof to erase any chance of their slipping through the law's fingers. If all he accomplished was to run them out of the area, he knew he would always wonder who they were hurting.

"What are you going to do about Antonie?"

"Hell, Cole, I'm not sure, but she's damn well not going to go back to Mexico and she's not marrying Tomás."

"You going to marry her?"

"Yes, even if I have to tie her up to get her before a preacher. Degas is a fine name but not for my child."

He wished he had as much confidence as he was able to put into his voice. Antonie would well be finished with him and he would not really blame her if she was. Then again, she had never spoken of love either. What had led her into his arms had been "the fire" as she had called it and for all he knew, that fire could have fizzled out.

When he went back into the cabin he prepared some coffee. Cole had gone to relieve Justin who was bringing most of the horses to the cabin. No one had eaten since last night and Royal, with what he could find in the place, started to make breakfast. That started, he brought coffee in to Antonie, O'Neill and Oro.

"Ah, this tastes much better than warm tequila which Raoul serves," Antonie sighed after savoring a mouthful of coffee.

"How's it look, O'Neill?" Royal sat down on the other bed.

"She will heal. With luck these shallow cuts will not scar."

"I am getting a very big collection, eh? Add the one on my arm and the one under my ribs and that could make five."

"Which is five too many," Royal grumbled. "How is the baby?"

"A man of great subtlety," Antonie murmured, causing O'Neill and Oro to laugh quietly. "The child is fine."

"Are you sure, lass? That is the one thing that needs watching. No pain or pressure?"

"No, O'Neill. The child moves even now. It is well settled."

"How settled?" Royal asked, fighting the urge to put his hand on her abdomen and to feel his child himself.

"You think maybe it is now yours?" Antonie snapped.

"Don't be an ass. It would be nice to know just when I'll become a father."

"In a little less than three months," she muttered, her weariness and the situation with Marilynn making her short tempered.

"Good God," Royal breathed, realizing that that took them back to the first night or shortly thereafter.

For a moment his thoughts were sidetracked. With all the trouble and the cattle drive, he had not realized how time had slipped by. His thoughts then became a hasty cataloging of all that had occurred during that time.

She had done lot of hard riding, spent hours in the saddle, been shot at, been hit and on and on. Through all that she had been carrying their child. Antonie had been carrying on like a ranch hand and a hired gun at a time when a woman should be coddled and cared for. She could not only have lost their child but done herself a great deal of harm.

"You are sure you have so little time left?" Oro asked while Royal was caught up in his thoughts. "It does not show at all."

"*Si*. When I got to thinking back, that is the length of time I came up with."

"You went on a long, hard cattle drive while pregnant?" Royal snapped.

"I did not know I was with child when I went."

"Well, just when did it occur to you?"

"There is no need to be sarcastic. What do I know of these things?"

"You must have noticed something."

Antonie scowled at Royal, wondering what was putting him in such a temper. She was the one in pain. It seemed to her typical of a man to think that, just because she was a woman, she should know certain things, things no one had ever told her.

"I noticed a thing or two but there could be many reasons for these things, eh? How am I to know my stomach thickens not from too much food but from a baby? You think Juan or Manuel or Julio or Oro or

336

Tomás or any of the other *banditti* sit me down to say, 'Antonie, this is what will happen if you get with child?' Did you?"

"Enough. You made your point." Not ready to give up, Royal added, "You could have talked with a woman when, well, when things started to happen that had nothing to do with whether you were eating well."

"I did when I got back to the ranch. Stop yelling at me."

"I'm not yelling."

"*Sí*. You are. Between your teeth and quietly." She flashed a glare at the laughing Oro and O'Neill. "Why did you not notice?"

Royal felt a light color seep into his cheeks. He should have noticed something. Despite all the misunderstandings that had kept them apart for a time there should have been an interval here and there when nature put a short halt to their enjoyment of each other.

"She has you there, laddie," O'Neill said jovially, then turned to ask Antonie, ignoring Royal's scowl, "Got a name for the babe?"

"*Sí*, I have, O'Neill. I will call my son Juan Ramirez." Her eyes narrowed when she saw Royal's expression. "You do not like that?"

"You're spoiling for a fight, aren't you, darlin'," O'Neill murmured, laughter trembling in his deep voice.

"Juan is a fine name. Juan Ramirez would be a fine name too if it did not belong to the most notorious *bandito* in Mexico. I will not have my child named after a *bandito* who was one of the most wanted men for over a thousand miles around."

"*Sí*. He was the best. And, this is my child and I

337

will name him what I want." Her look dared him to argue.

It was a dare that Royal was preparing to heartily accept when Justin suddenly walked in, saying grimly, "Someone's headed this way."

"One rider," Cole said as he followed Justin in. "I think you can guess," he added with a meaningful look at Royal.

"Now maybe we can get our proof." Royal started toward the door.

"One sight of you fellows and whoever it is will be off before you can blink," O'Neill said stopping Royal's confident advance.

Royal frowned at O'Neill, knowing what the man said was true. "You have any suggestions?"

"I do. You stay hidden here and I will meet this envoy." O'Neill stood up and dried his hands. "The only ones of Raoul's men who I knew are lying out there. No one knows me around here. I also think I look suitably rough and nasty."

"Only to those who don't know you," Antonie said with a small smile.

"You think you can convince the one coming well enough to get some information?"

"Royal, this *gringo* before you could sell a glass of water to a drowning man," Oro said. "He also knows enough about *banditti* and their ways to act like one. Even if the one who comes did not know you, none of you could do that."

"I reckon you're right." Royal sat back down. "I want a confession."

"Get you as much of a one as I can. Any hard proof as well, I suspect."

"The paper to hang them with would be wonderful. I'll settle for whatever you can get, O'Neill. A confrontation will at least send them to their heels. Hard proof will put them where they can't pull this stunt again and that would be fine."

"Aye and I'll do my best to get it. I've an idea or two on what'll suit. Not a sound out of you, no matter what you hear. Just keep in mind that I'm playing me a game or two. I've got to convince this person that I'm one of Raoul's mad dogs and if I do it right it just might be convincing you too." As he went out of the door, he paused and added, "If this is a false alarm or anything goes wrong, I'll be sure to let you know."

Shutting the door, he went into the other room only to hastily return with most of the breakfast Royal had begun. Returning to the outer room, he settled himself at the table with a small breakfast and a cup of coffee. As he waited, he tossed around a few ideas on how to conduct himself.

Within the small room, Royal took O'Neill's place on the bed by Antonie. Cole and Justin settled themselves on the other bed. They all ate quietly and quickly, finishing by the time the rider reached the cabin. Everyone watched the door, their bodies tensed as they listened closely. Antonie watched Royal move to the door. She too was tense but not only because of what was to happen. She felt that Royal knew who was coming and she dreaded watching how he would react.

Chapter Twenty-four

O'Neill hid his surprise when a slim, lovely redhead entered the cabin. He met her narrow-eyed look with perfect outward calm as his mind worked feverishly. Things fell into place suddenly and he nearly smiled. Instinct told him that this was the woman responsible for the trouble between Royal and Antonie.

"Who the hell are you?" Marilynn snapped, her gaze moving over O'Neill with an appreciation she was not able to hide.

"Liam O'Neill, ma'am. And you?"

"Where's Raoul?"

"Ain't here. Waiting for him myself."

"No one's here?"

"Just you and me, darlin'."

She preened slightly beneath his leer. "I've never seen you with Raoul before."

"I been resting, you might say."

"Really. Perhaps I don't believe you."

Liam suddenly grabbed her arm, twisting it in a way that brought her to her knees by his chair, an intimidating action that succeeded in cracking her cool facade a little. "No one calls Liam O'Neill a liar."

Marilynn's cool facade was slipping but not because

of fear. Here was a man she knew could display all of the refinement of a fine gentleman yet also knew how to display his superior strength to a woman. He could give her all the subtlety that Raoul and his ilk lacked. In this man, she could have the best of both worlds, the gentlemanly airs her station in life required and the brutality her body craved. Simply the thought of such a combination was a heady one.

"He couldn't leave. There was a job he needed to do first."

"Ah, you mean killing that little bitch of Juan's."

"Yes, he said he would do it."

"Done. He didn't leave the bitch on the cross here for few'd see her. He's gone to put her where notice'll be taken."

"At Royal's doorstep." She could not hide how she savored the thought. "Did she take a long time to die?" There was a pleased, even eager, tone to her voice.

"Well, now, he did say something 'bout that. Said she'd proven to be all he would have expected of Juan's *niña*. Reckon that means she lasted a long time." He hid his disgust when he saw how that news actually aroused the woman.

"God, I wish I had been there to see it. When will Raoul return?"

"He didn't say. He told me to make myself at home."

"That does not include me."

"No?" That ain't how he put it."

"That pig forced me to pleasure him and his men. Look, I brought the last of the money but he promised me proof."

"Looks a healthy sum. You really wanted her dead, didn't you," O'Neill drawled.

341

"Yes," Marilynn hissed, "and I wanted to see it. I wanted proof."

"The blood on the ground beneath the cross should be proof enough. Now, Raoul, he told me you always gave a, shall we say, bonus. I'm thinking I'll collect it this time."

"No," Marilynn struggled when he grasped hold of her but was careful not to break his grip. "You can't force me to play your whore."

Seeing how her eyes kept flicking to his groin, Liam demanded, "Can't I, darlin'? Raoul told me you like it rough and often."

"Get your filthy hands off me."

Antonie watched Royal as Marilynn made her protests, protests Antonie knew to be false. His gaze was riveted to the door and a frown darkened his features. She could not, however, discern just what the frown meant.

Royal was struggling with indecision. He wanted a confession and told himself that Marilynn deserved no consideration. His gentlemanly instincts were aroused, however, by what sounded like treatment too rough for a woman. Cursing softly, he wished he could see Marilynn's face through the battered door. Then he would know how to act. But what he heard next quelched any doubt.

"Tell me how he does it," Marilynn urged.

"You'd like to hear that, would you?"

O'Neill's descriptions of Raoul's tortures made Antonie shudder for she had come too close to personally enduring them. Oro's hold on her tightened in sympathy. She tried hard to concentrate on what was being said, to heed every word of the confession O'Neill was leading Marilynn into.

"Of course I would have done a few things differently." To Marilynn's clear enjoyment, O'Neill elaborated. "How does that compare to the skill of your Mexican lover?"

"He was not my lover. It was business. I needed him to clear a few obstacles out of my way."

"Well, there's one that'll never bother you again. Skinned like a rabbit."

"I suppose you expect that bonus now." There was eagerness in Marilynn's voice.

"I'm a man what likes to sip his pleasure, make it last. I don't need to take it as fast as Raoul."

"Raoul was a pig."

"But he served, eh?"

"Oh, but not like you can. I know it. Raoul does not know how to treat a woman."

"Now, lass, here sits an expert. I know just what you need."

Antonie felt disgusted by the ensuing recital as well as how clearly it was exciting Marilynn. She wondered where a man like O'Neill knew of such sick behavior. Trying to ignore it, she looked at the others in the room. Cole, clearly having guessed Liam's game, looked sardonically amused. Justin looked shocked while Royal's face was unreadable. Since Liam was leaving them in no doubt as to how Marilynn found her pleasures, Antonie could only wonder if Royal was struggling to hide a deep hurt. Then Liam said something that pricked at her sense of humor. She thought he had said it for their benefit because he knew they were listening. She pressed her face against Oro's trembling stomach to smother her ill-timed laugh.

"Take me. Please, take me. God, I want you to do all those things to me."

"And more, no doubt."

"I do have a few ideas of my own," Marilynn purred. "You can't leave me like this. Arouse me then push me aside."

"Don't fret, slut. I've no liking to do my riding in a chair."

"There's beds in there. Please don't leave me like this."

"What? No one at home to do the job?"

"None like you. Only gentlemen of refinement, weak men who don't understand the things a woman needs."

"Not like Raoul, eh?"

"Raoul was barely bearable. I could use a man like you. Raoul hasn't done as well as I thought he would."

"Got some more obstacles to clear away, have you?"

"Five. Then I'll have the biggest spread in the land and you could be at my side."

In an attempt to convince him, Marilynn outlined all her plans. With a little prodding and a great deal of flattery O'Neill got her to confess to everything. By interspersing his interrogation with promises of giving her all the twisted loving she could desire, he kept Marilynn eager to talk, to finish discussing business so that he could satisfy the needs he had aroused in her.

"Five is it? That'll take some thought. Come on, wench, I know many a way you can work to change my mind," he said at last.

When the pair began to walk to the door, Antonie's gaze flew to Royal. She nearly ground her teeth in sheer frustration when she saw that his features held about as much expression as a rock. Even as she feared it, she had hoped for some revelation of how he felt about Marilynn. She could still only guess at that and her own feelings, her own doubts and fears, made

344

that a far from successful venture.

The door was flung open and, for a moment, they all stared at each other. Marilynn's features held shock and disbelief but that quickly changed to anger, blended with fear. Liam leaned idly against the door jamb watching them but mostly looking at Marilynn.

"Sure 'n didn't I just forget that we had company."

"You bastard. You tricked me." Marilynn flung herself at Liam, her fingers curled onto claws.

Without pause, Liam curled up one large fist and connected it firmly with her jaw. Marilynn fell in a limp pile at his feet. Idly, he nudged her with his foot, musing aloud that he may not have pulled his punch as much as he had thought to.

"Liam," Antonie breathed in honest shock, "you hit a woman."

"I hit scum. You know I like women. A good woman like you, lass, can wrap me round her wee finger. I'd cut off my arm afore I'd hurt one of the fair sex, be they whore or nun. This," he nudged Marilynn again, "is filth. This sort can't feel any pleasure unless there's pain and humiliation. That sickness taints everything in them. It makes them able to want a whole family dead just so they can have a cattle empire. This is no woman but a sick beast wearing a woman's fine skin." He looked at Royal. "Her saddlebags on the table hold some proof."

Little was said as they collected up the saddlebags and restrained Marilynn. Royal's silence troubled Antonie but she did not press him. If he cared for Marilynn at all, this revelation of what she was and what she had planned to do had to hurt. Antonie could not stop herself from wondering if his silence was a result of his pain.

They did their best to keep Antonie comfortable for

the ride home but her head was fogged with pain and exhaustion by the time she got there. She was only vaguely aware of Royal carrying her upstairs and placing her on one of the beds in the room with Tomás. Somehow she managed to say enough to ease the fever-ridden Tomás's worries, but then she slept.

Royal and Cole delivered Marilynn to the sheriff who immediately sent men after her father. By the time they had reached town, Marilynn was in a raging fury and said all that was needed to get herself hanged. It amazed Royal that he had been so blind to her character. Hastily leaving the sheriff's office to escape the verbal filth she directed at him, he was ashamed of the time that he had thought her better than Antonie.

It was not until later, as he sat with his family, that he realized he may have erred yet again. Liam was entertaining Oro who was confined to his bed, his abused leg raised and covered in compresses. Therefore, only his siblings joined him in the small library for an after-dinner drink. They sat quietly, shocked by the events of the last twenty-four hours.

"Are you really going to marry Antonie?"

"Yes, Pattie, I am and quickly. If nothing else," Royal said dryly, "I've got to use all the time I can grab hold of to talk her out of naming the baby Juan Ramirez if it's a son."

Patricia smiled a little. "That could cause a little bit of trouble and there's been enough of that already."

"You should've told her what you'd planned with Marilynn."

"Really? What should I have done, Justin? Turned to her in the night and casually informed her that I planned to seduce Marilynn in the morning?"

"More or less. Tony ain't stupid. If you'd have told

346

her of your suspicions she'd have understood. She might not have liked the method of interrogation but she wouldn't have misunderstood as she did and bolted."

It was something Royal was all too painfully aware of. "I know," he said in a quiet voice laden with guilt.

"That's not saying this all could have been prevented," Justin said hastily. "Raoul's wanted her dead for a long time."

"True," Cole agreed. "An old feud. As often happens, it was bequeathed from father to child. As Oro said, Raoul saw Juan in Tony."

"It's over now, thank God. Do you think they'll hang Marilynn?"

"I don't know, Pattie," Royal answered. "They will lock her up though and her father will probably hang."

"Our neighbors," she faltered. "Ones we thought our friends. It's hard to comprehend."

"Greed, Pattie," Cole drawled. "Simple as that. They wanted it all. What's frightening is that they almost succeeded. That they didn't we owe to Tony, Oro and Tomás. They pushed Raoul to recklessness and Tony pushed Marilynn to it." He looked at Royal. "Marilynn could see better than you where Antonie was concerned. Women can sense when another woman's a real threat."

"Strange little creatures, aren't they," murmured Royal.

"Thank you very much," Patricia huffed, glaring her her three chuckling brothers.

Maria entered with a snack and Justin asked, "How are your patients?"

"Doing well. The *señorita* sleeps and so does the boy. It was good for him to know that his sister, she was safe. It eased his mind and he will heal better now. He is strong. *Sí,* and so is the *señorita.*"

"The baby?" Royal ventured, unable to stop worrying about what harm could have been caused by Antonie's ordeal.

"A strong child. He clings and thrives. Once the baby is well begun, *Señor,* it is hard to shake him free. The *señorita,* she knew how to act. That too helped. No bad fear or shock to hurt the child."

Relieved, he nodded, understanding what Maria meant. Antonie had known what she had faced. Her courage and the pride that kept her from cowering before her enemy had strengthened the child. A woman's state of mind could affect the child she carried and Antonie's had held firm, refusing to succumb to hysteria or shock. Fortunately, she had not had to hold out for too long. Even Antonie had to have a breaking point or, at least, her body did.

Even now, with her safe within the walls of his home, the aftertaste of fear was in his mouth. He wondered if he would ever forget how she looked tied and naked and so very helpless, Raoul preparing to sear her soft flesh. Royal knew he would never be able to forget how nearly he had lost her.

Liam wandered in a while later and Patricia quietly slipped away to join Oro. Royal could see that his brothers were as curious as he was about the big Irishman, but they held their questions until he was seated with a brandy and a fine cigar. The laughter in the man's eyes told Royal that Liam was well aware of how they felt.

"I'm a bounty hunter," he announced carefully, watching their faces closely.

"Of course," Cole groaned. "I would have recognized the name except that I was preoccupied. 'Bring 'em back alive' O'Neill."

"Er, isn't that dead or alive?"

"Not with Liam O'Neill, Justin."

"A bounty hunter friendly with a *bandito?*"

"Well, now, Royal, the man saved my life. I owed him and so I'd never go after him. He knew that. I also don't bother to hunt down men like Juan was. Sure way to die unless you've got an army behind you."

"I'd gotten the feeling that you'd ridden with them," Royal said slowly.

"Did, but not on this side of the border. Against their enemies on that side. Government or otherwise."

"So you've known Antonie for a while."

Liam nodded. "Got yourself a fine woman there."

"I know," Royal said quietly.

" 'Course, ain't telling just how long you'll have her if you don't tell her what you were up to with that whore."

It passed through Royal's mind that he should tell Liam to mind his own business but instead he murmured, "I thought I ought to wait until she's better."

"And you might be talking to thin air when you do. She's got it in her head that you wanted that redhead. Don't know what you're wanting to say to Tony but I'd clear up that misunderstanding real quick, for Tony's not about to take second place even if the other woman's locked up somewhere."

Seeing the truth in that, Royal later found himself at Antonie's bedside. He intended to let her know why he had been holding Marilynn. All the rest, such as getting married, could be discussed later, when she was stronger.

She looked so small and young as she lay sleeping. He felt a strong urge to protect her even though he knew she did not really need that. She was a woman to stand at a man's side, not behind him.

So caught up was he in studying her that he was a little startled to suddenly find her looking at him. Her eyes were heavy lidded with sleep but clear of a fever's brightness. He fervently hoped that they would stay that way, that her ordeal could be so easily recovered from.

"Tomás?" Her gaze flew to the young man's sleeping form.

"He's going to be all right, honey. Here, Maria left some broth and a potion. You need plenty of rest. This lot'll see to that."

"I will be washed from the bed, eh?"

He smiled a little as he helped her sit up. "Can you manage?" he asked as he handed her the bowl of hearty broth.

"*Sí.* I am exhausted is all. My hurts were little ones."

Antonie tried to concentrate on eating. She was filled with questions but afraid of the answers. The picture of him holding Marilynn came to mind all too easily. With it came a pain that easily surmounted all her bodily ones.

"I have to talk to you," he began when he took the empty bowl from her and handed her the potion.

"*Sí?*" She gulped down the potion, wishing it would work on her immediately. "About what, *querido?*"

"About Marilynn," he began a little awkwardly.

"I am sorry. I was hoping you would not find out what she is. Then too, I wanted you to because she was a danger to you. It was a very bad situation. Still, it is sad that it could not be other than it was."

"It was certainly a shock to see her so clearly. I had suspected her though, Antonie."

"You had?" She forced herself to listen calmly, to

suppress all hope until she was sure of how he felt about the matter.

Royal nodded, reaching to take Antonie's hand between his. "It suddenly penetrated this thick skull of mine that she was the only one who could have been informing Raoul. She'd also been seen in the wrong places at the wrong times. Nobody had seen her actually meet Raoul, however. It was all supposition. Not a scrap of real hard proof."

"If you knew that, why did you want to marry her?"

"I didn't."

Shaking her head, Antonie muttered, "Now you make no sense, *mi vida*."

"There was one thing I always knew about Marilynn. She was vain. I knew I could get her to believe that I would marry her, probably even that I was besotted. In doing that, I'd hoped to make her slip. I fully intended to give her information that was false, that she would then deliver to Raoul."

"Oh. And I ruined this plan?"

"No. It was set for next week. In a way, you did the same thing because it was Marilynn who told Raoul where to find you."

"*Sí.*" She fought the effects of the potion for she wanted to hear all he had to say. "She met me as I was leaving. I told her." She grimaced over her own stupidity. "I nearly got Tomás killed."

"You couldn't know, Antonie. It took a long time for me to figure it all out."

"Juan taught me to speak carefully all the time, to trust few. She was not of your family, she was suspect and so I should have been more careful." She could not hold back a yawn and her eyelids began to feel very heavy. "I was angry and spoke with no thought."

"So has everyone at times. You can't go blaming

351

yourself." He helped her lie back down. "If we're going to start scattering blame, we better start throwing some my way because I started the whole mess by not telling you what I had planned." Brushing the strands of hair from her face, he added, "I have a lot of faults but I'm not a man to leave the arms of one woman and minutes later propose to another."

"I think maybe I would have thought of that later," she murmured sleepily. "Still, you were to have maybe married her."

"So everyone assumed. It was merely a plan, nothing was meant, either what was said or anything you saw me do."

"You looked like you meant it," she grumbled, unable to hold off sleep much longer. "I would not have liked that plan."

"I know. That's why I didn't tell you. I wanted to avoid an argument." He bent to brush a kiss over her mouth. "Go to sleep."

"I think I am going to have to," she sighed, falling asleep even as she finished speaking.

Royal smiled a little as he settled himself back in his chair by the bed. Maria would be in soon to watch over the pair. For a while, even though he was exhausted, he wanted to simply look at Antonie, to reassure himself that she was alive and would soon be well again. The fear that he had permanently lost her still left a bitter taste in his mouth. He watched her light breathing as if he had never seen it before.

His eyes drifted finally to her belly. He could see now that it was no longer concave, but slightly rounded. Very soon it would round even more with the growth of the child they had created together. Royal shook his head, knowing that it would take him a long time to get used to the idea that he was to be a father. Only now was he aware that he had taken absolutely no care to prevent such a thing, something he had always been careful to do in the past.

"You will see the truth of the child soon," came Maria's soft voice as she entered the room. "Very soon the *señorita* will show clearly. She does a little now."

"It is hard to believe when she is still so slim."

"The first child is slow to round the belly," Maria said as she took the seat he had just vacated. "If she was not sleeping from the potion, you could feel your child maybe but the potion puts the baby to sleep too."

"It won't hurt the child?"

"No, *señor*. I will not give her much after this night but her body needs the peace now. You go to your bed now, *señor*, I will watch them. I am thinking I will be needing you rested well to help me keep the *señorita* in her bed soon, eh?"

He smiled a little as he headed out of the room. "Most likely."

His bed was a welcome sight. Despite his concern for Antonie, he was exhausted. As he lay down, and almost immediately began to go to sleep, he sensed he would need his strength not only to see that Antonie took care of herself but that she married him. Somehow, he knew it was not going to be a simple matter of proposing and getting an acceptance.

Chapter Twenty-five

"Aces and fours. Two aces and three fours. Full house, darlin'."

Antonie's eyes narrowed as she studied the poker hand Liam was proudly displaying and laid out her own hand. "I have a full house too. Three aces and two nines."

"I only have two pair and an ace," Tomás said, his eyes alive with laughter.

"Ah, well, Antonie has won this hand," O'Neill collected up the cards. "My deal."

"I think we need a new deck, *amigo*."

"A new deck, love? Why?"

It was hard not to laugh at the extremely innocent look on O'Neill's almost too handsome face and Antonie could hear the laughter in her voice. "Because this deck has too many aces."

"Too many?"

"*Sí*. Six."

"No, it doesn't."

"*Sí*. It does. I counted them."

"Nonsense. There's ten."

"Ten aces?" she squeaked and then started to laugh.

"Yup. Ten. Aces are nice to have in a hand. Figured I'd put in enough for everyone." He grinned when Antonie and Tomás began to laugh.

Royal knew his knock could not be heard and

quietly entered the room. His eyes immediately went to Antonie. She wore her peasant dress, her hair loosely tied back into one thick swatch. The loose fit of her clothes did not entirely hide the rounding of her stomach.

He had waited to speak to her until he felt she was well on the road to recovery. Her wounds had been slight but the ordeal had been hard on her. Fears for the health of the child had made them pamper her and had kept her from protesting. Looking at her laughing so heartily with the two men made him think that they had been overly cautious.

Reluctantly, he admitted that some of his hesitation was due to a healthy dose of cowardice. He was not exactly sure what he felt for Antonie or what she felt for him, making it very difficult for him to think of a way of proposing marriage. He knew he might also have to find a way to convince her to marry him.

Since he had explained what he had been up to with Marilynn, he had taken things slowly with Antonie by courting her. He could only hope it had worked. Then he would not have to demand anything. He wanted her and he wanted the child that she carried in her womb to bear his name.

"Royal, he's cheating," Antonie said with a laugh when she realized that Royal had joined them.

"Lass, how can you say that? If I'd been cheating, I would have given myself all the aces."

"I think I would have suspected something if you had dealt yourself ten cards, O'Neill," Antonie said firmly.

"Ten?"

"*Sí*, Royal. There are ten aces in that deck."

"A fine card the ace," O'Neill murmured.

"Remind me not to play cards with you, O'Neill. You look better every day, Tomás."

"Ah, *sí*, soon I can hobble about your house like Oro, eh? Matching gimps, O'Neill calls us. I think I will shoot him."

"I think I would too," Royal said when he stopped laughing. "Antonie, could I speak to you, please."

"Certainly. Here I am."

"Cute." He took her by the hand and gently tugged her off the bed. "In private."

Antonie tried not to hide her nervousness as she followed Royal into his room. It was a struggle for he looked very serious. There were several topics of conversation facing them that could cause that look and she was not sure she was all that ready to get into any of them. She admitted to herself that she was being cowardly but she didn't care.

In her less sensible moments, she had found herself wishing things could go on as they had been. But that could not be and she knew it. The baby changed everything. They might not be ready for any decisions but they had to be made.

Sitting on the edge of the bed, she watched him a little warily. He had not been acting quite the same with her. There were some subtle changes in his treatment of her, none of which were disturbing her. What really troubled her was that he hardly ever touched her. She knew she had been in no condition to make love until very recently but he hardly even put his arm around her. Antonie admitted to herself that she was hungry for some sort of contact with him, even like that simple but brief holding of hands while he had helped her stand up a moment ago. She was beginning to fear that the fire in him, the one they had shared, had died.

"There's been a verdict on Marilynn and her father," Royal cursed himself for yet again being cowardly, using that topic to avoid the confrontation he

356

had to face. "Her father will hang and she will be sent to prison."

Her heart sank. There was only one reason she could think of for him to require privacy to tell her that news. He was saying that the battle they had fought together was ended and now it was over between them. The interest he showed in the child they had created was not strong enough to make him want to keep her around.

"She should hang too. She is as guilty as he is." She watched him closely as she spoke, trying to see how he felt.

"Marry me, Antonie."

She gaped at him. She had just about convinced herself that he was going to tell her to go. This abrupt proposal, half question and half command, was totally unexpected.

"Why are you looking so surprised? You must've known I'd ask you."

"I thought you were going to tell me to go, that the fight is done now and I must leave."

He moved to stand in front of her. At times she could be a source of great confusion to him. Any other woman would not only expect a proposal but demand one. She sat there thinking that he would send her and their child away and did not seem to be contemplating anything to change that callous dismissal.

"Antonie, in case you hadn't noticed, you carry my child," he said sarcastically.

"It is hard not to notice. I cannot button this skirt."

"Do you really think I would be so mean, so hard, as to just tell you to go?"

"What is hard? If you do not want us, it is best. Better to send us away than to hold onto us for only duty."

"Is that all you think I feel for you and the child?"

He looked as if she had insulted him, even hurt him and she replied a little weakly, "I cannot be sure. We had the fire, *si?* But, since I was taken by Raoul you have not touched me."

"Of course not. You were healing, recovering from your wounds, shock and exhaustion."

"No, I do not mean making love. I mean you have not even touched me. If Raoul had raped me, maybe his men too, I could think it was that but they did not. Still, you do not touch me. Here you ask me to marry you but you stand at distance and do not even take my hand. I am thinking the fire has died in you."

"Oh no, Antonie. Not by a long shot. It's still strong, maybe stronger than ever. That's why I haven't touched you."

"I do not understand."

"If I touch you, I'm going to want to make love to you. The longer we go without making love, the worse it gets. One of the ways to help keep myself in hand is to keep my hands to myself. Even talking about it has me aching for you." He smiled crookedly when her gaze fell briefly then her eyes widened. "I think it's become permanent."

"I am healed now," she said quietly, her passion immediately stirred by the evidence of his arousal.

"I know. You've been healed enough for that for a while if we were careful. I've been working up the courage to talk about getting married and I thought it best if we didn't make love until it was all sorted out. I even thought it'd make our wedding night a little more well, special, if we'd suffered a dry spell beforehand. I still do."

He still felt the fire for her and was not prompted by duty alone. Knowing this eased the knot that had formed around Antonie's heart but she hesitated and did not really know why. Before she had fallen into Raoul's hands his declaration would have been enough.

"What about Marilynn?"

"What does she have to do with this?"

"For a long time you wanted to marry her."

"Antonie, that woman made a fool of me. She wanted to take my land, kill my family. She did kill my parents. Even if I could forgive that, convince myself that she was forced to do such things by her father, I certainly couldn't ignore what was said and done at that shack, what she admitted to doing with Raoul and what she was ready to do with O'Neill."

"O'Neill had a time forgetting it too," she murmured, smiling despite her blushes. "He keeps wondering if he was a fool to let his sensibilities get in the way of a good, er, how did he put it?, shag."

"The man shouldn't talk like that in front of you," Royal said with a shake of his head and a half-smile. "Antonie," he continued seriously, "I have never had any deep feelings for Marilynn. When I found out the truth, I was angry because I'd been made a fool of and because our family had trusted her and her father. Even before that I'd begun to wonder why I had ever thought of marrying her. I suppose it was because she was, well, there and of my world."

"I am not," she said quietly and hurried on when he prepared to protest. "I am Mexican. Maybe not in blood but in soul, eh? I am a *bandito's* child. I do not know all these ways a lady must know. Maybe that will be a trouble between us later. A big one. Maybe you should think harder on this."

"I've done all the thinking I want to. I'll be honest with you, love. It took me a long time to forget how you were raised."

"You should not forget. It is what I am."

359

"I know. Forget's the wrong word. Let's say I suddenly saw it was not only Marilynn who made a fool out of me. I was doing a pretty good job of making a fool of myself. Marilynn was what the world would call a lady. She was raised in wealth and comfort, schooled well and all that but look at the rot it hid. It was suddenly clear to me that all that gloss and that fine background isn't what counts. In truth, I was seeing your background as far worse than it was.

"Juan was a hard man, an outlaw who lived by raiding. Still, he was not cruel. He didn't hate like some of them do. Given half a chance, he could've been a great man in the lawful world. He loved you and did his best to keep you out of his business. He knew his way of life was wrong and didn't want you to follow it. Oh, things could've been a lot better for you but there's not all that much to fault in that."

Impulsively, she kissed him. She then found herself in the midst of a very heated embrace but she did not pull back. When he suddenly pulled away and firmly set her at a distance, she was more than a little disappointed. The only thing that kept her from getting somewhat depressed was that she now had proof that he still really desired her, more proof than the earlier visual one. His kiss had held all the same fiery hunger that it always had.

"Enough of that. Are we getting married?"

"It is not just for the baby that you ask?"

"No, although I'd be lying if I said that wasn't a part of it. I want that child to carry my name. Look, I'm not good with words . . ."

"No, what you said is enough." She did not really want him to explain himself. She feared he would say a lot she might like but not the words that she craved and that would hurt. "*Sí*. We will wed. When?"

"Saturday. That's the first day the preacher could come out here."

"You have already asked the preacher to come?"

Royal grimaced then watched her warily as he admitted, "I wasn't planning on letting you say no."

"When did you get the preacher?"

"About a week ago."

"Why did you wait so long to ask me then?"

"Cowardice."

"You are afraid of me?" Antonie said, surprised.

"I was afraid I'd end up having to force you to marry me and I didn't want it to be that way."

"Force me? How could you force me?"

"Well, I hadn't really figured that out. That's another reason I hesitated." He smiled crookedly when she giggled. "Any other things you want to ask me?"

"*Sí.*" She took a deep breath to boost her courage, wondering idly why it was sometimes harder to talk to him than to face the whole of Raoul's army. "This is to be a real marriage?"

"I'm not quite sure what you're getting at but I'll tell you what's in my head as I think of what's ahead. We'll share a bed, we'll work together, enjoy the benefits together, have babies . . ."

"Can I get this one out first?" she asked pertly.

"I think I can allow that."

"How kind."

"Where was I?"

"Babies."

"Ah, Yes. We'll have babies, watch them grow and have their own, which we'll tell them how to raise, and," he looked at her sternly, "there will be no running off with handsome young men the minute my back is turned."

"*Sí.* And no saloons? Or Louise's? Or hot little bits on the side?"

"No and your language is atrocious. Hot little bits on the side?"

"That is what Tomás says many wives complain about."

"And he sympathizes beautifully then takes them to bed."

"*Sí.*" She grinned.

"That boy's going to get himself shot."

"There is a good chance, I am thinking."

"Enough talk about Tomás's meanderings," he sighed, "and bed. I've only got two more days to wait."

She had to look away to keep her composure, the warmth of his gaze heating her blood. "*Sí.* Two days. I will go and talk to Patricia and Maria." She started toward the door, glancing back at him as she opened it. "You could go and play cards with O'Neill," she suggested then laughed and hurried downstairs.

Patricia's pleasure over the news, as well as that of Maria and Rosa, pleased Antonie. The more fully accepted she was, the greater a part of Royal's life she would be and that could only be good for her marriage.

For the rest of the day, she was deeply involved in preparations for the wedding. Because it was such short notice and she was so visibly pregnant, it would only be attended by those at the ranch and a few very close friends. Royal was somewhat apologetic about that until Antonie finally got him to understand that she really did not mind. She did not know many people outside of the ranch anyway.

Although tired when she finally sought her bed, Antonie found sleep elusive. She felt a leap of excitement when a soft rap came at the door. It was only a little depressing when Patricia entered instead of Royal. She would much rather have spent the night making love but a nice chat would be pleasant. It

362

could well help her get to sleep. Whatever was keeping her awake could well be eased by talking it out. She just wished she knew what it was.

"I wasn't sure you'd be alone," Patricia said then blushed as she sat on the bed.

"Ah, Royal's being very much the gentleman. He says it will make the wedding night special."

"Interesting, certainly," Patricia said, then giggled and Antonie smiled. "It's rather nice too."

"You sound surprised. Do you not think your brother can be nice?"

"It's always hard to think of a brother being a lover or romantic or anything like that. I mean, a brother, especially an older one, is the one who tells you to shut your mouth or not to get underfoot or go away or glares at your beau so hard the poor fellow can't speak. I had four older brothers to do that to me."

"One died in the war, right?"

"Yes." Patricia sighed. "Denton. He was in between Royal and Cole. It was sad. I'd prepared myself for one of them to die though. I knew it would be a miracle for all three to come home safe and whole. It's a shame I didn't dislike any of my brothers like some sisters do. I hate anyone to die but it must help if you can say, well, at least it wasn't the one I liked or something. The really horrible thing about Denton is that they never found him. Not a trace."

"Oh. Then how do they know he was killed?"

"Because there was a big hole and his dead horse where they'd last seen him." Patricia shivered. "How did we get onto this subject?"

"You were talking about your brothers."

"Right. Royal. And you. Antonie, are you sure about this? It's just, well, you don't act like you're marrying the man you want."

"Ah, because I am not distracted or blushing or

dreamy?"

"Well, yes. Don't you love him?"

"*Sí*. I love him, but if you tell that to him I will beat you." Antonie realized that she was only half teasing.

"You haven't told him?"

"No. He has not said these words to me."

"So you don't say them."

"No. Did you think this was a love match like you and Oro?"

"I'm not sure. It's not just because of the baby, is it?"

"*Sí* and no. I cannot be sure he would never ask me to marry him but he does ask now because of the baby. He wants his child to carry his name."

"But he wants you too."

"*Sí*. I think so. There is a fire there still."

"How can you be so calm about it?"

"What is there not to be calm about?"

"You're getting married yet it all sounds so unromantic and getting married should be romantic. It's forever."

"Are you and Oro always romantic, loving and soft-eyed? I think not. Ah, *El Magnifico*." She scratched the swiftly growing puppy behind his ears when he crawled up onto the bed to lie beside her. "Get lonely under the bed?"

"He's going to be huge. Look, Antonie, I'm not so foolish as to think everything is loving all the time."

"I know. It is hard for me to explain. I would like to be the glowing bride and I am sorry I am not. I am glad to be a bride though. Do not think that I am not. Before I left and fell into Raoul's hands, I had hoped for it. I was going to tell Royal about the baby. I felt I had seen enough in him to know that it would not only be the baby that our marriage would be based on. There are other things than passion too. I was sure of it."

"Are you still sure of it?"

"I think so, but now that I face it, I wonder. This is normal, I think."

"Yes, I wondered about Oro, about me, oh, about everything. It's because it is forever."

"*Sí*. Forever. I will be honest. Something was troubling me and I see it now. It is forever and in my heart there is the fear that even with forever I won't be able to make him love me. A silly thing, really."

"No, of course it isn't."

"No? It is the only thing he does not offer me. He even speaks of faithfulness. To moan about what I do not have when I have so much is foolishness. It is the sort of thinking that will make things worse."

"How so?"

"Because I will get bitter, eh? It is not his fault. He never asked it of me. To blame him because I gave love and did not get any back is not right. He is not without feeling for me."

"That is certainly true. You should have seen him when you'd left him. It only made it worse that it was really his own fault."

"*Sí*. It was." She grinned when Patricia giggled. "He should have told me but he knows that, so it is forgotten."

"I'm not so sure he will forget," Patricia said quietly. "Or to forgive himself for being at least partly responsible for your ordeal. You came too close to being horribly tortured. That is something that is not so easy to forget."

"Ah, well, I will work on that. I never told him what Raoul was like. I knew. I knew too that Royal, even Cole, did not. Maybe they did not listen to the stories about Raoul. They are hard to believe. Royal could not know what would happen to me. Also,

365

Tomás and I did not take care. That was very foolish and we paid for it. Always we have watched and been careful. Not that time."

"You were upset."

"That is no excuse. If we had done as we were taught, and taught so well, I think I would not have been caught and Tomás would not have been shot. I would not have been brought so close to such a horrible death. It is my lesson and I am not one to forget such a lesson."

Watching Patricia closely and recalling the conversation she had had earlier with Oro, Antonie asked gently, "And now that I speak of lessons, tell me, *chica*, have you and that fool Oro made love yet?"

Although she gasped, then blushed deeply, Patricia shook her head. "His leg, you know. Riding out like he did set him back some."

"He must be getting, how you say, very grumpy."

Patricia giggled. "Very. Though, I catch him looking at me funny sometimes."

Antonie laughed. "He is thinking of what I said once but I see he did not really listen. Now I will tell you."

When Patricia left, Antonie snuggled down into her bed and laughed softly. Patricia had been very embarrassed but also very fascinated. Oro was in for a big surprise. Although Patricia's cheeks had still been bright red when she had left, there had been a determined glint in her eyes. Antonie felt just a little bit jealous. Patricia and Oro would be loving each other tonight while she was stuck in her bed with only *El Magnifico* for company. And he snored, she thought with a wry smile.

She firmly told herself not to be silly. In a way, Royal was right. This small period of deprivation would add something to their wedding night, make it a little special. They had been lovers too long to act or feel like newlyweds but at least they could have the enjoyment of the return of something they had both sorely missed. It would be almost as good, maybe better.

Yawning, Antonie let approaching sleep overtake her. The talk with Patricia had helped. She had faced the fear she had not really known she had. Although she had not conquered it, she could now view it with some sense of acceptance. It would no longer secretly gnaw at her. Perhaps, one day, she might even be able to laugh at it.

Briefly, Antonie wondered if Patricia was right. Maybe she should admit her love to Royal. She shook her head. If nothing else, she could well be burdening him with guilt because he could not return her feelings and she would be hurt. No, she decided as sleep exerted its irresistible pull, that would be a secret she would hold onto for a while longer. Perhaps luck would be with her and one day she would be free to surround Royal with her love and speak of it freely.

Chapter Twenty-six

Antonie found it hard to believe that in one hour she would stand before a preacher with Royal. She still remembered the talk she and Royal had had, word for word. Despite her immersion in the wedding preparations she felt a sense of disbelief. She supposed she would not fully believe it until the words were said.

She stared down at the three headstones in the small family graveyard. Soon she would be part of this permanence. Never again would she be in a different place every night or call home the small village where Juan had been born only because he stopped there a little more often than he did anywhere else. Here would be a true home. Here she and Royal would live, have children, grow old together and die. It was a thought that was both comforting and frightening. Such permanence would take adjusting to.

Suddenly, she tensed, her hand slipping through the concealed slits in her skirts to grasp the knife strapped to her thigh. She wondered who was creeping up on her even before she heard the soft rustle of a footstep. With a lithe grace not at all hindered by her pregnancy, she whirled around even as she drew

368

her knife. Crouched and ready to fight or throw her knife, she faced a tall, young man whose forest green eyes widened as his arms went up in a gesture of surrender.

"Easy, honey. Easy now. I'm not meaning you any harm. Phew. Never seen a woman move like that."

"What are you doing here?" she demanded as she signaled for him to toss his guns to her. "Slow and easy, *señor*."

"Hell, lady, I'm not going to hurt a woman," he grumbled even as he very carefully pulled his gun from its holster.

"Not now, eh?" She picked up the gun he tossed her way. "I asked what you are doing here."

"That's a long story. Look, does a desperado lug his kid around with him?"

Her eyes widened when he took a very careful step to the side. A basket was on the ground just behind him. Two small arms waved in the air, the tiny hands trying to grab the leaves moving gently overhead. Still keeping an eye on the man, she edged closer to peer inside the basket at the infant shaded by the tree it fruitlessly reached for.

"Boy or girl?" she asked as she sheathed her knife.

"Boy. His name's Camden. My gun?"

"Not yet, *señor*."

"Not very trusting, are you."

"No. There has been much trouble here. It is over, I think, but—" she shrugged.

"That trouble killed the elder Bancrofts?"

"*Sí* ." She frowned for there was grief in his eyes, a deep grief no stranger or casual friend would feel. "Not their son. That was the war." She smiled when the baby grasped her finger. "Strong. His mother?"

"She died birthing him. She was sickly," he added hastily, his eyes going to her stomach.

"Do not worry, *señor*. I know the dangers. I will beat them. I am sorry your wife did not."

"The rest of the Bancrofts?"

"They are well."

"Is something going on? Seems to be guests coming."

"I am to be married." The grin that tugged at his mouth reminded her of Royal.

"A little slow to get to the altar, aren't you?"

"Just a little," she murmured, smiling back.

"Which one are you marrying?"

"Royal."

"Yes, he'd dawdle."

A shock went through her. She suddenly knew who stood before her. The resemblance was in his lean face only slightly married by a scar that ran the length of the right side. She looked more closely at him.

"I think you dawdle too. The war was over in '65."

"And Gettysburg even longer ago. Centuries," he whispered. "How did you know?"

"The look is there."

"We Bancrofts have a look, do we?"

"*Sí.* I also know you are not under there." She pointed at his headstone.

"It was close. Very close."

"I think you'd better come to the house."

"I was hoping it'd only be family."

"There are only a few others. This marriage was decided quickly. It took a lot of thinking, there was a fight to win and I had to heal from wounds. Come." She stood up from where she had crouched by the baby, then lifted the basket. "I will carry the baby. I am thinking you will need your arms free." When he still hesitated, she grasped him by the arm and tugged him along. "You cannot hide here."

"It's going to be one hell of a surprise."

"*Sí*, and then they might be angry. You left them to think you were dead."

"There's something about being blown off your horse that rattles your memory."

"For so long?"

"My wife didn't want to remember. She knew but she didn't tell me until she knew that she was dying."

"And you have not forgiven her?"

"Not really, but I've come to understand. Besides, she gave me Camden. Who are you?"

"Antonie Doberman Ramirez."

"Hell, you don't look Mexican."

"I was not born Mexican. I was raised Mexican." As they stepped up onto the veranda he stopped again. "Only a little farther," she said, urging him to walk with her.

"This might stop your wedding."

"No, only delay it a little. Ah, here comes Royal. He probably thinks I tried to run away again."

"Do that often, do you?"

"Just once." Antonie smiled when Royal flung open the front door and scowled at her. "Here I am."

"Where've you been?"

"For a walk."

"What's that?" Royal stared at the baby.

"A baby. Not mine. Mine is still getting ready."

"Funny, Tony."

"The baby is his."

"I was just about to ask about him." Royal looked at the man standing by Antonie and slowly paled. "Jesus."

"Wrong resurrection," Antonie murmured, causing Denton to laugh nervously and Royal to glance at her a little wildly. "Someone put the bits together, eh?"

"It's impossible," Royal whispered even as he reached out to touch the brother he had thought dead

371

for so long.

"Why? You found no trace. This is why." Antonie kept her voice calm for she could see how deeply shocked Royal was. "Is it so hard to believe?"

"It's really you, Denton?" Royal asked hoarsely.

When Denton nodded, Antonie found herself completely forgotten. She followed Royal when, after tightly hugging Denton for a long while, he dragged his brother into the house. Standing back a little, she watched the reunion, then separated Maria from the stunned group milling around Denton. Drinks would be needed soon and the baby should be seen to. Antonie wanted it all done before the explanations started. She did not want to miss what promised to be a fascinating if perhaps sad tale.

To her relief it was only just beginning to be told when she entered the parlor again, setting the glasses and drinks in easy reach. Even as she moved to sit by Royal, he reached out and tugged her down beside him. She could feel the tense excitement in him and held his hand. Her wedding was forgotten for the moment but she did not really mind. It was only a delay and there could be no better reason than this.

"Damn it, Denton, we looked everywhere," Cole said hoarsely. "Came back and looked again."

"Hell, I was nearly buried and thrown pretty far. Even the scavengers didn't find me, although for a long time I thought they had."

"So who found you?"

"This old farmer and his daughter, Elizabeth. They were looking for his son. Found the boy's body. It killed the old man. He followed his only son to the grave by less than a week."

"And this Elizabeth took care of you?"

"Yes, Pattie, and it was a long time, a long slow healing." He touched the scar on his face. "This is only one of many and I'll always limp."

"Why didn't you send us word?"

"Simple, Royal. I didn't know who the hell to send word to. When I was blown off my horse, every memory was blown clean out of my head. Oh, there were little bits here and there but they never told me anything. I had my uniform and my wounds to tell me that I was a soldier who hadn't fared too well. That was it."

"You remembered nothing?"

"Not worth mentioning, Justin. Little pieces that flickered in and out and were mostly an annoyance. I'd grab for it, try for the whole and it'd slip away. It got so bad that I wouldn't even try."

"So when did you remember?" Royal asked.

"Not until Elizabeth told me what she had been hiding. See, I married her even before I was really healed." He looked around and when he saw the basket, collected up his son. "Camden Bancroft."

Antonie saw the quiet pride in the man's face and could hardly wait to see Royal with their child. She knew that whatever was or was not between them would not affect Royal's feelings toward his child. When he suddenly glanced her way, she could see the anticipation in his eyes and knew that she was right.

"Where is Elizabeth now?"

"Dead, Pattie."

"I'm sorry."

"I reckon I am too, in a way." Smiling at Patricia's shocked face, he said gently, "I married her because she was all I had. It's hard to explain. I don't think a body can feel more alone than when he has no idea of who he is or was. There was just Elizabeth. She called me John."

"So tell us how you remembered," Justin urged.

"It was a lot of things. Elizabeth was sickly when

she had the baby. She knew she was dying. That's when she told me what she'd done. She'd known from the start who I was but she said she was thirty-two, unwed, and, when her father and brother died, totally alone. So, when she realized I'd lost my memory she did her best to make sure it stayed lost."

"That's terrible."

"Well, it is, Pattie love, but, as time goes on, I understand her better. Anyhow, she took every bit of identification I had, put it in a little box and buried it. She told me my body'd been picked clean by the scavengers of all its valuables. She'd even cut the buttons off my uniform to substantiate her story.

"I don't know, I think it was everything together that brought back my memory. I'd just become a father, my wife was dying, finding out that she'd lied to me like that and then seeing the pitiful collection of things that told me who I was. It came back to me piece by piece as I traveled here. I left after Elizabeth died."

As everyone seemed to talk at once, marveling over the tale, Antonie nudged Royal. "It is good Elizabeth died, I think."

"You mean Denton might've killed her?"

"Worse. He would have hated her."

"You don't think he does now?"

"Not really. She died giving him a son and the truth. It takes away the bite from the hate. I think he also sees that she deserves pity. Either she loved him too much or she did not think much of herself." Antonie shook her head. "She might even have been a little *loco,* eh? Ah, now he wants to hear what you have been doing."

"Antonie said something about fighting?" Denton asked, looking at his brothers. "When did Ma and Pa die?"

"Let's start at the beginning. Raoul Mendez was hired by the Collinses," Royal began.

Antonie watched how their few guests listened as intently as Denton. She suspected it was the first time anyone outside of the whole business had heard the complete tale. A little smile touched her mouth as she thought about how quickly the story would now spread, especially since Royal was revealing a few things that had not been told at Marilynn's and her father's trial.

"Damn, I should've been here to help."

"It would've been good to have you, Denton, but we managed."

"I can see that. Only you, Royal, would get the help of one *bandito* against another."

"Juan was a *bandito*. Raoul was a pig," Antonie said quietly. "Now he is a dead pig."

"And roasting in hell, eh?" Oro said, grinning slightly.

"*Sí*, with Juan, Manuel and Julio turning the spit."

"You're that little girl everyone always thought he'd stolen," Denton said.

"*Sí*, but he did not steal me. I was alone so he took me up."

"And little Pattie married. Sorry I missed the wedding."

At the moment, Tomás entered, helped along by O'Neill. "Hey, I have hobbled down to see a wedding. Where is it?"

"Oh, m'God." Royal could not believe he had forgotten and looked at Antonie a little warily. "The wedding."

"The preacher has not run away, *querido*, although, I am thinking we best hurry for he likes the punch too much. We would not want him to forget his part, eh?" She smiled as he stood up, took her hand and helped her to her feet.

"Now, I can give you away," Oro said as he stood up.

"Ah, if I was not so beat up, I would give you away, little one," Tomás sighed dramatically.

"Well, if there's a dispute about who's to give her away, I'll do it," O'Neill offered.

"I could become insulted," Antonie drawled. "So many so eager to give me away." She grinned when everyone laughed.

"Wait, wait," Maria cried as she hurried forward. "There is something to do first." Grabbing Antonie by the arm, Maria pulled her out of the room. "This will take only a moment."

"Maybe it's not a good idea to keep waiting," Antonie said, only half teasing, as she let Maria pull her into Royal's study. "When did you sneak in here, Patricia?" she asked when they found her waiting.

"Just after Tomás came down. We were waiting for you to come back from your walk but then you brought Denton in and," Patricia shrugged then held up a dress. "For the bride."

Antonie was speechless as she stared at the dress Patricia held up. It was a lovely creation of creamy lace and silk. The dress she wore, the one she had bought after the drive, had seemed the loveliest she had ever seen. It paled in comparison to the one Patricia offered her. Antonie reached out to touch it.

"For me?"

"A bride should have a special dress."

"Where did it come from?"

"Maria and I made it."

"You did not make this in two days."

"Er, no. We couldn't. Come on, Maria, help me get her into this."

"Just when did you start making this?" Antonie

376

managed to ask even as Patricia and Maria started to undress her.

"Oh, all right, if you must know."

"*Sí*, Patricia, I must."

"When you got back from being held by Raoul and we knew you were safe."

"Ah, but you did not know that I would be marrying Royal."

"We-ell, he did mention it that night."

"Then why did he wait so long to mention it to me? You did not push him to ask?"

"Not an inch. Stop worrying so."

"*Chica*," Maria said gently, "men can tell the whole world that they will marry a certain girl, but they find it hard to tell the girl, eh? I do not understand but it is how it is. The *patrón* has wanted to marry you. I think even before he knew of the baby but such a thing gives a man the excuse, *sí?*"

"Antonie," Patricia said as she carefully put the other gown aside, "I can't guess at what Royal is feeling any better than you can but I do know that he wants to get married. He's not good with pretty words, I reckon. Not like Oro is." She grimaced. "Oro can say the moon is purple, *querida,* and I'd say, 'oh yes, Oro' by the time he finished pouring all his pretty words over me. Maybe if Royal was better with pretty words, you would not be so worried."

"I would probably worry that he did not mean them. I did not expect it to come to this and so I worry that it will not."

"Well, it will. As soon as we finish getting you all gussied up. We even have flowers for you."

"And so I will really look the bride."

"Exactly. You don't happen to know where everyone went yesterday, do you?" Patricia asked, worry lacing her voice.

"No, but I think they went to see the hanging."

"Oh. It's really over then."

"*Sí*, Over."

"You don't sound too sure, Antonie."

"Sometimes I do not feel too sure, eh?"

"But Henry Collins is dead, Raoul Mendez is dead and Marilynn is being sent to prison," Patricia insisted.

"She is alive."

"You would feel better if she wasn't?"

"I do not know. It is not vengeance that makes me think it would be better if she were not alive. I can hear Juan telling me that an enemy is always a danger as long as he is alive," Antonie mused.

"Well, that's a little harsh, isn't it?"

"No," said Maria quietly, "it is the way of it. A man like Juan Ramirez would know."

"He did not mean all enemies, Pattie," Antonie explained. "Only ones like Raoul."

"And you think Marilynn is like Raoul?"

"*Sí, chica.* There is something very bad inside Marilynn." Antonie made a face to illustrate her disgust. "There has to be if she could lie with a pig like Raoul and like it."

"What?" Patricia and Maria exclaimed.

"Ah, I see that you were not told everything. Even Oro did not tell you, Patricia?"

"He still thinks I am a little girl even after . . ." Patricia reddened. "Never mind."

"Aha, you followed my advice."

Still blushing, Patricia urged Antonie into a chair. "Hush, now you just sit there. We're going to do your hair and you are going to tell us what went on in that cabin."

"The preacher is getting drunk."

"Well, if he gets too bad, we'll dunk him in the

378

horse trough to sober him up. Now, talk," Patricia commanded.

Antonie dutifully told the women all the men had thought too shocking for them to know. She had to laugh sometimes for Maria and Patricia were blushing so brilliantly. When she had finished, she noticed that Maria was not really surprised and suspected that she had had some inner judgments that were now justified. Patricia still looked shocked and just a little confused.

"How is it that I never saw that in her?" Patricia asked. "Surely you would see it."

"Perhaps later. I think she had a sickness that was growing worse. Her plans were not working out and being with Raoul was feeding her sickness. Sí, even her pretty Anglo manners would not have hidden it for much longer, I think." She shifted restlessly in her chair. "Am I done? It grows late, eh? Royal may get tired of waiting," she jested, partly serious.

"You're ready. We don't have a nice big mirror but if you back away enough, you can see a lot in that little one."

Antonie just stared when she saw herself in the wall mirror. She found the change that clothes and hairstyle could wrought somewhat spellbinding. There was little doubt in her mind that she looked as fine as any rich Anglo lady could. As she prepared herself to return to Royal, she wryly mused that he might not recognize her.

Royal fidgeted and kept an eye on the preacher. Antonie was right. The man was certainly enjoying the punch. If she did not return soon so that they could get on with the ceremony, Royal feared that there would be another delay while they tried to sober up the preacher enough to read the service.

He suddenly realized that Denton had neatly managed it so that they had some privacy, as much as one could get in a room full of people. Royal knew it would take him a while to fully believe that Denton was alive. Even now he had to keep touching him as if to reassure himself that his brother was no chimera. Royal suspected that he would do that for a long while. Miracles, he decided, were unsettling things.

"That Oro fellow seems nice enough," Denton said quietly.

"Don't hedge, Denton," Royal said gently and smiled a little. "He wasn't what we'd planned on for Patricia."

"Yet you let them get together."

"I had to. They were both hurting. I hadn't seen it but they were trying to follow the rules, the rules that say a man like Oro shouldn't even touch a girl like Patricia because his mother was a halfbreed and his father was a *bandito*. He's a man and he was being a hell of a lot more gallant than many would be. Patricia was, by her own admission, throwing herself at him."

"Been any trouble over it yet?"

"Nothing big. A few folks have stopped coming round to see her."

"And she doesn't mind?" Denton asked, surprised.

"Not really. She's looking at it from the viewpoint that they weren't worth having around anyway. Oro might not be easy to get to know and a little hard but he's a good man and she knows it. She also knows it's his mixed blood they object to. It's funny but that seems to make it easier for her."

"She can blame it on ignorance."

"Probably. Well, at least I don't have to worry that the man she's married can't protect her."

"Hell no. Don't have to worry about that with you either."

"What do you mean?" Royal asked, curious.

"That little lady you're marrying can protect herself and you too probably if she has to." Denton laughed and shook his head. "Thought I was being quiet but she heard me and had that knife ready before I'd even guessed that she'd heard me."

"She had to learn to protect herself. It can't hurt."

"Don't get defensive. I'll admit that I wondered what the hell was going on but I've been talking to folks and it's not her that troubles me."

"But something does."

"Yeh. Are you sure about this, Royal? I married for all the wrong reasons. True, Elizabeth wasn't carrying my child at the time but my reasons were still wrong. It wasn't bad but it wasn't good either. It was day by slow day. Even though I didn't know who I was or where I could go, I thought of leaving a lot. I felt trapped. It's no good that way, Royal. Not for either of you. Elizabeth didn't get much joy out of her trick, only a little security."

"It's not just the baby, Denton."

"You love her?"

"Damned if I know. Maybe. I've been put to enough tests to know it's not just the baby and it's not just lust."

Antonie entered shyly at that moment and Royal caught his breath. She was beautiful. The soft cream colored silk and lace she wore was a perfect foil for her unique loveliness. Her thick hair was pinned up in a soft style revealing her slim neck. A circlet of flowers was set upon her head, the small purplish flowers matching her wide, beautiful eyes. As she moved toward him, emotion swelled in him.

In just a few minutes she would be his in a way that no one could argue with. The law would be on his side if any man was foolish enough to try and steal her away. The ring he was about to put on her finger would be as much of a brand as the one Raoul threatened to put on her hip. It would be a sign even the illiterate could read.

For one brief instant, he wondered about the step he was taking. Her dress was cut in such a way that her pregnancy was barely noticeable. He wryly supposed that it was natural for a man to feel a tremor of hesitation before taking such a big step but his bout of bachelor's nerves was extremely quick. There was no doubt in his mind about the rightness of what he was about to do. He could only wonder why it had taken him so long to get around to it.

"This is your last chance to run, *mi vida*," Antonie said quietly as he took her hand in his. "Shall I saddle your horse?"

"Only if you saddle one for yourself as well and you should not be out riding in your condition."

"Are you going to be a bossy husband?"

"Most likely and let's get to that preacher before he's too drunk to make me one."

Chapter Twenty-seven

The gold seemed to catch every beam of light and Antonie decided that gold was an exceptionally beautiful metal. She decided it was at its most beautiful when it was formed into a small band and placed on the third finger of her left hand by Royal Bancroft. The law now said he was hers. She could use the ring to prove it to anyone.

"I was beginning to wonder if he'd be smart enough."

Antonie smiled at Cole as he sat down beside her on the settee. "Hah. At first you wanted me gone."

"Not exactly but I will admit that I warned Royal not to really trust you. You had just nearly killed me, you recall."

"*Sí.* Juan was dead. I knew that even as I went after him. I would have killed you. You held a gun on me too."

"Yes, but I froze. I couldn't shoot you."

"I know. Know what I thought as I looked at you?"

"I think I'm going to regret asking, but what did you think?"

"Stupid *gringo.*"

He laughed and shook his head. "You hated us."

"Sí. You had just killed my papa. The hate only lasted a little while."

"Are you sure?"

"Sí. It was a fair fight. He lost. Juan always said I must be careful about hating. He said it was not to be given lightly. He said I must choose carefully whom I hate because it is a thing that takes a lot of you. Raoul I hated. He was a good man to hate."

"Well, there's a thought. I was a mite worried. Once I did start to change my mind about you, I wondered how you would feel about my part in that day's events."

"Juan was an outlaw and you were the law."

"Very cut and dried."

"That is how it must be. He would have killed you in the fight if he could have."

"Very true. Why are you scowling at that preacher?"

"I was just about to ask that myself," Royal said as he sat on the arm of the sette at Antonie's side.

"He is not a very good man of God," Antonie answered.

"Because he drinks?"

"No, Royal, because he does not approve of these marriages you ask him to perform and he does not hide it."

"I was hoping you hadn't noticed that."

"How could I not notice? He looks as if he thinks the whole Bancroft family is going to hell in a purse."

"Handbasket," Royal corrected with a grin.

"Same thing," Antonie countered.

"Of course."

"It is nice that your brother came home, eh?" Antonie mused aloud as she looked at Denton.

"It's a damn miracle," Cole agreed. "I'm still not sure I believe it yet."

"Ghosts do not have babies," Antonie pointed out.

"Now there's something to ponder on, Tony. I wonder what Denton'll do now that he's home? He's got that babe to think of. Maybe he ought to find a wife," Cole said carefully.

"Don't think he'll do that for a while, Cole. I think he's a little, well, bitter," Royal said.

"He does not need a wife just to care for his baby," Antonie said. "There is me, Patricia, Maria and even Rosa. He brought that baby all the way from Pennsylvania and the little boy looks fine. He may not even need our help."

"Very true. Think it's too early to start our wedding night?" Royal asked abruptly.

Blushing, Antonie gave her new husband an exasperated look then winked at Cole who had nearly choked on his drink. "Much too early. I think we must stay with our guests for a few more hours at least. Three sounds right."

"Three hours, hmmm?"

"*Sí*. Three hours."

"I think three minutes sound better."

"How rude. What about your guests?"

"I officially hand them over to Cole's care."

She stared at him for a moment then looked at Cole. "He is not joking, is he."

"Nope. Don't think he is."

"You've danced, been well kissed, eaten and drunk." Royal looked at her. "Only one thing left."

"You have stopped being a gentleman."

"Right. A man can only behave himself for so long."

Quickly eluding his grasp when he reached for her, she stood up. "Five minutes. Maybe ten. *Sí*, ten."

"Why?"

"Ah, you will see. Ten minutes."

Hurriedly fetching Maria, Antonie slipped away as

385

discreetly as possible. She needed some help getting out of all her finery. When she entered Royal's room, she had to smile. All her things were already neatly combined with his.

"He did not waste any time," she said in amusement as Maria began to help her get undressed.

"No. The *patrón* had me start bringing your things in as soon as you were up. It was no trouble. You did not have very much," Maria said carefully.

"It is not wise to have too many possessions when you move around a lot."

"Ah, *sí*. He did not see what was in that box."

"Thank you, Maria. I hope I won't look silly in it."

"Why would you look silly?"

Antonie patted her rounded stomach. "Pregnant and trying to look seductive?"

"You're not very big. It is the *patrón*'s baby. He will not see it as bad or ugly."

Not so so sure that he would not at least be amused, Antonie got out the box, opened it and slowly extracted a nightgown of sheer lavender silk. She had impulsively bought it when she had gone shopping with Patricia after the cattle drive and was glad now. A woman should have something different and, perhaps, frivolous on her wedding night. Giggling along with Maria, she hurried to finish getting ready for she suspected that Royal would wait only ten minutes and no more, perhaps less.

"Down, boy," Cole murmured laughingly. "Six minutes left."

"What the hell does she need to have ten minutes ahead of me for?"

"Considering the state you're in, probably to get ready to protect herself." Cole laughed and shook his head when Royal glared at him. "Probably wants to make herself especially pretty. It's her wedding night, remember."

"I'm not likely to forget."

"Clearly amused by Royal's impatience, Cole asked, "What do you want? A boy or a girl?"

"I'm not particular. Of course, if we have a girl, we don't need to have that argument about the name for a while."

"Haven't sorted that out yet, hmmm?"

"Nope. I was too busy concentrating on getting married."

"There's going to have to be a compromise, I reckon. She feels she owes Juan and wants to remember him in a way."

"Immortalize him?"

"In a way. Perhaps. The man had no children of his own. Not that he knew of anyway."

"Yes, I reckon it'll have to be a compromise. I'll have to think about it. Must be some nice neutral ground."

Royal was just about to go, although a laughing Cole told him there were still two minutes left to wait, when Maria slipped back into the room. Almost completely oblivious to the teasing that came his way, Royal left immediately. It was rather early in the evening to go to bed but he felt that an especially long night with Antonie was just what he needed at the moment.

Stepping into his room, he was only vaguely aware of the soft light and the gentle fragrance of flowers. All of his attention was fixed on Antonie, his every sense taken up with her. He dazedly shut and locked the door.

She stood by the bed looking shy, a look that contrasted wildly with the sensuous gown she wore. The lavender silk was not quite transparent, her soft curves only partly visible. It tied down the front, just off center, a thin line of creamy flesh visible between each bow. Her slim arms were bare and the neckline of the gown was so low he felt sure that the slightest movement on her part would free her breasts. When he saw how her nipples hardened as he stared at her, the hard tips outlined clearly against the silk, he started to move toward her, removing his clothes.

Antonie felt shy and nervous. She told herself that that was ridiculous, but even reminding herself of how thoroughly they had loved each other for so many nights in the past did not alter how she felt. This time she would be his wife. She suspected that the long stretch of celibacy they had just endured also added to her feelings.

Watching how rapidly he was disrobing as he approached her, she thought wryly that he clearly did not suffer such feelings. Desire had already tautened his features. She was more than pleased that he obviously did not find her the least bit silly as she stood there in her alluring nightwear so obviously pregnant.

"Impatient, *querido?*" she asked huskily when he finally stood before her, naked and fully aroused.

"Very impatient. Where did you get this confection?" he rasped even as he began to slowly untie the first bow.

"After the cattle drive. I was saving it for a special occasion."

Cupping her face in his hands, his lips played over hers. "Lovely but, right now, I think it'll be lovelier in a heap on the floor."

He kissed her hungrily and she clung to him. She was starved for him. It had been too long since he had even kissed her. Clinging to him, she gave a soft murmur of conciliation when he lifted her then gently laid her down on the bed.

When his lips left hers and began to follow the path revealed by the slow undoing of her gown, she wondered how he had the control to indulge in any foreplay. The touch of his lips upon her breasts was almost more than she could bear. Beneath her caressing hands she could feel the fine tremor of fierce need in his body yet his tongue curled lazily around her nipples and he suckled with a greedy idleness until she began to shift restlessly beneath him.

She wanted to enjoy the slowness of his lovemaking but she also wanted him now. As his kisses slid down her trembling body and he moved out of her reach, she clenched her hands. Antonie fought to control the passion racing through her but lost the battle completely when his lips touched the heated softness between her thighs. Despite her efforts to enjoy the pleasure of his intimate kiss, her release shuddered through her body an instant later.

A return of sanity was extremely brief for he barely gave her time to catch her breath before he skillfully began to resurrect her passion. As she hovered on the brink of a second release, she reached for him a little desperately. He drove into her even as her inner tremors began. Her legs closed tightly around him but he barely moved within her, his release pulled from him by feeling hers. As she held him close, she realized that his control had been a hard won thing, his passion kept right on the edge of consummation to ensure that she was not deprived of pleasure.

After washing themselves, Royal slid back into bed. He ran his hands over her body to feel the changes pregnancy had wrought in her. Her breasts were fuller and, he guessed by the reaction she had to his light touch, perhaps more sensitive. The tiny waist he had often grasped was just a memory. When his hands covered the roundness of her stomach, he felt movement inside and was briefly choked with emotion.

"Lively."

"O'Neill says he does the Irish jig."

Royal felt fiercely jealous. "O'Neill felt this?"

"*Sí.*" She bit back a smile over the jealous tone in his voice. "He likes babies. He is a doctor, you know."

"A doctor who's a bounty hunter?"

"*Sí.* I think that is why he tries so hard to bring the men back alive."

"Well, why isn't he practicing doctoring?" He moved to lie at her side and tugged her into his arms, his hand returning to rest on her stomach.

"He has never said and I have never asked. I think something disillusioned him or maybe the wrong patient died. He had also had trouble because he is Irish. Some people have a bad feeling for the Irish. He doctors if there is a need like when I was taken by Raoul. Maybe he just has a restlessness in him he needs to ride out first."

"That could be. He's what? Twenty-five? Twenty-six?"

"Twenty-seven. You went to the hanging?" she asked abruptly.

"Yes, me, my brothers and Oro. We saw Henry hanged and Marilynn taken to prison."

"You did not have to hide this from me."

"I didn't want to stir up old memories. It was a frightening time for you, an ordeal not lessened by your relatively minor wounds."

"I was very lucky and you arrived in time. *De nada.*"

"The things he threatened you with," Royal began hoarsely, his hold on her tightening slightly.

"Threats do not hurt, *querido*. When I think of that time I think only of how lucky I was. The fear is not there. I cannot be troubled over things that might have happened but did not."

"You didn't really want to see the hanging did you?"

"No. I do not like hangings. I will take your word that all was done right."

Royal kissed her forehead. "It's over now. Henry's dead, Raoul's dead and Marilynn's locked up."

"Tight?"

"Very tight. From what I've heard she might soon wish the town wasn't so squeamish about hanging a young woman."

"Do you have any regrets about her?" she asked quietly.

"No. One reason I went was to see if I was being unfair, if maybe she was just a sick woman who had been cleverly manipulated by her father. Far from it. Henry had been manipulated. He died because she was greedy, because she wanted to be a damn queen."

"No, *querido*, he died because he did not say no. Maybe he was weak or maybe he wanted it all too, but did not have the wit or the courage to try for it. She could not make her papa kill so many or plan to unless he wanted to, I think. No, for whatever reasons, he was her partner. He was not blameless."

"True. It would have been fairer if she had hanged too."

"*Sí*, but that is not the way it is done here. The prison she goes to is a strong one?"

"Yes. It's over, Antonie. Don't worry about that. She'll live out her life there."

Inwardly, he grimaced. His words had sounded confident but a little doubt gnawed at him. He would not tell Antonie about how Marilynn had used her sexual expertise on the deputy and nearly succeeded in escaping. There was no need to worry Antonie. The sheriff had sent a warning to the prison officials even though the man felt that they were probably well acquainted with Marilynn's type. Marilynn was gone and he was foolish to feel that it could be otherwise. He was just letting that look of insane hatred in Marilynn's eyes get to him.

"You frown so, *querido*. Is something wrong?"

"No, I was just thinking about the Collinses ranch and if I can buy it. Terrible thoughts to think on your wedding night."

"What would you do with so much land?"

"There's Cole, Justin and now Denton."

"They have land."

"A bit. However, if I can get hold of that ranch, we'd have a good sized spread each."

"A Bancroft empire."

"I reckon it does sound like that," he murmured and laughed.

"A little, but it would not be one, eh? There would be four ranches and four families."

"Five. Patricia's bit could be enlarged. Room for more too." His hand smoothed over her stomach. "Land's disappearing fast. It might not hurt to get some for the future."

He found it a little difficult to think about grand plans for providing for future generations of Bancrofts when Antonie's mouth teased his. Her tongue eased into his mouth and he sighed with pleasure. The way her small hands stroked his body had desire flooding him.

Antonie neatly eluded his attempt to hold her firm, to take control. She dotted his throat with soft kisses as her fingers found the sensitive nipples on his chest. Unable to completely avoid his touch, she shivered as his fingers reciprocated but she successfully fought the urge to give control over to him and simply enjoy.

With a leisureliness that had him groaning softly, she teased his nipples with her tongue then gently suckled. His stroking hands continued to arouse her and she began to slide out of his reach. She smiled against his taut stomach when her tongue dipped into his naval and he shook. His obvious signs of pleasure increased her own.

The cry he gave when her lips touched the tip of his erection was music to her ears. As her hands moved over his firm buttocks and strong thighs, she pleasured him with her mouth and tongue. She knew he wanted to enjoy her attentions for as long as possible so she kept her caresses slow and gentle, moving away from time to time to allow him a chance to regain some control. When his leg curved around her to hold her close she felt engulfed in his maleness and wondered a little wryly who had the most difficulty in controlling their passions. Her body was shaking as much as his was.

"Enough, honey," he rasped as, even as he turned onto his back, he reached for her. "I want to be inside you."

Straddling him, she eased their bodies together. "Like this, *mi vida?*"

She gave a cry of surprise when he suddenly sat up and hungrily kissed her. He then gently forced her to lean back a little, his arm supporting her back, as he began to greedily kiss her breasts. His other hand directed her hips in a subtle movement against his. Her hands tightly gripped his shoulders as her release tore through her. At the same time, his hands gripped her hips, urging a fast pace that very quickly had him joining her in her fall into passion's abyss.

"The tables were neatly turned," he said, satiation turning his voice husky, as he lay back down, taking her with him. "Good God," he breathed when, with her stomach pressed close to his, he felt their child move. "What's that feel like?"

"Sometimes a little strange," she replied as she eased the intimacy of their embrace to curl up at his side. "It does not always happen at a good time either. At first it felt like a fish but now it feels more like a baby."

"What do you want? A boy or a girl?"

"A strong baby."

"Yes, same here. A healthy baby."

"And maybe that it will slip out without me hardly noticing," she said dryly.

He laughed quietly then held her tighter. Although he was eager for the child he was far from eager for her to go through the birth. Denton's mention of his wife dying in childbirth was an unnecessary reminder of the dangers Antonie faced. Even though he had always been removed from it, he was not totally ignorant of the risks of childbirth. He was afraid for her but he was going to have to hide it. She probably had a few fears of her own and he would do her no good by adding to them. It was his place to soothe any fears she might express and give her added strength.

"Just make sure you're standing over some place soft," he jested. "I don't want my child starting out with a bang on the head."

"Ah, no, that would never do. Rattle his wits, hmm?" She tried to smother a yawn.

"Go to sleep, Antonie," he said gently.

"But it is our wedding night."

"And we're supposed to stay up all night caught up in lustful greed?"

"Sí. Something like that."

"I'll wake you up after you've had a little rest."

As she had gone to sleep, she had not thought he was really serious. When she woke engulfed in a passion stoked by his skillful touch, she decided she needed a little more time to learn when he was joking.

Then she wrapped her legs around him and rode to the heights with him.

"It is the middle of the night, *gringo*," she said sleepily as she cuddled up to him. "You woke me up."

"I said I would."

"I know but I thought you were not serious."

"Oh, I'm always serious about something like that."

"I'll remember that, *querido*. Can I go back to sleep now?"

Royal chuckled, his hand smoothing over her thick hair. "Mmmm. Go back to sleep. I'll try to behave."

She smiled against his skin. It was wonderful to be sharing a bed with him again. Even as she had been healing from her ordeal, too worn out to even think about making love, she had missed sleeping at his side. It was nice to simply know that he was there, to touch or to hold. Now, even the law said that they could share a bed.

It was still a little hard to believe that she was his wife. She doubted that her sleep drugged mind would find it any easier to grasp than when she had heard them say their vows and watched him slip the ring on her finger. There would probably be a few times in the future when she would have to firmly remind herself. She even wondered if she would ever really get over the wonder of it.

Breathing in his scent as sleep claimed her, she prayed that she would have the good fortune to make a few more of her dreams come true. There were a lot of them but she was willing to settle for just a few.

Antonie was happy with what she had. She knew it was nothing to scoff at. In Royal she had a good man who talked of fidelity and commitment. He wanted her to share both the work and the profits with him. He wanted her as a partner in his life, not just some decoration that just happened to be able to give him

395

children as well. It was no small thing but she could not fully stop herself from wishing for his love as well. As she finally gave in to sleep, she swore that, while she would never bemoan all she did have, she would never stop trying for that last dream.

Watching her as she slept in his arms, Royal smiled faintly. Like this, she looked so sweet, so vulnerable and in need of protecting but he knew that, if danger struck right now, she would be as quick and able to face it as he. It was a little hard to accept that he was not really necessary to her safety but he also found that it could be a comfort. He could not be with her every moment and, while he would still worry about her, he did not have the added burden of knowing that she was helpless. It had taken him a while to get used to her proficiency with a weapon but he was glad of it now. There was still a lot of danger in Texas.

His hand rested against her stomach and he felt their child move. Here was a danger neither she nor he could avert or beat no matter how good they were with a gun. No matter how hard he tried to stop himself, he envisioned all that could happen to her, every horror story about childbirth crowding into his mind. All he could think of was how small she was and how even a big strong woman like Bella Dickson had been taken down by childbirth.

He should have been more careful. It was something he had always been cautious about in the past. However, when he held her, he lost his reason. What she called "the fire" burned away all rational thought. He vowed that he would change that. If God was good enough to let her come through this unscathed, he would practice caution. Even if she proved strong and healthy enough to survive childbirth without trouble, he would not risk her life by keeping her belly filled with child until her body simply grew too tired. She was young and there was plenty of time for them to build even a sizeable family yet allow her plenty of time between each baby.

Despite his worries, sleep tugged at him. He rested his cheek against her hair as his eyes slowly closed. For a brief instant his arms tightened around her and he smiled when she murmured his name in her sleep. He might not be able to clarify what he felt about her, even to himself, but he knew he needed her and intended to hang on tightly for years to come.

Chapter Twenty-eight

"Ah, *muchacho,* you are supposed to be going to sleep," Antonie scolded gently as she picked Camden up. "You are dry and your little belly is full. Now is when you should nap. A little walk then back to bed and sleep, eh?"

She smiled as she strolled through the house, the infant looking all around as she went. It was good practice, she told herself wryly. Her own baby was due soon. Taking care of Camden had insured that she would not find an infant a strange, perhaps frightening, little creature.

Stepping out onto the veranda, she looked around, then shook her head. She was totally alone. It was a rare occurrence and she suspected that Royal would be furious when he found out. Seeing movement by the stables, she hastily corrected herself. She was not totally alone. Maria's son Sancho, a lively boy of eight, was still around. Even as she reminded herself of his presence, he smiled, waved and hurried over to her side.

"I think there is a storm coming, *señora,*" he said as

he poked at Camden playfully.

Looking up at the sky, Antonie realized how black it was growing. "*Sí*, it does look bad. Well, that will mean that the men will be coming in soon."

"*Sí*, if they are not caught by surprise. It happens sometimes. I hope Mama doesn't try to come home in it."

"Ah, no, that would not be good. I will have lunch soon. You can eat with me."

"I would like that, *señora*. It is strange not to have anyone around."

"Very strange," Antonie agreed.

And very bad planning, she added silently. Every plan had had Royal's approval but she was certain he had not realized how they were all made for the same day and how it would neatly result in a deserted ranch. He had tried to be subtle about her being closely watched but she had seen how he had arranged it.

Glancing at the threatening sky again, she half wished she had gone into town with the women to get supplies. At least she would have had adult company when the storm came. But she hadn't wanted to go. Her stomach had not grown too large but she was uncomfortable, today more so than usual. The thought of the bumpy ride in the wagon was still less attractive than being caught nearly alone in the house during a bad storm.

"You do what's needed outside for a storm and I will shut up the house, *chico*," she told Sancho. "Then we eat."

"*Sí, señora*. I'll get right to it."

Smiling faintly as she went back into the house, she took Camden back to his bed. The baby whimpered a little but finally went to sleep. Checking to be sure that everything was shut tightly as she went, she headed to the kitchen to get a meal for herself and Sancho. She did not feel hungry but she felt she ought to at least try to eat something. A number of people had impressed upon her the need of eating well for the baby's sake.

The storm hit just as she and Sancho finished their meal. Antonie stood spellbound by the sudden fury nature had unleashed. She then heard Camden wail and sighed.

"The thunder woke the baby, *señora*."

"*Sí*. Probably frightens the poor *muchacho*. You will stay in here, Sancho. In the house."

"*Sí, señora*. The men did not come back."

"No." She sighed and started toward the stairs. "We will have to brave this alone, Sancho. *Por Dios*, I hate storms."

They had been in the parlor for a while when Antonie suddenly tensed. Her continuous discomfort seemed to have gained an alarming regularity to it. Remembering one of the many things Maria had told her, she watched the clock for a while and felt her heart sink. Even in her ignorance, she could no longer ignore the fact that she was in labor.

"*Ay de mi*, why now?" she whispered.

"*Señora?*" Sancho looked up from where he played with Camden.

"Do you think the storm eases?"

"Well, the thunder and lightning are moving away, I think."

"*Sí*. They are not so loud, not right overhead."

"But it is still raining buckets, *señora*. The wind is still very strong."

400

She only had to listen for a moment to know that he was right. The wind was driving the rain against the windows with an almost alarming force. It had the strength to go on for hours. Even though the thunder and lightning had lessened, moved a distance away, it was still too bad to expect anyone to show up and lend a hand.

For a moment, she fought a blinding panic. With so many people around all the time, she had never once contemplated the possibility of being alone when her time came. The depth of her ignorance about what was ahead was enough to terrify her. She fought that fear that pushed her toward unthinking panic. Now was a time for clarity of thought and calmness. The fact that her only source of help was a boy of eight made it hard but she finally managed.

Although she had never seen a human birth, she had seen horses, even cattle, give birth. Juan had once said that the process was much the same for people. The slight lessening of her own ignorance brought her closer to being calm.

"Sancho," she said quietly, "I know you are a brave boy but you are going to have to be very brave now."

"Something is wrong, *señora?*"

"The baby has decided to come now." She almost smiled at the way his big dark eyes grew huge and went to her stomach.

"There is no one here. It can't come now."

"The baby doesn't care that we are alone. Ah, how I wish O'Neill had not left after the wedding but I'm going to have to do this by myself."

"Can you do that?" Sancho asked, his lips trembling.

"If an Indian woman can, I can. I have heard that

they go off alone to have babies. I will need you to help a little though."

"*Sí, señora.* Do you want me to get someone?"

"I think you would be blown off your horse, *muchacho*. No, stay here. We must heat water, get clean clothes and a few other things. While I am busy, I will need you to help with Camden and to keep watch and guard. Can you do that?"

"*Sí, señora.*"

"Perhaps we should lock the doors too."

"What if the others come back?"

"They will let you know it is them, then you can let them in," Antonie instructed him.

"Ah, *sí.*"

"Now, let's get some water heated. I will put it in pots you can handle for there will come a time when I might need some but cannot get it. Not much is needed. It is just for cleaning."

"Is it as messy as when a horse foals?"

"I think it might be. I cannot be sure, *amigo.* This is my first and I have never seen it done."

"Are you afraid, *señora?*"

"*Sí.* I thought someone would be here. Your mama, I mean, or someone like her."

"*Sí.* I think the *patrón* forgot today was the day the women go to get supplies."

She nodded and, after setting water on to heat, went to look for clean linen. A little smile touched her face as she saw how Sancho, holding little Camden, trailed after her. The boy looked very worried but she knew she could count on him to do whatever she told him to. She just hoped she would not have to ask too much of him.

By the time she had everything readied to her

satisfaction, she was having strong contractions. "All right, Sancho, you can put Camden in his bed there. That's right. Now, go downstairs and keep watch."

"Shouldn't I stay with you, *señora?*"

"No, *chico*. I must get into a nightgown and into bed. I will call you if I need you." She smiled. "Don't worry. If I call, you'll hear me. Now, if someone comes that we do not know and tries to come in, you are to come up here. Okay.

"*Sí, señora.*"

The moment he left, she got undressed. She was naked and just sponging off when her water broke. Struggling to clean up and get a nightgown on, she wryly mused that that could probably be considered convenient. She had the sinking feeling that it could well be her only piece of good luck.

Finally crawling into bed, she placed her knife near. The pain was growing bad enough that she was a little afraid that she might not be able to be clearheaded when the time came. She fought to endure the pain yet conserve her strength and keep her mind from becoming too fogged by pain and exhaustion.

"*Señora, señora*, we have help now," Sancho shouted as he raced into the room.

Caught up in a strong contraction, Antonie could only rasp "O'Neill" when the big man appeared in the doorway.

"Where the hell is everybody? Get some more water, there's a good lad. I have to wash up."

She could only watch in silent wide eyed amazement as O'Neill stripped down, washed up and put on clean trousers. He was certainly a lot of man, she thought a little wildly. As another contraction ripped through her, she thanked God for O'Neill as she was not doing very well at all at staying clearheaded.

"Sure 'n I'm real surprised that that man of yours would leave you alone," O'Neill muttered as he checked her progress.

"A mistake," Antonie gasped. "Do you always run about in bad weather?"

"I told you I'd be back to see the babe. A little rain won't hurt me. Now, you just concentrate on getting this babe out, lass. I'll do the rest."

"That will be nice," she whispered.

Royal stared out of the grimy window of the line shack they had sought shelter in. Although the thunder and lightning had lessened the rain still fell hard. He should be glad that he was out of it but he could not seem to relax.

"Pacing the room won't change the weather," Cole murmured as Royal walked by him again. "Your deal, Denton."

"What's eating at you, Royal?" Denton asked as he shuffled the cards.

"Damned if I know." He scowled out at the weather again. "I'm uneasy. Something doesn't feel right but I can't put my finger on it."

"Expectant father," Denton muttered.

"That's probably it." Royal shook his head. "Stupid. Maria is there."

"No, she ain't," Cole murmured, studying his cards.

"What do you mean, no?" Royal demanded.

"Hell, it's the third Monday of the month. Supplies."

"Yeh, that's right," one of the hands agreed. "My Deidre went too."

"And my wife," another said.

"Well, let me think." Royal ran a hand through his

404

hair. "Maybe I did remember that and her being without a woman's bothered me. But who else is at home?"

"Oro, Patricia, Tomás and Justin are working on Oro's house. This'll have caught them there," Denton offered.

"Old Pete went to get his teeth done," Jed said.

"Well, who the hell's at the house?" Royal yelled.

"Now calm down," Cole soothed as he counted out a card for each hand and member of the household. "Let's do this scientific like." His lips moving as he murmured each name, he slowly accounted for everyone.

"Who's this? There's only three cards left." Royal fought against a strong urge to panic.

"Antonie, Sancho and Camden," Cole answered reluctantly.

"My wife is alone at the ranch with only an eight-year-old boy and an infant?"

"Now, calm down. I might be wrong. Let me do it again."

"Don't bother. I'm going home."

Denton leapt to his feet to intercept Royal. "Look, you can't go out in this."

"Antonie can take care of herself," Cole said.

"Against *banditti*, Indians or the like, yes. But what the hell is she to do if the baby starts coming?" He curtly nodded when no one had an answer for him. "I'm going back to the house." Royal grabbed his coat, flung it on and left.

"Oh, hell," Cole muttered and stood up to reach for his coat. "No, you fellows stay here," he said when he saw the hands moving to follow. "Let's keep this idiocy in the family. Besides, even if she is having a baby, a houseful of soaking wet cowboys ain't going to do her a hell of a lot of good. You coming, Denton?" Cole started out the door.

"What do you think?" Denton followed.

"I think we're probably going to drown," Cole yelled above the fury of the storm.

Royal sensed his brothers close behind him but did not look back to be sure. He doubted he could see them if they were more than a few feet away. Despite his urge to hurry, he was forced to go slow because the rain made it hard to see as well as made the ground somewhat unsafe. If he had not ridden over every inch of the land almost from the day he was born, he was not sure he would be able to find his way back to the house. The wind drove the rain so hard that he had to stay hunched in the saddle, his face averted most of the time.

When he reached the ranch, he went to the stables first. The place looked deserted and no one answered his call. As Cole and Denton arrived only a moment after he did, Royal saw that the wagon was gone, which meant that the women had not returned. Adding to his increasing worry was the presence of a horse he did not recognize.

"Hell, never seen the place look so deserted," Cole muttered.

"We can see to the horses in a minute," Royal said even as he started toward the house. "I want to check on Antonie first."

He jogged to the house only to find the door locked. For a moment, he could not believe it but then began to pound on the door. It was several minutes before he got any answer, then a small voice demanded to know who it was.

406

"Sancho? That you? Open the door."

"You say who you are first."

"Damnit, Sancho, it's Royal. Open the damn door."

"Oh, *señor*, it is good that you came back," Sancho cried as he quickly opened the door and let the three men in.

Removing his coat and hat, Royal demanded, "Where the hell is everybody? Are they all gone?"

"*Sí, señor*. Only the *señora*, Camden and me were left here. Then the storm came. The *señora* had me lock the doors, *patrón*, so that no one could sneak in, eh? I have been watching the doors because the *señora* couldn't do it."

Although the boy did not seem overly upset, there was something about Sancho's mood that made Royal's heart skip a beat. "Where is the *señora*?"

"Up in her bed, *patrōn*. The baby decided to come. She said it couldn't wait."

The same fear that had driven him to race through the driving rain now froze him to the spot. He stared up the stairs, unable to believe that what he had feared was exactly what had happened. It did not seem possible that even in this matter things could not go smoothly.

"Antonie's having the baby now?" he croaked.

"*Sí, señor*."

Even as Sancho spoke a cry came from upstairs. Royal jumped then started to race up the stairs. After only a brief hesitation, the others followed. Coming to an abrupt halt in the doorway to their room, Royal froze again.

Antonie heard the disturbance even through her pain. O'Neill kept telling her that it would be a few minutes now but she felt as if he had been saying that

407

for hours. To see that Royal had come home despite the weather, seemed a mixed blessing to her. She had decided that childbirth had to be one of the most undignified things a woman had to endure and she did not really want Royal to see her like this yet she felt a need for his presence.

Royal did not believe his eyes, was not sure he wanted to. Antonie lay on the bed gripping the rails of the headboard, clearly in great pain. A huge, redheaded bare chested man was very interested in what was happening between Antonie's legs. Royal's stunned mind took a moment to recognize the man.

"O'Neill?" He took a step into the room.

"Don't get any closer to the lass 'til you get dried off and cleaned up."

"But . . ."

"If you're real quick, you might get to see this stubborn babe come into the world."

"Come on, Royal," Cole urged. "I'll help you. Denton, can you and Sancho see to the horses?"

"But . . ."

Tugging Royal down the hall, Cole said, "O'Neill knows what he's doing. If he says clean up first, that's what you will do. Just thank God that he showed up when he did, when he was needed."

"But where the hell did he come from?"

"Wondered the same thing when he arrived in the nick of time for Tomás. Come on. Let's move."

"Royal," Antonie gasped as she saw her husband towed away then, when the doorway was empty again, began to wonder if she had really seen him at all. "Royal was here?"

"He was, lass. He'll be right back. The man's been in the rain and mud and with horses. He washes up first."

"Must be clean, eh?"

"Damn right. Now. I figure you only have a few minutes to decide if you want him here or not."

"You'd keep him out if I asked it?"

"If I have to tie him up to do it."

"So undignified, this having babies."

"It is that, lass." He laughed then said quietly, "Aye, undignified but look at what you gain."

"*Sí*. He will want to be here. I think I want him even though I don't want him looking too much."

"Well, I'll see how he acts. I can't have him getting in the way."

"Soon?" she gasped. "It will be soon?"

"It will, lass. I know it doesn't seem like it to you but things are moving along smoothly and quickly."

Still doing up the buttons of a clean shirt, Royal hurried back to Antonie. Again he hesitated in the doorway. There was a tension in the air that quickly infected him. Then Antonie reached out her hand to him and he hurried to her side.

"Almost too late, Royal," O'Neill said almost absently. "When I say push, darlin', you push with all your might."

Spellbound, Royal watched as his child entered the world. He was only faintly aware of how tightly Antonie gripped his hand. The pain she was unknowingly inflicting did not seem important. He held his breath as he waited for the newborn child in O'Neill's big hands to show indisputable proof of life. The moment the baby cried, Royal closed his eyes in relief and felt Antonie's hand go limp.

"Alive," she whispered, smiled weakly and fainted. "O'Neill!"

"Only a faint," O'Neill announced with certainty after a quick check. "Nothing to worry about. You've got a fine son."

"A son," Royal murmured as he moved to stare at the baby O'Neill cleaned, despite the child's vociferous protests.

"Sounds healthy."

"Oh, yes." Royal laughed shakily then had to turn his attention to his nephew who began to cry in sympathy. "Denton," he called as he strode into the hall holding Camden.

Denton was before him an instant later, taking his son into his arms. "How's Antonie?"

"Fine. I have to get back."

"Wait." Denton grasped Royal by the arm.

"A boy," Royal answered before Denton could ask then, slipping free of his brother's hold, hurried back to Antonie.

After helping O'Neill clean up the unconscious Antonie, Royal sat by the bed and watched her sleep. He was only faintly aware of Cole delivering some food and drink for him, which he dutifully consumed but did not taste. Except for the times he responded to a compulsion to see that a new child really did sleep in the cradle in their room, his eyes never left the sleeping Antonie. He had to hear her talk to him before he could fully accept O'Neill's assurances that she was fine and would soon be as good as new.

He could not erase the sight of her body racked with pain. She was so small and delicate. Royal did not know how her body could take such strain without damage. O'Neill had assured him that none had been inflicted but he was not fully convinced of that yet. He wanted to see her awake and recovering, acting like the Antonie he had left only this morning.

Antonie woke up slowly. Her alertness accelerated when she became aware of the change in her body. For a moment she had thought it all a dream but the sense of emptiness and the persistent aching told her differently. Her gaze swept the room then rested on the child curled up in the cradle.

"Alive."

Sitting up quickly, Royal took her hand. "Yes, Antonie. We've got a son and he's very much alive."

She looked at him and smiled. "You came home."

"Yes. God, I'm sorry, Antonie. I should've noticed, should have made sure someone was here for you."

She put her fingers against his lips to stop his litany of guilt. "I should have noticed too. If not for the storm I could have sent Sancho for someone. O'Neill came and everything is all right."

"Is it? Are you all right?"

"*Sí.* O'Neill must have told you so."

"He did but," Royal shook his head, "there was so much pain and you're so small. I just thought, well, if I heard you talking again it meant O'Neill was right."

"Well, he is right. Even now the pain becomes a memory. I could use a drink though."

After helping her sit up, he handed her a glass of water. "O'Neill says you are to put the baby to your breast." Even as he spoke, he gently picked up his son and brought him to the bed. "Unless, well, I never thought to ask if you wanted a wet nurse for him."

Setting her glass aside, Antonie took her child into her arms, undid her gown and urged the sleepy child to suckle. "No. He is my baby. And, that is what these are for, eh?"

"We-ell," he sat beside her, enthralled by the sight,

411

"I can think of one or two other uses."

"Rogue."

"Probably."

"Juan Ramirez Bancroft. Nice, eh?"

Sighing, Royal said, "You know I don't really want my son named after a *bandito*."

"I promised Juan I would name my first son after him. On his deathbed. He said, 'I will be remembered. It is enough.'"

Closing his eyes briefly, Royal said carefully, "People like him are not forgotten quickly, Antonie."

"I understand your reluctance but I promised him," she said quietly. "He was my papa, Royal."

"I know. We'll compromise. Ramirez is all right. It's a common name. No one will know it's the name of a notorious *bandito*."

"Ramirez Bancroft? Is not Ramirez a strange first name?"

"I'd rather that than everyone getting my son confused with Juan Ramirez, *bandito*, most wanted man in the southwest for twenty years. On his birth papers we'll write Ramirez Juan Bancroft but call him Ram or R.J. It's common to shorten names. You can tell him all about Juan when he's old enough but at least he won't spend his life trying to explain why he's named after a *bandito*."

"You think people will still remember Juan when our son is grown?"

"There's a good chance of it. He was a part of this land for twenty years. He was a legend while he was still alive. His is the kind of tale that lingers. Sometimes the outlaws get more fame and are better remembered than the lawful."

"All right. Ramirez. Ram. Juan will understand.

You can name the next baby."

"That won't be for a while yet."

"Don't you want more than one baby?"

"I want a houseful but I also want you. We're going to be careful. We can let time pass between each child. I don't want to make you old before your time by keeping you pregnant. We're supposed to live so that we can see our children have children."

"And tell them how to raise theirs," she added with a smile.

"Exactly." He looked at her and their son and lightly hugged them both. "Thank you," he whispered, his lips pressed to her forehead.

"You are very welcome, husband."

Chapter Twenty-nine

"Patricia, what are you doing here? Is your house all done?" Antonie asked as Patricia entered the parlor.

"No, but I volunteered to come and help you." Patricia eagerly relieved Antonie of Ram. "Oh, he's so pretty. Your hair and Royal's eyes. I've always thought Royal has the finest eyes out of all of us."

"*Sí*, they are very fine eyes." Antonie grinned and Patricia laughed. "What have you volunteered for?"

"To watch the babies. Royal wants to take you on a picnic."

"But what about your house?"

"They don't really need me underfoot. Besides, I think Qro just as soon prefers I was not there to gawk at O'Neill when the man takes his shirt off. My goodness, there's a lot of man."

"*Sí*. I thought that when I saw him naked."

"When the hell did you see O'Neill naked?" Royal demanded.

"Oops." Antonie sent her scowling husband a sweet smile as he strode over to her. "When I had the baby."

"He wasn't naked when I saw him."

"He was only that way for a moment while he

414

washed up and put on clean clothes. Very startling, all that red hair. He wasn't as pale as I thought redheads were supposed to be either."

"I don't really want to hear about this." He grasped her by the hand and tugged her to her feet. "Now, if I've timed this right, you've just fed Ram."

"Sí, just finished."

"That gives us a couple of hours."

"Where are we going for this picnic?" she asked as he pulled her along.

"To the swimming hole."

"In the buggy?" she exclaimed even as he helped her into the seat.

"We're going in style today, ma'am."

She smiled and looked away. The idea of a picnic was very nice but she knew what he was really whisking her off for. Only yesterday she had been declared fully healed by O'Neill. When Royal had not made love to her last night, she had been hurt, not really believing him when he had talked of wanting to wait a little longer to be sure she was totally healed. This was what he was planning even then. Something a little special to celebrate the resumption of the physical side of their marriage. Whenever she felt doubtful about her assumptions, she just had to glance his way. The correctness of her guess was easily seen on his face and in his eyes.

"Here we are, m'lady."

He played the gallant lover as they ate the food Maria had packed. Antonie loved it. She felt as if she was being wooed. There was also a gentle seduction hidden in his words and actions. It was totally unnecessary but she loved that too.

"A very pretty dress. The little flowers in the print match your eyes." He touched her shoulder and felt her tremble.

"Maria and I made it. Well, Maria mostly. She is trying to teach me how to sew."

"How're you doing?"

"Not too well." She laughed and shook her head. "I can mend a little and stitch a wound, but dresses? No, I think not."

"Well, you don't really need to."

"I will keep trying. It is a good thing to know, I think."

"I've got the money to buy you dresses, to have them made for you."

"*Sí*. Now."

"Always, I hope."

"I hope too but?" she shrugged. "It is good to know how to do things if the money is not there. Money is fickle. You do not even have to do anything wrong for it to leave your hands. From what I have heard, you are lucky to have escaped the war with some money."

"And then came Marilynn. I see your point." He refilled her glass of with wine. "Is that why you're learning to cook too?"

"I could cook but not Anglo food. That is what I learn."

"You're becoming very domesticated," he teased, moving closer to her and starting to take down her hair.

She began to feel a little breathless. "It is not as I thought. There is always something to do. There is a lot of doing the same thing over and over but that is there in every job, eh? Even in ranching."

"Oh, yes. Raise them, round them up and sell them. Year after year. Antonie," he murmured and then gave into the overwhelming urge to kiss her wine-dampened lips.

With a soft sound of delight, she tossed aside her glass and wrapped her arms around his neck. She met his kiss with a hunger that equalled his. There was not an ounce of resistance in her body when he urged her down onto her back but then he suddenly pulled away. She stared at him in confusion as he propped himself up on one elbow and ran a hand over his face as he fought to regain control. It was clear that he wanted her as badly as she did him but he held back. It did not make any sense to her and she was sure that her utter confusion showed clearly on her face.

"Antonie, we have to talk first," he finally said quietly.

"Talk about what? I am all better. O'Neill said so. I have felt better for a while now. Why do you wish to wait longer? I didn't understand last night and I understand less now."

"I know. I don't want to wait. You should be able to tell when I'm aching for you by now."

"I thought I could."

"Well, you can and I am. Last night I hesitated, even though it was killing me, because I wanted our reunion, shall we say, to be a little special. Right now, I'm hesitating because we need to talk about having babies, or, rather, not having babies."

"Oh," she breathed in sudden understanding.

"I talked to O'Neill."

"*Sí.* So did I."

"You did?"

"In a way. He started it. Told me about growing up a good Catholic boy who believed implicitly in the Lord's order to go forth and multiply, that you didn't fool around with that but had as many babies as you could. His mother seemed to be constantly pregnant and, when he left, his sisters were doing the same."

"But that's just what I don't want for you."

"Neither does O'Neill. He said I am strong and can have many babies but that many babies can be five as easily as it can be ten. When he went into doctoring he began to learn a few things, things that changed his mind. He saw that maybe his mother didn't have to die before she was forty, that maybe there need not have been any dead babies. He said he was glad that you had seen that it wasn't really good for a woman to birth every spring like some bit of farm stock."

"And he told you what you can do? What we can do?" Royal wondered if there was a method he did not know of.

"Sí. He said I have many years to have babies. I can rest between births so my body will be strong which is good for me and good for the baby. You do not need to do anything. I will do it."

"I'm willing to do my share," he said quietly. "Hell, you wouldn't have to worry about it at all if it weren't for me."

"True. It would be very hard to make babies by myself," she said with a gentle laugh as she began to undo his shirt. "I do not want you to leave me quickly and I do not want something between you and me when we join. So, I will do it. As O'Neill says, the sponge is the least disruptive. Only a little less, how did he say it?, spontaneity."

Shivering slightly when her hand smoothed over his chest, he asked, "Hadn't you better get ready then?"

"I am. I did not go to the bushes a little while ago to answer nature's call."

He smiled slowly as he began to undo her dress. "Taking a lot for granted, weren't you?"

As she eased his shirt off his broad shoulders, she asked huskily, "Was I?"

418

"No," he whispered against her mouth as his hand cupped her breast. "God, how I want you."

Antonie was left in no doubt of that. She let him know that the need was fully returned. Later, as she lay sprawled beneath him, their breathing still not back to normal, she had to smile. They were going to have to do something about the way they could lose control when they had been apart for a while. The romantic interlude had turned into a frantic scramble to sate pent-up desire. They had not even finished disrobing.

"So much for a slow, easy session of lovemaking," Royal said with a laugh.

"I was just thinking about that."

"We-ell," he said as he rolled off her and adjusted his pants, then looked at his watch, "we still have about two hours."

Sitting up, she hastily pulled on her pantaloons and then did up a few buttons on her camisole. "Greedy. I have to wash up."

She blushed slightly and ignored his grin as she hurried to a spot by the swimming hole where she could tend to herself without him seeing her. Grimacing a little, she decided that contraception had its drawbacks. After a few times of watching Camden and Ram at the same time, however, she knew that insuring that she did not have one baby right after another was not only for the good of her body. It was for her sanity too, she thought with a grin, recalling how harassed she had felt.

Still smiling as she recalled one of those frantic times, she started back to Royal, then froze, unable to believe her eyes. A filthy, ragged Marilynn stood before Royal, a gun pointed at his heart.

'Don't panic, *chica*,' a well-remembered voice said in

419

her head. 'Time is important. Use it well. Think, *chica*. Plan.'

Her eyes went to her knife. It still lay where Royal had tossed it after he had untied the sheath from her thigh. If she moved carefully, she could get it without being seen. Slipping back into the full concealment of the bushes she had almost left, she started toward the knife and tried not to think of how she might not get there in time.

"So, you married the little bitch."

Royal gaped at the woman before him, a woman who should have been miles away and securely locked up. She did not look anything like the Marilynn he had known. The dull prison dress she wore had probably not been very flattering even when it had been clean and new. Her hair was a dirty tangle. Her eyes held a wild, vicious look that chilled his blood. He fought his fear and tried to speak calmly. There was always the small chance that he could talk her out of what she so clearly planned to do. Marilynn had been responsible for a lot of deaths and had planned to see a lot more people die but she had hired men to do it. There was a very small chance that she could not kill anyone herself.

"How did you get free?" he asked quietly as he hoped that Antonie would not try anything foolish.

"My dear stupid Royal, I learned long ago that most men think with what dangles between their legs. I also learned how to use it. To put it quite simply, darling, I humped my way out of prison. I was clean and I was new and of a better class than the trash they usually get in that place. I played coy for a while until I saw what route to take out of that sty. After that it was easy."

Thinking to use her obvious pride in that accom-

420

plishment to buy himself time, even if he wasn't sure how he would use that gain, he said, "It was hardly easy to come this far."

"Easy enough. Men think they're so strong, so smart, but all I have to do is open my legs or my mouth and I have them. And that's what I did all the way here. Guards, drifters, cowhands. It was only after I got within the last fifty miles of this place that I had any trouble. I didn't want to be seen, of course. I wanted to be sure to get here and make you pay."

"You'll never get away with it, Marilynn. This time they will hang you for sure."

"Oh, no. They'll never catch me this time. I've learned quite a lot about how to hide and survive. I've also learned how easy it is to kill a man. Oh, I knew you bastards were weak once a woman got hold of your sex but not how weak, not until I killed that drifter." She smiled. "It added something you know, to cut his throat just as he was spilling his seed into me. Of course, I won't bother to give you any pleasure. I'm going to simply shoot you. But, first, you will tell me where that little blond slut is."

"No." Royal tensed, ready to move in the faint hope of avoiding her shot.

Marilynn shrugged. "I'll find her, you know. I know she was here with you. She's probably just hiding. This might bring her out." Marilynn smiled as she fired her gun.

Antonie cried out when Royal's attempt to move out of the way failed. She stilled what horror she felt when he cried out, his hand going to his head as he collapsed. Even as she grabbed her knife and started to move, Marilynn fired again and Royal's body jerked. With a scream of fury, Antonie threw her knife.

421

A surprised look came over Marilynn's face as the knife buried itself in her chest. To Antonie's horror, the woman pulled it out and then looked at her. Blood poured from the wound but Marilynn did not fall, simply aimed her gun. As the shot rang out, Antonie threw herself to the ground, rolling toward Marilynn, hitting the woman's legs and bringing her down. Instantly, she leapt on her and fought to get the gun Marilynn still gripped.

As they wrestled in the dirt, Antonie was amazed at the strength Marilynn still had. She had to be bleeding to death yet Marilynn fought like a tigress. When Antonie finally managed to turn the barrel of the gun away from herself and toward Marilynn, she did not hesitate to fire. The force of the bullet's contact sent Marilynn flying backward. Unsteadily, Antonie stood up and knew that she was really dead this time. The bullet had entered right in the middle of Marilynn's forehead. After wrestling with the urge to empty the chamber into her, Antonie tossed away the gun and raced to Royal's side.

Forcing herself to be calm, even though her heart threatened to beat its way through her chest, she did what she could to clean and bind his wounds. The head wound was only a graze but the wound in his chest made her blood run cold. The bullet was still in there and she feared it would be difficult to remove.

She briefly wondered about racing home and getting someone to come after him but she could not think of leaving him alone. Grasping him under the arms, she dragged him to the buggy then balked. Although she was strong, she did not think she could lift the weight of a full grown man.

Using the side of the buggy she propped him against it. Then she got him upright and pushed the

422

top half of his body in. Whispering heartfelt apologies for her rough handling, she got in on the other side and dragged him into the buggy. Then, using the blanket they had so recently made love on, she tied his body to hers to insure that he would not slide or fall out while she drove.

Even as she started toward the ranch at a gallop, she realized that she had on only her blood-stained undergarments. "To hell with it. Forgive me for the roughness, *querido*."

Careening to a stop before the house, she untied Royal and leapt down as people appeared from the house and the yard. "Help me with him, please. *Por favor*, he is bad hurt."

Hands gently moved her aside and reached for Royal as a gruff voice demanded, "What's happened?"

"Sheriff? What are you doing here?" she asked absently, her eyes only flicking his way once before her gaze returned to Royal.

"I came to tell you that Miss Collins has escaped."

"*Sí*. She has. She is dead now. By the swimming hole. Is O'Neill here?"

"I'll get him, *chica*," Tomás said as he looked her over. "Are you hurt? There is a lot of blood."

"Marilynn's. Maybe Royal's. *Por favor*, get O'Neill quickly, Tomás." She hurried into the house after the men who were carrying Royal up to his room. "Someone must take the sheriff to the swimming hole," she called over her shoulder.

Maria caught up with her at the door of her room. Between her urgings and those of Jed and Tom who were tending to Royal, Antonie went to her old room to clean up. Once she got a good look at herself, she was glad she had let them persuade her to change her clothes. O'Neill would never have let her near Royal

423

with the dirt and blood she had on her.

As she cleaned herself, she struggled to keep her fears for Royal under control. She knew she would not do anybody any good if she gave in to the hysteria she could feel struggling within her. Screaming and wailing would change little. She would upset people, distract them from Royal who desperately needed all the help he could get and probably do herself little good as well. Antonie just wished that she did not feel so afraid.

Just as she came out of her old room, she saw O'Neill going into Royal's but that he was held back yet again. Ram did not understand how badly his father was hurt. He only understood that he was hungry. Taking her son from a pale Patricia's arms, she hurried back into her room.

Sitting in the chair and nursing her son helped her gain a little calm. It was an action so removed from the violence she had just endured that she was able to distance herself somewhat from the event. That newly gained control slipped a little when, just as she finished and was ready to go to Royal, the sheriff asked to see her.

"Please, I want to go to my husband."

"This'll only take a moment, ma'am."

"Perhaps it's just as well if you wait until O'Neill is done," Patricia said gently as she took Ram into her arms.

"I have seen bullets dug out before," Antonie informed them.

"But not out of Royal."

"No, not him. All right, Sheriff. What do you want to know?"

"Nothing much, ma'am. Just a quick telling of what happened out there." He shook his head. "I still don't understand how she got away and why I was only told about it today."

"Perhaps it was her method of escape or, well, the way she even got a chance at it."

"You know something about that?"

"She told Royal about it. Sex, Sheriff," she said flatly, too worried about Royal to be even slightly embarrassed by the subject. "She seduced her way out."

"Oh, hell, I warned them about that."

"Perhaps that is why they didn't tell you right away. I think you may find a few bodies littering her trail here although she only talked of one. She cut some drifter's throat."

"What happened by the swimming hole, ma'am?"

"I wasn't with Royal when she arrived but I saw her holding a gun on him. As she talked I crept toward my knife. I was not fast enough. She shot him and creased his head when he tried to move out of the way. While he was helpless, she shot him again. That's when I threw my knife. It was a good throw but she did not die. She pulled the knife out and tried to shoot me. Then we fought over the weapon. I won. That's it, Sheriff. Now it is really over."

"Yes, ma'am, I reckon it is."

Antonie did not say another word but hurried off to Royal's room. As she hurried in, Jed and Tom were just leaving. They each murmured a few well meant words of hope and sympathy as they went. Antonie shut the door behind them and turned to look at Royal.

Very slowly, she approached the bed where O'Neill was just finishing bandaging Royal. She thought it a little strange that the clean white bandages should make it look worse. It was chilling to see how pale he

425

was and how still he lay in the bed. She took a deep breath and then another as she felt herself begin to shake.

"Oh, hell," O'Neill swore as he pushed her into a seat he had placed near the bed, then forced a brandy into her hands. "Drink it all, lass, and while you're drinking you can tell me all that happened."

Between the talking and the brandy, Antonie felt herself grow a little calmer. "I am sorry, *amigo*."

"Don't be. By the sound of it, it was one hell of an experience. You kept your head when it was needed. That's what matters."

"I wanted to empty the gun into her," Antonie whispered. "She was dead but I wanted to shoot her again and again."

"Darlin', that's not so strange. You saw her shoot down your man. You were dealing with madness and violence. The important thing is that you didn't do that. Hell, she didn't die when she should have. That might've had something to do with it."

"Perhaps." She reached out to take Royal's hand. "She was *loco* and she shot him so coldly, almost with pleasure."

"It just might've been a pleasure for her."

"You can tell me about his injuries now. I am ready to hear about them."

"I wish I had more to tell you than I do. It's bad darlin' but I think you know that."

"*Sí.* The chest wound."

"Actually that's not what's got me worried the most. A clean shot and the bullet was easy enough to get out. He's strong and you got him here fast, got the bleeding slowed. It is a bad wound but I think he'll recover from that. It's that head wound that troubles me."

426

"It's just a graze," she said fretfully.

"Ye-es, a graze and I didn't see that it's cracked the bone or anything. Look, honey, I'll be honest with you. They haven't learned too much about head wounds, about the head and its innards at all. He's out cold, darlin'. That made it real easy to take the bullet out of him but that's the only good in it. It's a graze but a deep one, the bullet gave him a bad knock and it's close to the temple."

"He will wake up, *sí?*"

"He might wake up in a few minutes, a few hours, a few days."

She froze as she heard the words he did not say. "Or not at all. Is that what you tell me?"

"What I tell you, sweetheart, is that I don't know. All I know is that he's out, he's sunk deep if you know what I mean. I can clean the wound, help it heal, but that's it, short of praying that he wakes up soon with nothing more than a hell of a headache. It's wait and see, darlin'." He briefly clasped her shoulder in a gesture of comfort then started out of the room. "I'll go talk to Doc Fowler. He might have some information I don't have."

As soon as O'Neill left, Antonie indulged in the release of tears for a while. When she finally stopped crying, she felt weak physically but stronger emotionally. Fear for Royal still ate at her but she now found the fortitude to handle it, to even reach for hope. He was badly hurt but he was still alive. O'Neill admitted to little knowledge about head wounds, about those sleeps so deep that nothing seemed to reach the patient. Royal could wake up within hours. Whenever he did come back, she was going to be there.

Antonie found the following days a torture. Her hopes for his recovery were raised when he would reach a semi-conscious state allowing Maria and her to get some nourishment into him, then they would plummet when he would slip back into a deep unresponsive sleep. The others tried to cheer her, to ease her fears but they found it hard to hide their own worry.

One night as she sat by his bed and kissed the limp hand she held, she briefly faced the fact that he could die and shuddered. She knew she would go on but feared that she would never fully recover from the loss. There would be an emptiness within her that nothing could fill.

Suddenly all the words she had held back crowded into her mouth. It did not matter that he might not have the same feelings for her that she did for him. Now that she may have lost the chance to speak what was in her heart, she saw that pride that had kept her silent as a foolish thing. If, she took a deep breath and firmly changed that to 'when', when he came back to her, she would tell him all that she felt. To never have told him of her love was a regret she could not bear.

Chapter Thirty

Royal felt as if he had been buried in thick mud and was just now clawing his way through it to freedom. It took a lot of effort to open his eyes only to shut them against the brightness in the room. By the time he got them open for the second time, he realized that the room was not really bright at all but very dimly lit. It was also very quiet, the only sound he could hear being a soft snore and he started to turn toward it.

A tightness around his chest suddenly brought memories to the fore, causing his head to throb with pain and hid heart to stop with fear. Marilynn, insane and murderous, had attacked them, shot him. She had been looking for Antonie too. Seeing that the person by the bed was a dozing O'Neill, Royal's fear started to choke him. Where was Antonie? He refused to believe that she had fallen victim to Marilynn's madness, for the very thought of it threatened to make him as deranged as Marilynn.

"Antonie," he rasped, wondering why his voice felt as if he had not used it in a long time. "Antonie," he called again and, although his voice was little more than a hoarse whisper, the man at his bedside was instantly alert.

"Well, three hail Marys, you've decided to rejoin the living."

"Antonie?" He tried to sit up but O'Neill easily held him still. "Did Marilynn?" he asked weakly, unable to put his fears into words.

"Marilynn is dead."

"But Antonie, Marilynn was looking for her."

"Ah, so that's what's got you in a fever. Antonie is fine. She killed that madwoman. Antonie doesn't have a scratch, Royal. Not a scratch."

"Thank God." Royal felt weak with relief. "Where is she?"

"Resting. She's got a greedy son to keep fed and can't let herself get too tired. Try moving that arm."

When he did so, he winced but not only because of the discomfort it caused, the slight pull on the skin on his chest. His arm felt weak. It took a lot of effort to move it and he could not understand why.

"Pulls my chest. Why is that? I was shot in the head," he muttered as O'Neill helped him sit up and aided him in the drinking of a glass of water. "Damn. I'm so weak."

"That bitch shot you twice. Once grazing your head and then in the chest."

His hand automatically going to his chest, he muttered in confusion, "No bandage."

"Don't need one any longer."

"Another graze?" He grimaced when O'Neill gently prodded his chest, for the result was a slightly more than irritating twinge.

"No," O'Neill answered quietly. "It was a bad wound. Had to dig the bullet out."

"Then how can it be like this?"

430

"Because you slept through the healing," O'Neill said gently.

"Slept through it?" Royal croaked. "How?"

"That graze on your head. You've napped for a little over three weeks."

"My God. Why aren't I dead?"

"Well, a body can last a long time like that. Doc Fowler told me he'd known one that was out six months then woke up, weak but fine, fit as a fiddle after eating regular for a while."

"That's why I feel so weak."

"It is, although I think you're stronger than you might've been. You've been in and out, sometimes deep asleep, sometimes half-conscious. Antonie and Maria kept you well fed. No mere gruel for you. Damned unappetizing but they made you mashed food and fed you whenever you were able to be fed. Got that stuff so you could drink it really. They also took turns rubbing and moving that arm which helped, I think."

"How's Antonie?"

"As well as can be expected. She was set to stay right here but she's got a babe who needs her and needs her strong and healthy with her milk still flowing. I convinced her that she'd be doing you no favors if she let that responsibility slide. She didn't like hearing it but I reminded her about how that lad was you, a bit of you left behind if you slipped away from us."

"And there was a chance of that?"

"Yup. The longer you stayed out the greater the chance. There was also that chance that you'd come back not quite right but I don't see any sign of that."

"No? I'm still tired. Is that all right after three weeks of sleeping?"

431

"Yup. You're weak."

"I won't slip back?"

"No, I don't really think so. A few more days, some hearty meals and some exercise and you'll be getting back to normal. Don't fight the resting. That'll do you no good."

"I want to see Antonie," he protested even as O'Neill calmly saw to his personal needs. "Antonie."

"She'll be here when you wake up again," O'Neill said as he lay Royal back down then tucked him in.

Despite his efforts to stay awake and the hurried, emotional visits of his family, Royal fell asleep. When he woke up again, he was momentarily afraid that he might have lost another three weeks. His gaze shifted nervously around the room until it met Antonie's wide-eyed one. To his astonishment, she gave a soft cry, fell to her knees by the bed and started to weep.

"Antonie?"

"Oh, *querido*, I thought you were lost to me. I thought you were dead or, worse, that you would just slip away, little by little. Sometimes you seemed to come back and I would hope but you would slip away from us again."

He was touched by this display of emotion for him but he hated to see her cry and smoothed a hand over the top of her head in a soothing gesture. "Shush, Antonie. I didn't slip away, did I."

It was tempting to just leave it at that but she had made a promise to herself. God had seen fit to allow Royal to stay within the ranks of the living but she had seen how easily and suddenly she could lose him. She had seen how deeply she would regret never telling him how much he meant to her. Pride and cowardice wanted her to be silent now, now that he was going to be well and the frightening shadow of

432

death was receding. She could not let them win and tie up her tongue again.

Kissing the palm of the hand she held, she stared at it as she said quietly, "I was so afraid. There was so much I wanted to say, things my pride made me keep inside, things you were beyond hearing and might never hear. Then pride seemed such a small thing. It left me only with regrets and they were bitter. I promised myself that I would not let that happen again.

"I love you, *mi vida*. My life, that is what you are. If you had left me, I would have lived but not very well, eh? There would be such an emptiness, a hole even our child could not fill. *Por Dios*, it is hard to tell you," she whispered shakily, "but I made a promise to myself that I would speak.

"I saw the danger of you from the beginning but the pull was too strong. Ah, *sí*, I knew when you held me that I would place my heart in your hands. Sometimes, I fear it because it is so strong. That is one reason why I ran when I thought you would marry Marilynn. I feared you could make me stay as your 'little bit on the side', eh?

"Well, there, I said it, said what I must. It need not trouble you," she said and, quickly releasing his hand, stood up.

"Antonie," he croaked, stunned by what she had told him.

"I will get you some food, *querido*," she said as she practically ran out the door, not ready to face him.

Royal stared at the empty doorway for a moment in open-mouthed surprise then sank back against his pillows. A grin started to spread over his face as pure joy filled him. She loved him and, judging from what else she had said, had for a long time. He closed his eyes and savored the knowledge, finding it sweeter than he would have thought possible.

"Which ought to tell you something, fool," he scolded himself. "Just think on that for a minute."

"Think on what?" Cole asked as he brought a tray of food in and set it down on the table by the bed.

"Where's Antonie?"

"Said she had to see to Ram."

"So that's the game she'll play," Royal muttered.

"What?"

"Nothing. Who do I thank for getting me back to the house?" he asked as Cole helped him sit up.

"Antonie." Cole managed to help Royal eat his meal. "I'm damned if I know how she managed to get you into the buggy, tied to her so you wouldn't fall out and came home hell bent for leather. Didn't even bother to put her dress on. We thought she was hurt too for a bit 'cause there was a lot of blood on her."

"Marilynn's?"

"Yup."

Royal listened in amazement as Cole told him what Antonie had done. It was hard to believe that such a small woman could find the strength to get his body back home, especially after struggling with an insane killer. What she had done seemed a clear illustration of what she had just confessed to him and he ached to talk to her.

But she was not going to give him any chance to, which became very clear as the days slipped by. She always brought someone with her when she did come to visit him. She also continued to sleep in her old room. The way she seemed to be keeping a close eye on his recovery gave Royal an idea. With a grinning O'Neill's cooperation, he kept his full progress a secret from her. If she did not come to him, was intent upon eluding him, he did not want her to know when he was capable of chasing her down, for she would be sure to find some new way to escape any private meeting with him.

"Well, Royal, you're as strong as a horse," O'Neill declared one night, almost two weeks from what Tomás irreverently called his resurrection. "Isn't it about time to break out of the stall?"

"First tell me where the filly is."

O'Neill laughed. "Slipped into her own stall a short while ago."

"Without saying goodnight to her husband? Tsk, tsk."

"Ah and the stallion rears," O'Neill murmured when Royal hopped out of bed.

"Funny man," Royal grumbled as he pulled on his pants. "Well, the little coward can't run any more."

"Well, it wouldn't hurt to lock the door and pocket the key," O'Neill advised as he left. "That lass can be a slippery little one."

Antonie crawled into bed, sprawled on her back and stared up at the ceiling. Her honesty had turned her into a coward. She did feel better now that she had told Royal how she felt except that she was embarrassed. No matter how many times she scolded herself for being silly, she could not face him. The way he kept looking at her told her that he wanted to discuss what she had said and she wanted it to be forgotten.

She knew she would not be able to avoid him forever. He would soon be better and would certainly expect their married life to resume. It was a little puzzling that he had not done so already.

Even as she started to frown about that, she heard her bedroom door open. Her eyes wide, she watched a bare chested Royal enter, lock the door after him and place the key over her door. She could break her neck if she tried to get it, she thought a little wildly. Then she realized that he was out of his sickbed and marching toward her wilt all his former grace.

"What are you doing out of bed?" she squeaked, sitting up slightly.

"Well, you weren't coming to my bed," he said reasonably as he took off his pants and crawled in next to her.

"But you have been very ill."

"I'm better," he murmured as he turned onto his side and reached for her.

It was very hard to think when he held her so close. Antonie found her mind quickly clouding over with desire as he nimbly removed the shirt she was wearing as a nightgown. It felt so good to hold him, to feel that he was alive and well.

"Wait a minute," she muttered as she tried to wriggle free of his hold.

"A whole minute?" He loosened his arms enough so that, when her small hands pushed against his chest, she was able to put a little distance between them.

"You were sick."

"So I've been told."

"No, I mean, you were still in bed this afternoon."

"Maybe I was just waiting for you to join me."

When she pushed him again, he abruptly released her. She fell onto her back and he hurried to pin her down. He met her scowl with a sweet smile. There was no place she could run to now. He placed a gentle kiss on her mouth.

"You have been playing a trick on me," she accused him but her stern voice broke on the last word as, holding her wrists over her head with one hand, he began to fondle her breasts with the other.

"Well, yes, I reckon I was."

"What did you do that for? I was worrying that you were healing too slowly when all along you were getting better." As his finger toyed with her increasingly aching nipples, she gritted her teeth against a swiftly rising passion.

"I could see how you were eluding me."

"I was not," she gasped as his tongue caressed her nipples.

Ignoring that interruption, he continued, "so I thought I wouldn't let you know my progress. Then you couldn't run away."

Then hand that had been so skillfully touching her now sought the silky curls between her thighs. "I was not . . . I didn't . . . Oh, I can't think when you do that."

"Good. I don't feel like thinking either," he moaned as he slowly joined their bodies.

He rested his forehead against hers and sighed. Silently he gave thanks for her swift response to his touch. He had been too long without her to indulge in much foreplay. She clearly felt the same way. He was not going to be able to savor the feel of her warmth surrounding him for long. Even now his hips began to move as if of their own accord.

"It feels like coming home," he said huskily as he kissed her.

Antonie clung to him, her legs wrapping tightly around him. She was starved for him. It had been too long since she had held him close, had felt his body joined with hers. Breathing words of love in Spanish, she fought against losing control. His slow rhythmic thrusts felt good. It also felt as if he was relishing the feel of her. When they simultaneously lost the strength to go slowly, she was almost disappointed but it was a fleeting sensation erased completely as her climax engulfed her. Even as her ecstacy took her beyond thought, she heard Royal cry out her name and stiffen as he joined her in release. She held him close, as close as she could, as they slowly regained their senses.

Her first clear thought was a strong hope that this was how it would be, that they would simply return to what they had been before. The emotional confession she had made would be set quietly aside, remembered but not discussed. That hope was strengthened when his first clear thought proved not to be about her confession. She was surprised and confused when he abruptly left her arms and crouched over her.

"Damn. I didn't take care. Did you?"

"Oops."

"Antonie, oops is not what I want to hear. Damn it, Ram is only a few months old."

"Well, I had no idea you were coming to my bed tonight. I thought you were still sick," she added with a touch of accusation in her tone.

"We'll talk about that in a minute." He ignored her quick panicked look. "Maybe you ought to see about that now."

"Oh. Planning on a . . . um . . . a . . . ?"

"An encore? Yes."

"Ah. Well, if you would just turn to look toward the door for a while, *por favor*," she said as she started to get out of bed, wondering idly when she would stop blushing about the matter.

Doing as she asked, he said, "Not planning to bolt, are you?"

"You are watching the door and I think you would notice, *querido*, if I tried to creep out of the window."

438

"Quite possibly. Allow me to apologize now if my impetuosity results in something tangible."

"Huh?"

"If you get pregnant, I'm sorry."

"Oh. Well, it is said that while you are nursing a baby you cannot get pregnant."

"Really?" he drawled. "Are those the same people that say toads give you warts?"

She grimaced as she crawled back into bed. "Sí. I am afraid it is the same they."

"Then maybe we ought to start thinking of names." He turned and pulled her into his arms.

"It was only the once."

"Ram was only the once."

"Maybe. We are not sure. There is no sense in worrying, eh?"

"True. We can have that discussion you've been running away from."

"How about Caterine if it is a girl?"

"Antonie, why are you afraid of talking to me about what you said that day?" he asked quietly.

Staring at him, she frowned a little. That was a question she had not really answered for herself. She supposed it was fear, in a way. The confession was easy enough but to discuss it meant she had to hear about how her feelings were not returned.

"It does not need to be discussed. I needed to tell you. I was shown how easy it was to lose you and I did not want to bear the regret of words not said. It need not bother you," she said gently. "Maybe it was wrong. I should have said nothing."

"No." He gently kissed her. "We've been too busy saying nothing. The incidents with Oro and Marilynn should have shown us the trouble of saying nothing and the woe it can bring. We can't read each other's minds. There has to be talking or there is confusion, doubts and hurt."

"And you have been silent about things too?"

"Yes, although, a lot of my silence was because I simply didn't know my own mind. Maybe it's easier for women to simply accept how they feel, not question it much. Perhaps they see it clearly, know exactly what it means when they experience things like jealousy and need. I was always puzzled and surprised."

"Maybe," she said quietly, "some of that was because of who I am, where I come from."

His hold tightened on her slightly and he nodded reluctantly. "I am ashamed to admit it but, yes, some of it was. You weren't what I'd planned on."

"Everybody finds it hard to change what they had planned on. I planned on enjoying this fire then saying, 'adios, amigo.'"

"Just like that?"

"Just like that. It is what men do."

"When did you change your mind?"

"The first night, although, I did not really change my mind. I still planned on that. I just saw that it would not be easy. It took a while longer to see just how badly my heart had become involved."

"And what did you decide when you knew that had happened?"

Sighing, she decided that perhaps it was time to be fully honest. He knew how she felt now. There was really not much left to hide. How she had reached the point of loving him was really only incidental.

"I was rather dismayed but my feelings did not change my plans by much. I was still going to stay and enjoy until I was sent away. What else was there to do?"

"You could have told me what you were feeling."

"No. I thought about it but it is hard to swallow one's pride, eh?"

"Yes, I reckon it is. It's choked me a time or two."

"And there was always Marilynn."

"I'd told you that that was nothing really."

"*Sí*, but, too, you did not push her away. That was hard to understand at times."

"And it made it easy to think that I would choose her over you, ask her to marry me almost immediately after leaving your arms."

"It did, *sí*. I thought I was but a diversion, that is the word?"

"Yes, that's it. And when you said you'd marry me, did you love me then, Antonie?" he asked, aching to hear her say the words again.

She sighed and hid her face against his chest. "*Sí*, even before then I knew I had love for you, not just a fire, eh?" Feeling his chest move with a deep sigh, she said quietly, "It is no matter."

"No matter? Don't you want anything in return for such a gift? You have given me so much. Passion, your innocence, your loyalty and your love. Don't you expect anything for all that?"

"It would be nice," she answered honestly, "but it is not really necessary. You said we will have a sharing in our marriage and that you will be faithful to me. That is a lot. I understand this."

"So practical."

There was a hint of amusement in his voice that made her look at him. She did not think there was anything particularly funny about the matter. It seemed to her that he ought to be touched perhaps, pleased that his wife loved him or maybe a little embarrassed to be told of feelings he had not asked for and did not really return. There were a dozen

441

feelings he could have but she did not think amusement ought to be one of them. That seemed to be just a little bit cruel.

"See what happens when we say nothing? I can see your mind working furiously and in all the wrong directions. Tell me, Antonie, what did you think when I acted like an idiot over Oro? I scowled over dinner that night in the hotel because Baird was flirting with you. I chased you down that night because I got to thinking to Cole was picking up where he thought I had left off. When you took off with Tomás, I was ready to chase you right down without a thought of how it could disrupt my grand plan to expose Marilynn's treachery. Now, why do you suppose that was?"

"Because you are a possessive man?" she answered tremulously, not daring to trust her own judgment of the soft look in his eyes.

"I can see that you are as stubbornly blind as I was. That is what I told myself. You were mine and a man likes to hold onto what is his, doesn't want to share it, especially when it's the best he's ever had."

"The best?"

"Oh, yes, love, the best. That's one thing I've known for certain from the very beginning. After the time we spent apart during the drive, I knew I ought to start really thinking about how I felt about you and thinking about what I wanted for us, and from you, but I kept putting it off. There was enough trouble to allow me to avoid facing things. I told myself there wasn't enough time to do it properly.

"Christ, I had a good explanation for everything. Of course I'd be afraid for you even though you can take care of yourself because you are small and soft and female. Of course I needed you, for what man wouldn't need a fire like the one we share. That explained why I had such a need to know you would stay when the battle was over. The need to know you were fighting for me was because I was still stinging from Marilynn's betrayal."

"It all sounds very reasonable," she whispered.

"Of course it does. A man doesn't elude the truth as neatly as I did without using the best of logic."

"The truth?"

"Yes, the truth." He held her close. "I love you."

She clung to him tightly and felt an urge to cry, she was so choked with joy. He said it so calmly that she had no doubt that he meant it. It was a clear statement of fact. She was not sure that he would ever understand how much it meant to her to hear those words.

"Even when I came out of what O'Neill keeps calling my 'little nap', I tried to ignore it. The moment I recalled what had happened, I was terrified for you, as terrified as I had been when you were in Raoul's filthy hands."

"When did you see?" she asked hoarsely, still clinging to him as if afraid that he would prove to be an illusion and slip away, that this moment she had waited for for so long was only a dream.

"When you told me you loved me," he answered quietly. "God, Antonie, it felt so good, so damn good. I just lay there smiling like a drunken idiot and reveled in it, savored it. That's when I finally stopped making excuses for everything I felt. There was only one rational explanation. Once I admitted it to myself, it felt right. I knew I had finally faced the real truth. It explained even the things I'd felt and done that had left me confused. I love you."

"And I love you, *querido*. *Por Dios*, how I love you."

"Forever."

"*Sí*. Forever."

"Well, I think we ought to do something to celebrate this momentous occasion."

She looked at him and smiled slowly. "And you have an idea?"

"We-ell, you could always express your delight in our mutual affection by ravishing me."

"Ah, *querido*, what a good idea. You always have such good ideas."

"I've got years and years worth of them, love."

ROMANCE REIGNS
WITH ZEBRA BOOKS!

SILVER ROSE   (2275, $3.95)
by Penelope Neri

Fleeing her lecherous boss, Silver Dupres disguised herself as a boy and joined an expedition to chart the wild Colorado River. But with one glance at Jesse Wilder, the explorers' rugged, towering scout, Silver knew she'd have to abandon her protective masquerade or else be consumed by her raging unfulfilled desire!

STARLIT ECSTASY   (2134, $3.95)
by Phoebe Conn

Cold-hearted heiress Alicia Caldwell swore that Rafael Ramirez, San Francisco's most successful attorney, would never win her money . . . or her love. But before she could refuse him, she was shamelessly clasped against Rafael's muscular chest and hungrily matching his relentless ardor!

LOVING LIES   (2034, $3.95)
by Penelope Neri

When she agreed to wed Joel McCaleb, Seraphina wanted nothing more than to gain her best friend's inheritance. But then she saw the virile stranger . . . and the green-eyed beauty knew she'd never be able to escape the rapture of his kiss and the sweet agony of his caress.

EMERALD FIRE   (1963, $3.95)
by Phoebe Conn

When his brother died for loving gorgeous Bianca Antonelli, Evan Sinclair swore to find the killer by seducing the tempress who lured him to his death. But once the blond witch willingly surrendered all he sought, Evan's lust for revenge gave way to the desire for unrestrained rapture.

SEA JEWEL   (1888, $3.95)
by Penelope Neri

Hot-tempered Alaric had long planned the humiliation of Freya, the daughter of the most hated foe. He'd make the wench from across the ocean his lowly bedchamber slave—but he never suspected she would become the mistress of his heart, his treasured SEA JEWEL.

Available wherever paperbacks are sold, or order direct from the Publisher. Send cover price plus 50¢ per copy for mailing and handling to Zebra Books, Dept. 2345, 475 Park Avenue South, New York, N.Y. 10016. Residents of New York, New Jersey and Pennsylvania must include sales tax. DO NOT SEND CASH.